Treasure At Rainbow's End

Enjoy!

Dwight Hood Roberts

DWIGHT HOOD ROBERTS

Copyright © 2012 Dwight Hood Roberts

ISBN: 0615580858

ISBN 13: 9780615580852

Dedicated to the memory of my son

Dwight Rexal Roberts

Oct. 3 1962   Nov. 28 1990

CHAPTER 1

The bright, twinkling stars of a clear summer night slowly began to fade as dawn approached the vast Sonora Desert. Chirps and whistles broke the silence as stirring birds announced the coming of another day. Scattered among the desert flora, an army of Saguaros slowly appeared in the waning darkness, their arms pointing upward as if urging the sun to appear. A crouching cougar, the tip of his long tail nervously twitching, took a last lap from a murky pool, then slunk back into the cover of the cactus and stunted trees. High above the cougar's waterhole, on a ledge protruding from a towering mountain, Bo Logan, clad only in a faded pair of denims, watched the arrival of the dawn as he sipped coffee from a stained and battered cup. He was a tall, stocky man, a few inches over six feet, with bulging muscles in his arms and shoulders. A blond thatch of hair hung down past his ears, framing a rugged but handsome clean-shaven face. Goosebumps appeared on his body from the chill of the cold desert night, but he disregarded them as he watched and waited. Suddenly the edge of a blood-red sun appeared above the rugged horizon, shooting its crimson rays across the arid desert. The young man stared at the emerging red orb until the increasing brightness forced him to shift his eyes to the dusky desert below him, where the sunrise was slowly illuminating the waking land. Sunlight touched the very top of a range of mountains in the distance, and he elevated his eyes to watch them change colors as sunlight slowly inched down their jagged peaks. Feeling small and humble, he was captivated by the almost supernatural beauty of the desert sunrise, and questions entered his mind. *Why am I here in this place and time to witness this amazing sight? What else do I have waiting for me on this journey?*

With his questions unanswered, Bo watched as the magnificent sunrise finally came to an end and a soon-to-be-hot desert day began. Bo, still thinking about his questions, lingered as his memory returned to the time when, at nineteen, he left his home in Georgia and began his wandering of the West, searching for the adventure he had read and heard about. His travels first took him to Texas, where after a few years, he became a top hand with cattle. Later, after trailing a few herds of longhorn cattle up to Kansas, he turned out to be a pretty good hand with a gun. Bo had enjoyed the adventures of the cattle drives and the excitement of the railroad towns, but eventually it became boring to the restless young man. He began drifting, taking odd jobs here and there, always at a place he hadn't been before. Bo felt that something was missing in his life and he just needed to search for it.

Bo began this particular journey back in Texas just a few months ago, when he agreed to deliver a small herd of Herford cattle to Jose Perez's ranch just south of Nogales, Mexico. When he delivered the cattle, Senor Perez asked him to stay on and help get the beefy, white-faced cattle settled in to their new range. With nothing in Texas pulling him back, he took the job, but after a few months in Mexico he got itchy feet again and decided to ride north to Tucson.

The first day out of Nogales on his journey, he ran into a nest of Mexican bandits tormenting some poor blanket Indians. When Bo rode into their camp to ask them to stop, they turned on him with pistols drawn and rotten yellow-tooth grins on their faces. Luckily they were poor shots, so as they shot up some nearby cacti, he had time to draw his Colt forty-four and send them to a place much hotter than the Sonora Desert. The poor blanket Indians watched him with expressionless faces the whole time. When Bo untied them, they rode off into the desert without even a thank you. The next three days were nearly as bad. Bo found out that everything in the desert will either stick you or bite you, and some things will do both. He also discovered the scorching sun and the dry wind will quickly suck the moisture out of you. On the fourth morning, his canteens were empty, so late that afternoon when he found the small, murky waterhole at the foot of a small mountain, he didn't stop to see if the water was clean. Bo and his horse buried their faces in the warm water and drank their fill. Later, after filling his canteens, Bo moved up the mountain to a ledge and set up his camp. So far, the sunrise the next morning had been the best part of his journey.

Bo lingered for a few more minutes, lost in his thoughts, but finally he sighed and decided it was time to saddle up and hit the trail. He picked up the new stovepipe boots he had purchased in Nogales by the heels and turned them upside down. A large, yellowish scorpion fell from the left boot and scurried under a flat rock. Bo shook the boots again for good measure before he pulled them on. He tucked his faded-out denims into the boots,and slipped on his freshest calico shirt, then buttoned it up to its raveled collar. Next he reached for his gun belt, which he had also bought in Mexico. The fancy leatherwork on the rig had caught his eye when he spied it in a small leather shop in Nogales. It was perfect for his Colt, and after a little practice, Bo felt he was much faster getting his pistol out than before. He buckled it on, then pulled the Colt and checked to make sure it was clean and loaded. Satisfied, he began to pick up the rest of his gear and stuffed it into his saddlebags and his bedroll. Moments later, after he put out his campfire with leftover coffee and dirt, Bo reached for his saddle. As he picked it up, he glanced back toward the desert, and a dust cloud in the distance caught his eye. Slowly the saddle slipped from his hands as he squinted into the sun, trying to make out what was causing the dust. Bo pulled his hat lower to shade his eyes. Suddenly he could see what was coming, and a sense of dread seeped into his mind. A small band of Indians was riding toward the muddy water hole that was down the mountain below his campsite.

Bo had read in the newspapers that the Indian wars were over and almost all the Apaches were on the reservation. He had also read and heard talk of Geronimo raiding and killing, but he figured that as big as the territory was, he wasn't going to run into any renegade Apaches. The evening before when he had decided to make his camp on the large ledge of rock jutting out from the mountain, he thought he would be safe from any predators of the night. But he hadn't counted on these kinds of predators.

It's just my luck to be right where Geronimo is headed, he thought as he grabbed his rifle out of its saddle boot. Crouching low his six foot four inch frame, he slowly backed away from the edge of the ledge until he was out of sight from the Indians. Bo's first thought as he calmed down was to saddle his horse. If they saw him, his only chance would be to outrun them. Bo dropped to his hands and knees, then slowly crawled back to retrieve his saddle. He carefully pulled it to him as he slowly backed up to where he had staked out his horse next to the cliff. Cautiously looking to see if he was out of sight from the approaching band of Indians, Bo slowly stood up and slipped the bridle onto the horse's head. He threw the saddle blanket over the big dun gelding's back and grabbed the saddle.

"Hold still, Dunce," he whispered shrilly as the gelding shied away from the saddle. Bo was familiar with the stupid ways of his horse, so he stepped with him and set it on his back. Even though the morning was cool, sweat was popping out on Bo's forehead as he cinched up the saddle. Nervously he kept glancing over his shoulder at the edge of the ledge, expecting to see an Apache head pop up at any time. Finally Bo had the saddle buckled. He scurried back to where he had left his bedroll and saddlebags. He tossed them back toward his horse, then crawled closer to the edge. He slowly peeped over the rim of the ledge. The Apaches were still steadily advancing toward the waterhole, but apparently they hadn't seen him because they seemed to be in no hurry. Bo slowly backed away from the rim, then carefully turned to scramble back to his horse.

Dunce was gone! The horse had chewed off the limb he had been tied to and was nowhere to be seen. Frantically Bo looked around for the dun gelding. *He couldn't have gone far; the ledge isn't that big.* Bo was almost in full panic. Suddenly he saw a horse's tail swishing out from behind a large boulder next to the cliff. *There he is!* Bo grabbed his saddlebags and bedroll as he hurried to the boulder.

"Damn you, horse, you trying to get me killed?" He whispered nervously as he secured his gear to the saddle. Bo tied Dunce to another bush. "Why don't you just holler out and tell them where we are? Don't you know Indians eat horses?" Bo looked back toward the edge of the ledge. When he didn't see the Apaches, he calmed down a little. "Damn it to hell," Bo muttered to the horse as he nervously looked around for another way out. "I got a pack of renegade Apaches looking for someone to scalp, and if we don't find a way out of here, we are both cooked." He hopefully looked for a way up the mountain from the ledge, but it was almost straight up; not even a mountain goat could climb those cliffs. Discarding that idea, he studied the ledge where he had sat up his camp. It was in a half circle shape about two hundred yards wide, with each end against a huge cliff. The only way to get to the ledge was a trail that angled up from the water hole about fifty yards below. The east end of the ledge was bare rock with no cover, but on the west end of the ledge was a jumble of boulders and brush. Dunce had wandered off into the side with the boulders. *My only chance is to hide in the rocks and pray to God they don't come up here and find me,* Bo thought as he grabbed Dunce's reins and slowly led the horse through the huge rocks.

Bo had covered about fifty feet when he noticed a faint path that led through a narrow opening between two of the larger boulders. He looked through the gap, but it seemed to dead end against the cliff that rose above them. He looked around for something better, but this seemed the best place to hide. Cautiously looking for rattlesnakes, Bo entered the narrow opening and immediately had trouble with his horse. Dunce didn't want to come, but with a few curses and pulling hard, Bo finally persuaded the stubborn horse to follow him into the narrow space. Past the opening there was more room, and after securing Dunce, Bo pulled up a small salt-bush, went back out, and brushed out the tracks they had made. He returned for a few more of the small bushes to pile up in front of the opening between the boulders. Searching for more bushes, Bo went farther back toward the cliff, where a huge boulder sat next to the cliff. Bo noticed some small bushes beside it, so he squeezed through the larger creosote trees to reach them. Past the boulder he noticed another open area, and he could see there was enough room for a man and a horse to fit behind it.

Bo slowly made his way behind the boulder but suddenly stopped; he couldn't believe his eyes. There was a cave hidden behind the boulder, and it looked as if it was large enough for him and Dunce to squeeze into. He could get in there and hold them off for a long time if he had to. Bo hurried back for Dunce. He led him back to the narrow opening of the cave. Carefully watching for varmints, Bo stepped into the cave, pulling the horse behind him. For once Dunce didn't give him any trouble as he followed close behind his master. He finally seemed to realize that Bo was trying to save their lives. A few yards past the entrance, the cave opened up into a large room that was wide enough for Dunce to turn around in. Bo didn't bother going any farther; he tied the horse's reins to a rock formation rising from the floor, then returned to the opening, where he carefully squeezed back outside the cave to again brush out their tracks. Before coming back into the cave, he gathered up some more brush and arranged it in front of the cave entrance, hoping to hide it from any casual glance from an Apache. Bo's heart slowed, and he relaxed a little after he pulled one last piece of brush into the opening. He pulled out his Colt to check the cartridges again; satisfied, he slid it back into the holster, then pulled his Winchester from the saddle boot.

As he settled himself on the cave floor just inside the entrance, he cocked a round into the firing chamber. He waited.

Bo waited for what he thought was a long time. If the Apaches were looking for him, he had fooled them. The only sounds were the wind whistling through the rocks and Dunce shifting around in the cave. Soon it became dark.

Bo woke up. It was morning; he had fallen asleep during the night. Groggily he looked around the cave as he rubbed the kinks from his back. Abruptly he remembered why he was in the cave, and fear gripped his heart again. He quickly grabbed the Winchester that had fallen out of his hand and pointed it toward the cave entrance, but nothing was there. "Surely they would have found me by now if they were going to," he said to himself. Slowly he crept to the entrance and peeped out. The space between the boulders was empty. Carefully pushing the brush out of the way, Bo cautiously stepped out of the cave, his eyes darting from side to side. He slowly made his way back up the trail to where he had camped. A robber jay was pecking at something on the ground. Bo got down on his hands and knees, then slowly crawled toward the cliff that rose above the water hole. As he got closer, he went down on his belly, then pulled himself forward to peep over the edge. The water hole was deserted. Bo breathed a sigh of relief as he relaxed, but suddenly he tensed up again. The Apaches were in the distance heading south, away from him, the dust from their ponies slowly rising into a cloudless sky. He relaxed again, but even seeing them leaving, he was still careful. He eased back from the ledge and watchfully made his way back to the cave.

Dunce was impatiently waiting for him back at the cave. He nickered and pulled back on his reins.

"I know you're hungry and thirsty, boy, but we got to wait a while longer. I don't trust those Apaches; they might double back," Bo said to his horse. He would wait until noon and then take off in the opposite direction of the Apaches. Bo sat down to watch the entrance and made himself as comfortable as he could, but after an hour he got bored. He stood up to stretch his legs for a minute, but instead of sitting back down, he began to examine the cave. Bo was a tall man, but the roof of the cave was still two feet over his head. The walls were mostly smooth, and the floor was covered in a fine dust with a few small rocks scattered in it. Bo had no trouble walking as he made his way farther back into the cave.

This is a good place for snakes, he thought as he slowly walked into the darkness. *It would just be my luck to stumble into a nest of rattlers.* The light from the entrance grew dimmer as he continued farther into the cave. It made a curve to the left, and beyond that it became too dark for Bo to see where he was going. Not wanting to stumble into a crevice or bump into a low-hanging stalactite, he hastily returned to the entrance, where he made a torch out of a small bush and some rawhide. He lit it with a Lucifer, then proceeded to walk back into the cave. He slowly made his way past the first curve to where it ran straight for a little ways, but then it curved back the other way. As he went around this second curve, several bats flew out of a crack in the ceiling. Bo frantically swatted at the furry mammals with his torch as they circled his head. Abruptly the torch flickered out to a few glowing embers, then it was dark. "Damn it to hell; now I can't see anything, and I got bats flying around everywhere," he said as he ducked his head and waved his burned-out torch. He stood there for a minute with his arms protecting his head, hoping that all the bats were gone, but as his eyes adjusted to the dark, he noticed a faint glow in the distance. Carefully watching for more bats, he made his way farther into the cave. The glow became brighter as he walked toward it. After he had gone about fifty yards, he could see the source of the light. It was another entrance to the cave. Bo carefully walked to the opening, then paused for a second, his mouth open in amazement as he tried to understand what he was seeing. Slowly he stepped out into the daylight to something he had never expected to see.

"What's a place like this doing in the Arizona desert?"

CHAPTER 2

Nana scowled as he glanced up at the ledge high above their camp. He was becoming impatient waiting for Geronimo to send them up to kill or capture the white eye. He hoped they could capture him. He would enjoy hearing the screams from the white eye as they tortured him. He wondered what their leader was waiting for. They had been at the water hole for a day and a night, resting their horses while they tended one of their wounded. Geronimo knew there was a white eye on the ledge above him, but the chief refused to send his warriors up to get him.

"The white eye is still up there," he said. "Why do we not catch and torture him?" So far their leader had not answered them.

"No, I will not kill this white eye," Geronimo finally answered as he stepped into the firelight, his brown skin glistening in the light of the campfire. He held up his wrists that were raw from being tied, then motioned for all to see the burn marks on his body. "When the Mexicanos tricked us into their camp and were torturing Blue Wolf, the white eye came and killed the Mexicanos and freed us." Geronimo paused as he thought back to a few days ago, when bandits had tricked Blue Wolf and him into entering their camp to look at guns that the bandits said they wanted to trade for gold. They drank the whisky the Mexicans gave them, then went to sleep. When they awoke their hands were tied, and the Mexicans were torturing Blue Wolf with their red-hot knives. When they were through with Blue Wolf, they came to begin on him, but they were interrupted when the white eye rode into their camp.

Red Deer, one of the younger warriors, interrupted his thoughts. "Why did the white eye stop the Mexican bandits from torturing you?"

"Huh," grunted their chief. "No one knows what a white eye will do. He rode into the bandit camp when they were burning me with their hot knives. The white eye told them to stop, but the Mexicans told him they were going to kill him. When they went for their guns, the white eye's gun magically appeared in his hand, and he killed both of them. When he freed my hands and legs, he told me to go." He paused for a minute. "The Great Spirit has told me in a vision, this man is not to die." Slowly he looked at his warriors, his eyes staring hard. "We will not kill him." Geronimo looked toward the horizon where the sky was slowly getting lighter. He turned back to Nana. "We have buried Blue Wolf. The sun will be up soon; let us go."

The warriors knew that Geronimo would kill anyone who harmed the white eye. They reluctantly finished filling their water bags, then jumped on their mustangs. Geronimo led them south, back to their home high in the mountains of Mexico. None of them even glanced up to the ledge where Bo Logan had made his camp.

CHAPTER 3

Bo Logan couldn't believe what he was seeing. Nestled in between the jagged mountains was a small valley, complete with fresh water, huge trees, and lots of green grass. From the mouth of the cave, the land sloped down into a valley about two miles across. In the middle of it was a small lake surrounded by trees. Across the valley, a small stream flowed down from the higher mountains and into the lake. On the other side of the lake, Bo could see the stream continue flowing until it disappears into the trees. From where he was standing, he could see several meadows lush with grass mixed in with hundreds of evergreen trees.

I've heard talk of hidden valleys in the mountains, but I never expected to see one, he thought as he stood there for a few minutes looking down into the valley. The green grass caught his attention, and he thought of his horse. "I better go get Dunce and check on them Apaches again; I want to be sure they left for good." He turned and walked back into the cave. Bo didn't bother making another torch. He walked until the light faded into near darkness, and then he began feeling his way along the cave wall.

He was in the darkest part of the cave when suddenly somebody knocked him down. Bo's head struck the rock floor of the cave, and he was momentary dazed. When he came to his senses, he realized that someone was standing astraddle him in the dark. His heart pounded, and all he could think of was that the Apaches had finally found him. He grabbed for his pistol, but it had fallen out of his holster because he had undone the hammer thong. Frantically he ran his hands across the cave floor, trying to find his pistol. Suddenly he felt hot breath on his face, and he flinched. Something warm splashed on his cheek. It was coming closer; something long and wet slid across his face.

"Damn you, Dunce, I thought you was an Apache!" Bo exclaimed with relief as he wiped his face. He realized he had collided with his horse in the dark when he felt Dunce's tongue and smelled his familiar scent. He got up off the floor, still grumbling as he felt around for his pistol. He quickly found it, then, grabbing Dunce's reins, he led him back to the valley.

"Wait here, if you don't mind," Bo said as he tied the horse to a tree close to where the cave emerged into the valley. "If the Apaches find you, they might eat you; and if they don't, I might."

Bo took the time to make himself a good torch before he made his way back through the dark cave. He emerged from behind the large boulder, then cautiously crept back to the ledge. Once again, he peeped over the side. The Indians were completely out of sight. "I guess I fooled 'em," Bo said as he started back to the cave. "Maybe the Apaches ain't as smart as everyone thinks." He wiped out his tracks again, then piled brush in front of the cave entrance. He made his way back to the valley, where Dunce was impatiently chewing on the small tree where Bo had tied him. Bo untied the reins, then stepped into the saddle. He noticed a faint trail winding down into the valley, and, heeling Dunce, followed it down the slope. As Bo rode down the trail, he studied the valley. He could see the walls of the valley were almost all cliffs, as if it were an old crater or volcano. Apparently, the cave was the only way to get into the valley unless you were a mountain goat. Eventually he came to the bottom of the slope to level ground. As he entered a thick grove of trees, Bo saw something that disturbed him, and he stopped. Tree stumps. Someone had cut down trees here. He rode up closer to look at one. *Yep, someone cut it down with an ax; it wasn't a beaver.* "These trees were cut several years ago,"

Bo said as he rode on through the trees. Soon he came to another trail that had a lot of tracks on it. "Horse tracks, unshod!" he said. Bo turned Dunce onto the trail that continued in the direction of the lake.

He had only gone a little ways when he saw something else that made him stop. It was a small log cabin, almost hidden back in the trees. "Indians don't build cabins," Bo said to himself. He rode closer. The cabin sat back in a small clearing close to the stream, and when he got closer, he could see the roof and other parts of the cabin needed repairing. It appeared to be deserted. As he rode up to the door of the cabin, he saw something odd: above the door, someone had carved the words, **RAINBOW'S END.**

"Hello, anybody home?" Bo yelled. Nobody answered. Cautiously he dismounted, then tied Dunce to a bush. He examined the cabin as he slowly walked around it, calling again, but still no one answered. Bo was pretty sure that no one had lived in the cabin in a long time as he looked at the boards from the roof scattered around behind the cabin and a broken meat drying rack with vines growing up through it. Bo wondered if whoever built the cabin had just gotten up and left one day or if he had died here in the valley. *Maybe his skeleton is lying on a bed inside the cabin.*

Bo made his way back to the door of the cabin. He noticed a leather string sticking out of a hole in the center of the door. Carefully he pulled the leather latchstring out a few inches, then pushed on the door. Instead of opening, it fell back onto the dirt floor, a cloud of dust rising into the air around it. The leather hinges had been eaten or had rotted away. Suddenly Bo heard something inside making a lot of noise. His heart beating rapidly, he jumped backward and drew his gun. More noise came from the roof, and Bo quickly looked up. Three squirrels rushed out of a hole in the roof, ran to the edge, then jumped into a tree. They scampered up to the top, angrily chattering for being disturbed. Logan grinned as he holstered his gun, and then he slowly walked inside and looked around. A wooden bunk propped up on rocks stood against the wall to his left. On the wall opposite the door was a fireplace with a dutch oven built into one side of it. The hearth was big and well made, with an iron rod to hang pots on. A rickety table and two hand-made chairs were in the middle of the room. Pots and pans hung haphazardly from pegs driven into the wall by the fireplace, and shelves full of cans and sacks were on the other side. Dust and cobwebs covered everything in the cabin.

This place has been deserted for a long time, Bo thought. *Looks like someone just up and left one day and didn't come back.* He ran his finger through the dust on the table. *I don't think anyone has been here in over a year.* Bo's curiosity about the old place grew as he explored the cabin. *There is a mystery here to be solved,* Bo thought as he poked around the cabin. Maybe he would stay in the valley for a while and see if he could find out what had happened to the man who built the cabin and named it **RAINBOW'S END.**

When Bo went back outside to check on Dunce, he discovered the horse was nowhere in sight. The horse had already chewed off the limb he had been tied to and wandered off to who knows where. Frustrated, Bo followed Dunce's tracks back to the small stream, where he found him with his nose buried in the water, getting a drink. Bo let him drink his fill, then led him back to the cabin. He stripped off the saddle and bridle, then staked him close to the cabin in a patch of tall grass. Using his lariat, he hung the saddle from a high branch of a tree, out of reach of any creatures that may want to gnaw on it. Bo spent the next hour repairing the small corral behind the cabin. When he was satisfied that Dunce wouldn't be able to escape from it, he tackled the job of fixing up the cabin. He made some new leather hinges for the door out of his spare cinch strap and nailed it back up with a hammer he found in a well-stocked carpenter's box. He carried all the bedclothes outside to shake the dust out of them, then left them in the sun to kill any bugs that might have made a home in them. He repaired all the loose boards on the roof and then fixed the shutters on the two windows. Next Bo began cleaning the shelves and the floor. As he worked he wondered why someone had put so much work into building this cabin. Suddenly he saw something on the top shelf that gave him an idea what the reason might be. Scales, the kind miners use. Looking closer, he found a bottle of quicksilver and a few of the ribbed pans that miners use to pan gold. "He was a miner," Bo said. He searched the top shelves again and discovered several empty canvas sacks and ten leather pouches. "He must have found gold or he wouldn't have stayed here this long,"

Bo wasn't jumping to conclusions; he knew about gold. He had learned a lot about mining when he had worked in the mines back in Georgia. He knew that gold was found only in flakes, or dust, as the miners called it, and it would be carried in sacks; silver, on the other hand, had to be melted down from the ore and made into bars. Bo became excited as he began searching the cabin more thoroughly, hoping to find some gold. He looked in every nook and cranny and even checked for loose rocks in the fireplace, but an hour later, after a fruitless search, he was almost ready to give up. He was sitting on a chair thinking about hiding places when he noticed that the legs of the small cot were resting on large, flat rocks. Bo went over to the bed and pulled it off the rocks. He grasped one of the large rocks and began to slide it over to the side. Suddenly something struck his hand, and pain shot up his arm. "Damn it," he yelled as he jerked his hand away from the rock.

CHAPTER 4

"A damned scorpion!" Bo exclaimed as he cringed in pain from the scorpion's sting. He hurriedly put his finger in his mouth as he looked back at the rock to see where the scorpion had gone. Bo almost forgot the pain when he noticed the large hole in the floor that had been hidden by the flat rock. Carefully he reached for the rock and slowly moved it away from the hole. Suddenly the scorpion appeared from under the rock, running toward the safety of the cabin wall. "Gotcha," Bo yelled as he quickly crushed it with his boot. Bo checked to make sure it was dead, then turned his attention back to the exposed hole. He held the lantern for light as he leaned over and peered into the hole. Lying in the bottom were five plump canvas sacks. Bo gasped, then held his breath for a few seconds. Then, looking for more scorpions, he reached into the hole and picked up one of the sacks. He untied the leather string that kept it closed, then opened it and looked inside. "Gold," he said, "pure gold!" Shaking with excitement, Bo hurried to the cupboard, where he picked up one of the tin cups and set it on the table. Sunlight shining in from the open front door made the gold dust sparkle as he poured it into the cup. Bo stared at it for a few seconds, then ran his fingers through it to feel the texture of the gold flakes. "This gold came from quartz. The edges are still rough, and some of it is wire gold," he said. "Whoever this gold belongs to, he dug it out of a mine."

Carefully Bo poured the gold back into the sack, then laid it on the table. He went back to the hole in the floor to remove the other sacks from the hole. Taking them back to the table, he opened them all up; they all contained the same type of gold. His heart racing, Bo hurried back to the cot to check under the other rocks. He discovered that each one of the rocks had a hidden hole beneath it that contained bags of gold. Two of them, like the first hole, had five bags of gold hidden in them. The last hole had only two bags of gold, but it also contained a small wooden box. Bo removed all the gold-filled bags, then carried them to the table, where he checked the contents; it was the same type of gold. Bo gazed at the seventeen bags of gold as he figured the value. *There's over ten thousand dollars in gold sitting on that table*, Bo excitedly thought. *I could buy anything I wanted with that much money.* But suddenly his excitement began to wane as he remembered that it wasn't his gold. It belonged to whoever had mined it and hid it in this cabin. Bo's conscience would never let him take something that didn't belong to him. That was just the way he had been brought up, and that was the way he chose to live.

Bo was running these thoughts through his head when he thought about the box. He retrieved it from the hole, then set it on the table to examine it. The box was about six inches wide, nine inches long, and four inches high. It was well crafted out of hickory and had been well oiled to keep it waterproof. All of the joints were airtight. The lid had tiny brass hinges and fit snugly with a tongue and groove edge cut in to keep it bug proof. A brass latch held it closed, and it was tied with a leather strap.

Bo untied the strap, then opened the latch. As he slowly opened the box, a musky smell seeped from inside. As the light illuminated the contents, Bo was surprised to see only a few letters and a photograph. Bo picked up the picture and saw that it was of a pretty girl who looked to be about nine or ten years old. She was wearing a fancy dress, and her light-colored hair was in braids. Bo studied the photo for a few moments before he placed it on the table.

He picked up the letters to examine them. They were all addressed to Thomas O'Shay and were from the Perfect Lady Girls Academy in New York. Bo settled back in his chair and began to read the letters. From their content, Bo learned that Thomas O'Shay was a widower with one daughter. He had placed his daughter, whose name was Bonnie, in a girl's boarding school when he went out west to prospect for gold. The first letters Bonnie wrote to her father were addressed to general delivery in San Francisco. The last letter was dated four years ago and addressed to Tucson. Bo frowned. *Four years is a long time,* he thought as he put the letters and photo back in the box. *What happened to Thomas O'Shay, and where is his daughter now?* The question was still in his mind as Bo put the sacks and the box back in the holes and replaced the cot on the rocks.

CHAPTER 5

A knock on the door startled Professor Sylvester Dungerhill. He quickly shoved the French nude picture postcards he had been staring at into his desk drawer. "Come in," he called out.

The door opened, revealing a short, heavyset woman in a shapeless gray dress and black high lace shoes. Her round face was framed by her brown, ratty hair pulled back in a tight bun. Oma Stutdorf, the professor's assistant, swiftly lumbered to the front of his desk. "Professor, I have just received the latest bank statement, and we have a problem," Oma reported in a serious voice. "The school bank account is almost broke; in fact, we don't have enough money to pay next month's wages." She laid the bank statement on his desk and stepped back.

"Are you sure?" Professor Dungerhill said as he picked up the statement. The expression on his face changed from irritated to worry as he examined the figures on the paper. "How could this have happened? I thought we were in fine financial shape." He raised his head and looked at Oma, an accusing look on his face.

Oma put her hands on her ample hips and glared back at the professor. "I told you the school couldn't afford it when you gave yourself that huge Christmas bonus. Now you have to explain to Mister Vanderoche why the school is broke."

Professor Dungerhill slumped back in his chair. A touch of fear slowly spread in his mind. He had never thought it would come to this. He had been borrowing from the school for years to cover his gambling debts. He had always thought he would win big the next time and pay it back. Now there was nothing left to borrow. Mister Vanderoche would fire him, and no one else in New York would hire him. He would have to sell his house to pay off his debts. He shuddered as he thought of what they would do to him if he couldn't pay. Suddenly he thought of something that had been at the back of his mind for a long time. "What about the O'Shay account? How much money is left in it?"

A look of puzzlement came over Oma's face. "There are three thousand dollars left in her account, enough for three more years." Oma quickly glanced at the door, suddenly guessing at what he was thinking. She wanted to be sure she wasn't overheard. "That money is in a trust fund and can't be touched."

Professor Dungerhill smiled. "There are always loopholes in any contract. My name is on that trust fund along with Thomas O'Shay's and yours. All we have to do is claim that Mister O'Shay pulled his daughter out of school and we refunded his money."

Oma still looked puzzled. "But we haven't heard from Mister O'Shay in two years. How are we going to get him to sign?"

Professor Dungerhill sighed and shook his head. "I'm sure that if Thomas O'Shay were alive, he would have contacted us by now, so I presume he is dead." He leaned forward and looked her in the eye." I will forge his name."

Oma's expression changed to one of understanding. "Oh, I see what you mean." She glanced back at the door for a second, then turned back to Dungerhill with a fearful look in her eyes. "What will we do about the girl?"

"She will have to go," he said." An evil grin came upon his face. "I think I know just what to do with her."

CHAPTER 6

Bonnie O'Shay, a tall, shapely girl for her fourteen years, was one of the most popular girls in her school. Not only was she pretty, with blonde hair and blue eyes, she had a very outgoing personality and was friendly to everyone. She was very intelligent and made high grades in her classes, but she also had a lot of common sense. A lot of the girls in the school went to her for advice or help with their homework. On this particular day when her best friend, Lucinda Mayberry, came into her room, Bonnie assumed she needed help with her arithmetic again.

"Bonnie, would you help me with today's lesson in arithmetic? I just can't figure out this decimal system."

Bonnie smiled. "Oh Lucinda, I showed you how to do that yesterday."

Lucinda sat down on the bed next to Bonnie, who was sitting at her desk. "I know, but I still can't remember where to move the decimal when I multiply two numbers." She placed her notebook in front of Bonnie, then put her hand on Bonnie's shoulder. "You are so smart, Bonnie. I am so glad you are my best friend."

Bonnie smiled and picked up the notebook. She had great fondness for her friend, even though the girl was an airhead sometimes. Bonnie needed a close friend. She didn't have any family except her father, and she hadn't had a letter from him in two years. If it weren't for Lucinda, she didn't know what she would do sometimes. She was just beginning to explain to her about decimals for the umpteenth time when there was a knock at the door. Before she could say come in, Bertha Muddle, one of the teachers, walked into the room. She was a tall woman in her thirties, wearing a long, blue striped dress and white buckle shoes. She had dark, curly hair to her shoulders and a faint mustache under her pug noise. She was a big-boned woman with a deep voice. "Bonnie, Professor Dungerhill wants to see you in his office right away."

At first Bonnie wondered what he wanted her for, but then a wave of hope swept across her mind. It could be news from her father. She became excited. "Yes, ma'am," Bonnie said as she got up from her desk. She turned to Lucinda and put her hand on hers. "I'll see you later."

Bertha walked back into the hallway and stood by the door. Bonnie followed her out, then continued down the hall. Bertha, her eyes glistening with tears, watched until Bonnie was out of sight.

The door was open when Bonnie arrived at professor Dungerhill's office. She hesitated at the threshold when she saw him looking at something in his desk drawer. "You wanted to see me, sir?"

Sylvester jerked and quickly slammed the drawer shut. "Yes, Bonnie," He smiled and motioned her in. "Close the door, please."

Bonnie closed the door and walked to his desk. He nodded toward the chair beside her. "Sit down, Bonnie."

She slowly sat down in the chair as she watched his face, hoping to see a sign of good news. Instead, he was frowning.

"Bonnie, I'm afraid I have some bad news. We haven't heard from your father in two years, and I think it is time to assume that he is most certainly, uh, deceased."

A cloak of dismay seemed to fall over Bonnie, and she couldn't catch her breath. Tears came to her eyes. "Have you heard anything?" Bonnie asked with a glimmer of hope still in her mind.

"I telegraphed the sheriff in Tucson, which is the last place we heard from your father, and asked him to inquire about Thomas

O'Shay," Professor Dungerhill said. "He wired back that no one has ever heard of the man."

Bonnie slumped back in her chair. She couldn't think of anything else to say. Sadly she put her hands to her face and sobbed.

Professor Dungerhill watched her cry, his face not showing any emotion. "Bonnie, there are some more things we need to discuss," he said awkwardly after she had cried for a few minutes. Bonnie looked up at him as she dried her eyes with her handkerchief. "The money your father paid for your tuition here at the school ran out at the first of this current session. I was hoping that your father would send more money to pay the amount you owe, but he never did." Professor Dungerhill paused for a second, then continued. "With your situation now and the fact that the school is in financial trouble because of the recession, I have arranged to place you in an institution where you will learn a trade. You will be able to support yourself in the future."

Bonnie just stared at the professor. This was all happening too fast. Her mind couldn't comprehend what Professor Dungerhill was saying. "What am I supposed to do, sir?" she asked in a subdued voice.

"Go to your room, pack your things, and come back to the office," he told her. "Someone will be here this afternoon to pick you up and take you to your new home."

Bonnie's spirit was broken; puppet-like, she slowly walked back to her room. Lucinda was waiting for her when she got there.

"What did he want?" she asked.

"I have to leave the school," Bonnie replied as tears came to her eyes again. "He said my father is dead."

"Where will you go?" Lucinda put her arms around Bonnie and hugged her.

"I have to go to a place where I can learn a trade." Bonnie said.

"An orphanage?" Lucinda dropped her arms. She stepped back from Bonnie, a strange look on her face.

Bonnie turned to her best friend. "We can still be best friends, I will write to you."

"Yes, maybe you will live close by and you can visit." Lucinda said unemotionally as she picked up her notebook from the desk.

"I hope so." Bonnie said, feeling a little better. She dried her tears again as she turned to find a bag to put her things in. "Do you want to help me pack?"

"I really need to go do my homework. Without you here I will have to study harder to pass my classes."

Bonnie sensed something different in Lucinda but couldn't quite figure it out. "Go ahead and study, Lucinda, I need to be alone for a while, anyway." Bonnie watched her leave, then slowly began packing her things. Bertha brought her some boxes, and she put things in them that she didn't need right away. Bertha told her they would store them for her until she could get them. Finally, she was through. She took one last look around the room. This had been her home for four years, and she regretted leaving it. She picked up the picture of her father, which had been on her dresser. She studied it for a minute and then put it in her bag.

The giggles coming from the group of parasol-carrying girls standing in the parlor only intensified the ache of sadness in her heart as Bonnie slowly walked back to Professor Dungerhill's office. One of the girls saw her and whispered to another. The giggling stopped as they all turned to look at her. Two of them called out weak goodbyes, but most of them just stared and whispered behind their hands. Bonnie looked for Lucinda, but she was nowhere to be seen. Professor Dungerhill was talking to a man she had never seen before when she walked into his office. A woman was sitting in a chair beside him.

"Ah Bonnie, here you are," Professor Dungerhill said when he saw her, a smile on his face. "I want you to meet Mister Bart Mastard, and the lady is Martha Shatt. They are here to take you to your new home."

Bonnie was instantly repelled at the sight of Bart Mastard. He was a short, greasy-looking man with black, slicked-back hair that looked as if it had never been washed. He had on a rumpled, threadbare suit that looked as if it had come out of a rubbish bin.

When he stuck out his hand to her, she could see the dirt under his fingernails. He grinned, and his teeth were yellow. His breath almost made her sick, and his eyes seemed to be looking through her clothes. Hesitantly she shook his hand. She was relieved when he turned loose her hand. She turned to the woman, who had gotten out of the chair; she wasn't much better. The woman was tall and rail thin. Her clothes looked costly but were threadbare and worn. Her lanky hair was pushed up under a last year's hat, and she smelled as if she had poured a bottle of cheap perfume over herself. Martha put her arm around Bonnie and squeezed.

"I just know you will like it in your new home," she crooned to Bonnie. "You will have lots of new friends, and you will learn a trade so you can support yourself when you are all grown up."

Bonnie didn't think she could feel any worse, but this was too much. She burst out crying again, the tears flowing down her cheeks.

"It will be okay, dear," Martha said as she patted Bonnie on the back. "Come with me. We will go on to the carriage." She turned to Bart. "Will you get her bags?" Martha grabbed Bonnie by the hand and led her out of the office to a carriage parked in front of the school. Bonnie meekly climbed into the one-horse Studebaker and sat quietly sobbing. She was beyond caring about anything. Her whole life was coming apart, and it would never be the same again.

Professor Dungerhill watched as Bonnie and Martha left the office, his face emotionless. He turned to Bart.

"Remember, half of her wages go to me to pay her bill here at the school."

"I know, I know, you will get your cut. This ain't the first time we've done this," Bart said. "I've already got her job lined up; you will get your first payment on the first of the month."

Dungerhill smiled as he watched Bart, carrying Bonnie's bags, leave his office. This was working out fine for him. He went back to his desk. He opened the drawer where he kept the French post-cards and started browsing through them again.

Bonnie thought the ride through New York City would never end. They soon left the rich part of town and entered the business district. Smoke from the hundreds of factories settled to the streets, and the smell of rotting garbage permeated the air. People were everywhere, from workers with dirty work clothes to beggars dressed in rags. Vendors were selling all kinds of things out of their makeshift stalls that lined the sidewalks and alleys. Bonnie had never seen this side of the city, and she was scared. She was glad when the carriage passed most of the factories, but then they stopped in front of a large, two-story building that was in bad need of repair.

Martha got out of the carriage. "Come on, Bonnie, this is your new home." She stuck out her hand to Bonnie.

"I don't want to live here," Bonnie said. "This place is horrible. I can't breathe here."

Martha's face suddenly changed to anger. She grabbed Bonnie by the arm and slapped her hard on the face. She pulled Bonnie's tear-stained face closer to hers.

"Let's get something straight right now, fancy girl. This is your new home whether you like it or not. You belong to me now, and you will do as I say."

Bonnie opened her mouth in surprise. She had never been hit in her life. She stared at Martha, and the truth rushed into her mind. She was all alone; she didn't have anywhere else to go. She was dependent on these people. "Yes ma'am; I'm sorry. Bonnie hung her head. She would go along with these people and do what they wanted, but as soon as she could, she was leaving this place. She would go out West to look for her father.

CHAPTER 7

Bo's excitement from finding the gold was subsiding as his thoughts turned to the whereabouts of Thomas O'Shay and his daughter. He stared at the picture of the young girl again. A feeling of sadness and concern come over him as he thought about the O'Shays. Bo decided that he would do everything he could to find out what had happened to Tom O'Shay and his daughter Bonnie.

With that decision made, Bo's thoughts turned to the cabin. He was feeling hungry, but he wanted to finish cleaning and repairing the cabin before he ate lunch. Bo had seen a wooden bucket, so he took it to the stream and got some water. He started a fire in the fireplace and heated water in an old, blue, speckled teakettle he found next to the fireplace. When the water was hot, he poured it into a dishpan that matched the teakettle and washed all the kitchen utensils. He swept the dirt floor as well as he could, then cleaned the shelves and wiped the dust from the furniture. The sun showed mid-afternoon by the time he was finally satisfied that the cabin was as clean as he could get it.

By now Bo's stomach was screaming to him that he was hungry, and suddenly he realized he hadn't eaten since the morning he had seen the Apaches. His own grub sack consisted of only a little beef jerky, so he examined the cans of food on the shelves. He picked up a can of beans and looked around for a can opener.

"I guess Tom won't mind if I borrow some of his beans; that is, if they're not spoiled," Bo said. Not finding a can opener, he pulled out his Bowie knife and cut off the top. The beans smelled okay, so he set the can close to the fire to warm it up. He had found some flour earlier in a big tin, but it had a few weevils in it. He found a flour sifter and sifted out enough bug-free flour to make himself a few tortillas. These he cooked on a flat iron pan nestled in the hot coals. When the beans were warm, Bo poured them straight out of the can onto the tortillas, then wolfed them down with cool creek water.

"I'm as full as a tick on a Redbone coon hound," he said to himself later as he pushed himself away from the table. He sat for a few more minutes thinking about Tom and Bonnie O'Shay, wondering where they were now. Finally he decided he would explore the valley to see what other clues he could find that might help him in his quest. First he cleaned up his dishes, then went outside to where Dunce, to his surprise, was still tied right where he had left him. Even though Dunce had shortened a large patch of the grass around him, he still didn't want to quit eating when Bo untied him to lead him back to where he had left the saddle and bridle. "Sorry, boy, I know you're enjoying the rest, but I want to scout out this valley before it gets dark," Bo said to the dun gelding as he finished tightening up the saddle. Bo mounted Dunce, then urged him onto the well-used trail that ran past the cabin and wound through a grove of evergreens.

Bo had seen fresh tracks earlier, so he wasn't surprised when the trail faded out at a small meadow where two horses were grazing in knee-high grass along with several deer. He stopped Dunce and watched. The deer spotted him at once; one of them gave its sneeze-like warning before they all trotted back into the trees, their tails raised high. Both of the grazing horses raised their heads to see what had disturbed the deer. Spotting Dunce, one of them nickered as both of them trotted over closer. They hesitated when they were a few feet away and looked at the horse and rider for a minute, then they slowly eased closer. One of them, a bay mare, eased up to touch noses with Dunce. This brought the other horse up closer, a gray gelding; he had to touch noses with Dunce, too. He squealed, then seconds later both of them were pushing and snorting, trying to touch Dunce. They didn't seem to notice Bo until he swatted the mare when she bumped up against his leg. The horses finally settled down enough so Bo could examine them. Both of them were fat, but their feet need trimming. He also noticed that both of the horses had a T O branded on their hips, and the mare had the markings of carrying a pack rig.

"This mystery is getting deeper," Bo said to Dunce, who responded by swishing his tail at a deerfly biting at his rump. Whoever lived in this valley disappeared one day, and for over a year, probably two, hasn't come back. All the signs point to a dead man, but what had happened to him? Did he die here, or did he leave the valley and for some reason he didn't come back? My guess is that if he died here, he will be close to his mine, so I need to find the mine." Bo rode around the meadow until he found where the trail continued out through a gap in the trees. The other two horses followed him for a while, but they stopped to resume their grazing when he passed through the trees. Bo followed the winding trail until it split into two directions at a rocky slope that ran up to the bottom of the cliffs that surrounded the valley. The trail ran both ways along the bottom of the slope, seeming to follow the cliffs. Bo turned left and followed the trail that looked as if it had been used the most. He had only gone a little ways when he came to the place where the stream that ran across the valley disappeared into a hole at the bottom of the cliffs. Twenty yards upstream Bo spotted a small waterfall about three feet tall, and built beside it, where the water would run into it, was a sluice box.

"The mine has to be pretty close," he said to himself as he rode up to the sluice and examined it. It was about twenty feet long and built where it would carry the water back into the stream. There was no water running in it now because a gate that controlled the water was closed. Bo stepped out of the saddle and picked up some of the sand in the bottom of the sluice to examine it. Almost immediately he realized it was nearly pure gold. "There's enough gold in this sluice to fill a pouch," he mused. "The mine must be really rich." Becoming more excited by the gold, he quickly tied Dunce to a tree and looked around, trying to spot signs of digging. He noticed a side trail leading up the slope, so he followed it until he came to a cave at the base of the cliff. The opening was small, but as Bo peered inside, he saw digging tools leaning against one of the walls. Bo ducked his head and stepped into the cave, his heart beating faster and faster in excitement. He walked a few steps to the back wall of the excavation, where someone had been digging.

"Wow!" was the only thing Bo could say; he had never seen anything like this. It was the mine, but what a mine. There was a vein of quartz in the wall of the cave full of wire gold. Bo grabbed a pick and swung it into the vein. It crumbled under the pick almost like dirt. He picked up some of the crumbled quartz, then pulled the wire gold out of it. "I have almost a handful of gold!" Bo said after a few minutes. He was so excited he couldn't control himself. He began swinging the pick into the vein, digging out more of the ore until he had a small pile. He began crushing the ore with a sledgehammer so he could pick out the gold. Bo continued this routine frantically until he could hardly lift the pick any more. He finally stopped, sat down, and leaned against the wall of the cave to rest. After his breathing slowed down and he had rested a while, his gold fever abated and calmness returned to him. He surveyed the pile of gold he had dug out of the quartz. He had nearly enough to fill one of the leather bags. "Eight ounces of gold at about fifteen dollars an ounce is one hundred and twenty dollars. I dug this out in only about an hour," he said to himself as he put the gold into his pocket. "If the vein holds out, I could be rich." Getting excited again, Bo continued working but at a slower pace until he had filled both his pockets. Finally he reluctantly put down the pick and walked out of the mine back to Dunce. "Let's go, Dunce," he said as he mounted the dun horse. "I have to go back to the cabin and get some sacks."

Although it was mid-afternoon, Bo worked the mine the rest of the day until he had filled two of the leather sacks with gold. That night after he had eaten, he thought more about the man who had built the cabin and discovered the gold. He felt bad about not looking for more signs of what had happened to him. He decided he would search the valley for Thomas O'Shay before he did anything else.

The next morning Bo saddled up Dunce and started his search for more clues. First he rode all around the edge of the valley looking for trails or hidden canyons that would be another way out. When he couldn't find any other way in or out of the valley other than the cave, he began to crisscross the valley looking for clues. He looked for two days and covered the whole valley, but finally he gave up when he couldn't find any trace of O'Shay. He did find a few cows scattered around the valley and at least one bull because two of the cows had calves. On the second night as Bo was eating supper, he finally came to the conclusion that since the cave was the only way in or out of the valley for men or livestock, Thomas O'Shay had been alive when he left the valley. Bo decided that he would work the mine for a few more days and then go to Tucson to ask around about O'Shay. Maybe someone there knew what had happened to the miner.

The next four days, Bo worked the mine and filled four of the large sacks with gold. On the fifth day, as he was eating his supper, he decided that he would leave in the morning for Tucson. He would continue his search for O'Shay and also pick up some much-needed food and supplies.

Early the next morning, Bo saddled up Dunce, then rode out to catch the mare. He found the two horses grazing as usual in the small meadow. He roped the mare, then led her back to the cabin, the gelding following. Bo would have to take care of that problem later. When they got back to the cabin, Bo placed a halter and a packsaddle on the mare. Bo remembered how hot and dry the desert was, so he made sure he had plenty of water as he loaded his supplies on the mare for the trip. After he was finished loading the mare, he put four sacks of the gold he had taken from the mine into his saddlebags. Bo closed the door to the cabin, mounted Dunce, then, after a quick look around the area, headed for the entrance to the valley.

When Bo arrived at the entrance of the cave, he checked the dirt at the entrance for tracks but found only where a raccoon had entered and exited. Tying the mare's lead rope to his saddle, Bo walked and led Dunce through the cave; the mare followed right along just as if she had been there before. The gelding tried to follow, but Bo quickly put up a barrier to stop him. Bo could still hear him whinnying halfway to the other end of the cave. When they reached other end of the cave, the brush barrier was still in place and everything looked the same. Bo removed the brush, then led the horses outside, where he tied them to a small tree. He quickly replaced the brush at the cave entrance, then left the horses tied as he cautiously crept toward the rim of the ledge just above the water hole. His heart began racing as he slowly moved his head forward to peer over the edge and thoughts of Apaches camping below crossed his mind. The water hole came into view, and Bo breathed a sigh of relief; a mule deer was calmly drinking its murky water. It was a clear sign that no humans were in the area.

The bright sun was just beginning to warm up the desert as Bo made his way down the rocky slope to the water hole. He stopped to let the horses drink before he led them along the trail that would eventually bring him back to the main road between Nogales and Tucson. Initially Bo had been traveling on that road but had gotten off of it when he saw the sign that pointed toward the water hole. He hurried the horses down the trail until he came to the main road, then he turned west toward Tucson. He wanted to hurry to get out of the Apache country, so he continued to push the horses as fast as he thought he could without hurting them. But the day became increasingly hot, and after a while, he had to slow down. He had just emptied the water from his last canteen into his hat for the horses to drink when he glimpsed smoke coming from a building in the distance. Quickly he divided the water between the two horses and mounted Dunce. "Dunce, I think we found civilization."

CHAPTER 8

A slight breeze carried the familiar smell of horse dung mixed with hay to Bo's nose as he rode up to one of several hitching posts in front of the stage station. Slowly, testing his stiff muscles, he dismounted, then tied Dunce's and the mare's reins to the wooden post. It felt good to stretch his legs and straighten the kinks out of them. Bo started walking toward the front door of the stage station but paused to take a closer look at three other horses tied in front of the building. One was obviously an army horse with its McClellan saddle and USA branded on its hip. The other two horses, a bay with black legs and a blue roan, were branded with a Box S brand. They looked like good horses, but Bo didn't see any ropes or chaps on them like a working cowboy would have on his horse. He felt a tinge of caution but shrugged it off as he turned his attention back to the stage station. The wooden steps creaked as he stepped up to the large, roofed porch that shaded the front door. It was a large, two-story clapboard building with a false front rising above a balcony on the second floor. The large sign out front read, **Butterfield Stage Station**. A smaller sign under it read, **Saloon, rooms, entertainment. Bob Vail, prop**. When Bo pushed open the batwing doors, the usual saloon smells of tobacco and stale beer greeted him. It wasn't a smell he liked, but he knew that in a few minutes, he wouldn't even notice it. He stepped to the side and stopped for a few seconds to let his eyes adjust to the dim light inside the saloon. A bar made of rough planks laid over upright barrels ran along the wall to his left. Behind it were shelves with various bottles of liquor lined up on them. Several equally rough homemade tables were scattered around the rest of the room along with matching chairs. A steep set of stairs on the back wall ran up to a small balcony that had several cloth-covered doors lined up behind it.

The three men playing poker at one of the tables looked up when he walked in, then went back to their game. The bartender was wiping a shot glass, but his eyes were on Bo. He set the glass down and smiled as Bo walked up to the bar. He was a small, thin, middle-aged man wearing an apron over his corduroy pants and black garters on his white shirt. A light grey beard covered his jaws and chin.

"Give me a beer," Bo ordered.

Without a word, the bartender turned around, picked up a dingy glass mug, and filled it with beer until the foam ran over the top. He set the mug in front of Bo. "That'll be ten cents."

Bo reached into his pocket, pulled out a quarter, and pitched it on the bar. "Take out for two."

The bartender glanced at the coin as he picked it up then dropped it in a tin box. He dug around in the box until he pulled out a nickel. He scraped his fingernail across it before he handed it to Bo.

"It still has a little gold-colored paint on it from when some city slicker tried to pass it off as a five-dollar gold piece," the bartender explained.

Bo looked at the nickel for a second, then grinned. "I heard tell of a blind man who gold plated some of those V nickels when they first came out, then passed quite a few of them. When they caught him, they couldn't convict him because he was blind."

"The man who had this one was caught and convicted right here." The bartender motioned with his thumb to a window in the back of the saloon.

Bo looked out the window and solemnly nodded his head. Grave markers dotted a hill in the distance. He took a big drink of his beer. "Seems a little harsh to kill a man for trying to trick someone."

"This is a hard country, mister." The bartender said. "The cowboys out here work all month for twenty dollars, and the soldiers make less than that. Five dollars is a lot of money to them." He picked up a mug, examined it, and began to wipe it with his dirty rag. "Anyway, this feller was playing poker with some of the locals when he tried to pass it off in the game. One of the players, Sergeant Dooley, who had just transferred in from the East, scraped some of the gold paint off of one of the coins, then accused the man of cheating them. The man claimed he was innocent, but they found nineteen more on him when they searched him."

Bo emptied his glass, then pushed it to the bartender. The beer wasn't that good, but at least it was wet. The bartender drew a refill, then set it back in front of Bo.

Bo took a big drink. "Did they hang him?"

"Nope," the bartender said. "He went for his gun; four men beat him to the draw, pumped him full of lead."

Bo just shook his head as he turned around to look at the rest of the people in the bar. One of the men playing poker was a soldier. He was a medium-sized man with a smooth face and sandy-colored hair: a sergeant by the chevrons on his sleeve. There was only small change on the table, and most of it was in front of the sergeant. Suddenly one of the other players, a stocky, red-haired man with a flat nose, threw down his hand.

"That's it for me; I'm just about broke." He got up and lumbered over to the bar. "Give me a beer, old man," he said as he pulled a dime out of his pocket. In his haste, he fumbled with it; with a "clink" it fell into a spittoon. The bartender, who was just starting to fill a mug with beer, stopped when he heard the sound of the coin hitting the brass spittoon.

"God damn you, give me the beer." Flat Nose bellowed when he saw the bartender stop filling the mug.

The bartender shook his head. "I know that's your last dime; get it out and give it to me first."

Suddenly, Flat Nose reached across the bar and grabbed the bartender by his shirt. "Damn you, old bastard, don't talk to me that way," he growled as he pulled the bartender across the bar. "Your dime is in the spittoon. Give me my beer."

At first Bo thought it was an amusing situation, but when Flat Nose got rough with the old man, he got angry. Although he had been taught to mind his own business, he had also been taught to respect his elders. He grabbed Flat Nose by the arm and said strongly, "Leave him alone. I'll buy you a beer."

Flat Nose screwed up his face, then shoved the bartender back across the bar. He turned back to Bo, tilting his head to look up into Bo's eyes, "You ought to stay out of other people's business." Suddenly he swung a roundhouse punch at Bo. Bo saw the blow coming and blocked it with his left arm. He immediately swung his right hand, still holding the beer mug, against the head of his attacker. Flat Nose's eyes closed as blood spurted from his forehead, and he dropped to the floor.

Bo dropped the mug and glanced at the table where Flat Nose had been playing poker. The other drifter, a tall, thin man with a dark, bushy beard, suddenly stood up. His hand was on his pistol.

"You son of a bitch, I'll kill you," he shouted angrily as he pulled his gun from its holster.

Automatically Bo's arm moved to his Colt. "BOOM!" The roar of the forty-five shook the glasses stacked behind the bar. The bartender and the sergeant jerked at the sound of the blast, and the bluish smoke from Bo's pistol blurred the scene. Bushy Beard had been knocked backward and was now lying in a widening pool of blood. The army sergeant, who was still sitting at the table, was the first to move. He slowly raised his arms. "I'm not with these men."

Bo nodded, and the soldier relaxed. Bo walked over to the bloody body. Bushy Beard's gun was still in his hand.

"He's dead," the sergeant said indifferently. "You drilled him right through the heart."

The bartender came over to look. "That's the fastest draw I ever seen, mister. What's your name?"

Bo holstered his Colt. "Bo Logan's the name," He turned to the sergeant. "You saw him go for his gun first, didn't you?"

"Yes sir," the sergeant agreed. "It was a clear case of self-defense."

"Yeah," echoed the bartender. "We both saw it."

Bo heard someone on the porch and glanced at the door, his hand ready to draw. He relaxed as two people slowly came in.

"What's all the shooting about, Bob?" An old man who looked a lot like the bartender spoke. The other one was an Indian who had long, black hair and was dressed in white cotton pants and shirt.

"Just some guy with more mouth than gun, Shorty," the bartender said. "You and Lame Deer drag him on out back to boot hill and dig a hole. We'll say some words over him later."

"Hold up a minute," Bo said. "We need to wake up his partner so he can see that this was a fair fight."

The bartender looked at Bo. "Good idea, mister, but I don't think it will help you any. You just shot one of the Skinner brothers."

Shorty grabbed a bucket from behind the bar and went back out the door. Shortly he returned with a bucket of water and threw it into the face of the still-unconscious Flat Nose.

"Oh," he groaned as he woke up. "What's going on?"

"Your friend's dead. He pulled a gun on this man, but he got outdrew; it was a fair fight." The sergeant said.

"He was pretty fast," Flat Nose said thoughtfully as he rubbed his head. "If you beat him, you must be mighty fast. Don't matter though, you better start saying your prayers because he got two brothers who will be looking for you, and they won't play fair."

Bo muttered to himself, "I just can't stay out of trouble." He turned to the bartender. "Give me another drink—whiskey this time."

As the bartender poured Bo's whiskey, the sergeant helped Flat Nose off the floor. Flat Nose watched as Shorty and the Indian carried the dead man out the back door.

"Do you want them to load him on his horse, or do you want us to bury him out back?" The bartender asked.

"You bury him; I ain't going to smell him all the way back to Tucson. If John wants to bury him in town, he can send someone out to get him."

"What was Skinner's first name so they can put it on his marker?" Bo asked.

Flat Nose picked up his hat, put it on, and turned to Bo. "Willy Skinner is who you killed; his brother John in Tucson will put a price on your head." Flat Nose walked out of the saloon, mounted his horse, then spurred him to a gallop as he turned him down the road toward Tucson.

The bartender got some rags and slowly began wiping up the blood on the floor.

"John Skinner runs a saloon called the Silver Dollar," he said. "They say he's pretty mean. The other brother's name is Curt; he's the meanest one of the bunch. He tries to live up to his name. He skinned a man once just because he didn't like what the man had said to him. The last I heard, he was in the prison at Yuma."

Bo listened to what Bob said, then dismissed it from his mind. Bo never worried about someone's reputation. Most of them were exaggerated, anyway. The threats he would take care of as they came. "When does the next stage for Tucson arrive?"

"It's overdue now, but that don't mean nothing; it's always late," Bob said.

Bo thought for a minute. "I need to be on that stagecoach. Can I board my horses here until I come back? I'm going into Tucson for supplies, and I'll be back in few days. I'm going to try some prospecting back in the mountains."

"Sure, it's two bits a day for each horse. By the way, I'm Bob Vail, the owner of this place. You can pay me for the stage ticket, too. It's two dollars to Tucson. You want a round trip?"

"Glad to meet you, Bob," Bo said as he stuck out his hand. They shook, then Bo said, "No, just one way." Bo reached into his pocket to pull out some coins. He selected a five-dollar gold piece and handed it to the bartender. "Take out for two beers, too," he said as he pointed to the sergeant with his thumb. "One for me and one for Sarge." The sergeant, who had been listening all this time, walked over closer to Bo and stuck out his hand.

"Dooley's the name, Sergeant Dooley. Came to New York from Ireland in fifty-nine and joined the army, been in ever since."

"Bo Logan, born in Georgia," Bo said as he shook the sergeant's hand. "I don't like trouble, but it seems to follow me around."

Sergeant Dooly grinned. "I know what you mean; trouble follows me too, especially when I'm drunk."

Bo laughed as he turned to the bartender, who was bringing the beer.

"Bo Logan, huh," Bob said. "I've heard talk of a Bo Logan in Texas, fast with a gun, like you."

Bo took a long drink of his beer as the two men watched. He knew they were expecting some kind of answer. "I've been in Texas; worked for a small rancher with good water." He took another drink of his beer. "A big rancher tried to force the little rancher to sell. It ended up in a little shooting scrape."

"What I heard was ten men came to force the sale, but five of them were killed and the rest turned tail." The bartender said as he wiped the bar.

"I guess it grows with the telling," Bo said. "There were six men, but only three were killed."

"Oh," The bartender said as he wiped the bar again. "Well, you still got yourself a reputation. They didn't lie when they said you were fast; I seen it."

"The stage is coming."

Bo turned to the door when he heard Shorty yell from outside. The three men hurried to the door. A cloud of dust boiling up from the road covered the big Concord Stagecoach as it slowed down and stopped. A short, husky driver with a brown beard and an even shorter shotgun guard with a large mustache were in the driver's box. Both of them were waving their hats, trying to keep the dust off their faces.

"Draw me up a beer, Vail," the driver bellowed in a deep, gravelly voice. "I'm as dry as this dust."

"Me too," the shotgun guard yelled in an almost womanish, high-pitched voice. "He ain't no drier than I am." The two men crawled down from the stagecoach, then hurried into the saloon. Shorty and Lame Deer had already begun unhitching the horses so they could change them out for fresh ones.

Bo went over to his pack mare to pull off his pack. He threw it up on the top rack of the Concord, then crawled up to tie it securely. By this time, the driver and guard were back, and the fresh horses were hitched. Bo retrieved his saddlebags from Dunce, then crawled into the stage clutching it in his arms. He saw the bartender on the porch as the stage jerked to a start. He shouted at him as they rushed by, "I'll see you in a few days. Tell Shorty to give that dun horse some corn. I promised it to him."

CHAPTER 9

It was late at night when the stagecoach finally reached the outskirts of Tucson. Bo had dozed off but was awaken by the excited chatter of the other passengers when they saw the first houses on the outskirts of town. Bo roused himself and looked out the window. Nearly all of the houses were dark, their occupants deep in sleep.

"Does anyone know the time?" one of the passengers asked.

"It's about eleven," another answered.

After a few minutes, they began to see the businesses of the town. Most were closed, but a few glowed with soft lantern light, indicating someone working late. Bo's knowledge of Tucson was sparse, but from what he could see, it was a fair-sized town. During the trip one of the passengers, William Morgan, a merchant who was on his way to Tucson, explained to him that with the coming of the railroad and the end of the Apache wars, a lot of mining companies were moving into the area along with a few farmers and ranchers. Bo, having seen only the desert part of Arizona, was surprised to learn that a lot of the land in Arizona could be farmed. William went on to tell him that in the higher elevation of the mountains, there was a lot of land suitable for farming.

Finally they arrived at the stage station, which was located in the center of Tucson. The travel-weary passengers slowly crawled out of the coach and collected their bags. After saying good-bye to the merchant, Bo walked a block down the street to the nearest hotel he could see. There was no one behind the desk when he entered, but a middle-aged man wearing a white shirt, gray trousers, and shiny leather shoes was sleeping in one of the large, overstuffed chairs.

"Is anybody running this place?" Bo said in a loud voice.

The man in the chair jerked and opened his eyes. "Huh? Yes, I can help you." He got up from the chair and hurriedly walked behind the counter.

"I need a room for a few days."

"Yes, sir, we can fix you right up. I just need you to sign the register." The clerk pushed the large open book across the counter. "Rooms are a dollar a day in advance."

Bo picked a fancy quill pen out of its inkwell, shook a drop of ink off the tip, and signed his name on the book. He pulled three silver dollars out of his pocket. "Here's enough for three days." He laid them on the counter.

The clerk picked up the coins and smiled as he turned the register around to write the date and the amount by Bo's name. "Room ten, up the stairs and at the end of the hall," he said as he handed Bo a key he had removed from a pigeonhole behind the desk.

Bo took the key, picked up his gear, and walked up the stairs to his room. Hot, stuffy air with the smell of turpentine greeted him when he opened the door. He set his things down on the floor and lit a lamp on a table so he could examine the room. The only furniture besides the table was an iron-railed bed and a nightstand pushed up against one wall. A door to a small closet stood open to expose a few wooden clothes hangers on a wooden pole. The one window in the room faced the street and had white, lacey curtains hanging down each side. He had stayed in worse rooms.

Bo locked the door, then walked over to the window to open it and let in some fresh air. As he slid it open, music and laughter from a saloon down the street drifted into the room. Bo studied the street for a minute, locating the saloon and the other stores that were close by. He saw a few blue-clad soldiers walk out of the saloon, and he thought of Dooly. He liked the little Irishman, and he hoped he would see him again. Finally he closed the curtains, then walked to the nightstand, where he poured water from the pitcher into the wash pan so he could wash his face and hands.

After he dried them with a towel hanging on a peg, he undid his pack, pulled out his shaving gear, and put it on the shelf over the washstand. He hadn't brought any of his extra clothes because he intended to buy new ones while he was in town. He slid the saddlebags containing the gold under the bed. Bo unbuckled his gun belt, then carefully hung it on the bedpost before he sat down to pull off his boots. Pulling off all his sweat-soaked clothes down to his bare skin, he washed his body, then pulled on the only pair of clean underwear he had left. The air in the room felt cooler now, so he went to the window to lower it some. There was no balcony, so he didn't have to worry about anyone coming in the window unless they could fly. Bo was feeling pretty sleepy by this time, so he put his Colt under his pillow, blew out the light, and crawled into bed.

CHAPTER 10

John Skinner was sitting at one of the tables in his saloon frowning at the five mismatched poker cards in his hand when he heard someone yelling out his name. He turned his head to see Flat Nose Jack coming toward him, a serious look on his face.

"He's dead, John. Willy's dead." Flat Nose bellowed out loudly.

"My brother's dead! What happened?" The saloon became quiet as everyone stopped what they were doing and waited to hear what Flat Nose had to say. John glanced around, then got up from his chair. "Let's go to my office; you can tell me there." Flat Nose followed John into the office and shut the door. John, his face red with anger, whirled around, grabbed Flat Nose by his shirt, and pulled him up close to his face. "I sent you two to take care of an old man, and now my brother's dead? What happened?" Sweat popped out on Flat Nose's head as a wisp of fear filtered into his mind. John might kill him if he thought it was even close to his fault. "We were waiting for the place to clear out so we could do it, but then this son of bitch came in, and when I went to the bar to get a beer, this guy hit me with a beer mug and knocked me out," he managed to blurt out. "When I came to, Willy was dead."

"Why did the man hit you?" John asked angrily as he pulled Flat Nose even closer to his face.

"He said he didn't like my broken nose, but I just ignored him. The next thing I know he hits me with the mug," Flat Nose said.

45

"When I came to, they had their guns on me. They told me Willy was dead and for me to get out or they would shoot me. I looked over to where Willy was lying on the floor, and he had blood all over the front of his shirt."

John's face screwed up into a snarl. "Who killed him?"

"Vail said that the drifter outdrew him," Flat Nose said doubtfully. He paused as he looked up into John's angry eyes. "John, I could see Willy's gun was still in his holster. I think they just murdered him."

John didn't say anything for a second, then pushed Jack away from him. "Who all was there?"

Flat Nose felt relieved but knew he wasn't out of the woods yet. John was unpredictable when he was mad. "Sergeant Dooly was there and Vail. Me and Willy were playing poker with Dooly, and then this drifter comes in," Flat Nose said in a solemn voice. "Dooly was waiting on the stagecoach for the mail. I didn't see the old man or the Indian."

John went to his desk to sit down. He sat quietly for a few minutes, his thoughts going back to when he was growing up with Willy and Curt on their father's hardscrabble farm. John and his two brothers had always gotten along well together, but their father was mean and liked to use his fists on them and their mother when he was drunk. When they got older, they tried to stand up to him when he was in a beating mood, but usually they all got a worse beating because of it. Finally, one day they grabbed their father as he was beating their mother and beat him to death with sticks of firewood. They buried him out in chicken coop. John grimaced as he remembered burying his father. His thoughts returned to the present. Finally, realizing he had to do something, John looked up at Flat Nose. "Was this guy waiting on the stage, too?"

"Yeah, when I left, I circled around and hid in the brush for a while. I seen 'em carry Willy out to the hill and bury him, and then the stage came and the drifter got on the stage."

"What did you do then?" John asked angrily.

"I followed the stage on in to Tucson and watched the passengers get off. The drifter went over to the Tucson Hotel and got a room there."

"The bastards will pay for this," John said. He looked up at Flat Nose. "Okay, go get yourself a drink and then go find Sledge." He reached for a bottle of whiskey from the small table by his desk.

Flat Nose, relieved, watched him for a second, but John ignored him as he poured his drink. Hesitantly he turned and walked out of the office. The familiar sounds of the noisy saloon helped calm Flat Nose as he walked over to the bar. He motioned for Gimpy to draw him a beer. When Gimpy set it in front of him, Flat Nose took a quick swallow, then turned to the bartender. "Have you seen Sledge?"

"He went upstairs with Stella about a half-hour ago."

Flat Nose turned up his beer and drank the rest of it in one swallow. He set the mug down on the bar, then headed toward the stairs. He didn't like disturbing Sledge, but he was more afraid of John than he was of Sledge. He could hear Stella laughing inside as he knocked on her door.

"Get the hell away from the door or I'm going to shoot it full of holes," a gruff voice from inside growled.

"John wants to see you; it's important." Flat Nose said in a loud voice. He stepped to the side of the door in case Sledge started shooting. He waited for a few minutes and nothing happened. He was just reaching to knock on the door again when he heard someone fumbling with the lock. The door swung open; Sledge stood there naked, a half-full bottle of whiskey in his hand.

"This had better be important," he growled irritably.

Flat Nose Jack didn't say anything. The sight of Sledge naked surprised him. He was a huge man; over six feet tall and wide as a barrel. Black hair covered his entire body almost like the apes that Jack had seen in pictures. The hair on his head hung down in greasy curls to his shoulders, and a black shadow of whiskers covered his lower face. Flat Nose could see Stella sprawled out naked in the bed behind Sledge, her legs spread out waiting for Sledge to return.

"Willy is dead, murdered. John wants to see you right away." Flat Nose told him anxiously.

Sledge was silent for a few seconds, then said blandly, "When was he killed and where?"

"About noon, over at Vail's stage station," Flat Nose said.

"Who did it?"

Flat Nose cleared his throat and said, "Some drifter who came in looking for trouble."

"Was you there?"

"Yeah, but the drifter hit me with a beer mug when I wasn't looking and knocked me out," Flat Nose said, the sweat popping out on his forehead again.

Emotionless, Sledge stared at Flat Nose for a few minutes, then said, "I'll come down when I get through here; ain't nothing going to be done that can't wait." He turned, then slammed the door. Flat Nose could hear him lock it. He stood there for a few seconds, listening to Stella's voice as she laughed and giggled, then he turned to go back down the stairs, a tinge of jealously in his heart. Customers were two deep at the bar when he got there, and Gimpy was steadily drawing beer from the huge barrels. Flat Nose walked over to the end of the long bar, then went through the opening to the back of it. He selected a bottle of whiskey and picked up a glass, then made his way over to the employees' table by John's office door. Pouring himself a drink, he settled down to wait for John to send for him again.

John was still in his office, just sitting behind his desk, anger and revenge consuming his mind. Willy and Curt had been the only two people he could trust, and now Willy was gone. The drifter and the men who helped him kill Willy were going to wish that they had never been born.

CHAPTER 11

John Skinner was startled when someone walked into his office without knocking. He looked up, ready to chew on someone's ass until he saw it was Sledge. The huge man was like a loose cannon, and John, like everyone else, didn't mess with Sledge.

"You want to see me, boss?" Sledge asked in a loud, gravelly voice. "Flat Nose told me about Willy."

"Did he tell you who the bastards were who shot him?" John asked, his anger returning.

"He said it was some drifter."

"There were other men in on it, Vail and Sergeant Dooly," John said. He hesitated for a moment. "I want them all dead. I want you to round up some of the men, then ride out to the stage station and take care of Vail and his bunch."

Sledged raised his eyebrows. "I thought you had political ambitions. Everyone knows you and Vail was feuding; they'll think you had something to do with it."

"That doesn't matter to me," John said, a tone of indifference in his voice. "The bastards can think what they like. I just want to send a clear message that no one messes with John Skinner."

"You're the boss," Sledge said. He walked to the door. "I'll take care of it."

"Don't take Flat Nose. Send him in here. I got something else for him to do."

Sledge walked out the door without answering. Flat Nose was still sitting at the employee's table nursing his whiskey.

"Boss wants to see you."

Flat Nose nervously got up and walked to the office door. He knocked once, then carefully opened the door enough to stick his head in. "You want to see me, boss?"

"Come in. I got some chores for you to do," John said in a normal voice, his anger subsided.

Flat Nose scurried to the front of John's desk. "What do you need, boss?"

John leaned back in his chair. He liked it when his employees showed their respect. Someday he would have to teach Sledge some respect. "I want you to keep an eye on that drifter. Find out who he is and what business he has in Tucson."

Flat Nose scratched his head. "You want me to bushwhack him?"

"No, just let me know if it looks like he's going to leave town. I have something special in mind for him." Suddenly John pounded his fist on the desk. His face twisted up in rage. "I want him to suffer!"

Flat Nose jumped back at John's outburst and his hand went to his gun, but he hurriedly let it fall to his side. "Okay, boss, I'll get right on it," he said as he backed up toward the door. "Anything else, Boss?"

"Go!" John hissed.

Flat Nose quickly walked out the door, but he paused when he came to the table where he had been sitting. He reached for his glass of whiskey as he cautiously glanced back at the office door. John was standing in the door, glaring at him. Hurriedly he pulled his hand back, then walked as fast as he could through the saloon to the batwing doors. He didn't slow down until he reached the hotel.

The clerk at the hotel hesitated when Flat Nose asked about the stranger, but he knew Flat Nose worked for John Skinner, so he reluctantly opened the register to look up the names of the people who had registered that day. "This is him—Bo Logan; he paid for three days."

"Is he up there now?" Flat Nose asked.

"Yep, said he was going right to bed."

Flat Nose hurried back to the saloon and found John at the back table with Stella, her hand down between his legs.

"He's still at the hotel and gone to bed," he reported dutifully. "He's going to be in town for three days." He glanced at Stella and quickly turned his head.

John thought for a minute. "You be there when he gets up in the morning. I want to know where he is every minute of the day."

Flat Nose nodded. "Okay, Boss, I'll keep on it."

John turned back to Stella. "Come on, let's go to my office. I got an itch I want you to scratch."

Flat Nose watched as the two of them sauntered over to John's office. He hated it when Stella was with her customers. It was even worse when she was with John. Sadly he trudged over to the bar.

CHAPTER 12

Sunlight coming through his hotel room window greeted Bo when he opened his eyes the next morning. He reached over to the nightstand for his pocket watch to check the time.

It was almost nine o'clock. He felt as if half the day had been wasted as he crawled out of the bed. He reluctantly pulled on the same pants and shirt he had worn the day before. He would buy some new ones today and arrange to have the dirty ones washed. After buttoning his shirt, he sat down to put on his boots. He started to pull on his socks, but they were so full of holes he pulled on his boots without them. He washed his face, combed his hair, and strapped on his gun belt. Bo's stomach was telling him to find something to eat. But he wanted to take care of the gold first, so after putting on his hat, he retrieved the gold from under the bed and left the room. A different clerk was behind the counter looking through some papers when Bo got downstairs. "What's the best bank in town?" Bo asked him.

The clerk, an older man with a neat, grayish mustache, paused for a minute. "The hotel uses the Tucson National Bank. It's the biggest bank in town and is owned by a group of local businessmen."

"Where is it located?"

The clerk smiled. "Just turn right when you go out the front door, then go one block. You'll see it across the street."

Bo left the hotel, and following the clerk's directions, he easily found the bank. When he entered, there were several people ahead of him, and he had to wait in line for a few minutes. Finally, he got up to the teller. "I want to open up an account. Could I see the president of the bank?"

The teller stared at the tall stranger in the threadbare clothes and thought, *He could be a bank robber.* Slowly he lowered his hand to a pistol he kept under the counter. "Can I help you? Mister Johnson is busy right now."

"No," Bo answered. He had noticed the teller's movement. "I'll wait for him." He transferred the saddlebags from his shoulder to the counter, then opened it up a little so the teller could see the plump sacks inside.

"Yes sir," the teller said in a nicer voice when he saw the sacks. "I'll tell him you're waiting." He tapped on a door behind him, waited for a second, and when the door cracked open, he whispered to someone.

A short, dumpy man in a gray suit quickly stepped out. "Hello, I'm the president of the bank. My name's Walter Johnson. I understand you want to open an account." He motioned for Bo to follow him. "Please come into my office."

Bo followed Walter into his office. "Howdy, I'm Bo Logan," he said as he stepped into the room. Bo opened the saddlebags, then dumped the sacks onto the banker's desk. "This is what I want to open my account with."

Walter opened up one of the bags. He looked at the gold, then poured some of it in his hand as his eyes blinked rapidly. He smiled. "How do you want to handle this, Mister Logan?"

One hour later Bo walked out of the bank with two hundred dollars in his pocket and two thousand, eight hundred dollars in an account in the bank. He stopped on the boardwalk outside the bank to decide what he was going to do next. He was hungry and wanted to eat, but looking down at his worn-out clothes, he decided he would clean up first. He walked to the nearest dry goods store, where he bought two pair of blue dungarees, two shirts, socks, and underwear.

When he left the store, he went straight to a barbershop where he had seen a sign advertising baths. He got a shave and a haircut while he was waiting for his turn in the tub, but there was only one man ahead of him, and by the time the barber was finished, it was his turn. The hot water felt good as Bo slid his body into the large brass bathtub. He took his time washing up, but eventually the water cooled down, and his stomach kept protesting, so he finally got out of the tub and dressed. When he came out of the barbershop wearing his new clothes, he felt like a new man. It was late morning, and the day was already getting hot as he walked back to the hotel. Bo put the rest of his new clothes in his room, then brought his dirty clothes to the hotel clerk, who promised to send them to a laundry.

Now he would go find a place to get some breakfast. Earlier he had noticed a small café just down the boardwalk from the bank nestled in between a harness shop and a gunsmith. He headed in that direction. A few minutes later, he spotted the sign he had noticed before, a four-leaf clover and the words: **SHAMROCK CAFÉ**. As he opened the door, a bell above it tinkled and a woman's voice from somewhere in the back yelled out, "I'll be with you in a minute."

The café was small but had a long counter with stools running most of the way along the back wall. Tables with green-checkered tablecloths were scattered around the rest of the room. He could see the kitchen through an open doorway behind the counter. The breakfast rush was over, and the only people in the café were two old-timers at the counter, drinking coffee. Bo sat down at a table next to the front window and waited for the woman from the kitchen to come take his order. Seconds later a pretty girl carrying a pot of coffee came out of the kitchen. She stopped at the counter first to fill the cups of the two men seated at the counter, then, spying Bo, she grabbed a clean cup from a shelf behind her and hurried to his table.

"What will you have, sir?" she asked after she set down the cup and then poured it full of coffee.

Bo just stared at the young woman. He had been smitten by her as soon he saw her come out of the kitchen. His heart fluttered and seemed stuck in his throat. She was the image of the girl he always dreamed about. She had asked him something, but he couldn't remember what she said. Suddenly he came out of his trance. "I'm sorry, what did you say?" he asked apologetically.

"What can I get you, sir?" she asked irritably as she brushed her hair out of her face. She had seen this kind before. *They come into town once a year and act as if they haven't ever seen a woman.*

"I want four eggs, six slices of bacon, coffee, and a dozen biscuits," Bo answered, his eyes still locked on her face.

"Are you expecting company?" she asked as she wrote down his order.

"No, I'm just hungry."

The waitress rolled her eyes. "Let me guess: you just got into town for the first time in a year?"

Bo smiled. "No, but close. It's been about a month."

The waitress nodded her head with a knowing grin. "I'll go get your order."

As she walked back toward the kitchen, Bo's eyes followed her until she was out of sight. He paused for a few seconds, waiting for her to reappear, then suddenly blushed as he realized what he was doing. *She probably has a husband.* Bo turned to gaze out the window to take his mind off the pretty girl, but her face kept popping up in his mind. He had never felt like this before about any of the women he had met since he had left home. When he was still in school back in Georgia, he had liked a girl, but he was so shy he was afraid to talk to her. He finally worked up the courage to ask her to dance with him at one of the local barn dances, but it had ended ugly. She was the spoiled daughter of the local banker, and when he stepped on her foot, she called him a clumsy oaf and stormed off the dance floor. When the local town boys made fun of him, he took the toughest one out behind the barn and whipped him. He never went back to the school after that.

Bo was jarred out of his thinking when he heard footsteps behind him. He turned to see the waitress coming toward him with his food. With a smile she placed it on his table. "If you need anything else, just yell. I got plenty more eggs in the back," she said jokingly.

"I think this may be enough, but I'll let you know." Bo dug into his food like a starving wolf. After about half of it was gone, he realized how fast he was eating, and he sheepishly looked up to see if anyone was watching him. The pretty waitress was looking at him. He blushed and ducked his head, embarrassed. He wanted to hide from her, but suddenly he realized, no, he didn't want to hide from her. This woman was different, and his attraction to her was too strong; he wanted to be near her, to talk to her. He wanted to see her smile at him again. He raised his eyes toward her; she was still looking at him. "I told you I was hungry. I haven't eaten in about two days."

` "Oh," she said blandly. "And I thought it was my good cooking." She smiled at him, and Bo blushed again.

"It is good, ma'am. Food hasn't tasted this good since I left Georgia."

The waitress raised her eyebrows. "How long you been out West, cowboy?"

CHAPTER 13

Bonnie and her father were sitting by the lake enjoying a picnic lunch. A young man and woman were merrily laughing as they splashed water on each other while wading. Children were feeding the ducks and the geese. Bonnie looked up at her father and smiled; she was so happy.

"Get up; it's time for your breakfast," a voiced boomed in her ears. The lake and her father disappeared. Bonnie opened her eyes to the same crowded bed in the same crowded room where she had exhaustedly fallen asleep the night before. She groaned and rubbed her eyes; all around her were other beds full of young girls in different stages of waking up. Bonnie quickly climbed out of the small bed she shared with two other girls and pulled on the shapeless gray dress she had worn the day before. Her bladder felt as if it were going to burst as she hurried to the water closet at the end of the room to pee. Happily she found only two other girls in the four-toilet room, and she quickly relieved herself. Bonnie washed up at one of the rusted sinks, then rushed to the kitchen, combing her hair as she walked. She had learned early that if you were late getting to the kitchen, you sometimes had to go hungry until lunch. She got in line behind three other girls dressed much like she was and picked through the bowls, looking for one that wasn't cracked. Not finding one, she picked up the least cracked one she could see, then moved up to where a server was waiting to fill it with watery porridge from a huge pot. She inspected the cups of water lined up and picked the cleanest one she could find. Looking toward the tables, Bonnie saw Peggy sitting at her usual place and hurried to sit by her. Peggy, a slim, medium-sized girl with brown hair, was several years older than Bonnie and was her best friend. She had met Peggy on her first day at the clothing factory, and it was the best memory she had of that horrible day when her life had changed forever…

Martha had brought her to a large room lined with beds and showed her where she was to sleep. She went through Bonnie's things and picked out her everyday clothes, then pitched them on the bed. Her nice dresses and shoes she left in the bags.

"You won't need these anymore," she said. She pointed to a plain dress that Bonnie had worn to work in the school flower garden. "Take that party dress off and put this on. I'm taking you to work."

Bonnie obediently changed dresses, and afterward Martha took her to the factory, where she placed her beside Peggy. She never saw her nice clothes again.

"Good morning, Bonnie. Did you sleep well?" Peggy asked as Bonnie sat down beside her.

"Good morning to you, too. Yes, I was having such a nice dream, then Madam Shott woke me up." Bonnie took a bite of her porridge. "I'm glad today is Saturday. Tomorrow I can sleep late."

"Do you want to come to church with me in the morning?" Peggy asked. She was German, and she always went to the Lutheran Church on Sunday morning. Bonnie was Catholic, but sometimes she went with Peggy just to get away from the factory for a while. The only other place she was allowed to go was to the street vendors on Sunday afternoon. But she never had any money of her own to spend, so she usually didn't go. Half of her wages went to her school debt and the rest to Madam Shott for her room and board. Bonnie was content to just stay in the bed and read on Sundays.

"I don't think so. I want to sleep late, and then I'll finish the book I borrowed from Jane," Bonnie said, a tired look on her face. She was always tired. The hard work and the poor food had almost turned her body into just skin and bones, and she never had any energy.

Peggy smiled. "I don't blame you. I would like to sleep all day sometimes." The two girls finished eating in silence, both knowing that soon the clock would turn to five o'clock and they would have to be at their workstations. They were both assigned to one of the trouser rooms where pants were cut and sewn together. A girl would cut the two parts of the pants from a bolt of cloth using a pattern. Another girl would temporarily sew them together with a needle and thread, which was called basting. Then another would sew the pants together on a machine. The pants were then sent to another room where they were hemmed and the buttons sewn on.

When the whistle blew to announce the start of the fourteen-hour workday, Peggy sat down at her machine and reached for one of the basted pants piled up beside her. Lining up the seams, she placed them under the needle, then, with her right foot, began working the pedal that ran the machine.

Bonnie sighed as she sat down across the table from Peggy. She thought of how easy her life used to be as she picked out a needle, then threaded it with tan thread. She was almost resigned to the fact that she would never get away from this wretched sweatshop, but deep in her mind was a small glimmer of hope that somehow she would. As she began basting together pants from a pile of cut pattern pieces on her table, she recalled the conversation she had had with Madam Shott just the day before.

She went to her office and asked her how much longer she would have to work to pay off her debt. Madam Shott just laughed, then told Bonnie she would be an old woman before her debt would be paid off. She did hint to Bonnie that she could pay off her debt much faster by working in a brothel, but Bonnie, shaking with anger, left her office. She would never do that kind of thing; she would die first. Bonnie cried herself to sleep that night, racking her brain trying to find a way out of her terrible nightmare.

Bonnie sighed again and continued her work. Her eyes began to water, and she looked up at the lantern over her table. The chimney was covered with soot, and the wick was nearly out. She knew that soon her eyes would begin to ache from the strain of trying to see the stitches in the dim light of the windowless room. The only light was from the coal oil lanterns above each of the tables where the girls were working. Even though Bonnie knew she might get behind on her quota, she stopped her work and stood up on her chair to unhook the lantern. She carried it over to a shelf, filled it from the kerosene can, trimmed the wick, and cleaned the chimney. As she hung it back up on its hook, she felt a chill in the air, so she put on her shawl before she began sewing again. Winter had passed, and it was early spring, but it was still cold in the factory. The only heat for the workers was a small coal stove in each of the rooms. All the women wore coats or shawls. Bonnie had been at the factory for over two years now, and she had learned how to survive in the harsh conditions.

The first few weeks were terrible for her. Her fingers stayed sore from the needles, and the twelve- to sixteen-hour days kept her so tired that sometimes she wouldn't eat; she would just go to bed. Peggy was the one who helped her and kept her going when she had almost given up. Peggy showed her how to hold the needles and how to protect her hands. She would bring her food at night and make her eat it to make sure she kept up her strength. Bonnie didn't know if she could have made it without Peggy.

"Peggy, I'll go to church with you if you want me to," Bonnie said as she laid a finished pair of pants on her pile.

Peggy looked at her and smiled. "No, it's okay. Stay and sleep, then read your book. I am sure God will understand."

Bonnie smiled as she turned back to her basting. Her pile was getting shorter. She wanted to finish this order quickly so they would get to quit at seven this evening.

The next morning Bonnie lay in bed after the rest of the girls had left, enjoying being alone in the quiet room. She would get up in a little bit to scrape up some breakfast from the kitchen. She had just turned over on her side and closed her eyes again when she heard someone enter the room. Bonnie didn't bother to look to see who it might be. Probably one of the girls had forgotten something. Bonnie, not wanting to be disturbed, kept her eyes closed, hoping that whoever it was would soon leave. Oddly, she heard the door close and the lock click. The sound of footsteps approached, then stopped at her bed. Curious, she opened her eyes. Her heart skipped a beat, then raced as fear filled her mind. Bart Mastard was standing over her, his yellow teeth showing in a wicked grin.

"I think it's about time to teach you how to be a woman," he sneered as he pulled off his coat.

Bonnie couldn't speak at first. Her heart beat wildly. "I don't want to be a woman," was all she could say in a trembling voice.

"Sure you do; you'll like it. All the girls do it sooner or later. You could even make extra money doing it."

Bonnie realized that Bart was a strong man and he would rape her unless she could think of a way out of her predicament. Bonnie tried to force herself to calm down as her mind raced, searching for a way to stop this horrible thing. "I'm not going to do that until I'm married, and only with my husband." Bonnie cried as she frantically glanced toward the door, hoping someone would come to stop him. "Please leave or I will call Madam Shott."

Bart laughed and threw his hat on the bed, his greasy hair falling in his eyes. "Martha is the one who sent me in here. We got plans for you, girlie. You're too pretty to be working in a factory when you could be making us good money in the brothels." He grabbed her nightgown at the collar, and Bonnie screamed. Bart slapped her in the face. Bonnie tried to turn away from him, but he ripped off her gown and held her down as he crawled onto the bed with her. She screamed again, and he backhanded her; blood seeped from her nose. Lust gleaming in his eyes, he glared at her naked body as he held her down. She stopped struggling, then began sobbing.

"Please don't. I don't want to do this, please," she begged him.

Bart grinned. "That's a smart girl." he rubbed her small breast with his hand. "It will all be over in a few minutes, and you'll wonder why you didn't do it sooner." He unbuttoned his pants and pulled them down to his knees.

Bonnie could only think of one thing to do. She laid her arms back behind her head and reached under her pillow.

"That's a good girl, just lie back and enjoy it." Bart hissed as he grabbed her legs so he could spread them apart. She resisted, but with a savage grunt he pushed harder and opened them wide enough to move his body up between them. Grinning wickedly, he leaned down toward her face. Bonnie could smell his putrid breath.

"No!" she yelled as she brought her hand out from under the pillow. Clutched in her hand was a ten-inch hat pin, and with all her anger and frustration, she thrust it into his chest.

"What the hell! What have you done, you little bitch?" Bart exclaimed as he looked down at his chest. He reached for the hat pin, but his arm fell to his side, his strength gone. Slowly he rolled off the bed onto the floor. Lying on his back, he again turned his eyes to the hat pin sticking out of his chest, but slowly his eyes closed, and he lay still.

Bonnie jumped up from the bed and backed up against the wall. She stood there staring at his unmoving body. She felt panic at first when she realized that Bart was dead, but then a calmness settled over her, and her head seemed to be clear for the first time in months. *I've got to get out of here now. I have no other choice but to go to prison.* Her mind made up, she slowly walked over to Bart and kicked him; he didn't move. She went through his pockets and found twelve dollars and sixty cents.

An idea came to her. Bart was a small man; maybe she could put on his clothes and disguise herself. Quickly she removed his shoes and pulled off his pants and shirt. She glanced at his long johns but decided she didn't want them on her body. She quickly pulled on his pants and shirt. They were a little big, but they would do. She tried on his shoes; they fit loosely, but she laced them up tight so they would stay on her feet. She put on his coat and hat. With her hair pushed up under the hat, she could easily pass for a man.

She grabbed his arm and pulled him to the far end of the room. Struggling but with renewed strength, she rolled him into a bed. As she reluctantly removed her hatpin from his chest, she noticed that there was very little blood on it or around the wound. "I need some time to put some distance between me and this place. When they find him, maybe they will think he is just drunk," Bonnie said to herself as she covered him up and went back to her bed. She grabbed her comb, brush, and some other keepsakes, then put them in a pillowcase. She didn't take her dresses or underwear; she would have to make her way as a boy for a while, and she didn't want to give herself away by wearing girl things. She needed more money, though, if she was going to get out of the city. Suddenly she thought of Peggy. She knew where her friend kept the money that she was saving. Bonnie went to Peggy's bed, lifted the mattress, and stuck her hand into a slit in the mattress. She pulled out a long, thin bag and laid it on the bed. Bonnie felt guilty as she counted the hundred and twenty-six dollars that was in the bag. Bonnie took a hundred dollars and put the rest back. She found some paper and a pencil, then, with tears flowing, she wrote a note:

Dear Peggy, I am so sorry that I have to do this, but I have to get away from here. I will pay you back someday. I promise. Love, Bonnie.

Bonnie put the note in the bag and put the bag back in the mattress. After putting everything else back in place, she grabbed her pillowcase bag and went to the door. Slowly she unlocked it and peeped out. Seeing no one, she quickly slipped down the stairs. No one noticed Bonnie as she casually walked out the front door into the street. As she began walking down the sidewalk, Bonnie realized that she didn't know which way to go. A horse trolley was stopped at the corner, and a line of people was filing into it. Without hesitation Bonnie got in line, made her way into the trolley, and found a seat. This was the quickest way she could think of to get away from the factory. Bonnie was sixteen years old and alone. She wondered how much a train ticket to Tucson, Arizona, would cost.

CHAPTER 14

Bo didn't want to leave the café. Long after he had finished eating, he lingered so he could talk to the pretty waitress.

"Could I have some more coffee, Miss?" he asked her for the fifth time.

The waitress was at the counter pouring coffee for a couple of cowboys. When she was finished filling their cups, she walked over to his table.

"When you get free coffee with your breakfast, you like to get your money's worth, don't you?" she teased.

"Oh no, I'm not like that. I'll pay you for the extra coffee. I'm just not ready to leave yet, and I don't want to sit here without buying something," Bo said, his face blushing.

"Oh, that's OK. I was getting ready to throw it out and make some fresh, anyway," she said as she filled his cup. She looked at him and smiled.

"Thanks, ma'am," was all Bo could think to say. He wished he knew her name. He had just gotten up his nerve to ask her when the two cowboys came walking in.

"Well the outhouse is out back. You're going to need it, drinking all that coffee." she continued teasing. She seemed to enjoy seeing his face turn red. "By the way, since you're going to hang around here all day, you can quit calling me Miss? My name's Mary Smith. What's yours?"

Bo was caught by surprise. He never knew what to say to girls, and this one was confusing him. Bo had never met a girl as outspoken as this one, but he wanted to make a good impression. He scooted back his chair so he could politely stand up, but as he stood up the chair fell backwards; then, when he turned to grab for it, he spilled his coffee. Bo's face got redder still, and beads of sweat broke out on his forehead. He wished he could find a hole to crawl into.

"I'm sorry, ma'am; I'll clean this up," Bo blurted as he turned to pick up the chair. He turned back to see Mary with her hand in front of her face, trying to hold back her laughter. She quickly turned away, then picked up a napkin from another table. She tried to hold a straight face when she turned back to wipe off the table, but after a few seconds she began giggling and couldn't stop. Bo watched her quietly for a few seconds, then he grinned, and seconds later he, too, began laughing.

After a few minutes, they stopped laughing, and Bo stuck out his hand. "My name is Bo Logan, ma'am."

Mary looked at his him for a second and shook his hand. "Now that we are friends, you can call me Mary, Mister Logan."

Bo was blushing again. "You can call me Bo," he said, then blushed again when he thought of how stupid that sounded.

"What kind of work do you do, Bo? Or do you just hang around cafes all day?" she asked as she filled his coffee cup again.

Bo sat back down in his chair again and reached for his coffee cup. "I've done a little bit of everything: punching cows in Texas, driving freight wagons, working as a deputy sheriff for about a year in New Mexico. Right now I'm just drifting," he said, then added, "I'm thinking of settling down around this area, though. I might do some prospecting."

Mary laughed, but with a little disappointment in her voice. "So you're one of those fiddle-footed Texans I hear about."

Bo laughed. "No, actually I'm from Georgia, but I have fiddle footed in Texas some."

Mary thought, *I don't know why, but I like this guy. I hope he stays around for a while. I would like to get to know him better.* She smiled, and suddenly the bell over the door rang as several people came into the café. She would have to get back to work. This café was her only source of income, and she couldn't afford to lose business. She looked at Bo. "Well, back to work. I got bills to pay," she said as she turned to walk back to the counter.

"Hello, Fred. What can I get for you today? The special today is beef stew," Mary asked the customer in her most friendly voice.

Bo sat and watched her for a few minutes. He wished he could think of some reason to stay. He looked at his pocket watch, then got up from the table. He laid a five-dollar gold piece by his coffee cup, then walked toward the door.

It was nearly noon when Bo stepped out of the café, and the day was already hot. There was a permanent veil of dust in the air as horses and wagons filled the streets, traveling to their destinations. Bo hadn't seen so much hustle and bustle in one place since the time he had been in San Antonio during a fiesta. There was a general store across the street, the boardwalk piled with all kinds of merchandise. A fancy saddle in front of the saddle shop next door caught his eye. The next block up, he saw a saloon that took up the nearly the whole block. He had just moved his gaze farther up the street when he looked back at the saloon. The large sign hanging in the front of it read: **Silver Dollar Saloon**.

I don't think I'll be doing much business there, he thought. *I don't need any more trouble.* Bo put it out of his mind. He hoped that he wouldn't have any trouble with the Skinner brothers. It had been a fair fight, and he wasn't going to worry about it. He didn't know which way to go from the café, so he went to the harness shop next door. The smell of fresh cut leather greeted him as he entered the shop.

A man working on a saddle looked up when Bo walked in. "Can I help you?" the man asked.

"I'm looking for the sheriff's office. Can you tell me how to get there?" Bo asked.

"You go four blocks down this street and turn right on Main Street. You'll see the courthouse about two blocks down, and the sheriff's office is in the courthouse," the man said as he went back to putting the saddle together.

Bo thanked him and followed the directions to the courthouse. When he walked into the sheriff's office, there was an older man sitting behind a desk with his feet propped up on it, apparently asleep.

"Excuse me, sir, are you the sheriff?" Bo asked in a loud voice.

"What!" The man exclaimed as he hurriedly dropped his feet to the floor and opened his eyes. When he saw Bo was a stranger to him, he hurriedly began shifting through some wanted posters. "What can I do for you? I wasn't asleep. I was trying to remember someone's name. It always helps when I close my eyes." He looked up at Bo. "I haven't seen you around here before. Are you new in town?"

"Well, Sheriff, I just got into town last night, but right now I'm looking for somebody who might live in this area," Bo said, trying not to laugh.

"No, I'm not the sheriff. I'm the jailer. I used to be the sheriff, but I retired. You can call me Deputy Hogg, or you can call me Porky; everyone else does," Porky said.

Bo smiled; he wondered if this man was the town idiot. "Okay, Deputy Hogg, glad to meet you. My name's Bo Logan, and I'm looking for a man by the name of Tom O'Shay."

A worried look appeared on Porky's face as he heard the name, and sweat popped out on his forehead. He glanced down at the posters in front of him as he said in a low but fast voice, "No, never heard of anyone with that name." He looked back at Bo. "Maybe you need to talk to the sheriff, Mister. Maybe he knows this man."

"Where is the sheriff, Porky?" Bo asked. He had a funny feeling that Porky knew more than he was telling.

"He's on the other side of the county looking for some cattle rustlers. He won't be back for several days," Porky said. He began leafing through the posters again.

"Thanks Porky. Go on back to your nap. I'll come back in a few days." Bo walked back outside. He stood there for a while wondering what he should do now. He felt he needed to find Thomas O'Shay, but if he couldn't find him, he needed to find his daughter. As he was standing there on the boardwalk, a man walked by reading a telegram. Suddenly a thought hit him. He would send a telegram to the girl's school in New York and inquire about Tom O'Shay.

Bo made his way across the busy street and went into a dry goods store. A tall, slim man wearing an apron was up on a ladder trying to reach a bear trap that was hanging from the ceiling. He had a hold of it, but it was heavy and the ladder wasn't steady.

"Let me hold the ladder for you, Mister. I'd hate to see you fall and break something," Bo said as he grabbed the ladder.

"Thanks, Mister. I need to fix this ladder; the pegs are getting loose," the clerk said as he climbed down. He laid the huge bear trap on the counter, then stuck out his hand. "My name's Ronald Harbin. Anything I can do for you, let me know."

"Right now I just need some directions. I want to send a telegram," Bo said as he shook Ronald's hand.

"That's easy. Just go to the train station." Ronald walked to the door, then pointed down the street to his right. "Go down this street about six blocks, then turn left at Smith's harness shop. Go two more blocks; you can't miss it."

Bo glanced down the street, then turned back to Ronald. "Thanks, Mister Harbin. I'll need some supplies later, but right now I have to send a telegram." Bo walked down the boardwalk until he came to the street where he was supposed to turn left. As Bo walked he paid close attention to the stores he passed so he would remember them and not get lost going back to the hotel. Tucson was a lot bigger than he had thought. Walter the banker had told him that Tucson had over eight thousand people in the 1880 census. He said when they moved the capital back in 1877, the population really grew fast, and the railroad coming in 1880 just let them come in faster.

Bo's thoughts were abruptly interrupted when he heard a train whistle somewhere in front of him. A little farther down the block, the train station came into view, and just behind it, a big, black locomotive was sitting on the tracks belching black smoke.

A group of people carrying their bags and trunks was going into the station as Bo got there, so he followed them through the large double doors into a large waiting room. He stopped for a minute, looking for the telegraph office, then spotted it over in one corner. As Bo approached the counter, a man was pecking out a message, and Bo waited for him to finish.

The clerk stopped, paused for a minute, and turned to Bo. "Sending or receiving?" he asked.

"I need to send a telegram to New York City."

The clerk pointed to a stack of blank papers. "Get one of those sheets of paper and one of those pencils to write down what you want to send. It'll cost you one cent per letter, so you might want to keep it short and to the point."

Bo looked to where he was pointing, then took one of the sheets along with one of the pencils, which had been lying beside them. He thought for a few minutes, then wrote: *PERFECT LADY ACADEMY, NEW YORK CITY, LOOKING FOR THOMAS O'SHAY OR BONNIE O'SHAY PLEASE RESPOND, I WILL PAY FOR REPLY. BO LOGAN TUCSON ARIZONA.* Bo handed the paper to the clerk, then waited while he counted the letters.

"That'll be a dollar and twenty cents," the clerk said.

Bo dug around in his pocket for some coins. "When will they get the message?" he asked as he handed the money to the clerk.

"Oh, they'll get it today; at our office in New York, they got young men on those bicycle contraptions that deliver telegrams any time of the day or night," the clerk said. "But I don't know when you will get a reply. Write your name and where you're staying on that register over there."

Bo wrote his name and the name of his hotel on the register. The clerk read it, then looked back at Bo. "I sent your telegram as you were writing this down. I'll send the reply to your hotel when we get it," the clerk said, then added laughingly, "We don't have any of them bicycles, but Gerald, our delivery boy, is pretty fast." Suddenly, the telegraph sounder started clicking, and he turned to start writing down the incoming message.

Bo watched him for a minute, wondering how the man could make words out of the clattering of the telegraph. Someone had explained to him once that the letters were combinations of dots and dashes, but hard as he tried, he couldn't tell the dots from the dashes; finally he just shook his head and walked over to the ticket office. He thought that since he was there, he would find out how long it would take to travel on the train to New York City. The ticket master was very patient and helpful. Bo walked away reading a schedule the man had written down for him. A train left Tucson every day for San Francisco, and from there a train left every day for New York City. The ticket master told him he could be in New York City in six or seven days. Bo had always wanted to ride a train. Maybe a trip to New York City wouldn't be so bad.

As Bo began walking toward the exit, he heard a train whistle blowing. He turned to see another train coming into the station. This one was heading west, and Bo decided to watch for a while. The train had hardly stopped before conductors hurried to place small steps in front of each exit. As soon as they placed the steps, people swarmed out of the cars, many of them carrying bags or packages, and rushed into the station, where some of them milled around waiting for the baggage handlers to bring out their trunks and luggage. When the baggage arrived, they all crowded around the handlers shouting for their bags. As the passengers got their bags, they left the station, and soon most of them were gone. A few minutes later, the conductors walked around the station calling for the departing passengers.

"ALL ABOARD," echoed across the station until the conductors were satisfied that all of them were on the train. Bo waited at the station until the train slowly moved out, black smoke puffing and steam coming from the vents. Bo had seen a lot of people getting on the train, and he wondered where they were all going.

Maybe some of them were going to New York. As the train continued to pass by the station, Bo saw boxcars connected behind the passenger cars, and after the boxcars were several cars loaded with cattle and sheep. He didn't know what was in the closed-up boxcars, but he did see some soldiers looking out of the ones with open doors. The caboose finally went by, and he watched it until it was nearly out of sight. He pulled out his watch and looked at it: three o'clock. He was getting hungry again; he thought of Mary.

CHAPTER 15

A hint of shyness along with second thoughts flashed across Bo's mind as he reached for the café door. He wanted to see Mary very much, but what if she couldn't care less if she saw him? Did she like him, or was he just a paying customer? He hesitated just a second, then pushed the door open. Mary was at the counter talking to the banker Walter Johnson. She had a frown on her face, but when she looked up and saw Bo, she smiled. Walter glanced at Bo but didn't seem to recognize him. Mary grabbed the coffee pot and a cup and hurried to the table where Bo had sat down.

"Hello, Bo. Did you come in for some more of my coffee?" she asked with a smile on her face.

"Sure. Coffee and lunch to go with it." Bo said. He felt good when Mary called him by name. *She must like me a little bit, at least.*

"All I got left is beef stew and bread unless you want me to cook up something else, but it would take longer," Mary said with a tinge of caring in her voice.

"The beef stew sounds good to me," Bo said dreamily as he looked into her eyes. They were a beautiful shade of blue, almost like the sky. They were framed by her long, silky, blonde hair that hung down over her cheeks. Even the tiny beads of perspiration on her forehead were attractive.

"I think I have a little apple pie left. Do you want a piece of it?" Mary asked.

Bo was lost in Mary's eyes; he knew she had said something, but it hadn't registered in his mind. "What?" he blurted as he snapped out of his trance.

Mary slowly shook her head and smiled; she could hardly keep from laughing. "I said: do you want some apple pie to go with your lunch?"

"Yes," he squeaked as he nodded his head. Bo's face turned red as he thought about what he must have sounded like. "I would like some very much, thank you," he said in a more manly voice.

Mary shook her head, her lips curling upward as she went into the kitchen.

A few minutes later, she emerged from the kitchen with Bo's meal. She laid it down in front of him with a quick smile, then said, "Here you go. Would there be anything else?"

"No, I believe this will do me," he said as he looked up into her deep blue eyes again. They held his gaze, and he couldn't seem to pull away from them. She saved him by quickly turning her head. As she walked back to the counter, Bo stared at her back for a minute, then half-heartedly returned his attention to his lunch.

Mary's expression changed to worry when she went behind the counter to where Walter was waiting for her.

"Can't you give me a few more days to pay you the money? You know I'm good for it," she said in a low, desperate voice. "It's just that all the new furnishings and equipment cost more than I expected, and now no one wants to give me credit."

"You knew what the deal was when you bought the place. You had six months to pay the rest of the money. I can't help it if you can't make a go of the place," Walter said softly but sternly. He knew he had her over a barrel, and now he would just tighten the screws.

"I make good money here," Mary answered angrily, but keeping her voice low. "You told me all the equipment was nearly new, and like a fool I believed you. I should have known that I couldn't trust a man to tell the truth."

"Now, now, my dear, we can work something out. When the bank repossesses, I can rent you the building for a fair price," Walter said. He looked around the room; no one else was in the café but some cowboy sitting over by the window. He winked one eye then said in a lowered voice, "Or, if you want to pay me in something else other that money, you could do that."

At first Mary felt shocked at hearing the banker's words, then her anger took over, and she slapped his face. "I'm not a whore, Mister Johnson," She replied angrily. "I resent that insult, and you can get out of my café right now!"

Walter quickly stood up and glared back at Mary, his face scarlet with rage. "It won't be your café very long. You have until tomorrow to pay off your loan or the bank is taking it back." Suddenly Walter was jerked around by a powerful arm gripping his shoulder. A huge hand grabbed his coat front, lifted him to his toes and shook him like a dog shaking a rat. A face twisted up into a snarl came within six inches of his eyes. Fear swept through his mind; he wet his pants.

Bo had reacted instantly when he heard Mary angrily objecting to being insulted. *How dare anyone insult Mary*, he thought as he rushed to the counter and jerked the banker around. He grabbed the front of his coat, lifted him from the floor and shook him rapidly for a few seconds before he set him back down on his feet. Bo pulled out his pistol, then drew back his arm to pistol whip the banker—but he glanced at Mary first; she quickly shook her head no. Bo roughly shoved the banker back in his chair and leaned down into his face. "I think you had better apologize to the lady before I really get mad!" Bo said as his eyes narrowed to tiny slits.

"No! No, it was all a misunderstanding! She didn't understand what I said. I'm sorry!"

Bo glanced at Mary. She had a puzzled expression on her face, which quickly changed to one of gratefulness. "It's okay Bo; I've had to put up with men like him for years. They think because I'm on my own I will do anything to get by." She hesitated for a second, her expression changing to one of pride. "They are wrong, and I will say it again: I am not a whore."

Bo listened to Mary with mixed emotions. He admired her spirit and her pride; he realized he loved her more for it, but the man in him still felt as if he needed to protect her. He grabbed the banker's shirt and lifted him from the chair again. "He still doesn't have the right to insult you. I think I need to take him out back and thrash him."

"No, Bo. You would only bring down trouble on yourself. He is a respected banker in this town, and he said he was sorry."

Bo let go of Walter, and the banker fell back against the counter. He quickly straightened his coat and looked up at Bo. Suddenly he recognized him.

"Mister Logan, it's you. I'm sorry about this misunderstanding." He turned to Mary. "I'm sorry, Mary. I should have known that you weren't that kind of woman. I just had a lapse of judgment. I hope you will forgive me." The banker wrung his hands as he lowered his eyes. "I'm sorry about the payment, though; it's out of my hands. It's due tomorrow."

"How much is the payment?" Bo asked, not ready to forgive the banker.

Walter clasped his hands together in front of him as he meekly replied, "Three hundred dollars."

"She owes three hundred dollars on this place? Is that all she needs to get a clear title?"

"Yes, the bank sold it to her for five hundred dollars, and she paid half down. The rest is due tomorrow,"

Bo thought for a minute, then turned to Mary. "Mary, I'm going to loan you the money to pay off this note. You can pay me back any way or time you want to, no strings attached." He looked back at Walter, anger still etched on his face. "Draw the money out of my account to pay off her note. Bring her the deed to this place and the note paid in full, and no surprises. You just remember, I still think you need a thrashing."

Mary was speechless; this man she hardly knew was going to do this for her. A sudden suspicion crept into her mind. *Men always want something in return for their favors.* Quickly she pushed the thought from her mind. She liked Bo; he was the first man she felt she could trust. Maybe he was different.

"I accept your offer, Mister Logan. It seems I have no choice if I want to keep this place. I'll draw up a note for the money and sign it. I promise I will pay you back as soon as I can."

"A note is fine if that is the way you want it, but don't feel you have to be in any hurry to pay me back," Bo said. He turned to Walter. "Go get the receipt and the deed before I change my mind about that thrashing."

"Yes sir, Mister Logan, I'll be back in no more than thirty minutes with the papers," Walter said nervously as he headed for the door.

When Walter returned to the café, Bo and Mary were still talking. She had been telling him about her plans for the place, but the door opening stopped their conversation. Walter came up to Mary with his hat in his hand, then handed her the deed and the note. "Everything is signed, and the note is marked paid in full. Again I would like to say that I am sorry, and I hope you will continue to do business with me. I assure you that it will not ever happen again."

"Thank you, Mister Johnson. Now that you know what kind of a person I am, I will think about doing business with you. Good day, sir."

As Walter walked out the door, Mary looked at Bo and smiled. "I think the doing business speech was more for your benefit than mine." A concerned look came across her face. "I know it is none of my business, but can you afford to loan me that much money?"

Bo thought about it for a minute. "Oh, I have enough. I lucked into a little gold back in the mountains, and I put it in Walter's bank."

"Oh," Mary said casually. An old memory stirred in her mind, but she quickly disregarded it. Another thought came to her. "You know, I have big plans for this place. I could use a partner who would be willing to invest some money in expanding the building and hiring more help."

Bo was caught by surprise; he had never thought of anything like this, but it sounded interesting. "How much money do you need? I wouldn't mind investing in the Shamrock, but I got to warn you I'm not a very good cook."

Mary laughed. "I don't need a cook. Don't you like my cooking? I'll have you know that I cooked in a restaurant in San Francisco for two years."

"Yes, I love your cooking. I guess you need a dishwasher. I could do that." Bo grinned.

"No, seriously, if I had the money, I could add a new kitchen out back and expand this room so I could put more tables in. I could double or triple my business."

"How much money would you need?" Bo asked.

Mary thought a minute. "Two hundred would get us started, and we could do the rest as we go. The three hundred you paid off the loan with and two hundred more will make you a full partner."

Bo didn't think very long about the proposition. He would have said yes to anything she asked, just to be close to her. "Okay, Mary, I will do it, but on one condition: I'll have to be a silent partner for a while. I have some obligations I have to take care of first." Bo said as he held out his hand.

Mary hesitated, then shook his hand. "Okay, partner, it's a deal. We will split the profits fifty-fifty.

CHAPTER 16

Sledge lowered the spyglass from his eye. He wiped his brow as he walked back to his horse. The little bit of breeze coming out of the south wasn't enough to diminish the heat from the sun as it glared down on him and the four hardcases waiting on their sweaty horses behind him. They had ridden all night and half the morning to get to the ridge overlooking the small valley where Bob Vail had built his stage station. Sledge took one last look down at the station, then mounted his horse.

"There are only the two men and a squaw down there; let's ride," Sledge said as he heeled his horse down the steep grade. A crow sitting in a dead tree overlooking the graveyard was the first to give warning as the dangerous band of hardcases slowly rode down the hill. Sledge glanced at the graves as he rode past and noticed the one with the freshest dirt. He laughed to himself as he read WILLY SKINNER carved into the roughly made cross.

Your name on a cross won't help, Willy; you're still going to hell. Don't worry, though. I'm going to send you some company. Sledge motioned for Mad Dog and Horney to go to the back door as he led the rest of them to the front. Sledge could hear someone hammering inside as he dismounted from his horse. When he stepped into the saloon, he saw Bob Vail driving nails into the wall across from the bar. Dutch and Diablo spread out behind Sledge. Bob, hearing the door, smiled as he turned to see who had come in. When he saw

Sledge, his face changed to a mask of fear. He glanced toward the bar.

"Give me a beer, old man. I been riding all night," Sledge said. He could see that the old man had recognized him.

"Sure, Mister, beer for everyone," Bob said, trying to sound normal. He started toward the bar.

"Vail," Sledge said as he pulled his pistol. "It ain't that easy."

Vail lunged for the bar, trying to get behind it, but he was too late.

"BOOM!" Sledge's pistol roared, and gun smoke clouded the room.

Vail grabbed at his leg then fell to the floor. He painfully raised himself to his knees, then began to crawl toward the bar.

"BOOM!" The pistol roared again. Liquor bottles rattled on the shelves, and more gun smoke spread around the room.

Vail fell back to the floor as a bloody hole appeared in his other leg; he tried to pull himself along the floor with his arms.

"BOOM!" The pistol roared for a third time.

Suddenly his left arm wouldn't work. He looked at it; blood was gushing out of a jagged hole by his elbow. He screamed.

Suddenly Shorty, holding a shotgun, burst through the batwing doors. "What's going on Bob?" Shorty glanced at his brother on the floor, then at Sledge holding a pistol. He pointed the shotgun toward Sledge, but he had hesitated too long.

"BOOM!" Sledge shot again.

Shorty dropped the shotgun as he clutched at his stomach. Blood seeped between his fingers. Slowly he sat down on the floor then, leaned back against the wall. He writhed in pain; tears ran from his eyes. Sledge watched for a minute, then turned to one of the men who had came in with him. "Okay, Diablo, he's all yours."

Diablo, a small but husky Mexican, grinned as he pulled out his knife. He liked cutting up men, especially Gringos. He walked over to Shorty.

"Let me help you stop the bleeding, gringo," he said as he stuck the knife into the bleeding wound. Shorty screamed. A wide grin covered Diablo's dark, oily face. "We are just beginning, gringo. Save some screams for later." He twisted the knife.

Sledge turned back to Vail. The wounded man had pulled himself with one arm until he was behind the bar. Sledge turned to the other hardcase who had come in with him. "Dutch, drag him out here where he can watch his brother." Dutch, a tall, big-boned man with greasy blond hair, laughed as he hurried to the end of the bar. He grabbed Vail by his leg, then pulled the screaming man back around to the front of the bar, where he propped him up facing his brother.

"Vail, you know not to mess with John Skinner. Now look at what I have to do." Sledge said. He raised his pistol.

BOOM!" Sledge fired into Vail's unwounded right arm.

Vail screamed again. The pain was unbearable. Suddenly he heard someone else scream. He turned toward the screaming and noticed Shorty for the first time. A grinning Mexican was cutting off a finger from his brother's hand. Tears came to Vail's eyes as he began praying.

"Dutch, get Mad Dog and Horney and go find the Indian." Sledge said. "Me and Mister Vail got some more business to take care of."

Shorty was dead by the time Dutch returned. His blood oozed onto the floor from the stubs of his cut-off fingers and toes. Mad Dog and Horney barged through the door behind Dutch, dragging an Indian woman with her hands tied behind her back.

"We couldn't find the Indian buck, but we found his squaw," Dutch said. "We can have some fun with her before we kill her."

Sledge could see the despair in her eyes as she cut her eyes to Vail and then to Shorty. She turned back to Sledge. "I put a curse on you, devil white eyes. All of you will meet a painful death before the next moon of short days."

Sledge grinned. "Throw her over that barrel and tie her down."

Dutch and Mad Dog ripped the dress from the struggling woman as Horney positioned the barrel next to the bar. They threw her across the barrel and tied her hands to the bar.

"I'm first," yelled Horney as he unbuckled his gun belt. He pushed Dutch aside as he positioned himself between the legs of the woman. He was fumbling with his last pants button when Sledge grabbed his shoulder and jerked him to one side.

"You know I'm always first," Sledge said. He glowered at Horney as he undid his own buttons and reached into his pants.

Horney dropped his eyes. "I thought you was busy with Vail, Sledge. I didn't mean nothing ."

Sledge narrowed his eyes as a silent warning to Horney, then turned back to the woman. Brutally, he began assaulting her.

The mood changed, and the men laughed and joked as each man took his turn with the woman. Sledge grabbed Vail by his head and forced him to watch the brutal attacks until he finally decided to end it all. He pulled out his knife and slowly cut Vail's throat. "You will be dead in a minute, Vail, and all of this is your fault."

Bob Vail defiantly cut his eyes to Sledge as his lifeblood flowed from him. Somehow he uttered one last, short sentence: "Remember the curse."

Sledge laughed as he walked behind the bar. He pulled a bottle of whiskey off the shelf, took a big swallow, and threw the bottle across the room. Sledge grasped the woman's hair, then grinned as he tilted her head back. The woman calmly looked into his eyes as he drew his knife across her throat. Suddenly he felt a chill as her blood spurted onto the bar.

"What the hell?" Horney yelled as he quickly backed away from the body. "I was ready to do it again."

Sledge looked at him indifferently. "Burn this place to the ground."

Lame Deer, carrying an antelope on his back, had just reached the top of a hill that rose above the desert just east of the stage station when he saw five men ride away. He stopped and watched for a few minutes, then hurried toward the station. He was nearly there when he saw the smoke. He dropped the antelope and began running. The flames covered one wall and were crawling across the ceiling as he entered the station. He cringed when he saw the bodies, but he quickly pulled them outside. Sadly he gazed at his wife and the white men, who had been his friends. There would be time to bury them later and seek revenge. Now, he would try to save the barns and the horses. The stage would be coming in soon.

CHAPTER 17

The smoky smell of the factory district slowly faded as the horse trolley Bonnie was riding on made its way through the busy streets of New York City. The car had been almost full when she climbed aboard, but she had slid into one of the hard wooden seats next to a portly, middle-aged man who smelled of fish. Apprehension kept her in a steely grip as she sat hunched down in her seat. She glanced back toward the factory several times, expecting to see Madam Shott running after her and yelling for the police, but each time only a picture of normality met her eyes. She pulled Bart's hat down over her eyes, then ran her hands around the brim to check if any of her hair was showing from under it. A half hour passed, and the trolley rambled up to Forty-Second and stopped to let passengers off. Bonnie slid out of her seat so she could exit the car but had only walked a few steps when she heard someone yell.

"Hey you!" An icy fist closed around Bonnie's heart as she slowly turned toward the voice.

"You forgot your bag." The fish smelling man was holding her bag out to her. A flood of relief flowed through her body as she reached for the pillowcase full of her things.

"Thank you, sir," she said in a low voice that she hoped sounded like a boy's. She quickly made her way out of the car onto a brick sidewalk that was full of people hurrying to their unknown destinations. She studied the street signs for a few minutes; she knew the train station was on Forty-Second Street, but she didn't know which way to go. Finally she asked an elderly man who was standing on the corner with her if he knew which way was it to Grand Central Station. He nodded to his left, his hands busy holding a newspaper he was reading.

"Down that way about twenty blocks," he said as he scowled at her. Bonnie thanked him, then crossed the street to the other side, where other people were waiting for the next trolley. As Bonnie waited she noticed a strange network of cables suspended above the street, and she wondered what they were for. She soon found out when a horse trolley without any horses came toward her. Bonnie realized the car was attached to the cables above the street and that the cable was pulling the trolley along the street. She had heard of the cable cars, but this was the first time she had seen one. She watched in wonderment as the car full of passengers slowly made its way along the street to her corner and stopped as the driver pulled the brake. Almost immediately several passengers spilled out of the trolley and onto the brick sidewalk, scattering in every direction.

As soon as the door was clear, Bonnie hurried through it, looking for a seat. Luckily the car wasn't full, and as she settled into a seat by the window, she again looked for anyone who might be following her. Twenty minutes later the huge train station came into view, and Bonnie trembled as she began to feel the fear and doubt creep back into her mind. When the cable car stopped in front of the huge station, she was still trembling, but she got off along with the other passengers and walked with them toward one of the arched openings. As she approached the entrance, Bonnie thought of the unknown journey ahead of her and she hesitated for a second, but then she remembered her life in the factory and the degradation they had in store for her. Stoically she swallowed her fear, raised her head, and walked through the massive door into the largest train station in the United States.

Bonnie was no stranger to trains, but it had been several years since she had gone through this station on her way to her uncle's place in Pennsylvania. She had spent an enjoyable summer in Gettysburg, where he had owned a restaurant. She had been twelve, and the world was beautiful to her back then. Uncle Shaun and Aunt Lily didn't have any children, so they had treated Bonnie as if she were their own.

But it was different now. Uncle Shawn didn't live in Pennsylvania anymore; after Aunt Lily died with the consumption, he had moved west to California. Bonnie had received a letter from Shaun three years ago when he was in San Francisco, but she didn't know where he was now. Suddenly the noise of the station interrupted Bonnie's thoughts, and she remembered she needed to purchase a ticket. She began pushing her way through the hundreds of people milling around in the station and began looking for a place selling tickets to Tucson. She eventually came to a place where several ticket counters lined one side of a large room. She hesitated for a second, then moved into the shortest ticket line. The line moved fast, and after a few minutes she was next. She hesitated for a second, then stepped up to the bald-headed man patiently waiting behind the counter for her.

"Do you sell tickets to Tucson, Arizona, sir?"

"You can't get a ticket to Tucson. You have to buy one to Omaha, then change trains for San Francisco, and change again for Tucson," the clerk said in a monotone voice. "I can sell you a ticket to Omaha."

"How much is the ticket?"

"Twenty-one dollars."

Okay, I want one ticket." Bonnie put her bag down and counted out twenty-one dollars from the change and small bills she had in her pocket, then handed it to the clerk.

He counted the money, handed Bonnie a ticket, then turned to the next person in the line. "Next."

"Wait a minute, sir. Where do I get on, and when does the train leave?" Bonnie asked as she looked at the ticket and then at him.

The clerk turned his eyes back to Bonnie, an impatient look on his face. "It's right on the ticket: platform six, train number 2133, leaves at one o'clock." He turned his eyes back to the person next in line.

Bonnie picked up her bag, then read the ticket as she walked away from the desk. *Where is platform six?* She slowly walked toward the platforms, looking for signs that would indicate where she would board her train. Finally she spied the number five painted on a large brick column close to the tracks, and she continued along the platform until she came to the next one, which had the number six on it. A rumbling locomotive with steam rising from it was sitting next to the platform, and people were getting into the passenger cars. Bonnie pulled out Bart's watch to see what time it showed. It was one o'clock.

"All aboard," a man in a black uniform called out as Bonnie reached the passenger car door.

"Is this the right train?" she asked hopefully as she held up the ticket for the man to read.

"Yep," he said as he hurriedly read the ticket. "Go on in and find a seat. The train will be leaving in just a few minutes."

"Thank you, sir," Bonnie said with relief as she entered the car. Several empty seats were scattered around the car, and Bonnie settled into one by a window. A few minutes later, the train tooted its steam-powered whistle, and the train began to slowly move out of the station. Bonnie gazed around the car; it was only half full, and no one was paying any attention to her. She relaxed for the first time since Bart had come into her room that morning. Suddenly she felt exhausted; the strain of the day had drained all her energy. She leaned back in her seat, closed her eyes, and soon fell asleep.

Bonnie and her father were at the park enjoying a picnic lunch. The day was sunny and warm, and people were rowing their boats on the lake. Bonnie laughed at something her father said about a man in a rowboat. She turned to where he was pointing. She saw the man standing in the boat with his hands shading his eyes as he seemed to be looking for someone.

Bonnie thought the man looked familiar, but she couldn't be sure who it was. Suddenly the man looked toward her, and she recognized him. It was Bart! A wicked grin appeared on his face as he grabbed the oars and began rowing toward her. Bonnie wanted to run, but she couldn't seem to move. Closer he came, and Bonnie struggled harder, but to no avail. She turned to her father, begging for help, but he had his head turned and didn't seem to hear her. She pricked him with a hatpin to get his attention. Slowly he turned toward her. It was Bart. She screamed.

Bonnie woke up in a cold sweat, the click-clack sound of the moving train in her ears. *Where am I?* It took her a few seconds to remember where she was and why as she looked around the car. Sighing with relief, she turned her gaze to look out of the window, but all she saw was her own reflection staring back at her. Bonnie gasped as she saw her long, blonde hair spilling across her shoulders. Quickly she looked around to see if anyone was looking at her, but luckily everyone seemed to be asleep. Quickly she jammed the hat back on her head and pushed her hair back under it.

Bonnie sat for a while, thinking of her plight. She needed a plan. The first thing she would do when she got to Omaha would be to buy some more clothes. Some that didn't have the stink of Bart Mastard on them. She would cut her hair, and then she would continue on to San Francisco. Her stomach growled, and she remembered she hadn't eaten all day. Maybe the first thing she would do in Omaha would be to find something to eat. She pulled out the watch; it was a little past two. She leaned back and closed her eyes. Soon she was asleep again.

The next time Bonnie awoke, the train was pulling into a station. It was still dark, but she could read CLEVELAND OHIO on the sign above the train station. The conductor entered the car from the rear door, then began calling out for anyone who was getting off at Cleveland.

"Sir," Bonnie called as he approached her seat. "How long will we be stopped? Is there a place to get some food?"

"Thirty-minute stop," the conductor announced in a loud voice so everyone in the car could hear him. He looked down at Bonnie.

"There's some food stands just outside the station, son. Try the biscuits and ham."

"Thank you, sir," Bonnie said. She could feel her stomach growling as she grabbed her bag and followed the conductor through the car to the door. When Bonnie stepped off the train, she encountered a cold north wind blowing debris across the platform. She buttoned her coat as she began walking toward the station. Almost immediately the wind tugged at her hat, but she quickly reached up and held it down on her head until she entered the station. Pulling a scarf from her bag, she tied it over the hat to keep it in place, then went out the door on the other side of the station to a street that continued on into the town. She saw several different kinds of food for sale at the stands lined up along the street. At one of them she noticed that a jovial, middle-aged man with a long, flowing beard was selling biscuits filled with ham. Quickly she approached him.

"How much for the biscuit and ham, sir?" she asked as she bent over to examine them.

"Five cents each," he said.

"I'll take five of them," she said, the smell making her mouth water. After she paid him with a quarter from her pocket, the man wrapped them in butcher paper and tied the package with string. Bonnie took her package and started back to the train, but farther down the road, she spied a stand selling boiled eggs. Hurrying over to it, she bought four of them from a tall, thin lady who promised that they were fresh. As she was paying for the eggs, the train whistle sounded, so Bonnie started back to the train, peeling one of the eggs as she walked. Bonnie hadn't eaten anything in nearly two days, and she thought the egg was the best food she had ever tasted.

The conductor was standing at the door looking at his watch when Bonnie returned to the train. She hurried back to her seat, which she was happy to see was still empty, just as the train slowly left the station and began its journey west again. By the time the train caboose cleared the station, Bonnie had already consumed another egg and two of the ham sandwiches. She felt full, but now she was thirsty, so she walked up to the front of the car to the water barrel that the railroad kept in the cars for the passengers. As she drank from the tin cup chained to the barrel, she gazed around the car again, but nearly everyone was still asleep. When she went back to her seat, she put the rest of the food in her bag, then, using the bag for a pillow, she again went to sleep.

Bonnie awoke to the soft light of a dreary morning filtering through mist-covered windows. Worry touched her mind, as her first thought was that she would be late to her station at the factory, but quickly she relaxed as the clacking the wheels made at each joint of the track reminded her she was riding on a train. Through cautious eyes she watched as other passengers in the car began to stir and move around, some of them heading for the toilets at the end of the car. Feeling the need to go herself, she raised from her sleeping position on the seat. Immediately pain shot through her body as her joints and muscles resisted the movement from her awkward sleeping position. Fighting the pain, she got out of her seat, then slowly limped toward the toilets, trying to work out the kinks in her muscles on the way. The pain declined to a bearable level as she stopped in the women's line behind a woman holding her baby. At first Bonnie didn't understand why the woman turned and then stared at her, but suddenly she realized she was in the wrong line. With a low-voiced apology, she quickly moved over behind a fidgety young boy who had his hands over his crotch. *This is better for me*, she thought as she noticed that the women's line was a lot longer that the men's. In a few minutes she changed her mind when she noticed that the men's toilet would hold two people at a time. Slowly the line moved up, and soon only one man and the boy were in the line ahead of her. Bonnie was tempted to go back to her seat, but her urge to pee was too great, and she steeled herself to go through with it.

Soon it was her turn to go in, and she entered the small room. The boy was standing in front of a tin urinal as Bonnie entered, directing his yellow stream in a zigzag motion into it with both his hands. Bonnie quickly diverted her eyes as she took some pages from the Sears and Roebuck catalog hanging on the wall, then laid them around the toilet hole. The boy had finished his business and was buttoning up his trousers when he noticed what Bonnie was doing. He stopped and watched her for a second. Aware of his attention, Bonnie turned her back to the toilet hole, then pulled down her pants to her crotch while letting her shirt cover her front. Leaning forward to keep the boy from seeing that she was a girl, she slowly eased up her shirt as she sat down on the hole. Out of the corner of her eye, she could see the boy was still watching her as she urinated, but she kept her eyes on the floor until finally he left. Then a fat man came into the room, hurrying to unbutton his trousers. Bonnie was finished and ready to get out of the room, but she couldn't make herself get up until the fat man finished emptying his bladder. Finally he was through, and when he left Bonnie quickly wiped and pulled up her pants just as another man entered the toilet. Bonnie felt that everyone was watching her as she stepped out into the car. She quickly lowered her head as she walked back to her seat.

When Bonnie was settled back in her seat, she noticed that the train was passing through beautiful rolling hills dotted with neat farms and large areas of green forest. She watched for a while, fascinated with a way of life she had never seen before. Farmers were cutting the winter wheat in some places—some by hand and some with horse-drawn mowers. Bonnie enjoyed watching the scenery. She watched for a long time but soon grew tired again, so after eating another boiled egg, she lay across the seat and went back to sleep.

Bonnie was glad when the conductor shouted that the train would be arriving in Omaha in a few minutes. She was tired of sitting on the hard bench, and her body was aching. She would love to get off the train so she could purchase some more clothes. She had been wearing Bart's clothes for nearly two days now, and they had stunk when she put them on. Bonnie headed for the exit when the train finally came to a stop. She hurried into the station, wanting to find the ticket booth for the Union Pacific quickly so she would know how much time she would have in Omaha. She found the ticket booth just a little ways inside the station, and only a few people were in line. The line moved fast, and in a few moments it was Bonnie's turn. The ticket agent looked at her, a hint of skepticism in his face.

"What can I do for you, sonny?" he asked.

"I want a ticket to San Francisco, sir," Bonnie replied in her best deep voice.

The agent squinted for a second, then began to write her ticket out on a pad in front of him. "That will be twenty-four dollars, sonny. You traveling by yourself?" he asked as he handed her the ticket.

Bonnie counted the money out of her bag and handed it to the agent. "Yes, sir. I'm going to live with my uncle in San Francisco."

"The train leaves in three hours. Platform three." The agent cut his eyes to a man behind Bonnie and waited for Bonnie to move.

Bonnie hesitated for a second, then shouldered her bag and began walking toward the exit that would take her to the city. She had walked only a short distance when she arrived at the business district. Bonnie wanted to find a general store, but some frilly dresses in a dress shop window caught her eye, and she paused to look at them for a few minutes. Finally, with a deep sigh, she walked away, heading toward a store down the street with a huge sign out front that said it sold everything you could ever want or need.

The pleasing smell of fresh, new things greeted Bonnie as she walked into the huge store. The rows and rows of different items caught her attention for a few minutes, but soon she spied the men's clothes section in the back of the store. The first thing she picked out was a pair of long red underwear, or union suits, as they were commonly called. She had gotten cold during the night on the train, and these were her first priority. Next she picked out two pairs of blue denim trousers and then a couple of long-sleeve blue shirts. The store had a fitting room, and after Bonnie paid for the clothes, she entered a small cubicle on the men's side to change her clothes. Luckily the room was empty, but there wasn't a latch on the door, so she hurriedly stripped off her old clothes hoping no man would walk in.

There was a mirror in the cubicle, and she gasped when she saw the reflection of her nude body. Her once-full figure and ample breasts were gone, and a skeleton of a girl with just small nubs for breasts stared back at her. The harsh conditions of the factory and the minimal food had taken their toll on her body. Anger invaded her mind as she thought of this as one more thing that they had taken from her, and she hoped that all of them would pay for their crimes one day.

Bonnie didn't want to see herself anymore, so she quickly pulled on her underclothes. She had just finished buttoning her union suit when a man entered carrying a pair of new pants. Hurriedly she turned her back to the man, then slipped on the trousers and shirt. All the time she was imagining him staring at her, but when she nervously glanced back at him, he was already going out the door, his old clothes in his hand.

Bonnie picked up her old clothes and Bart's suit and stuffed them into the pillowcase, but now it was bulging and hard to carry. The store was empty except for the clerk when she left the fitting room. She asked him if he had a cheap bag that she could put her clothes in. He led her over to a shelf where he showed her a canvas bag for twenty-five cents.

"This one will be fine," Bonnie said as she began putting her spare clothes in it. Suddenly she remembered she needed some socks. The clerk helped her find the kind she wanted, and she bought two pairs that she slipped into the bag as well.

As she left the huge store, she noticed a barbershop down the street, and she sighed as she realized what she had to do. She sadly walked down the boardwalk toward it. The shop was empty of customers when she walked in, and the one barber was sitting in one of the barber chairs reading a newspaper.

"I want a haircut," she said in the deepest voice she could make. She pulled off her hat, and her hair fell to her shoulders. The barber, who had watched her walk in, got up from the chair and motioned for her to sit down.

"Son, you must live a long ways from a pair of scissors."

"We don't get in to town much," Bonnie said as she settled into the chair. The barber placed a cape over her, then grabbed his scissors and began to chop off her golden hair. Bonnie had mixed emotions as she watched her hair fall to the floor. She hated to see it go, but she felt relief that she didn't have to hide it under Bart's hat any more. Thirty minutes later the barber was through, and Bonnie had heard all the latest news and gossip of Omaha. She got out of the chair then looked at herself in a big mirror on the wall. *I look like a skinny boy,* she thought as she saw the reflection looking back at her.

"That will be ten cents, sonny," the barber said. Bonnie pulled a dime out of her bag and paid him, then pulled out her watch to check the time. She had an hour and a half before the train would leave. Bonnie felt the cold wind on her head as she walked out the barbershop door, and she took Bart's hat from her bag and put it on her head; it slipped down to her ears. Thinking she could put some paper in the hat to make it fit better, she pulled it off and looked inside.

"Wow!" she exclaimed as she pulled a twenty-dollar bill out of the hat; it had been folded and stuck in the inside rim. She ran her fingers around the rim, but the twenty dollars was all she found. She did find a coat of smelly grease inside the hat.

"Phew!" She said with a disgusted look as she pitched Bart's hat into a trash bin. Her head still cold, Bonnie hurried back to the general store.

"Where are the boys' hats, sir?" she asked the first clerk she saw. He pointed to a shelf of hats, and Bonnie hurried over and began looking through them. After trying on a few, she finally selected a gray one and paid the clerk for it.

Bonnie was ready to eat now that she had taken care of all the important things. She walked to a café she had passed when she first left the train. Only two other customers were in the café, and the waiter came to her table right away. The clock on the wall told Bonnie that she had only an hour before the train's departure time, so she ordered the daily special, which was ham steak and the fixings. In a few minutes the waiter was back with her order. Bonnie's eyes opened wide when she saw how much food was on the plate. She had never seen that much food on one plate in her entire life. She eagerly picked up her knife and fork and began to work on the food, but halfway through she finally had to give up and ask the waiter to wrap up the rest of the ham and a piece of bread for her to eat later on the train. Feeling stuffed for the first time in a long time, Bonnie paid for the meal, then hurried back to the train.

A heavy rain was falling when the train pulled into Cheyenne. It was mid morning, and Bonnie's stomach was growling; she had eaten the last of her food she had bought in Omaha for lunch the day before, and she hadn't eaten since. The train had only made two short stops since leaving Omaha, but they had been late in the night, and Bonnie slept through them. When she awoke the next morning, the conductor told her that they would stop for an hour in Cheyenne, and there were a few cafés close to the station.

Bonnie was one of the first passengers to get off the train when the conductor opened the door, and using her bag to cover her head, she ran across the road to the covered boardwalk. She was disappointed when she got to the first café; all the tables were full, and several people were waiting in line for an empty one. *There must be more close places to eat,* Bonnie thought as she walked farther down the boardwalk. Soon she came to a Mexican café about two blocks from the station and found a few empty tables. The smell of the spicy food enhanced Bonnie's hunger as she walked to an empty table. She was delighted when a waiter brought over a stack of tortillas and some butter as soon as she sat down.

"What can I get for you, chico? Do you want the special?" The waiter handed her a well-used, handwritten menu. Bonnie glanced at it but had no idea what anything was, so she handed it back to him. "Just give me the special. I have to hurry and eat so I won't miss my train."

"Oh, you are from the train. I will have your food pronto." The waiter hurried to the kitchen, where he rapidly spoke in Spanish to the cook.

Bonnie watched him go, then quickly buttered one of the tortillas. The waiter had been gone for only a few minutes when he returned with a plate of steaming enchiladas filled with beans and greasy meat. Bonnie dug into them with a ravenous appetite. She had never eaten Mexican food, but the spicy food was good. She quickly cleaned her plate. Her appetite sated, Bonnie took a last drink of water to cool off her mouth, then counted out money to pay the bill. She had just bent down to pick up her bag when suddenly her stomach rumbled and began to hurt. Bonnie paused for a second, then hurried over to the counter, all the time trying to keep from soiling herself.

"Do you have a toilet, sir?" she asked in a low voice, the sweat popping out on her brow.

The waiter looked at her, then nodded toward a back door. "There's an outhouse across the alley."

Bonnie hurried to the door with a quick "Thank you" to the waiter. She bolted across the narrow alley into a small shack that had four holes cut into a shelf that ran across the back. Hurriedly choosing the cleanest one, she dropped her pants and undid the flap on her union suit. She turned and sat down on the hole just in time as her bowels turned loose, rejecting the greasy, pepper-laden Mexican food. Bonnie relaxed and took a deep breath. Suddenly a sharp pain gripped her stomach, and again her bowels gushed out. Four times she thought she was through, but pain would come back and claim her again. She was feeling terribly exhausted as another round of pain and squirting had just passed when suddenly a man entered the toilet. He was a short, pudgy man with a scar on his face. Quickly he removed his pants, climbed up on the ledge, then squatted above one of the holes. Bonnie shrunk as small as she could and tried to not glance at the man, but his being only two holes down, it was impossible to keep him out of her mind.

"I never sit on the hole," the man casually said. "Spiders down there might bite you."

Bonnie glanced at the bare-assed man squatting next to her as the thought of a spider crawling on her butt crossed her mind. She cringed but didn't move. *Please, God, don't let a spider bite me.*

Suddenly, with a loud fart, the man's bowels turned loose; some of his waste splattered around the hole. Bonnie instantly vomited out all the food that was left in her stomach.

"God damn, boy! Watch where you're spewing that crap. You almost hit my clothes," the man on the hole yelled. He grabbed a few sheets of an old newspaper tacked to the wall and wiped his butt. He climbed down and put his clothes back on, trying to keep back away from the vomit on the floor.

"You just get off the train?" he asked.

Bonnie glanced at the man and nodded. "Yes." The man stared at her for a second, then walked out the door. Bonnie was glad he was gone. She was feeling better, and no more pains came to her stomach. She waited a few more minutes to be sure it was over before she wiped, then pulled on her clothes. She had covered the floor with the old newspapers and was reaching for her bag when the scar-faced man came back in the door.

"Give me your money, boy, and I won't hurt you," Scarface snarled as he pulled a pistol from his pocket. Bonnie stepped back in terror and looked for a place to run, but there was no place to go. She was opening her mouth to scream when Scarface hit her with the pistol. Bonnie sank to the floor as her mind went black.

"Wake up, boy, you're all right." Someone was shaking her. Bonnie opened her eyes. She was lying on the floor, and a man in an apron was standing above her. She was dizzy, and her head was aching. Bonnie tried to get up as the man reached down to help her. With his help she stood up on shaky legs and looked around. Her bag was gone. She reached into her pocket, and all her money was gone.

CHAPTER 18

The next morning found Bo still in bed as the sun slowly peeped into the open window of his hotel room. His eyes popped open as he felt the warm rays penetrating his skin.

Mary was expecting him at the café.

He had told her that he would come in early to help with the breakfast rush. Swiftly he jumped out of bed, mumbling as he pulled on his pants. His usual daily routine of early to bed and early to rise was getting all mixed up since he had met Mary. Last night he had stayed with her to help clean up after the café had closed, and it was way past his usual bedtime by the time he got back to his hotel room. He was buttoning up his shirt as he rushed out the door of the hotel, his face still dripping water and his hair sticking out from under his hat. The boardwalk echoed his rapid footsteps. Just before he got to the café, he slowed down to a normal walk.

The smell of sizzling bacon greeted him as he opened the door. At the ringing of the bell over the door, Mary and two early diners waiting looked up to see who was coming in. Bo's ears turned red in his embarrassment at being late. The two men, both local businessmen, turned back to their conversation, but Mary smiled at him and said in a teasing voice, "Good afternoon, Bo."

"I am a little late," Bo said with a sheepish grin. "I don't know what happened; usually I'm awake before the rooster crows." He hung his hat on the rack by the door, then hurried to the counter where she was standing. "What do you want me to do?"

Mary grinned. "I guess it's my fault for keeping you up so late last night, but you're here now, so go to the kitchen and cut off some more bacon strips, then get more sausage out of the root cellar." She looked up at his hair and shook her head. "You might want to comb your hair when you get a chance."

Bo obediently turned to do his chores. He put on an apron and started slicing bacon from the large sowbelly lying on the butcher block. He laughed as he thought, *If my friends back in Texas could see me now, they would hoorah me forever.* Bo grinned. He didn't care; this was the happiest he had ever been in his life.

Later, when the breakfast rush was over, Bo and Mary had time to talk about their plans for the café. Mary told Bo that a young Mexican woman had come by the day before looking for work, and she had told her to come back today.

"If she comes back, I'll hire her," Mary told him. It was only a few minutes later when the young woman came in the door. She was wearing a colorful dress, and her raven-colored hair was long and curly. She was short and pretty like a lot of Mexican women, but a desperate look on her face made her seem flawed. Bo noticed the young girl quickly crossing herself as she walked toward them.

"Remember me?" she asked Mary hopefully. "I was here yesterday, and you told me to come back today. I am hoping you have a job for me."

"Yes, I remember. You are Guadalupe," Mary said. "I might have something for you. Tell me a little about yourself."

"I am married and have a baby, Senora." Guadalupe answered calmly at first, but her voice broke, and her eyes became moist as she continued. "My husband, Carlos, worked for a rancher, but he broke his leg while breaking a wild mustang, and now he cannot work. The rancher, he tell my Carlos he no have a job, so we come to Tucson to live with my family." She paused and looked at Mary.

Mary looked at Bo, and he nodded his head.

"When could you start, Guadalupe?" Mary asked.

"I can start right now if you want me to," Guadalupe said, a pleading look in her eyes.

"Okay, you're hired. I will start you out at a dollar a day, and if business improves, maybe a small raise later."

Tears of joy appeared in Guadalupe's eyes. "Gracias, *Jefa*. Show me what you want me to do, and I will do it."

Mary smiled as she held out her hand. "Come, let me show you the kitchen. You can call me Mary."

Bo watched the two women for a while. Guadalupe was a fast learner, and soon she was doing all the work in the kitchen, and Mary was only taking orders and delivering them. Business would be slow until the lunch rush, and Bo decided to go check on his telegram. He walked over to where Mary was showing Guadalupe how to make the coffee. "Mary, is it all right if I go take care of some business, or do you have something you want me to do?"

"You go ahead, Bo. Guadalupe and I can handle it." Mary said cheerfully, then added, "If you could be back for the noon rush, it would be better, though."

"I'll be back by then, and I won't be late," he said as he started toward the door.

Mary smiled and shook her head. "We'll see."

Bo glanced back at Mary and smiled as he went out the door. He felt that Mary really liked him, and it made him feel good. He whistled as he strode down the boardwalk to the train station.

The telegraph was chattering and the clerk was writing down the message when Bo walked up to the counter of the telegraph office. He waited until the clerk was finished, then asked him if he had an answer to his telegram he had sent to New York.

"Sure do," the clerk said. "Came in this morning collect. Give me two dollars and forty cents, and it's yours."

Bo dug in his dungarees for the money. He took the telegram over closer to the window so he would have more light to read by. He sat down on a bench, unfolded the telegram, and read: *THOMAS O'SHAY DEAD STOP BONNIE O'SHAY PLACED IN ORPHANAGE.* Bo sat on the bench for several minutes trying to figure out what he needed to do. A deep sense of obligation to the young daughter of the dead Thomas O'Shay hung heavy in his heart. He couldn't leave her in an orphanage. He would do the right thing. He would go to New York and find her.

Bo started back to the café. He dreaded having to tell Mary he had to leave, but he felt it was the right thing to do, and he couldn't live with himself if he didn't try to help the orphaned girl.

He was on his way back to the café and still deep in thought a few minutes later when he heard someone call out Sergeant Dooly's name. The voice came from behind the batwing doors of the Tucson Saloon, and it sounded like someone was harassing Dooly.

"Why don't you soldier boys go back to where you came from, Dooly?" came the voice again.

Bo walked up to the doors to see what it was all about. He was met by several people coming out.

"Going to be a killing," one man said as he hurried down the street toward the sheriff's office.

Another man walked up beside Bo and casually remarked, "The soldier don't have a chance. Buck Horne is one of the fastest guns in Tucson, except maybe for Sledge."

"What's it all about?"

"I don't know. Horne just walked in and started goading Dooly."

Bo pushed through the swinging doors. Dooly was standing alone at the bar, a mug of beer in his hand, his pistol in his army-issue flapped holster. Buck Horne was facing Dooly not ten feet away, his arms down by his two Colts, his fingers twitching. Everyone else in the bar had backed up against the walls.

"I heard you Yankee blue bellies et the turds of your officers for breakfast," Horne drawled again. He stepped back a step, kicking a chair out of his way.

Dooly's eyes narrowed as he slowly set his beer mug down on the bar.

Bo, watching from the door, realized that Dooly couldn't beat Horne to the draw. Unless he did something fast, Dooly was a dead man. Taking a deep breath, he walked over to Dooly.

"Hey Dooly, when did you get back into town?" Bo asked loudly as he patted him on the back.

Dooly looked at Bo, glanced back at Horne, then back at Bo. Slowly he spoke in his Irish brogue, "Well, lad, I come in to town this morning to pick up some supplies. I thought I would take a wee drink or two before I started back, but this gentleman seems to have something against Yankee soldiers, and he is interfering with my drinking."

"My mother married a soldier," Bo stated calmly. He turned to Horne, whose face was turning red with anger. "Do you have a problem with women who marry soldiers?"

"I heard that only a whore would marry a Yankee soldier," Horne growled.

Bo never worried about dying. He figured when the Lord decided it was his time to go, then that was when he would go. He shook his head. "No, you heard wrong, but I guess as stupid as you seem to be, you would believe anything anybody told you."

Horne gritted his teeth. "Nobody calls me stupid."

Bo stepped away from Dooly and turned to faced Horne. "I just called you stupid, dumbass."

Horne growled and went for his Colts. "I'll kill you, you bastard!"

Bo saw Horne flinch just before he went for his pistols; automatically Bo pulled his Colt from the holster, cocked it as it came up, and fired.

"BOOM!" Gun smoke filled the air between the two men. Everyone in the saloon gasped.

Horne had his Colts halfway out of his holsters when suddenly he was slammed back into a table loaded with whiskey bottles and poker cards. Confusion and pain showed on his face for a second, and then he relaxed in death, blood gushing from his heart. It was quiet for a few seconds as the onlookers stared at the dead man, then the room erupted in a buzz of voices as everyone voiced amazement at how fast the stranger had drawn his Colt.

Bo waited a few seconds, looking around the room to see if anyone wanted to avenge the death of the local legend. Satisfied that no one was interested, he pushed out the spent shell casing and shoved another round in its place. He turned back to Dooly. "I know you're not a coward, Dooly, but you didn't have a chance against that gun hawk. Not with that army holster."

"You're right, lad, I appreciate your helping me out; I couldn't let the man keep on prodding me. I would have had to do something." Dooly said. He looked at Horne lying on the floor. "I would have been the one on the floor." He put his arm on Bo's shoulder, then nodded toward the bar. "Now, lad, let me buy you a drink."

A few minutes later the sheriff burst in through the batwing doors, his gun drawn. The crowd gathered around Horne's body drew his attention. Several people stepped aside to let him through as he walked over to look at the body. Seeing who it was, he whistled. "Okay, who murdered him? If you had a grudge against him, the law will probably go easy on you."

"Nobody murdered him, Sheriff," the bartender said. "As a matter of fact, Horne drew first."

The sheriff looked around the room. "Well, who killed him? Was it Sledge?"

"The cowboy standing there by Sergeant Dooly," the bartender said, pointing toward Bo.

The sheriff walked over to Bo. "What was this all about?"

Bo paused a minute as he set his mug down on the bar. "Well, Sheriff, the man had a problem with something he had heard about soldiers. I just told him he was stupid to believe everything he heard. I guess he didn't want to debate the issue, so he drew his gun to make his point. I had to defend myself."

The sheriff's eyes narrowed. "What's your name?"

"Bo Logan, out of Texas. I just got into town a few days ago. As a matter of fact, I went to your office looking for you a couple of days ago, but you were out of town."

"What's your business in Tucson, Logan?" the sheriff asked. "Why were you looking for me?"

"I was looking up an old friend, man by the name of Thomas O'Shay. You heard of him?"

The sheriff's face showed recognition for a second, but then he scowled, "Nope, never heard of him."

A voice at the door interrupted. "You need me in here?"

The sheriff looked at the man in the black broadcloth suit and said, "Yeah, Judge, we can do a quick inquest while you're here. Everyone says it was a fair fight, so I don't think there will be any charges."

The Judge walked over to the body and talked to a few of the witnesses. After a few minutes, he turned to the sheriff. "You can send for the undertaker to pick up the body. I declare this to be a clear case of self-defense."

Thirty minutes later the undertaker had picked up the body, and the swamper had cleaned the blood off the floor. The saloon returned to normal, except the chatter was all about the shooting. Bo and Dooly talked for a while, and during the conversation, Dooly mentioned he had family in New York.

"I'm going to New York City," Bo said. "I have to go find the daughter of a man I owe money to. The man died, and the boarding school where she was staying put her in an orphanage when she couldn't pay any more."

"The lass didn't have any other family?" Dooly asked.

"I'm not sure, but apparently not," Bo said.

"That's a shame, lad. How old was the lass?"

Bo wrinkled his brow in thought. "Somewhere around twelve, I think."

"More than likely they put her in a workhouse," Dooly said sadly.

"What exactly is a workhouse, Dooly?"

"Ah, lad, a workhouse is worse than a prison. They make them young folk work twelve to sixteen hours a day, feed them rotten food, and board them three and four to a bed. Then they keep most of their pay for their keep. What little pay they have left they have to buy their own clothes." Dooly shook his head and sighed. "I know because when I came over from Ireland, my dad was killed in an alley for his clothes and shoes, and my ma died of pneumonia.

They put me and my sister in one of those workhouses, but I run off and joined the army."

Bo looked at Dooly with concern and said, "What about your sister, Dooly?"

Dooly took a drink of his beer. "Oh, she's doing good now. As soon as I started drawing my army pay, I got her out of the workhouse and into a boarding school. Now she's married to a schoolteacher, and they have three kids. I go to see them when I get leave."

Bo smiled, relieved at the happy ending, but then he frowned, thinking of Bonnie O'Shay. "I think I'll catch the next train for New York, Dooly. I need to get her away from that as soon as I can."

Dooly lifted his mug and finished his beer. He paused, thinking for a minute, then turned to Bo. "If you can wait until tomorrow, I'll take leave and go with you—that is, if you don't mind."

Bo grinned. "I don't mind a bit. I was just thinking it would be nice to have you with me in that big city."

The two men raised their mugs one last time and clinked them together. "New York City!"

CHAPTER 19

When Bo left Dooly at the saloon and headed back to the café, his thoughts went back to his conflicting emotions between Mary and Thomas O'Shay and his young daughter. He felt obligated to find the little girl and rescue her from whatever place she had ended up in, be it a workhouse or an orphanage. In his heart he wanted to very much, but on the other hand, he didn't want to leave Mary. His heart ached every time he thought of her.

I've found the woman of my dreams. I don't want to leave her. Then his thoughts turned to Bonnie O'Shay, and his emotions swelled as he thought of her in imprisoned in a workhouse.

Her father is dead, and I have all this gold that is really hers.

"I have to go find her. I can't leave her there," he told himself as he finally decided what he would do. "I just hope that Mary will understand."

Mary was at the counter talking to one of the local Mexicans as Bo walked in the door. She looked up when she heard the doorbell. "Oh, Bo, there you are. This is Jose, Lupe's papa. He has agreed to build our kitchen."

"That was quick. Who is Lupe?" Bo asked.

"Guadalupe, our new help, silly. Jose was worried and came looking for her. I found out he's a carpenter."

"Oh, that Lupe." Bo walked over to Jose and stuck out his hand. "Soy Bo, mucho gusto."

"Mucho gusto, Senor Bo, soy Jose Luis Corona. You are the husband of the Senora?"

Bo could feel his face turning red. "No, we're not married; we're partners."

"I'm sorry, Senor; I did not mean to inquire into your private life," Jose said.

Bo glanced at Mary. She had her hand over her mouth, but he could tell she was laughing. He turned back to Lupe "No, we are just partners in the café. We don't do that—I mean, we don't live together."

"But she is your *novia?*" Jose asked.

Bo looked over at Mary. She was still giggling behind her hand, her golden curls framing her face and her blue eyes glittering with merriment. Suddenly his head cleared, and he said seriously, "I want her to be."

Mary stopped laughing and a puzzled look appeared on her face. She didn't seem to know what to say. Suddenly she grinned. "Okay, Bo, I'll be your novia. Now come on out back so we can decide where we're going to build this kitchen."

Bo's heart pounded. He felt light as a feather. With an astonished look on his face, he gazed at her as she walked to the back of the café. In a daze he followed her.

After Jose left the café, Bo and Mary didn't have time to talk about their relationship. The café started filling up with the noon crowd, and Mary and Lupe stayed busy waiting on the tables. Bo stayed in the kitchen, either washing dishes or helping prepare the food.

Later in the afternoon, after business slowed down, Bo was finally able to pull Mary aside to tell her his plans. "Mary, I have to go back East and take care of some business," he said. He paused for a second; he was hesitant to mention that it concerned a young girl. He didn't want to give her the wrong impression, so he carefully explained, "I owed a man money, and then he died. I've got to go back East to see that his family is taken care of. I should be back in two weeks."

Mary looked at Bo with questions in her eyes, "okay, Bo, I understand. I have Lupe now, and she has a brother I can get to wash dishes. We will make out."

Bo's heart felt as if it were swelling. He thought about what he was about to say; he swallowed and said, "I hope you meant it when you said you would be my novia. I like you a lot, and when I get back, I want to ask you a question that I hope you will say yes to."

Mary felt a sudden warmth flow through her body. She wanted to hear Bo ask her now, but maybe it would be best to wait. Her mistrust of men slowly filtered through the warmth of her love. Mary had only known Bo for a few days. Maybe she needed to find out more about him.

"Yes Bo, I like you too. I will be your girl. I also have a few things I need to take care of, so if you feel the same way when you get back, then we can talk about it."

"I'm glad you understand," Bo said, then hesitated. She was looking up at him, and her eyes were so blue. She opened her mouth a little as if to speak, but no words were spoken. She was so beautiful. He moved closer; she tilted up her head. Slowly they both moved their mouths closer, and they kissed.

Bo could hardly remember what happened after that. They talked more about the café, then he told her about his family in Georgia and about the time he had spent in Texas.

All too soon it was time for the supper rush, and they didn't have any more time to talk. The Shamrock was unusually crowded that night. It was after ten o'clock before they could finally shut it down. Jose was worried about Lupe walking home so late at night, and he came to walk with her. After they left Bo said goodbye to Mary with a kiss, then headed back to the hotel. He still needed to pack his things. Mary had suggested that he store his extra things in her room at the store so he could check out of the hotel and not have to pay room rent while he was gone. His train didn't leave until mid morning, so Bo would have a little time to help in the kitchen before he had to leave.

The next morning Bo got up bright and early, grabbed his things, and headed to the Shamrock. The morning rush was huge, so Bo didn't have a lot of time to talk to Mary, but they did discuss some things, and once they kissed in the kitchen. The rush was just about over and it was nearly train time when Dooly showed up. Bo told Mary good-bye, then after a quick hug, he and Dooly headed for the train. At the station they purchased their tickets and waited for the train. With all the rush, Bo hadn't had time to think much of anything, but as he sat in the train station, he wondered what the future would bring for Mary and him.

CHAPTER 20

It was after midnight, and only a few hard-core poker players were left in the Silver Dollar. John Skinner was in his office with Sledge, getting his report on the events at Vail's stage station, when suddenly there was a knock on his back door. John looked at Sledge, who shrugged and shook his head. John pulled open a drawer and removed a pistol. Holding the gun behind his back, he slowly walked to the door and cracked it open. Sheriff Cobb quickly came into the office.

"I'm surprised to see you here this late," John said as he went back to his desk. "What's up?"

"I guess you heard about Buck Horne," Cobb said. He sat down in one of the chairs and leaned over closer to John's desk. "This Bo Logan might be trouble. He's been asking about Thomas O'Shay."

John raised his eyebrows. "What did you tell him?"

Cobb cleared his throat. "I didn't talk to him, but Porky did."

John grimaced. "What did that idiot tell him?"

"He didn't tell him anything, John. He swore to me he didn't," Cobb said. He leaned back as he crossed his legs. "I got some more news about Logan."

"What difference does it make? He's going to be dead by this time tomorrow." Sledge sneered.

"You might want to rethink that plan," Cobb said. He sat back.

John reached in his desk drawer then pulled out a shot glass. He filled it from the whiskey bottle on his desk before handing it to the sheriff. "What did you find out, Cobb?"

Cobb wet his lips. "He deposited over two thousand dollars in raw gold in the Tucson National Bank." He paused for a second, then added, "It was the exact same kind of gold that O'Shay brought in."

John's body tingled. *Logan might know the location of O'Shay's mine.* He turned to Sledge. "Change of plans, Sledge. I don't want him killed just yet. Not until he leads us to the gold mine." He hesitated as a plan developed in his mind. "Go tell Flat Nose I want to see him."

Sledge, a look of annoyance on his face, left the room. A few minutes later he and Flat Nose came into the room.

"What's up, boss?" Flat Nose asked as he walked up to John's desk.

"Who's watching Logan right now?" John asked.

"Mad Dog is, over at the hotel," Flat Nose said. "But Logan went up to his room a couple hours ago. He's probably asleep by now. You want us to go take care of him?"

"No, "John said. "I don't want him killed now. I have other plans for Bo Logan." He pointed his finger at Flat Nose. "You just make sure he doesn't get out of your sight. If he leaves town, let me know right away."

Flat Nose backed away from the desk. "Sure, boss, I'll go check on Mad Dog right now." He hurriedly left the office.

John leaned back in his chair and smiled as Sledge closed the door. He felt good for a change. Things seemed to be going his way again.

"Pour us a drink, Sledge. I'm going to get the gold mine and my revenge." He turned to Cobb. "I don't need Curt in Yuma Prison any more. Tomorrow, get a writ from the judge, then send someone down there to bring him back. Tell the judge someone else confessed to the robbery and you have to set Curt free."

"Okay, John, I'll take care of it first thing in the morning." Cobb drained his glass and stood up. "I'm going; see you tomorrow." He walked out the back door.

John turned to Sledge. "I think I'm going to celebrate. Send Stella in here."

CHAPTER 21

The sky was overcast, and a cold wind was blowing when Bo and Dooly boarded the train for San Francisco. The smell of stale tobacco and body odor permeated the air as they shuffled down the narrow aisle of the car looking for a place to sit. They found a pair of seats together close to the front of the car, so they stuffed their bags into the overhead shelves and settled down on the cloth-cushioned benches to wait for the train to start. A few minutes later, the steam whistle blew three times, and the locomotive's wheels began to turn. As the train slowly pulled out of the station, Bo stared out the window, watching the buildings and houses going by faster and faster. He was fascinated by the seemingly effortless power of the huge engines. He glanced over at Dooly and noticed he was gazing out the window, too.

"This is something, isn't it," Dooly said to Bo. "I still don't understand how they get that steam to pull all this weight."

"It's a mystery to me, too, Dooly," Bo said.

The two men looked out the windows in silence for a while, keeping their thoughts and feelings private. Bo was thinking of Bonnie O'Shay again, wondering if he would be able to find the little girl. She didn't deserve the misfortunes she had been burdened with, and he wanted to change it for her. He hadn't thought much about what he was going to do with the young girl. Maybe he would bring her back to Arizona or to Georgia, where some of his family could take her in. She would need a good, loving family to care for her. His thoughts turned back to Mary. He liked her a lot; if she would marry him, they could take Bonnie in and raise her. He smiled. He would like that. It seemed as if all his thoughts lately had been of Mary. His carefree life of wandering the West that he enjoyed so much was shoved into a far corner of his mind whenever he thought of the beautiful young woman. A picture of her flashed into his mind, and he smiled again as he remembered their kiss. Yes, he would ask her to marry him when he returned with Bonnie. They would settle down on a little ranch and give Bonnie the home she had never had.

When the train pulled into Yuma around noon, the two men hurried off the train to the food stands set up across from the depot. The train had a thirty-minute stop before it continued on to Los Angeles, so they walked around as they ate the bean-and-meat-filled tortillas they had purchased.

Yuma was the location of the state prison, and a lot of businesses had sprung up to service the people who had moved in and worked there. Most of the original Mexican people who had first settled in the small village on the Colorado River had been poor farmers, but they began to prosper as jobs for them and markets for their crops were created. Bo and Dooly were walking through the farmers market when they heard the whistle calling the passengers back to the train.

Again the huge, black locomotive slowly pulled out of the station, then quickly picked up speed. Soon Yuma was far behind them as the train sped along on its ribbon of steel rails. The foothills of the San Jacinto Mountains they had been watching in the far distance for so long were now underneath them as the train slowly rose to the higher elevation of the Sierra Nevada Mountains. Evergreen trees began to appear around them as the train followed the rails higher into the rugged mountains. Eventually they were traveling in a forest that would rival many of the forests east of the Mississippi. The temperature fell as the train climbed into the higher altitude of the mountains, so the porter added wood to the stoves at both ends of the cars. The passengers donned their coats, and many of them covered themselves with blankets.

Bo was enjoying the view of the lofty mountains when suddenly the train came through a pass and he was presented with the beautiful sight of the Pacific Ocean in the distance. Bo was impressed as he stared at the rugged coastline, and he thought it was one of the most beautiful sights he had ever seen. He had seen the ocean down in Texas, but this was different. It wasn't the flat, sandy beaches of the Gulf of Mexico but huge waves crashing onto the cliffs and rocks. All too soon the train came off the mountains, and the view was gone. It was dark when they pulled into the growing little town of Los Angeles, and the train stopped only long enough to load the mail and a few passengers. Dooly left the train to buy a couple of blankets from a Mexican woman selling them by the depot. When the train pulled out of the station, he had already wrapped himself in one and was asleep. Bo stayed awake for a while, but soon he, too, was wrapped in a blanket and asleep on the seat.

It was afternoon when the train arrived in Sacramento. Bo and Dooly grabbed their things and left the train, heading for a hotel to spend the night. Tomorrow morning they would catch another train to Ogden, Utah, where they would change trains again, but this time they would be leaving the Southern Pacific Railroad to travel on a train of the Union Pacific Railroad. There was a nice hotel close to the depot, and they rented a room with two beds. Bo wanted to take a bath and clean up, but Dooly was eager to go to the nearest saloon and get a drink.

"You go ahead and get your bath," Dooly said as they were putting away their bags. "I think I'll eat something here at the hotel first and then go over to that saloon across the street and get me a whiskey. I need something to dull all the aches in my bones from that train ride."

Bo laughed. "I know how you feel. As soon as I clean up, I'll join you."

After Dooly left, Bo began taking off his boots. In a few minutes the hotel clerk and a bellhop brought a big brass tub into his room and began filling it with hot water. In just a few minutes, the tub was ready, and Bo settled into the hot bath. He just lay in it for a while, enjoying the soothing warmth as it penetrated his body and relaxed his muscles. He almost went to sleep, but when the water began to cool off, he began washing himself. The water was gray when he stepped out of the tub, and he felt a lot better. He dried off, then put on a set of clean clothes. After combing his hair, he set his Stetson on his head and headed out the door.

Dooly smiled as he walked out the hotel door and saw the brightly lit saloon across the street. The train ride had been long and tiring, and the best way for him to recuperate was to have a few whiskeys. Laughter and music, along with the usual saloon odors, greeted him as he stepped through the swinging doors. Dooly immediately went over to the crowded bar, where he squeezed into a spot between two men in railroad overalls.

"A whiskey, my good friend," he said to the bartender when the apron-clad man went by delivering a double handful of beer mugs to the end of the bar. "I been on the train from Tucson all day, and I need a wee bit of tonic to quiet me nerves."

Suddenly the men around him looked at him. There was a wave of whispering, then quietness spread out from Dooly until the whole saloon was quiet. Dooly, noticing the silence, looked around the room.

"What's going on?" he asked.

"Can't you read?" The bartender said as he pointed to a sign over the bar.

NO IRISH OR DOGS ALLOWED

Dooly studied the sign for a moment, then said with a grin on his face, "You got it all wrong, fellows. Actually, I'm an American. I just talk like an Irishman because of my parents."

The bartender stared at Dooly for a few minutes, a confused look on his face. "Okay, but you ought to try to learn to speak American. A lot of people around here don't like the Irish."

The silent crowd suddenly began talking again, most of them seemingly satisfied with the explanation and the outcome of the situation, but one of the men showed disappointment on his face. He was a tall, slender man with a black mustache under his long, red-veined nose. His black, greasy hair stuck out from under a dirty grey Stetson that looked as if a bird had crapped on it. His clothes were like a cowboy's but without the wear from working on the range. Two pearl-handled pistols hung low on his hips in fancy quick-draw holsters.

"I think you're trying to fool us," he drawled, glaring at Dooly. "I think you're a stinking, thieving Irish piece of shit."

Some of the patrons in the saloon showed their agreement with shouts and back patting, but most of them just watched, wanting some excitement to spice up their night. Dooly was quiet for a minute as he studied the red-nosed man. He didn't want to get into a gunfight with this local bully, but he knew he had to defuse the situation or fight.

"I respect your opinion, this being America and us all having free speech, but I'll have you know that I just took a bath before I came in here, and I don't stink. You must have smelled some cow manure on your boot." Dooly paused for a minute as he watched Red Nose. Then he added, "I do resent you implying that I am a thief. If you think I stole something, take off them guns and I'll meet you in the alley out back so we can settle this with our fists."

Red Nose looked confused. "I ain't going to go anywhere. You got a gun, if you're a man use it. If not, crawl out of here on your belly like a good dog."

The room suddenly became quiet again. The patrons hurriedly backed away from the two men to get out of the line of fire.

Dooly was in a dilemma: he wasn't a coward, but he knew he couldn't get his gun out as fast as this gun slick. He had just decided that the only thing he could do was to grab some of the free peanuts on the bar, throw them into the face of his antagonist, then jump him before he could get his gun out.

"Dooly, you starting the fun without me?" Bo had heard the exchange of words from the door. He was wishing that Dooly could work it out, but when he saw the gun slick was going to keep pushing, he felt he needed to step in. He knew Dooly was a courageous man, but he was no quick draw. If this went any further, Dooly would be killed. He looked at Red Nose.

"I heard what you said about the Irish. My mother was Irish, and I resent what you said. In my opinion you have horse shit for brains."

Once again, murmuring filled the room. The crowd hurried to move out of the field of fire. Some of them rushed out the doors.

Red Nose looked stunned. "Cowboy, you're going to have to wait your turn. I'm going to kill this Irish bastard first and then I'll have time for you half-breeds."

Bo took a few steps closer to Red Nose. "I don't think so. If you pull your gun, I'm going to blow out your horse shit brains."

Red Nose went for his guns.

"BOOM! BOOM!" The two shots rattled the glasses on the wall. The crowd flinched in unison. Red Nose's guns were just out of his holsters when the shots knocked him backward. He only had time to blink once before he hit the floor, and his blood slowly began to color the sawdust on the floor.

The gun smoke in the room was already beginning to clear when Bo put his gun back into his holster. He looked at Dooly. "I hope you don't mind my stepping in again. My mother's Irish."

"I don't mind a bit, lad. Come on over here to the bar, and I'll buy you a beer if the bartender will serve us."

The bartender hurried over with two mugs of beer. "I have no problem serving you gentlemen; in fact, these first two beers are on the house. That asshole lying on the floor bloodying up my sawdust ordered me to put that sign up, then said he would hurt me if I took it down." As he spoke he ripped the sign off the wall.

"You won't have any trouble with the law; everyone saw that it was a fair fight." He pitched the sign into the trash.

The two men stayed at the saloon for one more beer after the local sheriff left, then they went back to the hotel. They wanted to get a good night's sleep before the long train ride the next day.

The next morning the two men went to a local café and ordered breakfast. The weather was nice, and they walked around some after they ate. Bo had never been to Sacramento, and he wanted to see some of the city. The train was scheduled to leave at ten that morning. So they walked around the town until nine, then they returned to the hotel, grabbed their things, and went to the station.

The rest of the trip was interesting. Bo enjoyed seeing the changing scenery as the train left the mountainous country west of the Mississippi and began to travel through the forest and the farmland of the East. Parts of it reminded him of Georgia where he had grown up.

By the third day, after they had crossed the Mississippi River, Bo was ready to get off the train. He was tired of just sitting and looking out the windows, and his butt was sore from so much sitting. When the conductor came through the car to call out that the next stop was New York City, Bo felt relieved and much happier. Minutes later the train entered the outskirts of the city, and Bo grabbed his gear and waited for the train to stop. Twenty minutes later he was still waiting. Bo was amazed by the size of huge city, and by the time the train pulled into Grand Central station, he was already wondering how he was going to find one little girl among so many people.

CHAPTER 22

Bonnie's head was pounding; she couldn't catch her breath, and her heart felt as if it had stopped beating. A cold chill spread throughout her body as despair crept into her mind; she burst into tears. The man hesitated for a second, then put his hand on her shoulder.

"Come to my store, boy, and I'll put something on that bump on your head. Where do you live?" The man in the apron asked her.

Bonnie stopped crying as she looked at the man. He was middle-aged, short and slim with graying hair over a long, pleasant face. The apron he wore covered black broadcloth pants and a white shirt. His shoes showed wear but were of good leather. She wiped her eyes, then whimpered, "I've been robbed, sir. A man took all my money." Even in her confused and hurting mind, Bonnie saw the concern in the man's eyes. When he held out his hand, she reached out to grasp it.

The man helped her to the door. "Follow me to my store. While my wife looks at that bump, I'll go get the sheriff."

Bonnie wiped her tears as she followed the man up the alley and into the back door of a dry goods store. A short, plump woman was behind the counter looking at a catalog. She looked up when she heard them come in.

"Who have you got there, Edward? Oh my God, he looks like he's been hurt!" She hurried to them. "What happened?"

"Someone waylaid the lad and stole his money back there in the outhouse. See about that bump while I go find the sheriff."

The woman felt the lump on Bonnie's head while her husband hurried out the front door.

"Lord almighty, child, you got a bump the size of a hen egg. What did he hit you with? I better put some monkey blood on that cut." She bent down to look under the counter.

"Monkey blood! What is that?" Bonnie asked, then cringed with pain. She had calmed down a little, but her head still throbbed.

"Oh, it isn't really monkey's blood; we just call it that. It's some of new kind of medicine with a long name that starts with an M, but everyone calls it monkey blood." She pulled the stopper from a large bottle of red liquid, then daubed some on the cut with a little cloth on the end of a wire that stuck out of the stopper. "By the way, my name is Corrine, but everyone calls me Cori. My husband's name is Edward. What's your name, boy?"

Bonnie started to tell the lady her name but suddenly she realized what she was doing; her mind whirled as she tried to think of a name. She thought of her father, then blurted out, "Thomas, my name is Thomas. But you can call me Tom."

"What is your last name, Tom?" Cori asked as she put up the monkey blood.

Bonnie reached into her mind again; she didn't want to use O'Shay because the law might be looking for her and because she had heard that a lot of people didn't like the Irish.

"My last name is Jones; I'm Tom Jones from Pennsylvania. I was on my way to my uncle's place in San Francisco." Bonnie paused for a second as she looked at the woman to see how she would react.

"Oh you poor boy. You were on the train?" The woman asked as she wrapped some gauze on Bonnie's head.

"Yes, but I got off the train to eat. But then I got sick at my stomach, so I went to the privy. That's when the man hit me and stole my money."

A bell ringing at the front of the store interrupted their conversation, and they turned to see who it was. Edward walked into the store, followed by a man wearing a shiny badge on his vest. Bonnie's first reaction was to shrink back in fear as thoughts of going to prison for killing Bart filled her mind. She waited, trembling, as the two men approached.

"This is Deputy Blaise Fest; tell him what you told me," Edward said as he walked up to the counter with the deputy.

With a sigh Bonnie retold the story of her robbery to the deputy.

"Can you describe him, Tom? What did he look like?" the deputy asked.

"He was short and kind of pudgy, with a scar on his face," she said. Her confidence increased as she saw concern on the deputy's face. "He was about your age, deputy, and he was wearing black broadcloth pants and a blue shirt. His clothes looked like they had a lot of wear."

The deputy thought a minute. "I might know who he is. Sounds like one of our local thugs."

Bonnie felt a little better after hearing what the deputy told her. Maybe she would get her money back. She glanced up at a big clock sitting on a shelf. "I think I missed the train, sir. What am I to do now?"

"Don't worry about that, Tom," Cori said as she put her arm around Bonnie. "You can stay with us tonight. Tomorrow we'll put you back on the train." Bonnie looked up at Cori; she could sense the compassion of the woman. Thoughts of her mother crossed her mind. Cori looked back at her and smiled.

"If the deputy doesn't find your money and clothes, we can find something for you here," she said as she gave Bonnie a squeeze.

Edward looked at Bonnie, then smiled as he nodded his head. "The train will be here at the same time tomorrow, so the deputy will have plenty of time to find your things. Isn't that right, Blaise?"

"Yes, ma'am. We'll do the best we can, but if we don't find him pretty quick, the money will be spent. I'm going to check back at the office first, then me and the other deputies will go look for him. I'll let you know if we find anything." The Drakes and Bonnie watched as Deputy Fest left the store, then Cori turned to Bonnie.

"Come with me, Tom. I think you need some rest. We have a spare bedroom upstairs where you can lie down for a while."

CHAPTER 23

Lame Deer watched as the westbound stage pulled into the yard of the burned-out stagecoach station. He had a fresh team in harness waiting for the big Concord passenger coach. He had rescued the horses from the burning barn, but the fire spread fast and he didn't have time to save the feed and hay that was stored there. Luckily the harness shed didn't catch fire, and neither did another shed where there was more hay and oats stored. He was nervous as the stage pulled into the yard; the white men might blame him for the fire and the deaths.

"God O' mighty, what happened here?" yelled Bull as he drove the stagecoach into the yard. The air still hung heavy with the smell of burned wood as he climbed down from his perch and lumbered up to Lame Deer. "Where's Vail?"

"They are all gone." Lame Deer said as he pointed toward the graveyard on the hill.

"Did they all die in the fire?" Bull asked as he moved his eyes to the burned-out stage stop.

Lame Deer hesitated as Squeaky and the passengers crowded around him. "No one died in the fire. They were all killed by white men."

Three passengers had gotten out of the stage. One of them, a middle-aged man who had a leather tan face like a cowboy but was dressed in a broadcloth suit, walked up to Bull and Lame Deer.

"How do you know this Indian didn't kill 'em?" He paused for a second. "Why is he still alive?" Anger showed in the man's face as he recalled old memories. "My first wife was killed by this same type of murdering savage."

He started to say something else, but Bull interrupted. "Just keep your mouth shut; you don't know anything about this place. This Indian has worked for Vail for five or six years, and Vail trusted him. Let's hear his story."

"Yeah, tell us what happened here, Lame Deer," Squeaky, who had walked up, said in a sympatric voice.

Lame Deer turned to Bull. "I was in the hills hunting. I shot an elk and was on my way back. When I got closer to the station, I heard guns. I hurried, but when I got here, five men were riding out, and the station was on fire. I rushed in and carried out Mister Vail and Shorty." Lame Deer's face changed to sadness, and his eyes became moist. "They were all dead, shot many times and with their throats cut." He tried to continue, but he had to force the words out. "I went back in for my wife; I could see that they had torn the clothes off of my woman and used her while she was tied to the rail of the bar, then they cut her throat."

No one said anything for a few minutes. Finally Bull spoke softly. "Who do you think did it? Did you get a good look at 'em?"

"I think one of them was the big man, Sledge. It looked like him, but he was far away when I saw him. One of them was Diablo, the Mexican. Shorty had many knife cuts; that is the way of Diablo."

Bull mulled over Lame Deer's words for a few minutes, then turned to Squeaky. "Why don't you hitch up the fresh team? Maybe one of these gents will help you," he said as he glared at the passengers.

"I'll help him. The sooner I get my wife out of here, the better," the rancher said. He followed Squeaky toward the fresh horses. His wife, who was somewhat younger, paused for a moment as she looked at Lame Deer, then hurried after the two men.

Bull looked at the other passenger. He was a tall, husky man in his thirties with blond hair. He was dressed in a grey, Western-style suit with shined-up brown boots, and he was wearing a nickel-plated Colt on his side. The man pushed up his grey felt Stetson, then stuck out his hand.

"This is as good a time as any to introduce myself. My name's Rex Roberts, United States marshal."

Bull hesitated, then stuck out his hand. "You should have spoke up and taken charge, Marshall. You could have handled this better than me."

"You were doing all right; I couldn't have handled it any better. I just need to look around a little before we leave. Let's go over and look at the burned-out station. I want to look at those bodies, too. If you think Lame Deer is telling the truth, then I believe him, but I still have to look at the bodies."

Marshall Roberts and Bull poked around through the fire, but the building was so completely consumed that it was impossible to tell anything about what had happened there. Then Bull found a shovel, and the two men walked to the small cemetery to uncover the shallow graves. It was just as Lame Deer had told them—both men had been tortured and killed.

"This don't look like Apache work; it would've been a lot worse." Bull said as they looked at the bodies of Shorty and Vail.

"I agree, and Indians would have cut off their privates." Rex stared at the bodies for a few more minutes. "I've seen enough. Let's cover them back up."

"Yes, sir, Marshall." Bull grabbed the shovel and began shoveling.

Later, as they walked back to the burned-out station, Rex turned to Bull and said in a low voice, "Bull, I don't want anyone to know that I'm a marshal. I need to work undercover in Tucson for a while. I would appreciate it if you could keep this quiet."

"I won't tell a soul, Mister Roberts," Bull said. "But let me tell you this: watch out for Sledge. He's a bad 'un. He works for John Skinner, and at one time Skinner wanted this place."

"Thanks, Bull. I already had my suspicions about John Skinner," Rex said as they walked. "What do you know about Sheriff Cobb?"

"Not much. I know that he hangs out at Skinner's Saloon a lot, him and Judge Mills." He paused for a second and then said, "One other thing: there was a shooting out here a few days ago that might have set this off. John's brother, Willy Skinner, and Flat Nose Jack were out here, and Willy got into a shootout with this stranger and lost. He's buried out back, too."

Rex stopped walking. "Stop a minute, Bull. I don't want the others to hear us talking. Who was the stranger?"

Bull stopped and turned to Rex. "Bo Logan was his name. Big hombre out of Texas. He rode on into Tucson in my coach. That's his horse over there, that dun gelding in the corral."

Rex rubbed his chin. "I know Logan from down in Texas. He was on the right side of a range war and settled it real quick. The last time I heard about him, he was a deputy sheriff." He turned back toward the stagecoach. "Come on, let's go back to the stage."

When Marshal Roberts and Bull got back to the stagecoach, it was hooked up and ready to go. Squeaky had already tied Dunce to the back of the stagecoach to take to Bo in Tucson. Bull walked over to the corral, where Lame Deer was forking hay to the tired horses that had been unhooked from the stagecoach. He waited until he was finished, then said, "I don't know what the head office is going to do, Lame Deer. I'll report to them as soon as I get to Tucson, and they'll send out more feed and supplies right away." He paused. "And maybe someone else to run this place." He paused again for a second. "As far as I'm concerned, you could run this place as well as anybody, and I'll tell 'em that."

Lame Deer looked up at Bull, a blank expression on his face. "You know they will not let me run this station, Bull. No one would trust me but my friends; you and Squeaky are all that are left. Tell the office I will stay until they send someone, then I will go. I don't think I can live like a white man any more. I think I will go back to the reservation."

Bull looked down at the ground. "You're right. Maybe someday it'll change. "Bull stuck out his hand. "Sorry about your woman,

127

Lame Deer. Maybe I'll see you sometime when I'm at the Navajo reservation."

Lame Deer grasped Bull's hand and looked him in the eye. "No, Bull, you will have to come to San Carlos. I am Apache."

The stage had just gone out of sight when a small band of Apaches rode out of the trees. One of them was Geronimo. Lame Deer wasn't surprised when the war chief rode up to him. "The white men didn't blame you, little brother? I was waiting to see if they would kill you."

"Only one of them, the rancher Preston, wanted to kill me. The whites who know me believed me."

"Do you want to ride with me to Mexico? The Mexicans are easy to kill."

Lame Deer looked into his brother's eyes. "No, I have someone to kill here. I will wait in the hills and watch for them, and then I will torture them for a long time for what they did to my wife."

CHAPTER 24

Bonnie and her father were sitting by the lake, and Tom was laughing at two young lovers sitting on a bench. Suddenly the man stood up and walked toward Bonnie. She looked back at her father, but he was gone. She looked back at the man coming toward her. It was the scar-faced man. Suddenly he was closer, and he had a gun. Bonnie screamed.

Bonnie opened her eyes. She was in a strange bed. Confused and with her head pounding, she looked around. At first she thought she was back in the workhouse and she needed to hurry and dress so she wouldn't miss breakfast, but then she realized she didn't recognize the room or even the bed she was in.

Where am I? Why is my head hurting? She lay back down and tried to think, but her head was hurting so much she began to cry.

A strange woman came into the room. "Good morning, Tom. How are you feeling today?" Cori Drake said as she walked over to the window to open the curtains.

Bonnie hesitated before she answered. "I have a splitting headache, ma'am. I can't remember how I got here."

"Well, no wonder you have a headache; you were conked on the head and robbed. Don't you remember?" Cori felt the knot on Bonnie's head. She walked over to a shelf on the wall, picked up a white bottle, then poured out a white powder into a spoon. "I have some headache power for your headache." She dumped the powder into a glass on a little table by the bed. She poured water into the glass from a pitcher, stirred it with the spoon, then handed the glass to Bonnie. "Here, drink all of this down."

Bonnie was still in a daze, but she obediently took the glass and drank the medicine. She grimaced at the bitter taste. "Thank you, ma'am." She handed the glass back to Cori, then paused for a minute as her mind began to clear. The memory of the robbery slowly came back to her. "I think I am beginning to remember what happened now." She looked up into Cori's eyes. "Thank you for being so kind."

"Think nothing of it, Tom. We are God-fearing people, and it is our duty to help people in need. You just stay in bed and rest. When you are ready, there are some biscuits and gravy on the stove and some ham hanging in the cupboard. I will be downstairs in the store."

Bonnie lay back in the bed as Cori left the room. Her head was still throbbing, but not as badly as it was earlier. She closed her eyes; it was good not to worry. Cori was so nice to her. Bonnie fell asleep.

Several hours later Bonnie awoke feeling much better. She stayed in the bed for a while, going over in her mind the recent events and trying to figure out what to do next. Not finding any answers and suddenly feeling hungry despite the beating her stomach had received from the spicy Mexican food the day before, she decided to take up Cori's offer of food. Looking around, she saw her clothes neatly folded on a dressing table. She dressed, then washed up at a bowl on the bedside table. In the kitchen she found a covered plate of biscuits and a bowl of gravy sitting on the stove and a ham covered with cheesecloth sitting on the counter. The aroma coming from the food intensified Bonnie's hunger; she quickly got a plate from the cupboard and loaded it down with biscuits and gravy, along with several slices of the ham. She ate until her hunger was sated, then she cleaned up her mess and went down to the store.

The store was large and packed with all kind of dry goods. Cori was behind the counter waiting on a large woman who couldn't make up her mind on what bolt of material to buy. Edward was out front on the boardwalk straightening up some barrels and boxes. Bonnie walked over to Cori, who didn't seem surprised to see her.

"Can I help you do something, Mrs. Drake? I feel much better now."

Cori looked at Bonnie, thought a minute, and said, "If you feel like it, I could use some help. Do you know your arithmetic?"

"Yes ma'am. I have eight grades of school."

"That's good, Tom. Could you stay with Mrs. Collins and help her with this cloth? I need to help Mrs. Lackey with her grocery list."

Cori walked away, and Bonnie took her place. Mrs. Collins looked up at Bonnie. She seemed unhappy that Cori had left this young boy to help her.

"What do you know about cloth, boy? I need some cloth to make some sofa covers, but I want some that will wear well," she said in a doubting voice.

"I've worked in a sewing shop," Bonnie said with a hint of pride in her voice. "I know about cloth." She looked at the bolts of cloth that were on the counter. "None of these will last for very long. Let me look in the rack for some that will last." She walked over to a rack full of bolts of cloth. Soon she found what she was looking for and brought it back to the counter. "This cloth has a heavier thread, and there are more of them to the inch. This one will stand a lot of wear."

Mrs. Collins looked at the cloth and then at Bonnie. Her expression changed to a smile. "Do you have this in a dark blue?"

Bonnie worked in the store all morning. By noon she was running the big brass cash register, taking the money and giving change. The Drakes seemed pleased with her.

Later in the afternoon when she was taking time to eat lunch, Deputy Fest walked into the store. "Just the one I want to see," he said to Bonnie when he spied her behind the counter. "I want to let you know that we found your bag in the alley last night. It still had some things in it, so I don't know if anything is missing. Also, I found the guy I think robbed you, but he wouldn't talk. Could you come over to the jail so you can identify him?"

Bonnie thought for a minute. "I guess so. She looked up at Cori, who had just walked up.

"It's fine, Tom. Go with Deputy Fest. We can manage here, although you have been a great help to us. We will talk more when you come back."

Bonnie's mind began to drag up her fears and doubts as she followed Deputy Fest to the sheriff's office. She was nervous as he led her through the front room past a desk and a wall full of wanted posters. She could see in her mind one of them with her picture on it and maybe a reward. They entered a room with several cells made of iron bars and with iron doors, and Bonnie shivered as she imagined herself being in one of the cells. Most of the cells had men in them, and several glared at her and made rude remarks. She was glad when the deputy finally stopped at one of the cells and pointed to the man inside.

"Is this the man?"

Bonnie's heart raced as she looked into the cell. Scarface was staring back at her through the bars. "Yes, sir. He is the one who hit and robbed me."

"You lying little bastard. You are the one who should be in here." Scarface said as he looked at the deputy, "He come on to me wanting money for favors, then he grabbed at my privates. I had to hit him to get him off of me. I didn't take any of his money."

Bonnie was shocked at the man's lies. Her mouth fell open as she turned to Deputy Fest. "He's lying, sir. I am not that kind of person." Tears came to her eyes.

"Look at the little fag cry. You can tell he's queer." Scarface sneered.

Deputy Fest turned to Bonnie with an angry expression on his face. "Come on, let's get out of here." He took her by the arm then led her back to the office. "I know the son of a bitch is lying, but I didn't find any proof on him. I don't think a judge would call for a trial just on your word against his. I may have to turn him loose."

Bonnie stared at the deputy in stunned silence. Her thoughts were rattling around in her head as she tried to make sense of what he had said. Realization came to her that she didn't want a trial; a trial might bring trouble for her. It might send her back to New York. "I guess you're right, Deputy Fest," she said. "Do you have my bag here?"

"Yeah, right here." His voice sounded apologetic as he picked up Bonnie's bag from behind his desk and handed it to her. "Check it out and see if anything is missing."

Bonnie looked inside; everything seemed to be there, even her hat that Scarface had knocked off of her head when he hit her. Quickly she looked under the rim; the twenty-dollar bill from Bart's hat, which she had transferred to her new hat, was still there. "Yes, sir, it's all there."

"He probably saw someone coming, so he ditched the bag before he could go through it." Deputy Fest said. "I'm sorry, Tom. If I don't find any witnesses by morning, I'll have to let him go. He's already asking for his lawyer." He shrugged, then motioned for Bonnie to follow him as headed for the door. "Come on, I'll take you back to the store. We will see if the Drakes will let you sleep there for another night. Tomorrow I can put you back on the train. You do still have your ticket, don't you?"

Bonnie fumbled in her pocket. "Yes, it was in my shirt pocket," she said. "But will it still be good?"

"The railroad will honor it if I tell them to," Deputy Fest said as they walked down the boardwalk. In a few minutes they were back at the store. Cori was behind the counter, and the deputy told her what happened.

"I can't believe this thug is going to get away with this. Can't you do something?" Cori asked, a frown on her face.

"Nothing I can do now, but someday we will catch him red-handed, and then he will get the maximum sentence," the deputy said. "I got to go now. I'm late for our city band practice, but I wanted to ask if you can you take care of this boy for a while until he's ready to continue his journey."

"We would be glad to; in fact, if he wants to work for us to earn money for his trip to San Francisco, he can stay here as long as he wants," Cori said, glancing at Edward. "We have already discussed it." She turned to Bonnie. "Would that be satisfactory? We can pay you fifty cents a day with room and board."

Bonnie immediately responded with a yes. She had been thinking the same thing and was hoping they would ask. For the first time in a long time, she relaxed.

As the days turned into weeks, Bonnie became comfortable with the Drakes. The bad dreams eventually faded, and she was enjoying her life for the first time since leaving the boarding school. She liked working at the store, and she was very fond of the Drakes, but in a corner of her mind, Bonnie was still troubled by the desire to find her father. She knew that someday she would have to make the decision to leave, but she kept putting it off because she was enjoying her life so much with the Drakes. Bonnie didn't know that the next time she went out to the alley to empty the trash, the decision would be made for her.

It was middle afternoon and the day was windy, overcast, and cold. Bonnie went into the kitchen to begin peeling potatoes for supper, but when she saw that the kitchen trash can was full, she carried it to the alley to dump into the city trash bin. A light snow was falling, and she hurried to the trash bin, glad that she had slipped on her jacket. She had just emptied the waste can when she heard someone come up behind her.

"Hello boy. You want to come back to the privy with me?"

Bonnie froze when she turned and saw Scarface standing behind her. A wave of panic swept across her mind. She stared at him and couldn't speak.

"I'll give you back your money if you'll ride my mule," Scarface said as he fondled his crouch.

Bonnie knew what Scarface was talking about; in desperation she glanced toward the back door of the store, hoping to see Cori or Edward coming to her rescue. But in her mind she knew they weren't coming. She would have to get out of this fix on her own.

"Leave me alone or I'll tell Deputy Fest," Bonnie said fearfully. She tried to walk around Scarface, but he grabbed her hand and pulled it to the front of his pants where he thrust his groin against it.

"Feel of it; it won't hurt you. You might like it," he said with a sickening grin, showing his yellow teeth. Desperately Bonnie tried to pull her hand away, but he was too strong. She started to scream, but he put his arm around her neck with his hand over her mouth. He grabbed her around the waist with his other hand and began dragging her toward a small storage yard behind a gun shop. Bonnie's heart was racing as she frantically looked for help, but no one else was in the alley. She felt helpless as Scarface pulled her behind some large crates and threw her to the ground, knocking the breath out of her.

"Keep your mouth shut, boy, or I'll kill you," Scarface hissed as he knelt down and began unbuttoning her pants. Frantic with fear and trying to catch her breath, Bonnie tried to stop him. But even though her hands were free, she was no match for the grown man. All she could do was weakly pull at his hands and pound on his chest. Bonnie suddenly felt him pull her pants down, and she tried to scream, but Scarface punched her in the stomach, and again she struggled to breathe. He leered at her as he reached down and began opening the front of his trousers. Bonnie was exhausted, and she could only watch as her arms dropped to the ground.

"That's a good boy; just relax and enjoy it." Scarface grinned, apparently thinking she had given up. Tears appeared in Bonnie's eyes as she felt so helpless. She wondered if he would kill her. Would she go to heaven, or had she lost her chance when she killed Bart? She thought of the things she had read in the Bible.

Help me God, she prayed in her mind. *Forgive me for killing Bart; please don't let this happen to me.* Suddenly Bonnie remembered the small paring knife she had been peeling potatoes with. She had put it in her coat pocket when she began picking up the peelings to carry to the garbage. She reached into her pocket for the knife. She grasped it just as Scarface, who was now astraddle her, grabbed her hips so he could flip her over on her stomach and undo the flap on her underwear. Bonnie couldn't let that happen. She pulled the knife from her pocket, then, as he turned her over, she slashed out with the knife.

Scarface frowned and grabbed at his neck; a deep gash was spurting out a river of blood. He tried to talk, but only his lips moved. He collapsed, and Bonnie quickly pushed him away. She stood up, then hurriedly pulled up her pants. She wanted to run but could only stare at Scarface as he lay on the ground. Her mind reeled with thoughts of going back to the sweatshop, or worse, going to jail. She searched her mind for a way to escape, but all she could think of was to run. She was so happy with the Drakes and she didn't want to leave them, but finally she realized that she would have to go. Suddenly a plan came to her: she would hide the body, then go tell the Drakes that she wanted to leave on the night train to San Francisco. Anxiously she pulled the lifeless body closer to the empty crate and flipped it over his body, then with a dead branch, she dragged leaves and trash over the bloodstains.

With luck, the snow will cover the ground, she thought as she removed her bloody apron and tossed it into the trash bin. Bonnie rechecked the ground to be sure she had covered up all traces of the confrontation, then she hurried back to the store. She found Cori behind the counter and waited for her to finish with a customer before she told her she wanted to leave that day.

"But why so soon, Tom? We have enjoyed you being here. Is there a problem?"

"No. I've enjoyed staying with you, and I will always remember your kindness, but I just need to go on and find my uncle in San Francisco."

"I'll worry about you, Tom," Cori said, her lips quivering. She grasped Bonnie by the shoulders and looked into her eyes. "If you can't find your uncle, you just come on back here. You can live with us."

Tears came to Bonnie's eyes as she hugged Cori tightly. She almost wished she could stay and let Cori be the mother she had always wanted, but thoughts of Scarface lying dead under a crate told her she couldn't. She pushed herself away from Cori, then wiped her tears. Boys weren't supposed to cry, and she wasn't ready to tell Cori that she was really a girl.

"Thank you for everything. I promise I will come back if I can't find him, but I also promise I will come back someday to visit you if I do."

"Well, go pack your bag, Tom. The train will be here at ten tonight," Cori said softly as she walked toward a woman waiting at the counter. She glanced back and wiped a tear from her eye as Bonnie hurried up the stairs.

A cold wind was blowing in from the west as the train pulled out of the station. Bonnie finally relaxed but was sad as she watched Cori waving at her from the station. She had been apprehensive when Deputy Fest met them at the station, but he had only come to explain to the stationmaster why Bonnie had missed her train the first time. Apparently no one had found Scarface's body. She sighed as Cheyenne disappeared in the distance behind the train. She gathered her blanket up around her, then leaned back in the seat. She shuddered as the realization came to her that she was on her own again. Just her against the world.

CHAPTER 25

*B*onnie and her father were sitting by the lake watching the young lovers strolling in the park. It was a warm day and there were boats on the lake. She noticed a policeman walking down the path toward them, and she turned to tell her father, but he was gone! She looked back to the path, and the policeman was closer. He pulled out his gun and grinned. He came closer. It was Scarface! She tried to get up to run, but she couldn't move! She heard a train whistle.

Bonnie woke up; sunlight was streaming through the window next to her seat. She squinted as she turned her eyes away from the bright light to look out the window on the other side of the car. The mountains were gone now, replaced by low, rolling hills covered by small, neat farms. Various shades of green fields covered the landscape as far as she could see. The climate was warmer, and Bonnie removed the blanket from around her shoulders and folded it up. People were stirring around in their seats, chattering excitingly with one another and gathering their things. The train's whistle screeched, and Bonnie felt the train slow down. Little unpainted houses began to appear alongside the tracks. Soon larger business buildings replaced them, and in the hills she saw larger white houses with neat, fenced yards. Suddenly, billowing steam vented from the train engine, and the whistle blew several blasts. The train was moving much slower now. Gradually it became even slower until, with a screech of its brakes and the clanking of its cars, it finally came to a halt in front of the train station.

"San Francisco! Last stop, San Francisco!" the conductor yelled as he came down the aisle. Like the start of a horse race, people quickly moved into the aisles and began filing out of the train. Bonnie patiently waited for an opening, then gathered her bag and blanket to join them. Slowly the line of people shuffled out the door and down the steps to the platform. Bonnie was one of the last in line, and she finally stepped down from the train to find herself in an entirely different type of weather from what she had experienced the day before. It was sunny and warm, with a slight breeze that carried the salty smell of the ocean. Looking up, she saw seagulls flying above the trees. Bonnie felt a sense of calm and contentment as she watched the birds, but then her worries returned, and she frowned. Would she find her Uncle Shawn? Bonnie hadn't really thought much about what she was going to do when she got to San Francisco, but she knew she would have to start asking questions somewhere.

Bonnie walked into the station looking for someone who could give her some information about the city, but it seemed that everyone was in a hurry to get wherever they were going and didn't have time to talk. Finally she gave up and walked over to a bench to sit down until she could figure out what to do next. After a few moments, when most of the crowd had left the station or boarded the train, Bonnie spied the telegraph office. She got up and walked over to the counter, where a young man was listening to the clatter of the telegraph and writing down a message. When he finished, he looked up at Bonnie. "Can I help you?" he asked.

"I was wondering if you could tell me where the police station is. I need to find someone," Bonnie said.

"Sure. Just go to your left when you leave the station and walk about ten blocks down the street. You can't miss it. Only we don't call it a police station; it's the sheriff's office," he said.

Bonnie felt a little more hopeful. She thanked him then left the station. She was still a little apprehensive about going to the law, but she followed the man's directions and eventually found the sheriff's office. When she went through the door, a short, middle-aged man was sitting behind a desk drinking coffee and looking at a wanted poster. He set the cup down when he saw her walk in. "What can I do for you, boy?"

"I'm looking for my uncle," she said. "I was wondering if you could help me."

"What's his name? I'll see if he is in one of the cells," he said as he slowly got up from his chair.

"Oh, no sir, he's not in jail—at least I don't think he's in jail. I just arrived in San Francisco, and I need to find my uncle. He wrote me from here."

"He wrote you from the jail?"

"No sir, from San Francisco."

The jailer looked at her with a frown on his face. "San Francisco is a big city, son. I don't know everybody who lives here. What's his name?"

"His name is Shawn O'Shay, sir. I think he may have opened a restaurant here," Bonnie said.

"Nope, never heard of him. Do you know the name of his restaurant?"

Bonnie's heart sank. She just now realized how hopeless it was to find her uncle in such a large city. She had only visited him a few times when he lived back East. She did remember the name of his restaurant, though.

"Back in Pennsylvania he had a café called the Shamrock, sir. He may have used the same name out here."

The jailer thought for a minute. He reached up, took off his hat, and scratched his head. Suddenly his face changed. "I think that's the name of a café down by the wharf. If that's your uncle's place, it's in a rough part of town. I wouldn't be caught down there after dark if I was you."

Bonnie's mood changed as the small shadow of hope in her mind grew larger. "Could you tell me how to get there, sir?"

The directions the jailer gave her were easy to follow, but it was a long way to the waterfront, and it was almost noon before she finally found Water Street. It was a wide, graveled street that meandered along the edge of the water, and as Bonnie walked along it, she could see the waves crashing on the rocky shore. She was fascinated by the waves, but then she spotted a harbor seal and stopped for a few minutes to watch as it swam among the rocks looking for food.

Spying a small pier, she made her way down to it and stuck her hand down into the salty water. As Bonnie touched the Pacific Ocean, a sense of satisfaction crossed her mind. Bonnie realized she had accomplished something; she had set out to do something, and she had done it. Never again would she be in doubt of what she was capable of doing.

With renewed determination and courage, Bonnie returned to the street to continue her quest to find her uncle. Eventually she came to the harbor, and even though Bonnie had seen the ocean before when she lived in New York, she had never been to the docks where ships from all over the world came to load and unload their various cargos. She was amazed when she saw how many ships were anchored in the harbor of San Francisco. She paused for a minute, just gazing at the different ships, wondering what distant land they had come from. Where were they going when they left San Francisco?

Finally turning and looking farther down Water Street, she saw the wharves, where more ships were tied to the docks. She hurried toward them to get a better look. When she got closer, she saw people milling around everywhere, loading and unloading ships or loading the cargo into wagons. More wagons rumbled up and down the street, some leaving with loads and others, empty, returning to load up again.

Bonnie, fascinated with all the commotion, watched for a few minutes until she remembered why she was there. She began asking some of the workers about the café, but most of the people she asked only shook their heads without stopping what they were doing. A few of them pointed down the street. Frustrated, Bonnie kept walking down the street. She wondered why everyone was in such a hurry. Eventually she came to an old man sitting on a keg, smoking a pipe and watching the workers.

"Sir, do you know where the Shamrock Café is?" she asked the man to his back as she walked up to him. The old man turned his eyes toward Bonnie, paused, and pointed across the street.

"Why, it's right there across the street, boy. Are you blind?"

When Bonnie turned to look, she was instantly filled with happiness and relief. There it was, nestled in between two saloons. It was a nice enough looking place—solidly built with smooth sawmill lumber and large, glass-paned windows. It was painted green, and there was a sign over the door that read, **SHAMROCK CAFÉ**. Bonnie thanked the man, then hurried across the street to the café.

The clamor of people laughing and talking greeted Bonnie as she walked to the door and looked inside the café. The dining room was huge but crammed with tables full of people eating or waiting to eat. Others lined a counter, eating standing up. A few anxious people waited at the door for an empty spot to appear.

"The line's back here, sonny. Wait your turn."

Bonnie turned to the man who had spoken. "I was just looking for the owner, sir. Would you happen to know his name?"

"I think his name is Shawn," the man said. He pointed inside the café. "That's him at the payout counter collecting the money."

Bonnie looked where the man was pointing; the man he had indicated kind of looked like Uncle Shawn, but she wasn't sure. She decided to go talk to him. She looked back at the men waiting in line. "I'm just going inside to talk to the owner, not to eat." She made her way through the crowd to the counter. "Sir, could I talk to you for a minute?" she asked the man when he was finished collecting from one of the diners.

"If you are here about the job, just go back to the kitchen and start on those dishes. I will talk with you when the noon rush is over," the man said, then turned to take a customer's money. Bonnie stood there for a second, then looked for the kitchen. *What else do I have to do? I might as well be working.* She saw a waiter hurrying toward the rear of the café carrying dirty dishes, so she followed him. The kitchen was just as busy as the dining room. Cooks and waiters were scurrying everywhere.

A bald man across the room shouted at her, "Are you the new dishwasher?"

Bonnie looked at him. Piles of dishes were stacked everywhere around him. "I think I am, sir."

"Get busy, then. We don't have time to chat," Baldy said to her as he nodded toward a pile of dirty dishes. "You start on those over there. Scrape them out and then put them in this tub of water; wash 'em good, then put them in this other tub. I'll take them from there."

Bonnie found a dirty apron and tied it on. She grabbed a stack of dirty plates then scraped and slipped them into the hot water. No one had to tell her how to wash dishes. All the girls in the sweatshop had to work shifts in the kitchen, and Bonnie had become quite good at washing dishes. She had even learned to be a fair cook.

Slowly the pile of dishes receded until Bonnie was keeping up with them as they were coming in. She even had time to help Sam, the other dishwasher, dry some. She found out that he was really a waiter but had to wash dishes when the last dishwasher quit. Finally the noon rush hour was over, and everyone relaxed. Bonnie was sweeping the floor in the kitchen when the man who had been at the pay counter came in.

"Baldy tells me that you did a great job on the dishes. Apparently you've done this before. What's your name, lad?"

Bonnie hesitated for a second before she spoke; she still wasn't sure if this was her uncle. It had been a long time, and this man had a beard.

"My last name is O'Shay, sir. You don't mind hiring the Irish, do you?"

The man stared at Bonnie for a minute. "No, I don't mind. In fact, I'm Irish myself; in fact, my last name is O'Shay. Where would you be from, lad?"

Bonnie's heart seemed to skip a beat. She felt lighter, and her mind seemed to open up.

"I'm from New York, sir, but I did have an uncle in Pennsylvania. He had a wife name Lilly, but she died. I think my Uncle Shawn moved to California."

"Who are you, lad? Do you know me?" Shaun gasped.

Bonnie was choked with emotion. She tried to talk, but her mouth didn't seem to work. She finally spoke as tears filled her eyes. "My name is Bonnie."

Shawn's mind fluttered with emotion as he tried to absorb what he had just heard; waves of tingling sensations coursed through his body. He studied her face. Realization abruptly hit him like a slap on his face.

"You're Tom's Bonnie!"

CHAPTER 26

Bo felt a strange, hemmed-in feeling when he stepped out onto the platform at Grand Central Station. He wanted to turn around and get back on the train so he could get away from the hundreds of people who surrounded him. He had never seen so many people in one building in all his life. They were everywhere—getting on trains, getting off trains, or just walking in crowds down the walkways between the tracks. Bo counted eight trains in the station, and these were the ones being used. He could see others in huge repair shops on either side of the main building. For the first time in his life, Bo didn't know what to do. He turned to Dooly, who was behind him. "Dooly, lead the way. I have no idea which way to go."

"Just follow me, lad. I've been here a lot of times," Dooly said as he took off through the crowd with Bo close behind. The crowd thinned out some as they left the station, but there were still lots of people on the street. Dooly led them to a cable car stop, where they waited for a car that would take them to the section of the city where his sister lived.

"What makes this thing go, Dooly? I don't see a steam engine," Bo asked as the cable car pulled up to their stop.

"See that cable up there on that post?" Dooly said as they were getting on the car. "Well, there's a big steam engine somewhere that is moving that cable, and the cable is hooked to the cable car."

"I can see it now," Bo said as he looked up at the cable. He then looked into the car. It was full of people. "Dooly, how are we going to fit in this crowded car?"

Bo enjoyed the ride even if he did have to stand and hold his bag. Eventually, though, the crowded car discharged some of its passengers, and not as many got on. So after a few blocks, Bo and Dooly were able to sit down. Several minutes later they came to a stop just before the street crossed a river. Dooly led them off the car, and Bo thought they were at their destination. "Are we there yet?" he asked hopefully.

Dooly just shook his head as he led him across the street to another trolley stop. After waiting for a few minutes, they caught a horse trolley that carried them farther into the city. Bo was beginning to wonder if they would ever get there when Dooly finally led them off the trolley into a nice neighborhood with narrow, two-story brick homes built close to the street.

"This way, lad. It's just a little farther," Dooly said as he shouldered his bag and began walking.

Bo followed, looking at the brick buildings as they made their way down sidewalks also made of bricks. Dooly finally stopped in front of a brown brick building that looked exactly like all the others and announced, "Well, this is it. I hope she's home; I didn't have time to wait for an answer to my telegram."

"How do you know which one is hers? They all look alike to me," Bo asked half jokingly.

"See this number?" Dooly said as he walked up the steps and pointed to some numbers by the door. "This is her number. He knocked on the door, and in a few minutes a woman who looked to be in her thirties came to the door. She was a short, pudgy woman with sandy blonde hair who looked a lot like Dooly. She screamed when she saw him, then grabbed him in a smothering embrace. "You look good, Donny! How are you doing? Oh, it's so good to see you. Wait until the kids get home. They didn't want to go to school today just in case you arrived," the woman said as she turned him loose.

"You look good, too," Dooly said. "I didn't know if you got my telegram." He turned to Bo. "Bo, this is my sister Kaci. Kaci, this is my friend Bo Logan."

"It is a pleasure, sir. Come on in the house. I bet you men are hungry." Kaci led them into the house. It was nice inside, with neat, white curtains and pictures hanging on the walls. The floors were carpeted, and the walls had flower-covered wallpaper. They all sat down in a small living room and talked for a while. Dooly and his sister exchanged news about their lives, and then Kaci began telling stories about Dooly. After a while the conversation turned to Bo and his reason for coming to New York. Bo told her the story of Bonnie O' Shay.

"Oh, the poor lassie," Kaci said. "The workhouses are terrible. I was so blessed to have a brother who got me out of the one I was put in." She hugged Dooly again. "I'm going to fix us some food first, and then you two can go right to the police station to see if you can find out which workhouse the girl is in. You can't get her out of there any too soon."

Kaci went into the kitchen, where she fixed them a fine lunch of fried potatoes, beans, and ham. The food reminded Bo of his mother's cooking, and soon they were talking about Ireland. Bo enjoyed the meal, but as soon as they were through, he and Dooly left to go to the police station. It was only a short trolley ride this time, but when they got there, they were sent from office to office looking for information on the workhouses. They eventually ended up at city hall, where they found the address of The Perfect Lady Boarding School.

"Let's go, Dooly. They will know where she is," Bo said as Dooly showed him the address. They hurried out the door to the street, where Dooly flagged down a hackney.

"This will be the quickest way to get around now, but it will cost us more," Dooly said as he got in the hack.

"Cost doesn't matter, Dooly. Like Kaci said, we can't get her out of there any too soon," Bo said as he crawled in after him.

Soon they were in a different part of the city where big, nice houses lined the streets. The traffic was sparse, the hackney made good time, and in a few minutes they pulled up in front of a large wooden building spread out over a large lot and surrounded by huge elm trees. Flowers lined the brick walk to the front door, and a large garden full of vegetables was off to the side of the main building in an open area.

"Just wait for us here. We have other places to go," Bo told the driver. He walked to the door, Dooly following. It was unlocked, so they went inside to a small room connected to a hallway. A woman sitting behind a desk looking at some papers looked up and asked, "May I help you?"

"Yes, ma'am. I'm looking for some information about one of your students, Bonnie O'Shay."

"I don't think we have a Bonnie O'Shay. Is she supposed to be here now?"

"I don't know when she was here, but I know she is not here now. I was told she ran out of money for her schooling and then was put in an orphanage. Do you have records of your past students?"

"Yes, we do, but I can't give them out unless you are her parent or guardian."

Bo was beginning to get frustrated. About that time, a tall, thin woman in her thirties walked into the room. "Did I hear you say Bonnie O'Shay?" she asked.

"Yes, I did, ma'am. Do you know what happened to her?" Bo said.

"She was here a few years ago." The woman said, then paused for a second. "I remember her well; she was here for four years."

"Do you remember why she left?" Bo asked, almost in a whisper.

The woman's face turned sad as she began to answer. "The poor dear, her father went out West, and he never returned. Professor Dungerhill told her she was out of money and that he had to send her to an orphanage, but instead he sent her to a workhouse."

"Do you know which workhouse?" Bo asked.

"No, I don't know," the woman said apologetically.

"Where is this Dunghill? I want to talk to him," Bo said, his eyes blazing.

"He's not here anymore," the woman at the desk said. "He was fired last year for stealing from the school. Mister Vanderoche filed charges on him, but he never went to trial. He jumped bail and disappeared."

"Do you have a file on Bonnie? Maybe it would tell us where she went." Bo asked.

"I'm sorry, sir, but we had a fire two years ago, which was probably started by Dungerhill, and all the files were destroyed," the woman at the desk said with a sigh. She turned to the other woman. "Do you know anything else, Bertha?"

Bertha seemed to be searching her mind, her eyes turned toward the ceiling. Finally she said, "I remember seeing Martha Shott's carriage here the day Bonnie left—at least I think it was hers."

Bo turned to the woman at the desk. "Do you know her?"

"No, I don't know her. I wouldn't associate with such trash," said the woman disgustedly. "But I've heard she runs one of the worst sweatshops in the city, a garment factory." She paused for a second, then added, "I have no idea where it is located; you'll have to go down to the garment district and ask around."

Bo turned to Dooly. "Do you know where the garment district is?"

"I can take you right to it," he said.

Bo turned back to the woman. "Is there anything else you can tell me?"

"No sir," she said apologetically. "I do believe that some of her things were left here; they are probably still in the storeroom."

"Don't throw them away. I intend to find her, and she might want them back," Bo said. He paused for a second, then added, "Thank you, ma'am, for all your help, and you, too, Martha. If you think of anything else, send a message to Mr. Dooly's house. The address is 3456 West Thirty-Second Street."

"I will," the woman said. She hesitated for a second, her face nearly in tears. "Mister Logan, when you find her, please tell her we are sorry."

"Tell her for me, too," added Bertha, a sad look on her face.

"I will, and thank you," Bo said. He turned and with quick steps headed for the door, with Dooly right behind him.

Dooly instructed the hack driver to go to the garment district, and soon they were out of the residential district and into the crowded city streets. As they passed the numerous blocks of stores and businesses, Dooly explained to Bo that the workhouses were legal but there were certain rules to be followed. A lot of the sweatshops didn't follow these rules, so they were very leery of anyone snooping around asking questions. The best strategy would be to suggest to the people in charge of the factories that there was some money in it for them.

Bo agreed, so they began to discuss different strategies they could use. Thirty minutes later, they arrived in the district. Huge buildings lined the street, with smaller clothing shops scattered in between. Hundreds of people were scurrying up and down the brick sidewalks, most of them carrying clothes or pushing carts full of clothes.

"Stop here," Dooly yelled to the driver. He stopped, and Bo and Dooly crawled out of the hack. Bo paid him and turned to Dooly,

"Where do we begin?" Bo asked as he gazed at the two- and three-story buildings that haphazardly lined the streets as far as he could see.

"We just start asking people who are carrying garments. One of them will know her," Dooly said. He began searching the sidewalks, and after a few minutes, he saw a man coming toward them pushing a cart full of men's pants. Dooly motioned for him to stop, but the man only looked at Dooly as he slowly pushed the cart.

"I don't have time to stop. I have to get these pants down to Goldman's store."

"Do you know Martha Shott?" Dooly called out as the man walked by.

"Her factory is back that way," he said, motioning with his thumb behind him.

Bo and Dooly began walking in the direction the man had indicated, and in a few minutes they came to the first factory. The door was unlocked, and they walked into a small, unoccupied office containing a desk cluttered with papers and a couple of stiff-back chairs. They tried a door in the back of the office, but it was locked. A strong smell of glue hung in the air, and it was beginning to make Bo feel a little dizzy. He was about ready to leave when a man entered. "Can I help you with something?" he asked as he sat down at the desk.

"We're looking for Martha Shott. Does she work here?"

The man frowned then spit into a spittoon next to his small desk. "I don't know what your business is with her, but I wouldn't have that bitch anywhere close to my factory."

"I've never met the woman," Bo said. "But I have business with her about one of her workers."

"I wouldn't call them workers," the man said. "They're more like slaves." He hesitated for a second as he shook his head. "It's people like her who give the rest of us a bad name. I treat my workers fair."

"Do you know where I could find her?" Bo asked hopefully. His concern about Bonnie was steadily deepening.

"You can find her so-called garment factory on the next block, the building on the corner." The man sneered. You can't miss it. It's the worst-looking building in the whole district."

Bo thanked the man, and he and Dooly returned to the street and hurried to the next block. The first building they saw on the other side of the street was a two-story wooden structure in bad need of repair and some paint. Boards were hanging loose from the siding, and panes were broken in every window. A huge sign on the roof was barely readable.

Bo's first reaction was disgust, but it soon turned to anger as he thought of the Bonnie having to work in that kind of a place. "This building looks like it is about to fall down. This must be the place."

The noise of sewing machines greeted them as they entered the door. A grubby-looking man was sitting at a desk reading a newspaper. "Can I help you?" the man said as he lay the paper down. Suspicion was in his eyes as he shifted them from Bo to Dooly.

"Yes, sir, I'm looking for Martha Shott,," Bo said. "I have something for her, some money that is owed her."

The man's expression changed as he relaxed. "Oh, she's in her office, second door on the right as you go down this hall."

Bo and Dooly walked down the hall until they came to the second door. It was unlocked, and they walked in. A rail-thin woman with dark, stringy hair was sitting at a small desk. A short, greasy-looking man was sitting beside her, his hand down between her legs.

"Can I help you?" the woman asked in an irritated voice as she quickly smoothed out her dress. Their faces were red, and the man quickly stood up.

"I'm looking for one of your workers. There may be some money coming to her, and I need to talk to her. Are you Martha Shott?"

Martha's expression slowly changed to a smile when she heard the mention of money. She cut her eyes toward the greasy man, then back to Bo. "Yes, I'm Martha Shott. Which worker are you looking for? A lot of them borrow money from me."

"Bonnie O'Shay," Bo said as he studied her face.

Martha looked disappointed at first but then raised her eyebrows. "I'm sorry to tell you that she is no longer here. She ran away, owing me money." She paused for a second. "That was after she lured one of my employees into her bed and killed him for the money of mine he was carrying."

"Where is she now?" Bo asked, wondering if she was lying. Doubts slowly crept into his mind.

"We haven't seen her since; she is probably dead if she flashed the money around in this neighborhood."

Bo anxiously turned to Dooly. "What do you think?"

"I think she's lying about something," he replied without hesitation.

"How dare you accuse me of lying. Who are you, anyway?" Martha sneered at Dooly.

"Let's just put our cards on the table, Martha," Bo said bluntly. "You will get the money she owes you when you produce her."

Martha paused for a minute, searching Bo's face. "I'm telling the truth; she is gone. I can prove it, but I won't unless you give me a hundred dollars."

Bo was quickly losing hope of finding Bonnie. In desperation he glanced at Dooly,

"I think she's telling the truth about her not being here. I don't think she knows where she is, because if she did, she would tell you for the money," Dooly said.

Bo turned back to Martha. "How can you prove it?"

"I'll let you talk to her best friend and any others you want to. They will tell you that she is gone."

"Okay, I can't leave here without confirmation that she is gone. Bring me her friend, and let Dooly go talk to some of the others. I'll give you fifty dollars when you bring her and fifty more when I am convinced you are telling the truth."

"If you split it up, I want seventy-five when you're convinced. I know you will be," Martha said.

"You got a deal," Bo said. He reached into his pocket for his money pouch, then pulled out a fifty-dollar bill. "Go get her friend."

Martha turned to the man and nodded. He walked out of the office. A few minutes later, he returned, followed by a young woman with short, brown hair and wearing a gray, shapeless dress. She seemed to be in her early twenties, but her eyes were blood-shot and runny.

"Peggy, this man wants to talk to you about Bonnie O'Shay," Martha said. "Just tell him the truth." Martha turned to Bo. "Fifty dollars, please."

Bo handed the money to her and said, "I want to talk to her alone."

"Fine by me," Martha said as she took the money. She looked at Dooly. "Come with me. I'll take you to some of the others you can talk to."

Peggy's eyes turned to Bo as the others left the room. "Do you know where Bonnie is?"

"No, I don't even know Bonnie. I was hoping you could tell me something about her," Bo said. "I know of her father in Arizona. I've been looking for her. How long was Bonnie here?"

Peggy paused for a minute with her eyes closed. "She was here for about two years. I liked her right away, so I kind of took her under my wing and helped her. We were best friends. I don't know what happened exactly, but one Sunday, which is our only day off, Bonnie decided to sleep instead of going to church with me. When I came back, there were a lot of policemen here. They said Bonnie killed Bart Mastard and stole his clothes and money." Peggy hesitated for a second. "I haven't told this to anyone else, but a few days later, when I looked into the place where I hide my money, I found a note from Bonnie. She had taken a hundred dollars from me, and in the note she said she was sorry and she would pay me back someday." Peggy opened her eyes, then looked at Bo. "I don't blame Bonnie for what she did; I forgave her that same day. I hope the money helped her get away from this life. I pray for her every day. I just wish that I could have been with her when she ran away."

Bo was stunned; all kinds of thoughts ran through his mind. "Do you think she killed this Mastard for his money?" he asked her in a soft voice.

Peggy frowned and shook her head. "No, I'm sure that Mr. Mastard tried to..." she hesitated for a second, "force himself on her, like he has done to a lot of the girls." She closed her eyes again and grimaced. "I think she had no choice but to give in to him or to fight him." She paused again, "She kept a hat pin under her pillow. I think she stabbed him with it."

Bo was silent for a few minutes while he digested the information. Finally he looked at the girl. "Peggy, why haven't you left this place?"

"I owe more money than I can make here, and if I did leave, I'd have nowhere to go." Peggy said.

Bo was astounded at Peggy's predicament. How could some people treat others this way? He thought for a moment. "Peggy, I owe it to Bonnie to help you. Go pack your stuff; I'm taking you out of here."

Peggy stared at Bo in disbelief for a minute then hurried to her room to pack.

A few minutes after Peggy had left the room to get her things, Martha came back in with a smile on her face. "Well, are you satisfied?"

"I think I am, but I want to talk to Dooly first," Bo said. "By the way, I'm taking Peggy with me when I leave."

Martha narrowed her eyes. "She owes me money. She is under contract to pay me, and I could have her thrown in jail if she leaves."

"You'll get your money. Let me see her account, and I'll pay it," Bo said.

Martha grinned. "Sure, just give me a moment to find it." She went to a large wooden filing cabinet. While she was looking in the files, Dooly came back into the room, a grim look on his face.

Bo looked at his face and asked softly, "What do you think? Is she telling it like it happened?"

"Most of what she said was true. The lassie ran away wearing the clothes of Mastard to disguise herself. No one has seen her since she left." Dooly paused for a second, then added, "There are a lot of girls working here who live in the city with their families; none of them that I talked to have seen or heard of Bonnie since she ran away." He looked over at Martha and added, "They don't think Martha knows what become of her because she was very mad for weeks after the lassie left and took it out on the other girls."

Bo thought for a moment. "She had money; she could have left the city, maybe still dressed as a boy."

They were interrupted when Martha called from the filing cabinet, "I found her account." She brought it to her desk and opened it up. "She owes the company a hundred and twenty dollars," she said, pointing to a ledger with Peggy's name on it. "She personally owes me another hundred," she added.

"Let me see where she signed a note for it." Bo said.

"Here it is," she said as she pulled out another sheet of paper filled with figures. Bo looked at the paper. Suddenly the door opened, and Peggy came in carrying a small, worn-out carpetbag.

Bo turned to her. "Peggy, look at these figures and tell me if they are correct." He motioned her over to where the ledger was lying on the desk. While the girl was looking at it, Bo looked at the paper again.

He looked up at Martha. "This only says she owed you forty-two dollars."

Martha ran her hand over her stringy hair as she glanced up at the ceiling. "I haven't added everything for this week yet. I've been too busy."

Bo cut his eyes back to Peggy, who was still looking at the ledger. "Is it right, Peggy?"

Peggy glanced at Bo and then back to the book. "She hasn't subtracted my wages for this week yet, but other than that, it's correct."

"How much is your wages?" Bo asked.

Peggy dropped her eyes as she softly said, "Twelve dollars."

Bo frowned as he turned back to Martha. "I'm going to give you three hundred dollars. Write me a receipt and be sure that it says Peggy doesn't owe you or the company any more money."

Martha began began writing on the ledger, then she wrote on the sheet. She handed them to Bo. "It's a pleasure doing business with you. Now give me my money."

Bo looked at the papers for a minute, then reached into his pocket for the three hundred dollars. As he handed it to her, he said, "Here's your money. Now I have another deal for you. If Bonnie ever shows back up here and is charged for killing Mastard, I want you to contact me. If you tell the truth to the police that Mastard was trying to rape her and if they drop the charges, I'll pay you one thousand dollars."

Martha paused for a moment before she answered. "I accept the deal, but if you find her yourself, remember she is still wanted here until I drop the charges."

"I understand," Bo said. He turned back to Peggy. "Come on, let's get out of here."

Martha watched them leave, then walked to another door in her office and knocked on it twice. The greasy-looking man opened the door and walked back into the room.

"Well, what happened?" he asked as he sat down in her chair behind the desk.

Martha smiled as she looked down at the man. "I think this man was partners with Tom O'Shay and has a lot of money. We can get our share if we can come up with the girl."

"But she disappeared a long time ago. I don't think she's in the city or she would have showed up." Sylvester Dungerhill said, a frown on his face.

"I know, but I was thinking," Martha said, "if she had enough money, she probably took the train to Tucson to look for her father. Why don't you take a trip to Arizona to see if you can find out anything. If nothing else, we can trick this Bo Logan into thinking we have her, and then when he shows up with the money, you can kill him."

"I'll go pack my bag."

Bo, Dooly, and Peggy left the factory and caught a trolley to go back to Kaci's house. When they had gone a little ways, Bo turned to Peggy. "Where is your family, Peggy?

Peggy turned to Bo with tears in her eyes. "I don't have any family in America that I know of," she said sadly as she wiped her eyes. "I was just a little girl when my mother and father left Germany to come to America. Both of them died on the ship and another family took me in, but when they couldn't find work, they had to put me in an orphanage." Peggy trembled as she paused and took a deep breath. "When I was ten, they put me in the workhouse."

Bo was almost in tears as he listened to her story. She began crying, and he thought to reach for her hand to console her, but Dooly was already grasping it in his two rough paws and telling her that things would be all right now. Bo waited until Peggy had stopped crying, then cleared his throat. "Peggy, I don't want you to worry. I will see that you have a job and a place to stay."

When Kaci saw them come in, her first thought was they had found Bonnie, but when she heard the whole story, she was disappointed. She greeted Peggy with compassion though, and soon Peggy began to relax. Kaci's husband Todd and their two children, Robert and Lyda, had just returned from school, and Bo was introduced to all of them. Bo didn't have time to think about Bonnie for a while, but later at the supper table, they discussed her and what they should do. During the conversation Bo asked Peggy to tell him about Bonnie.

"Bonnie has corn silk hair and blue eyes," she told him. "She was normal sized when she came to the workhouse, but she soon became very thin like the rest of us. She was always tired, but she was a good worker, and after she learned how to do her job, she was able to keep up with her quota."

"Did she ever tell you about her family?" Bo asked. "I understand that her mother was deceased."

"She couldn't remember much about her mother; she died when Bonnie was only four," Peggy said. "Her father was from County Cork, Ireland, and worked for the railroad before he went out West to look for gold." Peggy paused for a moment. "Bonnie told me that she had an uncle and that she used to stay with him sometimes. She said she didn't know where he was now because his wife had died and he had gone out West, too. She only got one letter from him, and at the time he was in San Francisco." She paused for a second as she searched her memory. "I think she said his name was Shawn."

Bo pondered for a moment. Something had been bothering him, and he didn't know what it was. Something wasn't right. Suddenly it came to him. "Peggy, how old is Bonnie?"

Peggy paused as she counted on her fingers. Finally she said, "She turned seventeen on August the sixteenth a few months before she ran away. Now she would be nineteen years old."

Bo paused in thought as he tried to imagine the pretty little blonde-haired girl in the picture he had found in the cabin as a grown young lady. Finally he said, "All this time I thought I was looking for a little girl. I'm looking for a young woman." Bo turned to Dooly. "Dooly, I don't know what else to do but go to San Francisco and look for Bonnie's uncle. If I leave tomorrow on the train, can you take care of Peggy and bring her back to Tucson with you when you come back off your leave? I'll leave some money with you to pay for her room and board."

"Sure, Bo, I'll be glad to watch over her," Dooly said softly as he looked over at Peggy.

Kaci grinned then turned to Bo. "Don't worry about her, Bo. She can stay here with us until Donny goes back off his leave," Kaci said. She looked over at Peggy and smiled. "Or she can stay here with us until she is ready to go out on her own."

Bo turned to Peggy. "Peggy, if you come to Tucson, I'll see that you are taken care of. If you don't want to come, I will leave some money with you to get you started in whatever you want to do."

"I have a little money, but I want to get out of this city and make a fresh start," Peggy said. She looked over at Dooly and smiled for the first time in a long time. "I will come to Tucson, but I promise, whatever you spend on me I will pay back."

Bo smiled. "We can worry about that later. Right now I have to get ready to leave first thing in the morning."

CHAPTER 27

A newly hatched blowfly soared into the air from the shit pit under the prisoner's outhouse at Yuma prison. It meandered around for a while, tasting the air for anything rotten enough where it could lay its eggs. By chance it flew close to a small barred window on an outside wall of the huge Yuma prison, and instantly a smell from inside the small cell attracted it. Expertly flying through the bars, it honed in on a man lying on a bunk. It circled once, then landed on the sweat-beaded face of Curt Skinner as he lay resting on his bunk after busting rocks out in the hot sun all day. Curt swatted at the fly, missed, then swatted again. This time he smashed it.

"Fucking flies," he said as he wiped the smashed insect off his forehead. *I'm getting damned tired of this place. This was the worse idea my brother ever had.* He looked over at his cellmate, who was lying on the narrow bunk on the other side of the cell. *We should have tortured the bastard until he talked.*

"Paddy, I been thinking. I'm getting out of here soon. If you tell me where your mine is, I can use some of the gold to hire you a good lawyer who can get you out of here."

"I told you before, my name ain't Paddy," the man on the bunk said without opening his eyes. He was a medium-sized man with sandy hair tinged with gray.

"I thought all of you Irishmen were called Paddy. Anyway, just draw me a map and I promise to get you out of here," Curt said indifferently.

The Irishman slowly shook his head. "And I told you before, I only found a small pocket of gold, and I dug it all out. There was no more."

"How come you told Big Mike you had a mine and it was full of gold?"

"I was just funning Big Mike. It was a joke."

Curt's face turned red. He wanted to hit the man, but he knew he couldn't whip him. He had already tried once, and his jaw was still sore. He was about the same size as the Irishman, but his muscles weren't as big or as hard. A few days ago he tried getting some of the other inmates to rough the Mick up, but he soon found out that the Mick was friends with all the Mexicans, and he couldn't get enough white men who would go against them. He was about to say something else when a guard walked up to the door.

"Curt, get your stuff. Looks like you're going home."

"About time my brother got me out of here," Curt grumbled as he grabbed the few things he had in his cell. He sneered at the Irishman as he headed out the cell door. "See you later, Paddy."

The guard shut and locked the cell door. He looked at the Irishman, winked, and softly said, "I bet you're glad to get rid of that blarney." He turned without waiting for an answer, then followed Curt down the hall.

Curt walked into the warden's office to find found Sheriff Cobb waiting for him. He wasn't surprised to see him. Cobb had been working with the Skinner brothers for a long time—him and Judge Miles. They could get people out of prison just as easily as they could put them in.

"About time you got here, Sheriff," Curt said as he winked at the sheriff. "I told you I didn't steal that cow."

"Well, the real thief confessed. A Mexican we picked up for being drunk." Sheriff Cobb said with a warning look on his face. "Come on, you're free. Let's go. I got some bad news for you, too."

"What kind of bad news?" Curt asked as they walked out of the warden's office.

Sheriff Cobb looked at Curt. "Willy is dead."

"What! When did this happen? Who killed him?" Curt asked.

Sheriff Cobb paused and said, "Willy was shot when he was out at Vail's stage stop. John had sent him and Jack out there to take care of Vail, but this saddle bum steps in and kills Willy."

"Willy was fast. Was it a fair fight?"

The sheriff thought for a moment. "Jack tried to make out that the bastard might have shot him without warning, but I found out later this man has a reputation as a fast gun. His name is Bo Logan, and he killed some men in a range war in Texas."

"That don't mean he's fast," Curt said. "He just might be sneaky."

"He outdrew Buck Horn in a fair fight at the Tucson Saloon; a lot of people witnessed it," Sheriff Cobb said. "I wouldn't cut him short; he's fast. Some say faster than Sledge."

"That'll be the day. Why hasn't John taken care of the bastard?"

"John thinks he knows where the Irishman's mine is," the sheriff said. "He came into town with some of the same type of gold that O'Shay had put in the bank. Then he asked me if I knew where Tom O'Shay was."

Curt sifted through all the new information, then dismissed it. "Enough of this talking; I need whisky and a woman. What time is the train leaving?"

Sheriff Cobb hesitated for a second. "It should be coming in right now. You might have time for the whiskey...."

Later that night when they arrived in Tucson, the saloon was the only business open. Curt got off the train and hurried up the street toward the brightly lit building, the sheriff close behind him.

"I have to go over to my office," Cobb said when they were nearly there. "Tell John I'll see him in a few minutes." The sheriff walked up the street toward his office. Curt sauntered into the saloon and stopped just inside the door. The noise of the patrons slowly subsided as they noticed him standing there. Most of them knew that Curt had a fierce temper and that he had been away in prison, so now they waited to see what would happen next.

John, who was playing poker with Walter and Dutch, looked up when he noticed the saloon had gone silent and saw his brother standing at door. "About time you got here," he called loudly as he threw down his cards. He hurried over to Curt, shook his hand, then put his arm around his shoulder. "Gimpy, give us a bottle of Curt's favorite," John yelled as he led Curt over to the bar.

The noise in the saloon quickly returned to its former volume when everyone realized that nothing exciting was going to happen. John smiled as he watched Curt turn up the bottle and take a big drink. He started to say something but paused as he looked around the room. He nodded toward his office. "Let's go to my office, Curt, and I'll fill you in on what's been happening around here."

The two brothers slowly made their way to John's office, with Curt being stopped repeatedly by people wanting to shake his hand and offer congratulations. John closed the door behind them and settled down in his chair behind his desk. Curt was silent as he pulled up one of the other chairs and sat down with his feet on John's desk.

"Well, how'd things go? I hope they weren't too hard on you down there in Yuma," John asked as he studied Curt's face.

"No, wasn't too bad. Our friend took care of me. Hardest part was not having no woman." Curt grinned as he raised his hand and wiggled his fingers. "But I had that problem well in hand."

"Yeah, I bet you did," John laughed. "But let's change the subject. Did you find anything out from the Mick?"

"No, that son of a bitch kept insisting that he only found a pocket of gold, and he dug it all out," Curt said. "The lying son of a bitch; I would have beaten the shit out of him, but that damn Mick guard always seemed to be close by."

"Well that's probably for the best. I have a change of plans."

"Yeah, what's that?" Curt took a long drink of whiskey.

John leaned back in his chair. "A cowboy blew into town with some gold. Johnson over at the bank told me it's the same type of gold that O'Shay brought in, and the man has been asking around about O'Shay."

"Damn it John, I'm tired of your plans." Curt said as he leaned forward and looked John in the eye. "You could have got me out of the prison a lot sooner, but your fucking plan for me to buddy up with O'Shay and find out where the gold mine was located was plain stupid." He took another long drink and slammed the bottle down on the desk.

John shook his head. "It wasn't that simple to get you out, Curt. Remember you got yourself caught over in Maricopa County. Sheriff Bell and me ain't exactly friendly. I had to wait until I could find someone stupid enough to confess to your stupid mistake." John glared at his brother as he grabbed the bottle of whiskey, poured himself a drink, and then threw it down his throat. He wiped his mouth. "Why in the hell didn't you just steal the cattle and leave? Why did you have to hang around and skin that Mexican?"

Curt leaned forward in his chair; a frown appeared on his face. "I just wanted to have some fun, John. I didn't know the sheriff was that close behind me."

John leaned back in his chair. "Well, thank God they didn't hang you." He poured his glass full again, then raised it to his mouth as he looked Curt in the eye. "What's done is done, and now you're out, so go get yourself a woman and celebrate."

Curt paused as he glared at John for a minute. He was still mad at John for leaving him in prison so long, and he wasn't going to forget it this quickly. Suddenly he heard a woman laugh out in the saloon. He slowly rose from his chair, and then, without another word, he snatched up his bottle and headed out the door. .

CHAPTER 28

Gentle rain was falling from a leaden sky when Bo's train pulled into the station at San Francisco. His mood matched the clouds as he gathered up his things and made his way off the train. His search for Bonnie O'Shay seemed almost hopeless. He had run the information he had gathered on her through his mind a hundred times on the long trip across the country, and he always came up with the same conclusion. The last time anyone had seen Bonnie was that Sunday morning when she disappeared. She could be anywhere in the country by now. Or she could be dead. If Bo couldn't find her here in San Francisco, he didn't have anywhere else to look.

The rain had turned into a downpour by the time Bo made it into the station. He stood by the door for a while hoping it would stop, but after a few minutes, when it showed no signs of letting up, he sat down on a bench to wait it out.

As he sat in the station, his thoughts turned to his beautiful Mary, whom he hoped was waiting for him in Tucson. He had been thinking about her a lot lately. It seemed that he couldn't get her out of his mind. He wished he could just catch the next train to Tucson and go to her. *No, I have to check out all the clues I have on Bonnie, or I will always wonder that maybe I didn't go far enough and maybe she was at the next place to look.*

Bo waited awhile longer for the rain to stop, but after thirty minutes when it still didn't let up, he desperately dashed down the street to the closest hotel. A tall, thin bellboy was putting mud rugs on the marble floor when Bo entered the hotel. Bo hesitated, not wanting to track mud inside. He wiped his boots across one of the rugs.

"Sir, you can come on in," the desk clerk called as he waved for him on up to the counter. "If you track a little mud, the bellboy will clean it up."

"Thanks," Bo said as he carefully made his way across the floor. "Does it rain like that much here?"

"All the time," the desk clerk said as he turned the guest book around for Bo to sign. "How long will you be staying with us?"

"I'm not sure; I'll pay you for two days now and let you know tomorrow if I will stay longer." Bo reached for the pen, but when he raised his arm he got a whiff of himself. He said, "I'm going to get something to eat after I go put my things up, but I'd like to take a bath when I come back."

"No problem, sir. I will have a tub sent up right away. Come by the desk when you get back, and I will see to the hot water sir," the clerk replied with a smile.

Bo signed his name, paid for two nights, and in a few minutes he was climbing up the stairs to his room. After he put up his things, he went down to the hotel restaurant and ordered his supper. He was eating when he noticed a man over in a corner who looked familiar, but he couldn't recall who it was. It worried him for a while, but he soon put it out of mind as he left the restaurant and headed back to the desk to arrange for the hot water. He also arranged to have his clothes washed before he went up to his room.

The warm tub was relaxing and restful, but when Bo went to bed, he lay awake for a long time worrying about Bonnie. Finally, late in the night, he fell asleep, but when the dawn began brightening up his room through the open windows, he instantly awoke, ready to begin his quest for the young girl. He had shaved the night before and laid out his clean clothes, so all he had to do when he got up was to get dressed. After Bo combed his hair, he took out his Colt from his carpetbag and strapped it on. He hadn't worn it on the train or in New York City, and the weight of it felt good on his hips. Bo pulled on his hat, went down to the hotel restaurant, and ordered the morning special for his breakfast. As he waited, he thought of the familiar-looking man he had seen the night before and looked around for him, but didn't see him. He quickly put him out of his mind when his food was served, and he dug into his breakfast. Bo was anxious to start his search for Bonnie, so he hurriedly finished his food and paid the waiter.

It was only seven o'clock when Bo left the hotel, but already the boardwalks were full of people hurrying along on their daily chores. Freight wagons carrying everything from raw materials to finished products traveled the streets along with carriages, horses, and even a few bicycles. Bo cautiously made his way across the busy street, then walked the few blocks to the sheriff's office. The door was open when Bo reached it, and he walked in. A short, older man was sitting behind a desk drinking coffee. He looked up when Bo walked in.

"Can I help you?" he said as he set down his cup. "I'm the jailer."

"Yes sir," Bo said. "I'm looking for a young woman who might have came through here looking for her uncle about two years ago. Her name was Bonnie O'Shay, and she was looking for Shawn O'Shay."

The jailer picked up his coffee and took a sip. "Have a seat, son." He set it back down as Bo pulled up a chair. The jailer took off his hat, then scratched his head. "I remember someone coming in here looking for O'Shay, but I think it was a boy. I sent him down to the docks where O'Shay had a restaurant, can't remember the name of it right now, but the boy left, and I haven't seen him since." The jailer took another drink of his coffee. "I did go down there and eat at that restaurant a couple of times. I didn't see the boy, but I was waited on by a girl who sure looked a lot like him. Maybe it was some of his family. I was going to ask O'Shay about the boy, but I never got the chance."

Bo felt his heartbeat increase, and his skin began to tingle as he listened to the jailer's words. It had to be her; Shawn didn't have any children. "Where is this restaurant?" he softly asked as he leaned forward, the tension building in his body.

"Oh, it ain't there anymore," the jailer said. "That whole area burned down about six months ago. Everybody in the restaurant was trapped inside and burned to death."

Bo slumped back into his chair; it seemed as if a cold, dark wind swept over his body. "Were the girl and her uncle killed?"

"Don't know for sure about the girl, but the fire marshal was sure that O'Shay was dead," the jailer said as he picked up his coffee again. "Found him and a woman in his office, but the woman was burned so bad she couldn't be identified. They identified O'Shay by the gun he always carried and the big silver cross around his neck. Everyone assumed the girl was his niece who lived with him."

Bo leaned back in his chair. In his mind he could see Bonnie with her uncle, happy at last, but then, her happiness cut short by a deadly fire. Tears came to his eyes. He was silent for a few minutes as he tried to compose himself. Finally, in a choked voice, he asked, "How did the fire start?"

"Nobody knows; the fire marshal thinks it started in one of the saloons when a whole storeroom full of whisky exploded for some reason. The saloon was right next to the restaurant. The whole block of buildings on that street burned down and part of the docks across the street."

Bo slowly stood up. "What's the best way to get down to the docks, sir?"

"Just keep going down this street until you get to the ocean, turn right, and follow the street that runs along the wharves. It's just a little ways until you get to the burned-out section," the jailer said. He hesitated for a second. "They already cleaned up a lot of the mess and started rebuilding,"

Bo turned for the door but stopped and turned back to the jailer. "I would appreciate it if you would contact me in Tucson if anything else comes up about Bonnie O'Shay. Just send it general delivery to Bo Logan."

Bo left the sheriff's office and started walking along the crowded boardwalk toward the ocean, which he could see on the distance. A hackney was waiting for a fare in front of a hotel on the next block, and he hired it to take him down to the docks. When he got there he asked around, but everyone he talked to said no one had escaped from the burning restaurant. A couple people did confirm that indeed, Bonnie O'Shay had come to live with her uncle and worked at the café.

"Yeah, I knew O'Shay. I ate at his place all the time," one of the dockworkers told Bo. "They had the best food around, and it was cheap for how much they give you. It's a shame that it burned down and a lot of people died." The man pulled out his pipe. "I'll miss O'Shay and that pretty niece of his. The way it happened, they didn't have a chance." The man stuffed his pipe with tobacco, then lit it. He took a puff, looked at Bo, and said, "It was nice to have a café this close to the docks. I think the man who owned the property sold out, and now they're going to put a warehouse there." He took another puff on his pipe and paused as he looked toward the burned-out block. "I won't miss the saloons, but I sure will miss seeing that café with the four-leaf clover sign out front."

The words of the man disheartened Bo even more. He sat there for a minute just looking out at the ocean. The wind from the bay suddenly seemed colder, the day less bright. The screech of a gull jolted Bo out of his thoughts as it flew above them, looking for an easy meal. Bo got up from the crate he was sitting on and said softly, "Thank you, sir, for the information. I guess I'll go back to my hotel now. I got to get up early to catch the train to Tucson."

He was thinking about Bonnie as he made his way back up the hill. A sense of helplessness filled his mind. As he walked he reviewed all the facts he had been told about Bonnie. Everything added up to the conclusion that Bonnie had died in the fire, but something still bothered him. Something still wasn't right.

Bo finally arrived at the hotel. He collected his bags then checked out of the hotel. There was nothing else he could do but go back to Tucson.

CHAPTER 29

It was night when Sylvester's train arrived in Tucson. The chill of the desert night had already descended upon the town, and he pulled on his coat as he made his way down the almost empty streets toward the brightest lights he could see. A twist of fate brought him to the Silver Dollar, where not only John Skinner and his brother were sitting at a table drinking, but also Sheriff Cobb and Walter Johnson.

Flat Nose Jack was standing at the bar jealously glaring at Sledge as the big man was groping Stella. Mad Dog, standing on the other side, nudged Dutch and pointed at Jack. "Look at him. I think he's in love with Stella."

"Hell, everyone's in love with Stella. They all want to poke her," Dutch said. "I think I'll love her when Sledge gets through with her."

"I don't mean like that," Mad Dog said. "I think he would marry her."

"You're joshing me; nobody could be that dumb," Dutch said. He looked past Mad Dog at Flat Nose and then back to Mad Dog. "You know, you might be right."

Both men burst out laughing and slapping their legs.

Flat Nose turned around and glared at them. "Fuck both of you. Stella would quit whoring if she had a man to take care of her."

The mood was broken as Flat Nose noticed a duded-up stranger walking in their direction. The derby-crowned newcomer walked up to the bar on the other side of Dutch and ordered a beer. Dutch and Mad Dog stopped their guffawing to see what had caught Flat Nose's attention.

Sylvester had been served his beer and was bringing the mug up to his mouth when he noticed the men looking at him. He took a sip, then set the mug back down on the bar. He forced a broad grin to his face as he turned toward the three ruffians.

"Could I buy you men a drink? I just got into town with some merchandise to sell, and I'd like to get acquainted with some of the locals. You look like people I could do business with."

"Sure mister, I'm Dutch, that's Mad Dog and the ugly one is Flat Nose," Dutch said as he pointed out his two buddies.

"What kind of business are you in, mister?" Mad Dog asked.

"I'll show you in a minute," Sylvester said as he pulled a silver dollar out of his pocket. "First let's get those drinks." He turned to the bartender. "Give these men whatever they want."

The three men broke into smiles as they turned to the bartender and loudly ordered the expensive Kentucky bourbon that was always kept on the top shelf behind the bar. Sylvester watched them with amusement as they gulped down their drinks only seconds after the bartender poured them. With hope for another round on their faces, they turned back to Sylvester, but he only chuckled as he opened his carpetbag.

"I sell postcards," he said as he pulled out a large paper envelope.

Flat Nose laughed as he sat his shot glass back on the bar. "Hell, what would I do with a postcard? I can't even write."

Dutch grinned as he said proudly, "I can write. I went to school for six years."

"Yeah, but you only got to the third grade," Flat Nose said. "How about you, Mad Dog? Can you write?"

"I can write my name; that's all I need." Mad Dog replied smugly. He turned to Sylvester. "I don't think you're going to have much luck here, mister."

Sylvester smiled. "You got it all wrong boys, when you see these postcards, you won't even think about mailing them." He pulled out one of the cards and handed it to Dutch. His eyes grew larger, and a big grin appeared on his face as he stared at the postcard.

"Whoa Nelly, where in the hell did you get this? How much do you want for it?" Dutch exclaimed. "I got to have one of these."

Mad Dog and Flat Nose crowded around Dutch to look at the picture. Flat Nose kept reaching for it, but Dutch kept pulling it out of his reach.

"Just hold it still, so we can all look at it," Mad Dog hollered. "Shit, I can't even see it for you two assholes."

As Flat Nose put his hand down, Dutch held the postcard so they could all examine it. A woman, completely naked, stared out at them from the picture. She was smiling and had her hand down between her legs. With the other hand she had her index finger up in the familiar "come to me" gesture.

"Damn, will you look at that," Mad Dog said. "I think I'm in love."

John Skinner, sitting at his usual table playing poker, had looked up when he heard the men loudly chattering over at the bar. "What are you men getting so excited about?" he asked in a loud, commanding voice.

Flat Nose turned and said, "You got to see this boss; it's a naked woman."

John was curious. He had seen a picture of a naked woman once but it had been handed around so much that the image was in bad shape. What stayed in his mind was the way she was fondling herself. He folded his hand and walked over to the men at the bar. With the expression of a scolding father, he reached out his hand; Dutch reluctantly gave him the postcard. John stared at it for a second. He turned his eyes back toward Sylvester as he put on his best poker face. "How much do you want for this, Mister?"

Sylvester grinned. "You're just the man I wanted to see. My name is Sylvester Dungerhill from New York City, and I deal in this type of exotic postcard."

"I'm John Skinner. I own this place," John said. "How many of these do you have?"

Sylvester glanced at the other men standing around them, then turned to John. "Do you have an office where we could discuss business privately? I mainly deal in wholesale, and I like to do business with only one man in a town."

John hesitated for a second. "Sure. Come with me; we can talk in there." He started toward his office. Sylvester glanced at the three men, winked, and followed John into his office. He waited as John went to his desk and sat down. John motioned for Sylvester to sit in the other chair, then watched as Sly laid the picture on his desk where he could look at it. He wet his lips then looked up at Sylvester. "Let me see what else you got."

Sylvester dug into the envelope and pulled out some more postcards. He laid them in a row in front of John. All of the cards were different women in different poses. Most of them were smiling and gesturing.

"I can let you have these for fifty cents each if you buy two hundred of them," he said, his eyes studying John's face. "I guarantee you'll be the only one in this town who will have them."

John could feel a stir in his groin again as he looked at the new pictures. *These are good,* he thought. *It's almost like you're looking through a door at her.*

John reached for a bottle of whiskey on the table beside him. He filled two shot glasses, then handed one to Sylvester. He thought about the five hundred soldiers out at the fort. John took a sip of his whiskey before he replied. "I think I could handle about five hundred of these." Then he thought of something else. "I want to be the only one selling these postcards in Yuma, too."

Sylvester hesitated for a second as the figures whirled in his head. He sipped on his whiskey. This deal was better than what he had thought he would do. He had to pay only a nickel apiece for the cards. "I think we can work out an agreement. I haven't shown you the best stuff yet." He ran the numbers in his head for a minute. "If you can buy one thousand cards, I'll do it." He reached back into his bag and pulled out another big envelope. He opened it and sifted through the cards inside. He picked out a few and pitched them on the table.

John's eyes almost popped out of his head as he stared at the pictures. "Where in the fucking world did these photographs come from? I haven't ever seen anything like this." The picture was of a woman and a man on a bed in a position for sex. The woman was slightly plump and beautiful. The man was young, with large muscles and a handsome face.

"I have a supplier in France." Sylvester said. "I have them shipped to me, and I wholesale them to other people like you." He leaned back with a serious look on his face. "I have to get a dollar apiece for these, but you can more than double your money. I have seen these sell for as much as five dollars in New York."

"That's a lot of money for around here," John said. "The soldiers don't make but eighteen dollars a month."

Sylvester thought for a moment. "I tell you what I'll do. If you buy five hundred of the ones with just the women and five hundred of the couples; I'll let you have the lot for fifty cents each. That would be five hundred dollars total."

John thought about the deal for a few seconds and said, "It's a deal. Do you have that many with you?"

"Yeah, I have that many in my trunk plus these samples. I came here straight from New York," Sylvester said.

"We have a deal then," John said as he stuck out his hand. Sylvester reached out, and the two men shook hands.

"I left my trunk over at the train station in storage, but I have about fifty of both types in the envelopes, and I can give you these now, and in the morning I'll get the others. Can you can pay me for the hundred now so that I'll have a little spending money?"

"Sure, let me get the money." John turned, opened his safe, and counted out fifty dollars. At the same time, Sylvester was counting the pictures.

"I was wondering, Sylvester," John said, handing Sylvester the money. "You said you came straight to Tucson. I don't usually get into another man's business, but I just about own this town, and I may be able to help you with anything else you might have in mind."

Sylvester paused for a moment as he put the money away in his purse. Maybe he did need a partner in this deal. He didn't know anything about the West. He decided to feel John out. "Perhaps you could help me; I'm looking for a man by the name of Thomas O'Shay."

John paused for a moment, then carefully replied, "I've heard the name before; there was another man who came looking for this O'Shay."

"Was his name Bo Logan?" Sylvester asked.

John slowly took a sip of his whiskey. "Yes, I believe that was his name. Is he a friend of yours?"

Sylvester paused for a second. "No, is he a friend of yours?"

John leaned forward in his chair. "No. As a matter of fact, the son of a bitch killed my brother, and as soon as I find him, he's a dead man."

Sylvester swallowed and leaned back in his chair as he thought for a moment. "It might be in your best interests to let him live for a while longer. I assume you know about the gold mine."

John leaned back, a surprised look on his face. "What do you know about it?"

"Nothing really, except that there is one," Sylvester said. "You see, I worked in a boarding school for girls in New York, and O'Shay sent his daughter to my school. When her money ran out and we hadn't heard from O'Shay, I let her stay at the school for two years without paying. The owner found out about it and fired me, after making me pay back all the money she owed. He put her in an orphanage. With my reputation ruined, I had to earn a living any way I could." He paused and took another sip of the whisky. "That's why I'm looking for him."

John paused for a second. "Do you know where Bo Logan is?"

Sylvester finished his whiskey, then poured himself another. He filled John's glass before he set the bottle back down. "Let's put all our cards on the table. Tell me what you know, and I'll tell you what I know."

John picked up one of the pictures, looked at it for a second, and set it back down. "I don't know if you know anything that would help me. I staked O'Shay in that gold mine, and it's half mine," he said. "You help me, and I'll pay you back your money with a little extra to pay for your expenses."

Sylvester looked at his whiskey and thought about John's offer. It seemed that John held all the aces, but maybe he could still make some money out of this deal. Who knows, things could change in his favor. He sipped his whiskey, then looked back at John. "I think Bo Logan knows where the mine is. He was carrying around a lot of money. I asked him to pay me what O'Shay owed me, but he laughed in my face and told me I wasn't getting a dime from him." He paused for a second as he sipped again. "I followed him to San Francisco. But I lost track of him, so I came here to look for O'Shay."

John sat stone-faced for a second, then asked, "What was Logan doing in San Francisco?"

"Looking for O'Shay's daughter. I expect he has found her by now and is heading this way."

"I thought you said she was in an orphanage," John said.

Sylvester leaned forward in his chair. "She ran away. She has an uncle in San Francisco, and I think Logan stopped to get her."

John glanced down at the postcards as he thought about the new developments. He looked back at Sylvester. "This may work out for me, one way or another. I know where O'Shay is, but I couldn't get him to tell me where the mine is located. Maybe I can use the girl to get him to talk." He took a sip of his whiskey and looked back at Sylvester. "You hang around and let me know if he has the girl. You need a place to stay? I got a couple of rooms upstairs that are empty."

Sylvester said, "I could use a room." He paused for a second as he wet his lips. "I noticed that you have a few working girls, too. Do you have any young ones?"

John stood up. "Come on, I will introduce you, but don't even think about taking Juanita. She's new, and I'm breaking her in myself."

CHAPTER 30

Marshall Rex Roberts, wearing his undercover working cowboy clothes, was playing poker at one of the tables in the Silver Dollar when he spied John and Sylvester walk out of John's office. He pretended to be looking at his cards as he watched them walk over to the bar, where John handed Sylvester a room key. John was motioning for one of his girls to come to him when Rex was interrupted.

"Are you going to bet or fold?" Walter Johnson asked him, a hint of impatience in his voice.

Rex glanced down at his cards. He didn't have anything worth betting on. "I guess you got me this time," he said as he threw down his cards.

Walter grinned as he pulled in the pot. "About time I won one. I thought I was going to be skunked tonight."

"Looks like your luck is changing, Walter," Rex said as he pulled in the cards and began shuffling them. "Who's the new guy over there at the bar with John?"

Walter glanced toward the two men. "I've never seen him before." He turned to Dutch, who had just joined the game. "Who is he, Dutch? You were over there with him at the bar."

Dutch turned to look. "That's the fellow from New York, Dungerhill. He sells postcards with photographs of naked women on them. I was going to buy one but before I could, John walked up and they went off to the office. Now, I'll have to pay twice as much for one."

"You work for him, don't you Dutch? Maybe he'll let you have one at cost," Rex said, fishing for information. Rex had been hanging around the saloons of Tucson for a week trying to gather information, but so far he hadn't learned much except that the sheriff and Judge Mills were in cahoots with John Skinner.

"Hey, you're right. He might," Dutch said.

"He ought to just give you one Dutch, as much as you do for him," Rex said. "You know, I'm still looking for a job. You think John would give me a job?"

"I thought you were looking for ranch work. Didn't you go out to the Bar Seven? They were hiring last week," Dutch said as he reached for his beer. He scowled when he saw it was empty and turned back toward Rex. "Come on, Rex, deal the cards before you wear them out."

Rex began dealing the cards. "I thought about riding out to the Bar Seven, but then I remembered I have a bad back, and besides, them cowboys don't make much money."

"The way you're winning, you don't need to work," Walter said as he looked at his cards. "I'll open with a dollar."

"I call," Rex said as he pitched out his dollar. He had a pair of jacks. "Yeah, but my luck has been good. What about when it turns bad again?"

Dutch looked at his cards. "I'll call," he said as he pitched out a silver dollar.

Rex picked up the deck and dealt everyone three cards.

"I'll bet another dollar," Walter said.

Rex looked at his cards. He had drawn another jack. "Let's make it two dollars." He threw the two dollars in the pot.

Dutch looked at the three cards he had drawn. "Let's just make it five dollars," he said as he pitched in a five-dollar gold piece.

Walter looked at his cards again. He thought for a minute and pitched five silver dollars into the pot. "I'll call."

Rex noticed that Dutch didn't have any more money in front of him. He thought he had him beat, and Walter, he was sure he could beat. Walter was a plunger, betting on everything. If he wanted to keep on good terms with Dutch, he would have to let him win. "I'm going to fold, men. I think one of you has me beat," Rex said as he threw down his cards.

Dutch grinned as he laid down his cards—three sixes. "Read 'em and weep, boys."

Walter threw down his cards. "I've had enough, boys. I'm going home."

Dutch laughed as he pulled in his pot. "You ain't going to be any luckier at home, Walter."

Walter walked off muttering to himself. "I don't know why I have to put up with that trash."

Rex watched Walter for a second, then started gathering up the cards. "Now you can afford to buy some of those pictures, Dutch."

Dutch laughed. "You know, that's a good idea. I'm going over there right now and see what's going on. I don't like to play with just two people, anyhow." He stood up and was just about to turn when Rex said to him, "Dutch, how about asking John if he could use another man? Tell him I'll do anything he wants."

"If I get a chance, I'll ask him." Dutch said as he turned and started toward the bar.

John was laughing at something Mad Dog had said as Dutch walked up. "Boss, you going to share those pictures?"

John turned. "Sure, Dutch, for a dollar each. How many do you want?" John laughed as he reached into his pocket and pulled out five of the pictures. He had only brought out the ones with the single woman. Later, when the boys had bought all of these up, he would bring out the better ones. "Here, look at these and pick out the ones you want. I want you boys to show them around and sell them for me. I'm tired of paying you guys just to hang around here."

"Sure, boss, I'll sell some for you," Dutch said as he took the cards. "By the way, that guy I was playing poker with over there is looking for a job. Said he would do anything you wanted."

John looked across the room at the man , who was still sitting at the poker table playing solitaire. "I might hire him when we get the mine. What do you know about him?"

"He told me he rode with the Lardman Brothers up in Wyoming, but that was a few years back," Dutch said as he looked up from the pictures. "He said his name was Whitey something."

"Tell him to hang around. I might have something for him in a few days." John said absently as he saw Juanita coming down the stairs. He turned back to Dutch. "I'll take those pictures out of your pay. Show them to the guys and then tell them to see Ed. He'll have them for sale at the bar." He smiled as he turned and walked toward the stairs.

Rex watched John as he strutted over to the stairs and then went up with his arm around the young Mexican girl. The girl was pretty, and for a second Rex felt a tinge of desire, but he thought of his wife and brushed it aside. He had married just a few years ago and already had three daughters. He loved his job, but he sure missed his family. *I need to wrap this assignment up so I can go home. I just need a little more evidence and a few more statements.* Rex picked the cards up and began shuffling them again. He looked up when he heard someone come through the squeaky batwing doors. It was Sheriff Cobb, and he walked over to the table next to John's office door where Flat Nose was reared back in his chair looking at one of the postcards.

"Where's John?" he asked Flat Nose.

Flat Nose looked up from the picture of the naked woman. "He's upstairs with Juanita. He ought to be down in a minute."

"What you got there, Flat Nose?" Sheriff Cobb asked as he sat down across from him.

"It's some postcards with naked women on them." Flat Nose said without looking up. "John bought a bunch of them from some dude from New York and is selling them at the bar for a dollar apiece."

"Let me see what you got," Sheriff Cobb said. He reached out his hand.

Flat Nose reluctantly handed the picture to the sheriff. "That's my favorite one. She looks like a girl I took to a dance once, back in Missouri."

Cobb looked at the picture. "Did you see her like this after the dance, Flat Nose?"

"Hell no, she wouldn't even let me kiss her that night. She said I was crude."

The sheriff laughed as he handed the picture back. "Here, you need this worse than I do."

Watching from across the room, Rex decided to walk over and see if he could find out anything. "Jack, you and the sheriff want to play some poker?" he asked as he walked up to the table, cards in hand.

"I'll play a few hands," Flat Nose said.

"How about you, Sheriff? You game?"

"Yeah, I'll play until John gets down here. I got to talk to him when he gets here."

Rex settled down into a chair, then shuffled the cards. As they played, Rex pumped the two men for more information.

They had been playing for about thirty minutes when John walked up to the table. "Cobb, I need to see you in my office," he said. "That is, if you don't mind, Sheriff. I just want to be sure it was all right if I sold some postcards with naked women on them. I wouldn't want to break the law, you know."

The sheriff stood up and tossed his cards on the table. "Sure, John, show me what you're talking about."

Rex watched the two men walk into John's office. He had noticed the inflection in John's voice. It was as if the sheriff was working for John. He had already been told by some of the men he had confided in that John owned the sheriff and Judge Mills, but so far he hadn't found anyone who could stand up in court and testify with any solid evidence. He looked at Flat Nose. "You want to play head up?"

Flat Nose had gotten out his picture and was looking at it again. He looked up at Rex. "No, I think I'll wait for Stella and spend my last two dollars with her."

CHAPTER 31

John's mind was working fast as he walked into his office. As he sat down at his desk, he glanced at the postcards lying on it for a second, then shoved them into a drawer. "You want a drink, Charley?" he said as he reached for the whiskey bottle on his desk.

"I'm always ready for a drink, John." Cobb said as he pulled a chair up to the front of John's desk. He waited patiently as John set two shot glasses on the desk and filled them with his best whiskey.

John pushed one of the glasses across the desk toward Cobb. "I've been trying to sort out this thing about the gold mine," John said as he raised his glass to his mouth. He sipped the whiskey, licked his lips, and added, "I think I've wasted too much time on O'Shay. When we railroaded him to prison four years ago, it was to get the money he had in the bank." John paused as he sipped his whiskey. A scowl appeared on his face. "That idiot Walter didn't tell me the deposit was gold until almost two years later, when I told him that Curt reported to me that O'Shay had been telling people at the prison he had a gold mine. That's when I sent word back to Curt to buddy up with O'Shay and find out if he did have a mine." John tossed his whiskey down his throat and poured himself another.

"What's your point, John? I already know all of this," Cobb asked.

"Now, Walter tells me that this cowboy, Bo Logan, the same one who shot Willy, brought in the same type of gold that O'Shay had deposited." John sat back in his chair, his mind racing to make sense out of all this information.

"And he was asking about O'Shay, too," Cobb said. "What do you think, John?"

John thought for a moment. "I want you to find Mills first thing in the morning and get a writ to bring O'Shay back to Tucson for a new trial." John paused as he took a drink of whiskey. "If I get him here, I can either starve it out of him or beat it out of him. One way or another I'll get it, and I don't care which."

"Okay, I'll get the writ, then go get O'Shay tomorrow," Cobb said.

John thought for a minute. "Don't bring him to the jail. Take him out to my place and lock him in the barn. I'll send one of the boys out to guard him until we're ready to work on him." John hesitated for a second. "Something else—the guy from New York, Dungerhill, tells me he knows Logan, and he is pretty sure that Logan knows the location of the mine." John paused for a second as he sipped his whiskey. "He also told me that Logan is on his way back to Tucson, and he may have O'Shay's daughter with him." He paused again and added, "If he does, we grab her and use her to force O'Shay to tell us the location of the mine."

Sheriff Cobb leaned back in his chair and crossed his legs. "What does this Dungerhill want out of this?"

"He informed me that O'Shay owes him money, and I told him I would pay it to him if he helped me." He paused. "He's the one who sold me the postcards."

Cobb grinned. "Yeah, I saw one of them. Flat Nose couldn't keep his eyes off 'em."

"Hell, I haven't even brought out the good ones." John chuckled and took another sip of his whiskey.

Cobb uncrossed his legs "What are you going to do about Logan? He's pretty fast with a gun; he could be dangerous."

"I think Sledge can handle him," John said. "If he can't, then we can always bushwhack him. We wait until O'Shay talks, though. I want Logan alive until we're sure we have the mine."

Sheriff Cobb nodded, then a serious look crossed his face as he pulled off his hat and ran his hand through his hair. "John, after this deal is over with, I'm through. I want to go back to Mississippi, where the rest of my family lives."

John looked at Cobb a few seconds. "Sure, Cobb, that's fine. I can run one of the boys for sheriff to take your place."

Cobb grimaced as he leaned forward. "John, you and I are friends, but I know how you operate. I want you to know that I have every crooked deal that we were in on together written down and put in a safe place. I've given instructions to a lawyer in San Francisco to open the box if I am murdered. I hope you understand that I am only trying to protect myself. When I arrive in Mississippi, I'll send you a telegram to tell you where the box is located."

John leaned back in his chair. "I understand your thinking, Charley. But what if someone else robs you or something and you are murdered? What then?"

"I guess you had better see that nothing happens to me, then," Cobb said. "I'm going home now; I'll see you in the morning." Cobb got up slowly and walked out the door.

John sat at his desk for a while, thinking about what the sheriff had told him. Finally he walked out into the saloon. Flat Nose was still sitting at the table, ogling his postcards.

"Flat Nose, go tell Stella I want to see her in my office," John said.

"She's still up in the room with Sledge, boss. He's going to be pissed off."

"Fine, don't bother him. Go get Juanita for me."

CHAPTER 32

Mary was humming one of her favorite songs as she dug into the cash box to find change for the five-dollar gold piece Bull had just handed her. Business had never been better at the café, and she was bringing in a lot of money, but that wasn't the reason she was extra cheerful this day. She had received a telegram from Bo this morning, and it had changed her day. Bo would be coming in on the train tomorrow, and Mary was so excited she could hardly wait to see him. When Bo had left Tucson two weeks ago, Mary had mixed feeling about the young cowboy. She liked him and she was attracted to him, but deep inside she still had a strong distrust of men. However, as the days passed by, her feelings for Bo intensified until she finally admitted to herself that she missed him a lot. She missed his shy nature when she teased him and he way he would blush. She remembered the deep sense of being protected as Bo shook Walter Johnson when he had insulted her. He was her knight in shining armor whom she had read and dreamed about. Her heart ached when she thought of him; she was ready for him to return.

"Your change, sir. I hope you enjoyed your meal," she said cheerfully to Bull as she handed him his change.

"Yes, ma'am, I sure did. Me and Squeaky eat here every time we're in town. We wouldn't eat anywhere else."

"Thank you, Bull. I really appreciate your business." Mary said sweetly.

"By the way, have you heard from Bo?"

"As a matter of fact, I got a telegram this morning; he's coming in on the train tomorrow." She said with a smile. Mary cut her eyes toward a man who was waiting behind Bull to see if maybe he was in a hurry, but the man was looking the other way.

Bull noticed her glance, and not wanting to hold up the line, turned to go but paused and looked back at Mary. "When you see him, be sure and remind him his horse is down at the livery barn." He then said in a more serious voice, "I don't guess he knows about the killings out at Vail's place, so you may have to tell him what happened, if nobody else does."

"Okay, Bull, I will," she said.

Bull headed for the door where Squeaky was waiting for him. "Come on, Squeaky, let's go. The passengers are waiting on us."

Squeaky frowned as Bull walked past him. "I ain't the one holding us up. You're the one always wanting to stop and talk." He turned, still muttering to himself, and followed Bull out the door.

Mary laughed as she watched them walk out, then turned to the man who was next in line. He was a tall, wiry, middle-aged man wearing a broadcloth suit that had seen better days. Greasy hair stuck out from his black derby hat, and his face was covered with a black beard. He handed her his ticket and a silver dollar without saying anything.

"Thank you, sir," she said as she looked up at him. He was staring at her, his eyes open wide as in surprise. "I hope you enjoyed the meal."

The man quickly lowered his head and muttered, "Yes, it was fine." He turned and hurried out the door as if he was late for something.

Mary frowned as she watched the man go out the door; something about the man seemed familiar. She thought about it for a minute but put it out of her head as another customer came up to pay his bill.

Mary stayed busy for the next hour until finally, only one man was left sitting at a table. Mary walked back to the kitchen, where Lupe was cleaning up the counter. "I think the run is over. When Juan catches up with the dishes, send him out back to help Jose."

"Si, Senora," Lupe said. She looked over at Juan. "*Prisa Juan, papa esperate.*"

"*Si, hermana,*" Juan replied as he put a stack of clean dishes on the shelf. He was thirteen years old and proud that he was working. It didn't matter that he gave most of his pay to his mama. That was something to be expected. His brother-in-law Alberto was laid up with a broken leg and couldn't work, and the family's needs came first.

He looked over at Lupe. "Alberto told me that when he gets well, he will help get me a job on a rancho, and I will have a fine horse."

"You would do better to stay away from the ranchos. You saw what happened to your brother," Lupe said. "I am learning how to do this job, and someday I will open my own restaurant. You would do better to learn from papa and be a carpentero. Now, *prisa*, go help Papa."

Mary laughed. "Lupe, why do the boys all want to be cowboys?"

"Ha," Lupe said sarcastically. "It is not just the boys; it is the men, too."

The bell rang at the front door, and Mary turned to look. A tall, sandy-headed man was coming in, and when he saw her, he walked to the counter where she was standing.

"Good afternoon, ma'am. I'm Rex Roberts. Are you Mary Smith?"

"Yes, I am. What can I do for you?"

Rex looked around the dining room; it was empty now except for him and Mary, "I wanted to ask you about Bo Logan. I was told he was your partner in this café."

"Yes, he is." She paused for a second. She had never seen this man before and she was suspicious, but she was also curious. "What did you want to know?"

"Well, the first question is, where can I find him? I need to talk to him," Rex said.

Mary noticed Rex was dressed much like a lot of other cowboys who drifted into town. This man seemed different, though. His clothes were clean and neat, his boots were shined, and his Stetson hat wasn't sweat stained and bent out of shape. His hair was neatly trimmed, and he was clean shaved.

"What do you want to talk to him about?" she asked.

Rex paused for a second, then pulled his marshal's badge out of his vest pocket. He cupped it in his hand as he held it up for her to see, and then he quickly slipped it back into his pocket. "Ma'am I would appreciate it if you wouldn't reveal that I'm a United States marshal." He hesitated. "I'm investigating certain people in Tucson, and I'm not ready to reveal myself just yet."

Mary asked, "What do you want Bo for?"

Rex glanced around the room again. He turned back to Mary. "Bo Logan is in mortal danger."

CHAPTER 33

Bonnie thought her life had changed for the better when she found her Uncle Shawn in San Francisco. After the shock wore off from their first meeting, Shawn invited her to his quarters in the back of the café, where they talked for a long time. She told him of the school and how her father had seemed to disappear from the face of the earth. She told him of the workhouse and how she eventually escaped. He was silent as she told him of her adventures on the train and the stay in Cheyenne with the Drakes. She didn't tell him about the attack from Scarface or the fact that she had killed him. She didn't tell him of killing Bart at the workhouse, either. She just didn't seem to think that she needed to tell him everything. When she finally stopped talking, she had tears in her eyes. With tears in his own eyes, Shawn took her hand. He told her she was very brave and he was proud of her. She could move into his spare bedroom to live with him for as long as she wanted.

So Bonnie moved into the small bedroom, and once again she felt as if she had a home. She thought that her life had finally changed and she would be happy. She went to bed that night with a smile on her face. She had a wonderful, dreamless sleep. In the days that followed, Bonnie's life did change, and she was happy. Her fears of pursuit for the killing of Bart and Scarface diminished to a faint memory in the back of her mind.

The first thing Bonnie did the day after she found her Uncle Shawn was to hire a hack to take her to a women's store. She was excited when the driver stopped in front of a huge store with windows full of ladies' clothing, but she was overwhelmed when she saw all the items. Everything a woman would want was displayed on the rows and rows of shelves in the huge store. Bonnie seemed in a daze as she walked around the store. Her emotions churned inside her, and she would reach out and touch things as if to see if they were real. She picked up a pair of bloomers; it brought tears to her eyes as she remembered the underwear she had worn at the sweatshop. She wandered over to the windows to look at the dresses that were on the manikins. They were beautiful, all different colors and decorated with bows and ribbons. Looking at them brought back memories of her days at the boarding school, when all the girls would try to dress in the latest fashions. For a moment she was back at the school picking out a dress to wear to the theater, but a voice from behind her brought her back to reality.

"Could I help you find something, young man?" A sales women who had been hovering nearby asked with a disapproving voice.

Bonnie jumped, then quickly turned around, the bloomers held closely to her bosom. "Ma'am?"

The woman shook her head and rubbed her right index finger across her left. "Have you no shame, young man?"

Bonnie was puzzled. *What had she done wrong?* Suddenly it dawned on her: *she still looked like a boy!*

"I'm a girl!" she blurted. She blushed as she quickly pulled off her cap.

The saleswoman stared at her for a minute, then said, "You don't look like a girl."

Bonnie was frustrated. "But I am a girl." She sighed. "It's a long story, but I had to dress up like a boy for a reason."

"I don't believe you. You are just trying to lie your way out of an embarrassing situation."

Bonnie felt her anger rising. *How could she convince this woman that she was a girl?* There was only one way she could think of.

"Ma'am, I can show you embarrassment." Bonnie dropped her cap to the floor and followed it with her coat. She reached up to the top button of her shirt and undid the button, then the next, then the next. The saleswoman just stood there not moving, seemingly undecided on whether to turn her head or watch. Bonnie undid the last button and pulled open her shirt. Her two diminished but womanly breasts jutted out for all to see—more than enough though to prove she was a girl.

The saleswoman's face looked puzzled, but she didn't speak.

Bonnie reached down and began unbuttoning her trousers.

Suddenly the saleswoman realized what Bonnie was doing. "Stop! That's enough; I believe you." She hurried to Bonnie as her eyes swept across the store, looking to see if any men were around. She quickly pulled Bonnie's shirt closed and began buttoning it. "I am sorry," the woman stammered. "I didn't realize...I mean, I just couldn't believe..."

"That's okay, ma'am," Bonnie said. "I fooled a lot of people into thinking I was a boy, but now I can go back to being a girl." She pushed aside the saleswoman's hands and finished buttoning her shirt. "Now can you help me find some girl clothes?"

Bonnie spent the next hour picking out clothes. After she found some underwear and stockings, she looked at the dresses. She loved the party dresses, but she only had the money that the Drakes had paid her, so she only bought work and house dresses. She also bought a bonnet and some scarves to wear while she waited for her hair to grow out again. The last items she bought were two pairs of shoes; one pair to work in and a nice little dainty pair to wear when she wasn't working. Bonnie was tired when she finally found everything she needed and had paid the lady for her purchases. She gathered up her packages and headed out the door to catch another hack to take her back to the café. It so happened that the same hackney driver picked her up.

"Take me to Water Street, please. The Shamrock Café," Bonnie told him as she got in the back.

"Yes, ma'am, I know exactly where it is. I picked up a fare there a couple of hours ago." He thought for a second, then turned to look at her. "You know, you look kind of like the boy I picked up there. Do you have a brother?"

"No," Bonnie said. She chuckled softly to herself. "He was just a friend of mine."

Bonnie leaned back and closed her eyes. She was delighted to get back into girl's clothes. She never wanted to see those boy things again. Too many bad memories were associated with them. She would burn them when she got back to the café. Suddenly the hackney hit a bump, and Bonnie opened her eyes. A huge, old Catholic Church was looming in front of her. An idea formed in her mind.

"Driver, would you stop in front of the church and wait for me?" she called. "I have a quick errand to run."

The driver pulled the horses to a stop. Bonnie picked up the package of boy things, then climbed out of the carriage. She walked to the church, pitched the package into the poor box, and returned to the hack. Now Bonnie felt better. The reminders of her past were gone, and she would begin her new life in San Francisco as a woman.

That night as Bonnie showed Shawn all her new clothes. She told him that she wanted to keep working in the café.

"You don't have to work, Bonnie," Shawn said. "This is your home now, Bonnie. You've gone through some rough times, and you need to take it easy for a while."

"No, Uncle Shawn, I insist," Bonnie said, a stern look on her face. "I feel fine now that I have found you, and I want to work. Besides, I need to earn my own money."

With a smile Shawn shook his head. "You're just like your dad—bullheaded. Okay, you can work."

Bonnie hugged Shawn. "Thank you, Uncle Shawn." She stepped back and tilted her head to one side. "One other thing, Uncle Shawn. I don't want to wash dishes forever and I wouldn't mind cooking, but I am pretty good with figures, and I believe I could help you run this place."

Shawn grinned. "You know, I was just wishing the other day that I had someone to help me do my books. You got yourself a deal, lassie."

The next morning Bonnie was up before dawn. The day before she had noticed that the kitchen was in bad need of a cleaning, and she wanted to do it before the workers arrived. She lit a lantern, then made her way through the dark dining room to the kitchen. As she entered, the light from her lantern revealed what seemed like a never ending rush of roaches trying to hide. Bonnie shuddered as she watched them run; visions of the kitchen in the garment factory flashed through her mind. *I'm not going to work or eat in a place that filthy again*, she vowed as she examined the room. Most of the dishes were clean, but the stoves and ovens were covered with layers of spilled food, which had turned to a greasy, gooey coating. The floors and counters weren't much better. Shaking her head, Bonnie began lighting the other lanterns in the kitchen, cleaning and filling them as she went. She put on some water to heat up, then swept the floor. Next, using knives and scrapers, she cleaned as much of the goo off the stoves and floors as she could. When the water was hot enough, she wiped clean the stoves and mopped the floor. She was just finishing up when the cook arrived.

"Did you do all of this?" he asked as he glanced around the kitchen. "I have never seen it this clean."

"Yes, I cleaned it, and I'm going to see that it stays clean," Bonnie said proudly.

"You did a good job," he said. "By the way, my name is Sherman. What's yours?"

"I'm Bonnie," she said. "Bonnie O'Shay."

Bonnie put in long, hard days at the café, but it was nothing compared to the work she had done at the factory. She enjoyed life for a change, and the hours at the café pasted swiftly. Bonnie became friends with Dixie, who was Sherman's wife, and some of the other women who worked at the café. Bonnie's beautiful blonde hair had grown back in the year and a half she lived in San Francisco. She was becoming a beautiful woman, and a lot of the men who came into the café flirted with her. She would talk to men, but when they tried to get too friendly, she would cordially brush them off. After all her bad incidents with men, it was hard for Bonnie to trust them, especially when they grinned or leered at her.

But as the weeks went by, her confidence grew, and she slowly learned to talk to men. She even got to the point where she would flirt back with some of them, but that was as far as it went. In the back of her mind, there was always that distrust that kept her from forming any kind of relationship with a man. The only exception was her Uncle Shawn. They became close, like most families, but as the months went by, she began to realize there were things about Uncle Shawn that were less than desirable. He was very nice the first few months she lived with him and they got along well, but later on he fell back into some of his old habits. Shawn liked his whiskey, and gradually he began to like it a little too much; there were times he would come home late at night falling down drunk. What was even worse was that sometimes he would bring home one of the local whores to spend the night with him. They would try to be quiet, but Bonnie could always hear them through the thin walls of their living quarters. Reminding herself that no one was perfect, she would pull the covers up over her ears to try and block the sounds of their lovemaking.

Bonnie was grateful to her uncle for taking her in, and she committed herself to working hard at the café. After washing dishes for a few weeks, she began cooking. She learned fast, and soon she was in charge of the kitchen. By the time she had been with Shawn a year, she was running the café, and Shawn was spending his time at the local saloons, drinking, gambling, and whoring.

One day as the noon rush was winding down, Shawn came up to the counter from out of the back. His clothes were mussed up, and his hair wasn't combed. He looked as if he had a hangover as he stumbled up to the counter. "Bonnie, I need some money. Give me what you have in the till," he ordered gruffly.

Bonnie studied his face. "Shawn, I need the money to pay the grocer. I've already put him off once."

"Just give me the money," he said. "This is my place, and I'll do what I please."

Bonnie reluctantly reached into the till, grabbed all the big bills, and handed them to him. "Here, take it, but we won't have anything to serve the customers Monday."

Shawn grabbed the money and headed toward the door. Tears welled in Bonnie's eyes as she watched him walk out the door and turn toward the saloon. She would talk to him tomorrow. It was Sunday, and the café would be closed.

Bonnie woke early the next morning and dressed for church. She called out for her uncle, but he didn't answer, so she carefully peered into his room. He was still asleep or passed out; she didn't know which, but he looked terrible. He had bruises on his face as if he had been fighting, and his knuckles were skinned. Bonnie shook her head, then hurried out the door to catch the early mass at the big Catholic Church on the hill. She would talk to him later.

After the service was over, Bonnie slowly walked down to the waterfront. She had things on her mind, and she wanted to go to a quiet spot and think. She liked Sundays down at the docks. She wandered around, watching the gulls as they scrounged for food. There were sometimes seals in the harbor, and she smiled as she noticed two of them playing among the piers. A few gulls hovered over her in the air, but when she didn't feed them, they soon flew away to other likely places to look for food. Bonnie finally sat on a bench to rest as she thought about what she should do. She was a grown woman now, and she needed to get on with her life. She didn't think she could live with Shawn any more. He was ruining his life, and she couldn't do anything about it. She had saved her wages; she had almost seven hundred dollars hidden in one of her bags. Bonnie thought of her father; she still had to find out what had happened to him. Suddenly she made up her mind: she would take the next train to Tucson to look for him. Relieved that she had finally made a decision, Bonnie walked back to the café. It was noon when she got there. Shawn was in the kitchen, a bottle of whiskey sitting in front of him.

"Shawn, I need to talk to you," Bonnie said in a serious tone. "I'm going to Tucson to look for Dad."

Shawn looked surprised, but then a scowl came on his face. "So you're going to run out on me. Well, I got news for you, girl. I'm all you got now. I'm your guardian, and I've arranged a marriage for you, just like in the old country."

Bonnie's face flushed red with anger, and her eyes flashed as she said in a low warning voice, "Don't even think about trying to stop me. I don't know what happened to you or why, but you are a drunk and a whoremonger, and I'm not living here anymore." Furiously Bonnie stalked to her room and began throwing her clothes into one of her carpetbags. She was reaching for her other bag when abruptly she felt something hit her on the head, and her mind went black.

Her head pounding, Bonnie woke up in a dark room; the smell of whiskey filled the air. She tried to move, but her arms were tied behind her back and her legs were tied at the ankles. A chilling wave of fear swept across her body. She started to call out, but her mind cleared and the calm logic that had gotten her through her lifetime of troubles took over. She began to think about what would be the best thing to do. If she cried out, she might only call unwanted attention to herself. She needed to try to get the ropes untied first. She could wiggle her hands some, so she didn't think her circulation was cut off. She struggled around until she was sitting up. Her eyes slowly adjusted to the low light, and she saw that she was in a large storeroom with cases of whiskey and other liquors stacked almost to the ceiling. She noticed a door a few feet from where she was sitting, and she began scooting herself backward toward it, but suddenly she felt something stick her leg. She scooted around and felt with her tied hands for whatever it was that stuck her. She was rewarded with hope when she felt the jagged, broken neck of a whiskey bottle. Carefully she picked up the sharp glass with her tied hands, and then, turning on her side, she hurriedly went to work sawing the rope holding her legs. As soon as she cut them, she laid the broken neck on the floor and started moving her tied hands under her butt and down her legs. She got them to her ankles and seemed stuck, but she took a deep breath and exhaled. She leaned forward and pulled her legs tight against her body. Suddenly she had her tied hands in front of her. She found the broken neck again and put it between her knees. Quickly she rubbed the rope tying her hands back and forth across the broken glass, and soon it was cut enough for her to pull apart. Slowly she rose, then carefully walked toward the door. As she got closer, she heard talking in the next room. She put her ear against the door to listen.

"Okay, Shawn, you carried out your part of the deal. Here's your IOUs," a man's voice said.

Bonnie flinched; it was Gordon Stiles from the saloon next door. He was a middle-aged man with a large, red birthmark on his face. He came into the café quite often to eat. He didn't say much, but Bonnie couldn't stand the way he leered at her. Then she heard Shawn's voice.

"What about the money and the whore?" he asked.

"Go take whichever one you want. I'll bring the money to you in a moment," Gordon said coldly. "I want to check on my bride-to-be."

"I'm going back to clean up a little. Just send Shelia over with the money," Shawn said.

The talking stopped, and Bonnie heard footsteps coming toward her. Unexpectedly, she heard another voice.

"Did you get rid of the Mick?"

"Not yet. I'm leaving that for you to do, Sheila. I want you to go over there and get him in bed. Bring a bottle of his favorite whiskey, and when he is good and drunk, slip him the poison I gave you," Gordon said. "I want it to look like a heart attack."

Bonnie tensed. *No matter how sorry Uncle Shawn has become, he doesn't deserve to die.* She had to help him. She went back to where she had left the broken glass, picked it up, then hurried back to the door. She positioned herself to the side and waited; soon she heard footsteps coming toward the door again. A key rattled in the lock, and suddenly the door was flung open. Gordon, with a lantern held high above his head and a gruesome leer plastered on his face, stepped into the room. Bonnie, without a second thought, jabbed the jagged glass into his neck. He screamed as he grabbed for his neck, dropping the lantern. It fell to the floor, and with a whoosh it broke and spilled flaming kerosene across the floor. Gordon stumbled across the room, holding his neck, blood gushing out of a deep slash. He fell against a stack of whiskey cases, and they came crashing down. The whiskey from the broken bottles added to the flames. Bonnie watched for a moment, then ran out the open door.

In the next room, she almost stumbled over her packed bags, and she quickly grabbed them as she headed for a door at the far end of the room. The door was latched, but she quickly unfastened it and hurried through to the yard at the back of the saloon. Smoke was pouring from the windows now, and Bonnie ran to the alley to get away from the building. Suddenly the entire end of the saloon next to the café exploded in a burst of flames. Bonnie was knocked to her knees, but she got up and turned to look back at the inferno. The fire was spreading fast; the café was engulfed in flames as she watched. If her uncle was in there, he was surely dead.

With mixed emotions she walked up the alley to a street that led away from the docks. It was night, and she didn't want to stay around. She walked up the hill until she came to her church, and she went inside. As she slipped into one of the pews, she began to think about her options. She was alone again. She didn't have any money, she had killed another man, and she had caused a fire that might burn down half the docks in San Francisco. Bonnie was suddenly compelled to look up at the cross behind the altar. A statue of Jesus was on the cross, with the blood on his wrists and the crown of thorns on his head. Bonnie bowed her head and prayed.

Jesus, I could really use some help right now.

Bonnie raised her head. She seemed calmer now. She looked over at her bags beside her. She opened one and looked through it. All the clothes she had put in it were still there. She opened the other one. Shawn must have packed this one; he had put all her things in it, including her handbag. Slowly she loosened the string that held it closed, then pulled it open. Rolled up in a tight wad was the money that she had saved. Bonnie, her heart beating faster, retied the bag and put it back. She grabbed the two bags and walked to the door, but as she started to go out, she stopped, turned, and looked up at the cross.

"Thank you, Jesus. I know what to do now." Bonnie stepped out the door. When she got to the street, she turned to look back at the docks. The fire that was covering the sky. *Goodbye, Shawn. I hope you find peace.* A mixed feeling of hope and excitement filled her mind as she hurried up the street toward the train station.

Two days later the train pulled into the station at Tucson. As Bonnie stepped out onto the platform, she looked toward the dusty town with a weary smile. She had spent a sleepless night on the train, and she was tired as she walked toward the main part of town carrying her bags. She was looking for a nice hotel when she saw a sign in the window of an empty building that got her attention. The sign read: **FOR SALE SEE WALTER JOHNSON AT THE TUCSON NATIONAL BANK.** Bonnie looked into the window and saw that the building had been a restaurant, and an idea formed in her mind. She looked up the street and saw the bank just a few buildings away, and she quickly walked to it and entered. Two men were standing behind a tall counter. One of them turned to her.

"May I help you, Miss? I'm Walter Johnson."

Bonnie looked at him and smiled. "You're just the man I'm looking for. I'm interested in buying that building just down the street that you have for sale."

Walter smiled, showing his perfect teeth. "That's a very good location. I'm sure we can make a deal on it." He paused as he looked her over from head to toe. "I can let you make payments on it if you qualify. What did you say your name was?"

"I didn't say, but it's Smith. Mary Smith."

CHAPTER 34

As Sylvester sat in the café eating his breakfast, he couldn't get the face of the young woman who waited on him out of his mind. Now she was working behind the counter, and he studied her face again. He had tried not to stare at the young girl as she scurried around the café, but his eyes kept drifting back to her. Her face seemed familiar, but he couldn't put a name to it. As he watched her, a man at the counter said something to her, and she smiled at him. Instantly it came to him, and his heart skipped a beat. The young girl looked just like Bonnie O'Shay. Her face looked the same, only more mature—the cool blue eyes, the golden hair framing her face; it had to be her. Sylvester remembered the last time he had seen her; it was at the garment factory over two years ago when Martha Shott had pointed her out to him while making some nasty remark. Bonnie had been thinner then and her hair had been covered, but he had recognized her. Suddenly Sylvester realized he was staring at her, and he quickly looked out the window. He sure didn't want her to recognize him.

His thoughts turned to the money he could collect from John if it really was her, and he racked his brain, tying to think of some way to tell for sure. He thought back to when she was at the school, and all of a sudden he remembered that she had a small scar on her left arm. Bonnie had fallen on a sharp rock, which had cut her arm. When she had come to his office crying, he had decided not to spend money on a doctor but to clean and bandage it himself. The cut was deep and when the wound healed, it left an L-shaped scar just above her elbow. He would have to try to see the scar. Then he would be positive it was she.

Sylvester finished his breakfast, then went to the counter where Bonnie was collecting money from another customer. He waited until she was through with him, then held out his money for the meal. He kept his eyes on her arm. She took his money, and to his relief he saw the scar, a pale white L, on her bronze skin. Elated, he grabbed his change and hurried out the door.

"Watch where you're going, you idiot!" A man driving a wagonload of hay yelled at Sylvester as he jerked his horses to a stop. Sylvester, shaken by the near miss, slowed to a more normal walking pace the rest of the way to the saloon. Pushing through the bat wing doors, he spied John sitting at his regular table with some of his men.

"Could we talk in your office?" He asked John as he approached the table. He glanced at the other men at the table. "I have some news you need to hear alone."

"Sure," John said as he pushed his chair back to stand up. He walked to his office, not even glancing back to see if Sylvester was following him. John lit the coal oil lamp hanging in the ceiling and sat down in his chair. He looked up at Sylvester, who was still standing. "What is it you want to tell me?"

"I just saw someone who will solve your problems," Sylvester said. He stepped over to the chair in front of the desk then sat down. "I know how to make Tom O'Shay talk."

"We tried making him talk. He keeps claiming he don't have a gold mine." John snorted. "Sledge worked him over yesterday until he was almost unconscious, and he still won't talk. I'm beginning to believe him myself."

Sylvester said, "You just don't have the right leverage. There's a way to make him talk." He leaned back in the chair. "I know where his daughter is."

John stared at Sylvester for a few seconds. Finally he said, "Where is she? If I had her in my grasp, O'Shay would beg to tell me where his mine is located."

Sylvester paused as he put his hands together, interlocking his fingers. "I need to know what I'm getting out of this deal. This is some crucial information. I should get a part of the mine."

John stared at Sylvester for a second. "I'll give you ten percent—that is, if your information pans out."

Sylvester smiled. "She's just down the street. She runs the Shamrock Café."

"The blonde with the blue eyes? You told me you hadn't seen her in a few years. How do you know that's her?"

"I know because she looks like her, and she also has a scar on her arm that she got when she was at my boarding school."

John thought for a moment. "We need to take her out to the ranch. That Mick won't believe us unless he sees her."

"She might be a problem to grab; she's tougher than she looks. She killed a man with a hat pin back in New York," Sylvester said.

"You forget I have the law on my side. I'll get her out there the easy way." John leaned back in his chair and crossed his legs. "Go find Sheriff Cobb and tell him to come to my office."

Sylvester headed for the door. He paused, then looked back at John, who was lighting a cigar. "What will you do with the girl when you have the mine?"

John winked. "I can't just turn her loose. When we get through with her, I might sell her down below the border." He blew smoke toward the ceiling. "Maybe we can get one of those photograph gadgets to make some pictures of her in the nude. I might want to try out some of those positions with her."

Sylvester frowned. "I want my turn, too. I think I should be first."

John smiled as he motioned for Sylvester to leave. When he was gone, John muttered, "That bastard will be the first to go, all right. He's going to be the first one I get rid of."

Sylvester ambled out into the saloon looking for the sheriff. John's men were all over at the bar watching Shirley, a new singer from Texas, sing one of her catchy songs. Finally he saw Sheriff Cobb sitting alone at one of the tables, staring into his mug of beer.

"John wants to see you, Sheriff, in his office."

Sheriff Cobb looked up from his drink. "Okay, thanks." He finished his drink and rose to see what John wanted. When he walked into the office, John was still sitting at his desk staring up at the cigar smoke rising in the air.

"You want to see me?" Sheriff Cobb asked.

"Yeah. Guess what? I just found out that the girl who runs the Shamrock Café is O'Shay's daughter," John said. "I'm going to use her to make O'Shay talk."

Cobb raised his eyebrows. "Are you sure about that?"

"I got it straight from somebody who knows her."

"You want me to arrest her for something?"

"No, I don't want to raise a ruckus," John said. "If my plan works, we can do this the easy way. Now listen, I want you to go to the café with one of the boys and mention Tom O'Shay's name in front of her. If she takes the bait, get her out to the ranch and put her in with O'Shay. Sledge and I'll come out either tonight or in the morning, and we'll see how much pain the daughter has to take before O'Shay spills his guts." John paused for a minute, then added, "It'll probably be in the morning before I get there. Just stay out at the ranch tonight; I don't trust Mad Dog and Dutch out there alone with the girl."

Sheriff Cobb gazed at the cigar in John's hand. He watched the smoke for a second and said, "Remember, this is it for me." He walked out the door, then hesitated for a second as he looked around the saloon. Spying Dutch over at the bar talking to Juanita, he headed that way.

"I need you for a little con job. Come with me and I'll tell you what to do as we walk."

Mary was cleaning off a table when Sheriff Cobb and Dutch walked into the café. "What can I get you, Sheriff?" she asked as she headed toward the kitchen with the dirty dishes.

"Mary, can you make up a few tacos for me? I got to go out to Dutch's place to see about someone, and I might get hungry before I get back."

"Sure, Sheriff. You want beef and beans?"

"Yeah, that'll be fine, Mary," Cobb said. "Make up about a dozen."

Mary went into the kitchen. "Lupe, fix up a dozen tacos for the sheriff, beef and beans."

"Si, Senora," Lupe replied. She was already placing tortillas on the grill to warm up. Mary went back out to the dining area. She heard Sheriff Cobb talking to Dutch in a low voice.

"What did you say the name of that fellow you found was?"

"He said his name was O'Shay, Sheriff. Tom O'Shay."

Mary's heart skipped a beat, then raced; hope clutched her chest. She hesitated for a second, took a deep breath, and approached the two men. "What happened, Sheriff? I heard you mention Tom O'Shay. I know him."

Cobb looked at Mary. "Dutch said this Tom O'Shay wandered into his place from out on the desert, said he was jumped by outlaws. We're going out there to see about him now."

Father's alive! A cold, heavy load was lifted from Mary's shoulders and replaced with a warm blanket. Her heart raced with excitement. "How badly is he hurt, Sheriff? May I come with you? He is my father," Bonnie quickly brought her hand up to her mouth as she realized what she had said.

."Your father? I thought your name was Smith?"

"I didn't want people to know I was Irish," Bonnie quickly replied. "It doesn't matter now. I want to go with you."

"Do you have a horse?"

"No. I can rent one at the stable."

"Just meet me there in ten minutes; I'll arrange for you a horse," Cobb said. "Oh, and bring the food."

Bonnie, her heart still pounding, hurried to her room to change. Her hands shook as she pulled on her riding clothes. Her mood kept changing from happiness to worry as she thought of her father.

Is it really father? Is he all right?

She pulled on her boots last, then, remembering the hot sun, she grabbed her hat. She secured it to her hair, then hurried out the door to the kitchen. Lupe had just finished wrapping the tacos in butcher paper for the trip.

"Lupe, I'm going with the sheriff to Dutch's place. I think my father is there, and he may be hurt." Bonnie glanced around the room. "I don't know when I'll be back, so you take care of things while I'm gone. Get Juan and Jose to help if you need them." Bonnie gathered up the food and rushed out the door. A wagon loaded with beer barrels rumbled down the street and narrowly missed Bonnie as she hurried across the street toward the livery.

"What the hell," the driver of the wagon shouted as he pulled back on the lines and stopped the mules in the street. He stared at Bonnie for a few seconds, then looked at the café. He pulled off his hat to scratch his head as he thought about it. Shaking his head, he put the hat back on, and then with a crack of his whip, he started the mules on down the street.

The four blocks to the livery seemed like a mile to Bonnie as she ran down the street. Sheriff Cobb and Dutch were already mounted and waiting for her, the reins of a dun gelding in the hand of Cobb.

"Do you have plenty of water?" she asked as she stuffed the tacos in the saddlebag and climbed on the gelding. Cobb pointed at the canteens dripping with moisture hanging on the saddles. He waited for Dutch to mount, then wheeled his horse around toward the street. They trotted their horses until they were out of town, then Cobb kicked his into a lope as he turned him into the road that ran west out of town. Bonnie, thankful that she had learned to ride when she was in San Francisco, followed close behind, while

Dutch stayed close behind them. Cobb kept up the pace, and soon the town was behind them out of sight. After a few miles, he slowed his horse to a walk, and Bonnie rode up beside him.

"How far is it to Dutch's place, Sheriff?" she asked. "Shouldn't we hurry?"

"There's no hurry. Dutch said the man is all right; he just needs some rest," Cobb said. "We'll be there in about a half hour. How about you break out some of those tacos? I'm getting a little hungry."

Bonnie pulled the tacos out of the saddlebag and handed them to Cobb. He took a couple out of the paper and handed them to Dutch, who had ridden up beside him. The two men finished the tacos in silence as they rode. Soon they came to a wagon track that led off into a canyon filled with mesquite trees and cholla cactus.

Cobb looked at Bonnie. "This way. It's only a few more miles." The road wound through the canyon for nearly a mile until it finally came out in a small valley. A small, whitewashed house was nestled in a small grove of willow trees, and a barn with a corral was behind the house. Cobb rode past the house to the barn, where he got off his horse and tied him to the fence. Anxiously Bonnie dismounted and followed Cobb into the barn. A man Bonnie had seen occasionally in the café was sitting on a stool in front of a door with a chain locking it. A rifle leaned against the door.

"How's everything going, Mad Dog? Is our guest awake?" Sheriff Cobb asked the man.

"I don't know. I haven't checked lately," Mad Dog said indifferently. He cut his eyes at Bonnie. "What's she doing here?"

An uneasy feeling slowly crept over Bonnie. She noticed Dutch was standing right behind her. She looked at Cobb, and he was grinning. "Where is he?"

"He's in that room."

"Why is it locked?" Bonnie started toward the door. Mad Dog stood and picked up the rifle, but the sheriff shook his head, and he stepped out of the way. Bonnie removed the chain and opened the door. A man was standing just inside the room. He held his hands up to shade his eyes as he tried to see who had opened the door.

Bonnie looked at the man and instantly recognized her father. "Father, it's me, Bonnie."

Tom O'Shay stared at Bonnie for a few seconds, then slowly spoke in a trembling voice. "Bonnie, is it really you?"

"Father," Bonnie said anxiously as she ran toward him. "I've found you at last." She began crying as she threw her arms around him.

Tom held her close for a minute, tears running down his face. They embraced for a while, then they stepped back to look at each other again. Tom lovingly gazed at his daughter for a few moments. Suddenly he frowned. With fearful eyes he looked at the sheriff. "Why did you bring her here? Are you going to turn me loose?" he asked.

Bonnie moved closer to him, then turned to face Sheriff Cobb.

"We figured you needed some help deciding if you were going to tell us where the gold mine is located. We thought she could help you decide," Cobb said. "You think about that until John and Sledge get here, and then you got to make up your mind." Cobb nodded to Mad Dog, "Lock 'em up."

Mad Dog swung the door shut.

CHAPTER 35

Fear and confusion crossed Bonnie's mind as Mad Dog closed the door to the small room. As she listened to him locking the chains she felt helpless. She turned to her father. "Dad, what's going on? Where have you been for six years?"

Tom looked at Bonnie, then clasped her hand. "Come over here and we will sit on the cot." He led her to the cot, and they sat down. "After I left you in the boarding school in New York, I came out here to Arizona to look for gold. One day I found a hidden valley out in the mountains, and in this valley I found a very rich gold mine." Tom hesitated, wiped tears from his eyes, then continued. "A few months later I came into Tucson to buy supplies and to put some of my gold in the bank. That's when my troubles began. Walter Johnson, the banker, went straight to John Skinner, the biggest crook in the territory, and told him I had put a lot of money in the bank. Skinner had the sheriff and Judge Mills in his pocket, so he arranged to have me arrested on a fake charge of robbery. They confiscated all my money and sent me to prison." Tom paused as he cleared his throat. "After I was in there for about two years, I got careless and confided to my cellmate that I had a gold mine. At the time I didn't know he was a friend of Curt Skinner, John Skinner's brother. Curt somehow got himself moved to my cell, hoping he could convince me to tell him where my mine is located. I told him that there was no mine, but he wouldn't believe me."

"How did you end up here, Father?" Bonnie asked.

"Three days ago the sheriff came to the prison and got me out. He brought me here and locked me in this barn." Tom looked toward the door then back at Bonnie. "Why are you here, Bonnie? When did you leave the school?"

Bonnie realized her father didn't know any of the things that had happened to her. She wiped her eyes and said, "Father, I had to leave the school four years ago. They told me the money was used up, so they sent me to a workhouse, a garment factory."

"Who told you that? I sent them enough money to take care of you until you were eighteen years old."

"Professor Dungerhill called me to his office and told me," Bonnie said. "He said you were more than likely dead and all the money was gone. He told me he was going to send me to an orphanage, but when the people came, they took me to a workhouse."

"A workhouse," Tom said. "I don't understand; how could people do that kind of thing?" He shook his head; tears came from his eyes again. "How long were you in the workhouse? How did you get away from it?"

Bonnie hesitated for a second. Should she tell him everything? She sighed. "Father, I'm going to tell you the whole story, so just let me tell it before you say anything. You might not like what you hear."

Tom looked at his daughter. The last time he had seen her, she was twelve years old. Now she was a grown woman; a beautiful young woman. He swallowed, then said in a low voice, "Okay Bonnie, tell me your story."

Bonnie looked into his eyes and began her story. "I was in the workhouse for two years. It was hard work, but I learned to sew and to cook. There was no way out for me. What little money I made went for my so-called past debts and my upkeep. One Sunday, when I was alone in my room, one of the supervisors tried to rape me." Bonnie hesitated for a second, then lowered her head and looked at the floor. "I killed him with a hat pin trying to protect myself." Her voice cracked, tears glistened in her eyes. "I put on his clothes and took what money he had." She paused to wipe her eyes. "I also stole money from my best friend."

Tom eye's watered up again as he reached out for Bonnie's hand. "You did what you had to do, Bonnie."

"After I escaped from the workhouse, I bought a train ticket to San Francisco with the money I stole," Bonnie said. "I was hoping I would find Uncle Shawn there. I was afraid the law would find me, so on the train I stayed dressed like a boy, and I used the name Tom Jones. I was doing fine until I got to Wyoming, but then I got into trouble again." Bonnie cleared her throat. "When the train stopped in Cheyenne, I was hungry. So I went to a café to eat, but the food made me sick. When I went to the toilet, a man hit me on the head and robbed me. A nice couple helped me and gave me work and a place to stay. I worked for them for several months, still posing as a boy." Bonnie paused and cleared her throat again. "One day when I was in the alley behind the store, I ran into the man who robbed me, and he attacked me again." Bonnie lowered her eyes. "He tried to rape me like he would a boy. I killed him with a paring knife."

Tom gasped. "My god, Bonnie, I'm so sorry." He hung his head and wiped at his own tears.

"I hid his body, went to my room, and packed my things," Bonnie said. "I told the Drakes I wanted to leave to find my uncle, and I took the next train going west." Bonnie paused to take a deep breath. "I finally arrived in San Francisco and found Uncle Shawn. I lived with him and worked at his café for nearly two years."

"So that's where he ended up," Tom said awkwardly. "I haven't seen him since he left Pennsylvania." Tom put his hands on Bonnie's shoulders. "Why didn't you stay with him, Bonnie? How did you end up in Arizona?"

"Shawn wasn't the same kindly uncle I remembered in New York," Bonnie said as she lowered her eyes. She looked at her father again. "He was moody, and he drank a lot. He also gambled a lot; I think he owed a man a lot of money." Bonnie pulled away from her father and looked toward the small window across the room. "He told me I had to marry the man so his debts would be paid off, but I refused. When I told him I was leaving, he knocked me out and tied me up. He brought me to the man's saloon, and they locked me in a storeroom. I woke up, got loose, and when the man came for me..." Bonnie paused for a second, then, with a trembling voice, she continued. "I cut his throat with a broken bottle."

Tom lowered his head and gritted his teeth. His breath came in gasps. Slowly he asked in a low sad voice, "What happen then?"

Bonnie squeezed her eyes shut for a second, then continued. "He dropped his lantern and it broke, catching the saloon on fire. The whiskey in the storeroom exploded, and in just a few minutes half the waterfront was on fire, including Uncle Shawn's café." Bonnie turned to look at her father. "I think he died in the fire." Bonnie stood up, then walked to the small window. A light breeze was blowing in, and she turned her face to catch it. Finally she turned back to her father, who was still sitting on the cot. "I got to Tucson about six months ago. Using the name Mary Smith, I bought a building from our friend Walter Johnson." Bonnie walked back to the cot then sat down. "I opened up a business, the Shamrock Café. I thought if you were still around this area and saw a café with that name you would come into it. I couldn't ask the law about you because I didn't know if there was any reward posters on me." Bonnie sighed as she leaned back on the cot. With a worried look on her face she turned back to Tom. "What do we do now, Father?"

CHAPTER 36

The air in the passenger car began to grow warmer as the train left the cool Pacific coast. The desert heat worked fast, and by the time the train arrived in Yuma, the passengers had lowered all the windows and taken off as many clothes as they could without being indecent. Bo was no exception as he loosened his collar and fanned himself with an old newspaper. Despite the heat he was still trying to put together in his mind all the information he had gathered about Bonnie O'Shay. His thoughts kept returning to what one of the dockworkers had said to him back in San Francisco— something about a four-leaf clover. *He said he would miss the café with the four-leaf clover on it.* Bo thought of Mary's Shamrock Café. It had a picture of a four-leaf clover. He would ask her about it when he saw her. He settled back and crossed his legs as he tried to get comfortable on the lightly padded bench seat. The sky would soon be dark, and there was still a long way to go. *At least the night will be cooler.* Using his coat for a pillow, he leaned against the window and tried to sleep, but the clacking of the track and the jerking of the train kept him mostly in a state of drowsiness. Finally, when he had just fallen into a deep sleep, the whistle blew. He awoke and sleepily looked out the window. In the dim light of the dawn, he could see Tucson slowly creeping up the tracks toward them. The sun was just peeping over the horizon as the train slowly pulled into the station. When the movement of the train finally stopped,

Bo gathered up his coat and bag and joined the other passengers in the aisle as they slowly shuffled their way to the door. When Bo stepped onto the platform, he searched the waiting faces for Mary, but he didn't see her. Disappointed, he waited for a few moments on the platform, hoping she would come, but finally he trudged into the station. He went to the baggage claim to retrieve his other bag, then, gathering it up, he started toward the door of the station. Suddenly Bo heard someone call his name, and he eagerly turned toward the direction the voice had come from. A man was walking toward him. He looked familiar, but Bo couldn't place him. Unconsciously he lowered his hand to his gun.

The man grinned. "Bo, don't you remember me, back in Texas?"

Bo suddenly recognized the man. "Marshall Rex Roberts! I couldn't place you at first, but yeah, I remember you now. What are you doing in Arizona?"

"I've been doing some undercover work," Rex said in a low voice when he got closer to Bo. He nodded toward a deserted bench down at the end of the station. "Let's go to that bench; I need to talk to you in private." He led Bo to the bench, and they sat down.

"I knew you were in this area because I heard you had a run-in with Willy Skinner out at Vail's station."

"News travels fast," Bo said. "Did you come all the way out here to ask me about the shooting? Vail can tell you what happened."

"No, I've been investigating John Skinner and his gang for some time now. I've had complaints from some of the prominent men in this county that he is running a lot of crooked deals. Bob Vail is one example."

"What about Vail? Bo said. "The last time I saw him was at the gunfight. I left my horses there when I took the stage to Tucson."

Rex grimaced. "Vail is dead. I came in on the stage just a few hours after it happened. They tortured and killed Vail and his brother Shorty, then raped and tortured an Indian woman. They tried to make it look like the Apaches did it, but Lame Deer, one of the employees and also the woman's husband, got back from hunting just as the bastards were leaving. He saw them from a distance, but he said it looked like Sledge and some of Skinner's other men."

"Vail was a good man; all of them were. What are you going to do about it?"

"I couldn't do anything then. An Indian doesn't make a very good witness in the courtroom," Rex said. "But I have more information now. I found out that John Skinner has the sheriff and a judge in his pocket. They've been sending innocent men to prison so they can take over their ranches and mines."

"Sheriff Cobb is working for Skinner?" Bo said. "Rex, I haven't been around here long enough to know what's been happening. What do you want me for?"

"I need someone I can trust to watch my back, Bo. I need a deputy."

Bo hesitated. He wasn't afraid to take the job; he just had other things to do right now. Finally he asked, "What are your plans, Marshal? I have some unfinished business to take care of first, but I'll help you as soon as I can."

Rex looked around the room, then turned back to Bo. "I need to arrest Judge Mills and Sheriff Cobb. I need to seize all of their records and check out each of the cases he has presided over since he took office."

Bo chuckled. "I don't know how much help I would be reading court documents."

Rex grinned, then said seriously, "I have men to do that Bo, but they aren't gunmen. They're clerks and secretaries." He cut his eyes toward Bo's pistol. "I need you in case we have gunplay."

"Okay, Marshal, but let me go see Mary first. I have a lot of things to talk over with her," Bo said. "Some of them can wait, but I got one thing I need to ask her that can't."

Rex paused for a minute as he thought about what he had to do, "I'll meet you at the café in about an hour after I get everything set up. I'll tell you what we're going to do then." The two men shook hands.

"I'll see you in an hour. Now, let's get out of here," Bo said as he walked toward the door on the Tucson side of the station. Rex followed close behind Bo as they wove their way through a crowd waiting to board the train. Just as Bo stepped out the door, he paused, then turned to ask Rex a question.

"BOOM! BOOM!" Splinters flew from the doorframe. Bo dropped to the floor.

CHAPTER 37

It was a little after two in the morning and John was sitting in his office thinking about his plan. He watched the smoke from his freshly lit cigar slowly rise to the ceiling as he tried to sort out his options. Finally, after a few minutes, he got up from his chair, put on his hat, and walked out the door. Flat Nose and Horney were sitting at his personal table looking at the postcards again. They didn't notice him until he kicked the chair that Horney was sitting in.

"Go round up everybody and bring them to the office. I got chores for you boys," he said.

The men jumped up and looked around the room.

"Dutch went with the sheriff, and Mad Dog is at the ranch, boss," Horney said. "We ain't seen Diablo and Curt, but Sledge is over there with Stella."

"You go tell Sledge first, then go find Diablo and Curt," John said. He turned to Flat Nose. "You go find the postcard man, Sylvester. He's in one of the rooms upstairs. Get him and come to my office."

The two men hurried off to do their errands, and John went back to his office. He was relighting his cigar when Sledge and Flat Nose walked into the office.

"What do you need, boss? You want me to take care of Logan?" Sledge asked as he settled into a chair.

"No," John said. "I want you to go with me to the ranch. We got a little persuading to do."

"I don't think he's going to tell us anything. I beat him until he was unconscious, day before yesterday, and he wouldn't change his story," Sledge said as he pulled out his knife and picked at a sore on his arm.

"You're not going to hurt O'Shay," John said.

"How are we going to make him talk then? Tickle his feet?" Flat Nose said. He began to laugh but stopped when John glared at him.

"I thought I told you to go get Sly."

"I told him. He said he would be here as soon as he got dressed."

John stared at Flat Nose for a second, then turned back to Sledge. "No, I just happen to have O'Shay's daughter out at the ranch. I don't think it will take a whole lot of persuading for him to tell us everything we want to know."

Sledge furrowed his brow. "Where did you come up with the daughter?"

"Sly found her over at the Shamrock," John said. "She's been under our nose the whole time, and we didn't even know it."

"You talking about the blonde who runs it?" asked Sledge. He grinned and grabbed his crotch. "I could do this one for free, boss."

"Yeah, the blonde, but we ain't going to do nothing until we know for sure where the mine is located," John said. Then he grinned. "Then we take turns, and I'm first."

Sledge shrugged. "Sure, you're the boss. I don't mind seconds."

"What about me, Boss? I want to be third," said Flat Nose as he rose from his chair. Sledge scowled at him. His glare was cut short when someone knocked on the door. Sledge got up and slowly opened the door. He relaxed when he saw who it was and opened it all the way. Sylvester and Horney walked into the room.

Sylvester glanced around the room, then turned to John. "You want to see me, boss?

"Yeah, I want you to go with me and Sledge out to the ranch. We're going to have a talk with O'Shay and his daughter about his mine." John turned to Horney. "Did you find Curt and Diablo?"

"Diablo was over at Lulu's Cantina, said he would be here in a minute. I couldn't find Curt. Stella said he might have gone out to the ranch," Horney said.

"What do you want us to do, boss?" Flat Nose said. "You want us to go with you, too?"

"No, you three are going to stay here and take care of Logan," John said. "I don't need him anymore, and he knows too much."

Flat Nose bared his stained teeth in a wicked grin. "I can't wait to get that bastard in my sights. I ain't forgot what he did to me at Vail's place when he killed Willy."

"Yeah, he killed my buddy Buck Horne too," Horney said. "Let's gut shoot him." The two men started toward the door, but Flat Nose, who was in the lead, paused and turned back to John. "We don't know where he's at, Mister Skinner."

"You imbeciles just wait; I'll tell you what to do in a minute," John said. He turned back to Sledge. "I want you to go up to the livery and get the horses ready. Take Sly with you."

"Okay, boss. I'm on my way. Do we need to bring any supplies with us?"

John thought for a minute. "Yeah, pick up some extra food. When O'Shay leads us to the mine, we might be gone for a few days."

As Sledge and Sylvester left the room, Diablo walked in. John motioned for him to wait, then he turned to Flat Nose. "You and Horney go to the train station and wait for Logan to come in on the morning train. If he ain't on that one, he will probably be on the evening train. Diablo will be there in a minute." Flat Nose and Horney shuffled out the door. John waited until the door closed behind them, then turned to Diablo. "I'm going out to the ranch to talk to O'Shay. I have a feeling that this time he will tell me where his mine is."

Diablo sat down. "What do you want me to do, boss?"

"First off, I want you to stay here to make sure that Logan is taken care of. I told those two to get rid of Logan, but I want you to see that they don't mess up. When Logan is taken care of, I want you to come out to the ranch. If we have already left for the mine, I want you to trail us. I've got a feeling that I might need to take care of Sledge somewhere along the way, and I want you there to back me up."

Diablo grimaced. "That won't be easy. He's fast on the draw."

"Shoot him from ambush," John said. "You stay out of sight, and as soon as we find the mine, you kill him."

Diablo licked his lips as he studied John's face, "What about me? What do I get out of this?"

John smiled. "You get a bigger cut, and you get to finish off O'Shay and his daughter."

A look of surprise came upon Diablo's face. "Where did this daughter come from?"

"It's the blonde from over at the Shamrock," John said. "I found out she's O'Shay's daughter. I'm going to use her to get him to talk."

Diablo flashed his teeth in a wide grin. He pulled out his Bowie knife and run his fingers down the blade. "I think I will enjoy this job, patron."

John grinned, but in his mind he shuddered when he thought about what the man was capable of doing. Diablo was crazy. He would have to figure out a way to get rid of him, also. He turned, picked up his hat off the hat rack, and pushed it on his head. "I got to go meet Sledge at the stable. I'm counting on you, Diablo."

Diablo sheathed his knife as he opened the door. "Si, patron, I will follow you and do as you say."

John followed Diablo out the door and locked it behind him. He went to the bar, where Gimpy was wiping a glass with his apron. "I'll be gone for a few days, Gimpy. If anyone asks about me, tell them I went to Yuma."

"Yes sir, Mister Skinner. I'll take care of things just like I always do," Gimpy said. John headed for the door. The dusty street was nearly empty as he made his way to the livery stable. Sledge and Sylvester were waiting for him when he got there.

"How far is the ranch, John?" Sylvester asked. "We don't ride horses in New York. Can't we take a buggy?"

John looked at Sylvester and said, "It's just a few miles. You need to get used to riding if you're going to live out here in the West." John stepped into the stirrup and swung into the saddle. He looked at the other two men. "Let's go." John whirled his horse around and kicked him in the flanks. The chestnut gelding surged into an instant lope, leaving a trail of dust as he carried John into the street and toward the west end of town. Sledge looked at Sylvester, grinned, then spurred his own horse into the street behind John. Sylvester watched the two men moving rapidly away from him. He reluctantly kicked his own horse in the flanks and took out after them, his butt bouncing in the saddle like a rubber ball.

CHAPTER 38

"BOOM!" Splinters peppered Bo's face as another bullet plowed into the floor. The crowd in the station froze for a second, searching for the source of the shots. Suddenly one woman screamed as she pointed at Bo. "He's dead!"

Like a herd of buffalo, the crowd turned and stampeded toward the other end of the station.

Bo quickly rolled to his left, pulling his Colt as he turned. Safely behind the wall by the doorframe, he stood up and peered over at Rex, who had bolted to the other side of the station door when he heard the first shot. Several women were still screaming and milling around at the back of the station, but a few of the men had pulled their guns and rushed to the windows. A few minutes passed with no shots fired. Rex, noticing the confusion in the station, pinned his badge on his vest.

"Everyone listen to me. I'm a United States marshal, and this is my deputy." The crowd became silent as he spoke. "Everyone stay behind cover while we see who is doing the shooting." He turned to Bo. "They are probably gone now." Bo peered around the doorframe. People were still running away from the station, shouting for help. He looked for likely hiding places for the gunman but saw nothing.

A man hiding behind a barrel slowly stood up and shouted, "I saw him; he had a rifle, and he ran that way." He pointed back toward the main part of town.

Bo ran to the man. "Did you get a good look at him?"

"No, but he was wearing a red shirt and had brown whipcord pants," the man said.

"I saw them go into the Silver Dollar saloon," a cowboy shouted from the crowd. "It was Flat Nose and Horney."

Bo's hands clinched. He turned to Rex, who had followed him out of the station. "I'm ready to get this over with. If they want to kill me, I'm going to bring it to them." He started walking toward the Silver Dollar.

Bo was still fuming when he got to the saloon, but he was careful as he peered over the batwing doors. Even though it was early in the morning, a few of the tables were occupied with customers. A few men were still playing cards from an all-night poker game, and others were just the ones who needed that morning beer. Bo's eyes swept across the room; He saw Flat Nose standing alone at the bar, but Horney wasn't in the room. Bo glanced at Rex, who had come up behind him. Then Bo slowly walked into the saloon, his eyes fixed on the bushwacker. Bo stopped when he was a few feet from Flat Nose; he could hear Rex behind him and knew his back was covered. Flat Nose, who had been staring at a glass of beer in front of him, turned his eyes toward Bo.

Bo pushed his hat back with his left hand as he calmly drawled, "I come to give you another shot at killing me, Flat Nose. The only difference is this time, you got to look me in the eye."

"I don't know what you are talking about. I've been here for the last two hours," Flat Nose said as he quickly glanced around the room for support. The saloon patrons stayed silent.

"I have a witness who saw you." Bo said. "Hand over your gun. You're under arrest."

"Under arrest for what? I told you I didn't do nothing," Flat Nose said irritably. He cut his eyes toward the balcony for a second.

Bo instinctively looked toward the balcony; Horney was standing next to a doorway with a Winchester pointed straight at him. Bo went for his Colt.

"BOOM! BOOM!"

Smoke filled the room as Horney tumbled over the rail then fell to the saloon floor with a crash; a small, red hole between his eyes. Bo realized he had only fired one of the two shots, so he quickly turned to Flat Nose, but the outlaw was down on the floor, blood gushing from a ragged hole in his chest. Rex was holding his smoking Colt and searching the room with his eyes.

"I saw that," shouted someone among the few customers who had sat in silence all through the incident. "You shot them without any reason. The sheriff will hear about this."

Rex turned to the man, who had gotten up and was walking toward the door. "Judge Mills, you're under arrest."

"Under arrest? Who are you?" Judge Mills screeched as he turned to face Rex. Suddenly he saw the marshal's badge on Rex's vest; a worried look appeared on his face. "What are you arresting me for?"

"Corruption; you're in the pay of John Skinner." Rex turned toward the bar. "Gimpy, you're under arrest, too."

Gimpy was reaching under the bar but stopped when Bo turned his gun toward him. "I'm just the bartender. I didn't do anything."

"You know who did." Rex looked around the saloon. "This saloon is closed. Everyone leave except the ones who work here." The room began to buzz with conversation as the people started leaving. Rex motioned for Judge Mills and Gimpy to sit at one of the tables. As Rex glanced around the room, he spotted Bull and Squeaky standing at the door looking in. "I need some help here unless you two got another run to make," he said to the two teamsters.

"No, we'd be glad to help. Don't have another run until tomorrow," Bull said. "What do you want us to do?"

"Just guard the prisoners while I search John's office," Rex said. "I'll have some other men coming soon, and we're going to be busy for a while."

"What about the saloon girls?" Squeaky squeaked. "You want us to watch them, too?"

"Yeah, them, too." Rex turned to Bo. "You go see about Mary. I got things under control here."

Bo holstered his pistol and started walking toward the café. He understood John Skinner might want him dead, but something about this whole situation just didn't feel right. He wondered where John Skinner was and what he was up to. Bo wasn't going to take any chances. Cautiously looking for trouble, he made his way to the café, but nothing happened. By the time he got there, he was thinking only of seeing Mary.

As he pushed his way through the door, he saw Lupe behind the counter. She turned to look as the bell on the door rang. When she saw it was Bo, a wide smile appeared on her face. "Oh, it's you, Mister Bo. I am so glad you are back. I know Mary will be, too."

"Where is Mary, Lupe?" Bo asked as he looked around the room.

"She went with the sheriff and Mister Dutch. She tell me her father is at Mister Dutch's place, and he was hurt."

"When did she leave with the sheriff?"

"It was yesterday evening, Senor. But she hasn't come back yet."

Bo pulled out his watch. It was seven o'clock. "If she returns, tell her I'm in town." He hurried out the door toward the sheriff's office. When he got there, Porky was asleep at the desk.

"Wake up, Porky. I want to know where the sheriff went yesterday." Bo said as he pushed the chubby deputy's feet to the floor.

"What! I was just resting my eyes." Porky rubbed his eyes and looked at Bo. "I don't know where the sheriff went." With an angry look he got up out of his chair and pointed to his badge. "I could arrest you for assaulting an officer of the law. Who do you think you are?"

Bo spied the keys to the cells hanging on the wall. He took two steps, then lifted them from their hook. "I'm a deputy United States marshal; you're under arrest." Porky's eyes opened wide and he started shaking; he fumbled for his gun but dropped it on the floor. Bo grabbed Porky by his shirt collar. Although Porky weighed over two hundred pounds, Bo roughly dragged him to one of the cells and thrust him into it.

Bo glared at the terrified man. "I'm going to ask you one more time: where did the sheriff go?"

"I think he went to Skinner's ranch," Porky said. "He told me him and Dutch had some business to take care of out there." Porky sat down on the cot and put his hands over his face. "I knew something bad would come of this. I swear I had to go along with them or they would kill me."

Bo studied the trembling Porky. This would be a good time to get some answers. "What are the sheriff's plans?" he asked.

Porky looked up at Bo. "If I tell you everything, will you turn me loose? I was afraid of them."

"That's up to the marshal and a real judge. But if you talk, I'm sure the judge will take that in to consideration. If you don't talk, I'm going to beat you until you do."

"They railroaded a man to prison on false charges a few years ago so they could steal the money he had just put in the bank," Porky said. "Judge Mills and Walter Johnson were in on it, too. Later, when Curt Skinner was in prison, he found out that the man had a gold mine. He told John, and John had the sheriff get the miner out of prison and took him out to Skinner's ranch."

Bo thought for a minute. "Who is this miner, and what has Mary got to do with it?"

"O'Shay, his name is Tom O'Shay," Porky said. "John wants the mine, but the man won't tell him where it's at. John found out that the girl down at the Shamrock Café is really O'Shay's daughter, so they tricked her into going with them to the ranch." Porky paused and swallowed. Tears were now coming from his eyes. "John's going to use her to make O'Shay tell him where the mine's at."

Without thinking about it, Bo slammed the cell door shut and locked it. His mind was elsewhere, trying to fit all the pieces of the puzzle of Bonnie O'Shay together. Slowly he walked to the sheriff's desk, then sat down. His mind whirled as he tried to sort out the pieces.

Bonnie was at the girl's school, and then she was sent to the workhouse. She escaped and took the train to San Francisco, where she found her uncle. Her uncle had a café with a sign that had a four-leaf clover on it, and Mary's café has a sign with a four-leaf clover on it. If Mary is Bonnie, then she didn't die in the San Francisco fire. But why did she change her name to Mary?

Suddenly Bo remembered that Mary was in danger. He rushed back to the cell. "Where is Skinner's ranch?"

Porky got up from the cot where he had been sitting. "It's west of town about five miles," he said. "I could take you there."

The sound of the front door of the jail opening interrupted their conversation. Wheeling quickly, Bo pulled his Colt. As the door swung open, he saw that it was Rex, followed by Ronald Harbin, Bull, and two other men he didn't know. They were leading Judge Mills and Gimpy. Bo holstered his pistol as he turned back to Porky, who had moved to the back of the cell.

A puzzled look was on Rex's face. "I thought you were going to see Mary."

"I went to the café, but she wasn't there," Bo said as he holstered his Colt. "Lupe told me she went out to John Skinner's ranch yesterday with the sheriff." Bo hesitated for a second. "I need to find Mary. She's in danger," he said anxiously. He cut his eyes to the other men in the room. "Can any of you tell me how to get to Skinner's ranch?"

"I can," Ronald said. "Take the road going west out of town past the stables. Go about five miles and then take the side road to the left that goes up through a high-walled canyon. The ranch is just down that road; you can't miss it."

"Yeah, that's right," added Bull. "It's the only side road that goes to the left. All the rest turn off to the right. You can find it easy."

"Thanks, men. I'm sure I can find it," Bo said as he turned to Rex. "I know you have things to do here, so I won't bother you to come with me, but I'm leaving right now."

"I hate to see you ride out there alone, Bo, but I know I can't change your mind," Rex said. "John and some of his men are still on the loose, so be careful." He thought for a second, then added, "As soon as I can finish up here, I'll come out there, so if you find more than you can handle, wait for me to get there."

"I will, Marshal," Bo said as he went out the door. He hurried down the dusty street to the stable. The old stableman was sitting on his stool mending a harness when Bo got there.

"I need my horse. They said the stage brought it here from Vail's place."

The man looked up and slowly said, "You mean that crazy dun-colored horse that Bull and Squeaky left here?"

"Yeah, that one. Where is he?"

"The sheriff came in yesterday to rent an extra horse, and he was in a hurry. He said he wanted a horse that was gentle for a woman, and that dun was the only horse here I knew was gentle." The man looked down at the ground and said apologetically, "So I rented it to him." He paused a second, then said, "That crazy horse thinks he's a human being. He gets out of everything I put him in and then follows me around everywhere."

Bo couldn't help but grin for a second when he heard the old man's story. "Look, Mister, it's OK; just get me a horse and saddle. I'm in a hurry, too." Bo noticed a saddled horse tied to the corral fence and started toward it. "Whose horse is that?"

"That's Walter Johnson's horse, the banker. You can't take his horse; he said he's going on a trip as soon as he collects some things from the bank."

Bo untied him and climbed into the saddle. "I don't think Walter Johnson is going to need his horse today or any other day for a long time." He turned the black gelding toward the westbound road.

The old man watched as Bo and the horse disappeared down the road in a cloud of dust. He pulled off his old, battered hat and wiped his brow. "Durndest thing I ever seen; the man stole the banker's horse. I guess I better go tell Porky."

CHAPTER 39

*B*onnie and her father were sitting under a shade tree at the lake watching the children play in the water. She wanted to join them, but something was keeping her from moving. She struggled, then finally rose to her feet. But when she started to walk toward the lake, a door appeared in front of her. She turned to her father, but he was gone. She turned back to the door, and it was open. Slowly she walked up to it to peer inside. Her father was lying on the floor of a tiny room. Suddenly someone pushed her inside the room, then slammed the door shut.

Bonnie awoke to the sound of a horse neighing somewhere close by. She was confused when she opened her eyes, and she slowly looked around the room, but then scenes from the day before flashed in her mind and she remembered. She saw her father asleep on the floor and she smiled, but then her thoughts turned to John Skinner, and her smile turned to a look of despair. Bonnie and her father had talked deep into the night about their predicament and what might happen to them. Bonnie still feared that they would be killed, but Tom had assured her that when he told John where the mine was, he would set them free. Bonnie still had her doubts, but weariness finally overcame her, and she dropped off to sleep on the small cot.

Now it was morning and Bonnie felt a need to relieve herself. Seeing no other choice, she went to the corner and used the rusting slop jar that had served Tom for the past few days. A few minutes later Tom grunted and opened his eyes. He greeted her, and they talked for a few minutes. Then, when he couldn't wait any longer, Tom used the same slop jar. A few minutes later, as they were both sitting on the cot, they heard someone rattling the chain; in a few seconds the door opened. Tom and Bonnie stood up. John Skinner, pistol in hand, stepped into the small room. "I see you two have been getting acquainted again. How long has it been? Six years since you have seen one another?"

Bonnie glared at John; she had seen the man in the Shamrock. Bull had told her that he was the owner of the Silver Dollar Saloon. She had never liked the way he looked at her. He reminded her of some of the riffraff she had to put up with at her uncle's café. "Why have you locked us up, Mister Skinner? What do you want?"

John scowled as he turned his eyes to Tom. "He knows what I want."

Sledge pushed his way into the small room, looked at Bonnie, and grinned. "I know what I want."

John looked at Sledge and frowned. He turned back to Tom. "I'll make it real simple. If you take me to the mine, you and your daughter go free. If not, I turn her over to Sledge."

Tom sank back down on the cot, a hangdog look on his face. He was beaten; he couldn't let anything happen to his daughter. "Okay, Mister Skinner, you win. I'll show you the mine." He hesitated. "You can let her go; I promise I'll take you to my gold mine."

"No, you show me the mine first, then I'll turn you both loose," John said. He turned to Dutch, who was standing at the door. "Get the horses ready and pack some grub. We'll leave as soon as we can get everything ready." He turned back to Tom. "You better not lead me on a wild goose chase. Sledge wants to get his hands on your gal real bad." He nodded to Sledge as he walked out the door. Sledge grinned at Bonnie, then winked as he left the room. They heard the chains rattle as someone locked the door. Then Bonnie turned and looked at her father; tears came to her eyes. She felt that old hopeless feeling coming back to her, and she was afraid.

Tom said, "It will be OK, Bonnie. With the Lord's help, we will come through this."

Bonnie turned her eyes upward and prayed. "Lord, I know you didn't bring me this far and then abandon me. Please watch over us, Lord, and help us defeat this evil."

John and Sledge were waiting in the barn for Dutch to come back with the supplies when they heard horses coming toward the ranch. John pulled his pistol as he watched the road but holstered it when he saw it was Curt and Diablo. He stepped out into the open when they got closer. They rode over to him. Both had worried looks on their faces.

"Hello, Curt. I been waiting for you. We're going to take a little trip." He turned to Diablo. "How did things go in town?"

"Everything got screwed up, patron. Flat Nose and Horney are dead."

John jerked; his eyes opened wide. "What? What happened?"

"We were at the train station this morning when Logan arrived. Flat Nose had a bead on him, but Logan turned just as Flat Nose pulled the trigger, and the shot missed him. Flat Nose and Horney ran back to the saloon, and Logan followed them. He killed Horney, and the marshal with him killed Flat Nose."

"Marshal? What marshal?" John asked. A touch of fear began to grow in his mind.

"There's more," Curt said. "This marshal arrested Judge Mills, Porky, Walter Johnson, and all of our employees at the Silver Dollar. And guess who the marshal is?"

"I don't know anything about a fucking marshal," John yelled irritably. "What the hell is going on?"

Curt glared at his brother for a second, then said slowly, "The big cowboy who has been hanging around the saloon. Turns out he's a United States marshal. He's been asking around about our dealings with the sheriff and Judge Mills. Logan is his deputy, and he's on his way out here."

John hesitated as he tried to digest all this new information. Suddenly he realized that all his plans were falling apart and he needed to figure a way out this mess. John had always had a backup plan for when he might have to leave town in a hurry, and part of it was that he had stashed a lot of cash in the safe at the saloon. But now he couldn't go back to town to get it.

"Damn the sorry bastards," he yelled. He turned as he heard someone behind him. It was Sheriff Cobb, Sylvester, and Dutch walking into the barn.

"What's going on, John? What's this about a marshal?" Sheriff Cobb asked.

"We're through in this territory, Cobb," John said. "A federal marshal is in Tucson right now closing me down." He grimaced and shook his head. "We need to run, but we need some time and money." He pointed at Dutch and Curt. "You two go up the canyon and ambush Logan and anyone else who's with him."

Sheriff Cobb looked confused. "Wait a minute, John. I'm still the sheriff. I'll go into town and straighten all this out."

John flared at the old sheriff's stupidity. "Damn you, Cobb! They've arrested Mills, Johnson, Porky, and all my employees. They already know everything! Do you really think that Porky is not going to talk?" He hesitated for just a second. "You know Mills and Johnson will spill their guts!" He paused, catching his breath. "You can go into town if you want to, but we are through around here."

Sheriff Cobb seemed to shrink as realization entered his mind. His face turned ashen, and he leaned back on the wall of the barn, seemingly unable to stand without support. He clutched his chest and slowly slid down the wall until he was sitting on the ground. He closed his eyes and went limp.

John watched the sheriff until he stopped moving. Shaking his head, he turned to find Mad Dog and Curt watching. "I told you guys what to do; why haven't you left?"

"What do we do after we kill Logan?" Mad Dog asked. "Where will we find you?"

"Just follow our trail. Curt can track us," John said. "Now hurry!"

Mad Dog started toward his horse. He cut his eyes at the body of Sheriff Cobb and hesitated as if he needed to do something, but Curt nudged him in the back and he hurried to his horse, the old sheriff forgotten. John watched the two men ride off toward the canyon, indecision whirling around in his mind.

Sylvester who had standing off by himself, walked over closer to John. "John," he called softly. "I think I can help you out. I'm not wanted for anything around here."

John turned to Sylvester with a small but desperate feeling of hope. "What do you have in mind? Make it snappy; we need to ride out of here pronto."

"Well, I was thinking…" Sylvester hesitated for a second as the thought of John pulling his gun and shooting him crossed his mind. He cleared his throat. "You could sign a bill of sale saying you sold the ranch and saloon to me a week ago, and that would keep them from taking it. I would run it for you until things blew over and you could return."

Eyes glaring, John reached for his pistol but paused. Sylvester's idea might work; besides, he had no choice, and he was running out of time. He would have to trust the man for now; he could always shoot him later. "Okay, let's go to the house, and I'll make out the bill of sale." John looked at Dutch. "You go get more supplies. We may have to take the back trails all the way to California."

"What are you going to do with them two in there?" Dutch asked, pointing toward the room where Tom and Bonnie were.

"I'll take care of them; you just go do what I told you," John said. He reached for his pistol as he walked toward the door. The chain was latched, so he motioned for Sledge, who had been standing by the door, to unlatch it.

"We're going to take the girl with us, ain't we?" Sledge asked in a commanding voice.

John hadn't thought about taking the girl. His only thought was he would get rid of a couple of witnesses. "Yeah, we can take her with us for now, then get rid of her later."

Sledge unlocked the chain and pulled the door open. Bonnie was sitting by her father on the cot, both of them staring at him with fearful eyes. They had heard everything and were waiting to see what John would do with them. Bonnie gasped when she saw the gun in John's hand. She turned to her father, a pleading look in her eyes. John raised the pistol and pointed it at Tom. His finger tightened on the trigger.

CHAPTER 40

The black gelding was a sound horse, and he liked to run. The road was fairly straight the first two miles, and Bo kept up the pace all the way, but at the first turn in the road he sensed the horse was beginning to tire, so he pulled him up into a slow lope. Even though his heart was telling him to race to Bonnie as fast as he could ride, he didn't want to wind break the gelding or he would be walking.

Eventually Bo came to the wagon-rutted road that led off to the north, and he guided the black toward the canyon. But as Bo studied the high walls above the road, the thought of an ambush crossed his mind. He noticed a faint trail that seemed to lead up to the top of the canyon wall, and thinking about the danger of an ambush again, he reined the gelding onto the trail. It turned out to be an easy trek up, with only a few places where the gelding had to really struggle. When Bo got to the top, he found the trail continued along the ridge, but the going was rough and slow.

Bo was beginning to wish he had just taken the road at the bottom of the canyon when a flash of light caught his eyes. He stopped behind a small saltbush so he could watch the trail ahead. Suddenly a man rode into view. Bo drew his pistol, then waited as the man rode closer. Bo recognized him as someone he had seen in town hanging around with Flat Nose a few times, and he assumed he worked for John Skinner. The man seemed to be looking for something in the canyon, but when he was just a few yards from Bo, he stopped and got off his horse. The man pulled his rifle from the saddle scabbard and crept to the edge of the canyon. He crouched behind a boulder with his Winchester ready; slowly he peered around it, his eyes looking down toward the canyon floor.

Slowly Bo rode out from behind the bush. "Drop the rifle. I got you covered," he demanded in a loud voice. Startled, the man quickly turned toward the voice. When he saw Bo with a pistol in his hand, he whirled the rifle around and pulled it to his shoulder. He began squeezing the trigger, but suddenly, a blow to his chest pushed him backward into the canyon. He screamed until he hit the rocky canyon floor of the canyon with a thud.

Bo waited and watched for a few minutes, then holstered his smoking pistol. He cautiously walked to the rim of the canyon to look down. Mad Dog was sprawled out beside the dirt road, his arms and legs spread out in awkward positions.

Suddenly chips of rock from a nearby boulder peppered Bo's face and a split second later, "BOOM!" The sound of the rifle shot echoed in the canyon as Bo dove behind the boulder. "BOOM!" Another shot sprayed more chips above him as he squirmed in tighter. From the angle of the shots, Bo figured they came from across the canyon, but he wasn't sure. He nervously glanced around, looking for smoke or movement. Seeing nothing, Bo waited a few more minutes, listening for any unnatural sounds, but all he heard was the wind blowing in the trees. Bo waited for a few seconds longer, then began to look a safer spot with more cover. He noticed another large boulder to his right and slightly behind him, so he eased down to his belly and slowly began scooting backwards to the other boulder. He inched back, nervously waiting for the next shot. *I'll never hear the one that kills me*, he thought. The shot never came, and he sighed with relief as he stood up behind the larger boulder. Safely concealed, he cautiously studied the area around him, looking for more cover. The ambusher knew his location, so he could be stalking him. Farther behind him, away from the cliff, was a thick growth of creosote. It would make excellent cover, but he would be in the open for a few seconds if he made a dash for them.

He had just decided to wait for a few more minutes and then make his try when he heard the sound of a horse running. It came from the other side of the canyon, and Bo was pretty sure that someone was riding away. With a burst of nervous energy, Bo jumped up and dashed for the brush. He plowed through the small bushes, but seeing a lager mesquite tree that would conceal him, he quickly dashed behind it. Bo peered around it with his gun ready as he studied the other side of the canyon. It was quiet and normal looking. Suddenly a squirrel off to his right and down in the canyon began chattering; immediately another one answered him from across the canyon. A robber jay screeched from somewhere on the other side, and Bo relaxed as he realized that the animal sounds indicated that the intruder was probably gone.

Slowly he moved from his hiding place and went back to where the gelding was still standing. With one last look around, he holstered his Colt, then mounted. Impatiently he spurred the gelding back on the trail and again headed for the ranch. Bo had ridden only a half-mile when he saw the ranch house nestled among some willow trees in a little valley at the end of the canyon. The ranch looked deserted, but he wasn't going to take a chance and ride straight up to the front door. He had already been ambushed once, and he didn't think they were through with him yet. Noticing a grove of hackberry trees behind a huge barn, he circled around out of sight of the ranch house and rode up to the grove.

Dismounting, Bo tied his horse to a bush, then slowly walked through the trees toward the barn. He stopped behind one of them as he came to the back of the huge building. Cautiously he studied the layout of the barn. Huge doors were open to a large hallway that ran through the middle, with stalls and pens on both sides. He didn't see anyone around, so he quickly dashed to the back of barn. The normal barn smells of manure and hay greeted his nose as he examined the interior of the barn. The stalls lining one side of the hallway were empty, but on the other side were some rooms with closed doors. The rest of it was a large, open area fenced in with wooden rails and containing a pile of hay.

As Bo's eyes adjusted to the dim light, he froze as he glimpsed someone sitting on the dirt floor, leaning against the wall. The man was staring at the opposite wall, and he wasn't moving. Puzzled, Bo realized that the man was dead. With his pistol ready, Bo slowly walked toward the body.

As he got closer, he was surprised to see that it was Sheriff Cobb. He leaned down looking for blood, but seeing none, he nudged the body down and turned it over. Still no blood. Bo was puzzled, but he didn't have time to worry about it now. He crept farther down the hall to a closed-in stall that had a chain hanging on its door. The chain rattled some when Bo opened the door, so he quickly stepped inside then glanced around. It was empty, but it looked as if someone had slept there. Bo carefully moved to the next room; it was full of saddle racks, but the saddles were gone. The next room had only sacks of grain. Bo looked around inside the barn again. Since the horses were gone, John and his bunch must have already left and taken Bonnie with them. But where did they go? Suddenly, Bo heard someone walking up behind him. He whirled, his gun ready to fire.

CHAPTER 41

"Wait a minute, Mister Skinner," Tom pleaded. "I have the perfect hideout for you at the mine."

"What do you mean, perfect?" John said as he eased off the trigger. He was open to any suggestions at this point.

"The mine is in a hidden valley," Tom said. He knew that he had only seconds to persuade John to spare them. "There is only one way in, and that is through a cave. They would never find you in there." Tom paused to catch his breath and added, "There is plenty of water, and there is game to hunt. There are even a few cows in there."

"All of this in the middle of the desert? You're lying."

Sweat poured down Tom's brow as he continued with his plea. "No, it's at the edge of the mountains north of here. Out past Vail's Station; we can be there tonight."

Silence filled the room for a few seconds as John considered what Tom had said. A horsefly buzzed around his head, and he absently brushed it away with his hand. Slowly he lowered his pistol and put it back into his holster. He stared at Tom. "You ride Cobb's horse." He turned to Sledge. "Get them mounted up. As soon as Dutch gets the supplies loaded, you and Dutch head for Vail's Station." John stepped out the door to look for Diablo. He was helping Dutch load the extra supplies on the mules. "Diablo," he called, "when you get through helping Dutch, you stay with me.

I got a few things to do here before I leave." John turned toward Sylvester. "Come on with me to the house. I'll draw up that bill of sale." Sylvester and John headed for the house as Sledge herded Tom and Bonnie to their horses.

"You help load the supplies," Sledge said to Tom. He turned to Bonnie. "Get on your horse." He grinned wickedly. "We're going to have some fun when we get to that valley."

Bonnie grimaced as she mounted the dun horse. She tried to think of ways to escape as they waited for Dutch and Tom to load the supplies, but it just didn't seem possible. There were too many of them.

When the supplies were all loaded, Dutch tied Bonnie's and Tom's hands with leather thongs, then helped Tom get up on Cobb's horse. Dutch mounted, and then, leading Bonnie and Tom's mounts, he followed Sledge into the desert.

In the house John searched his desk until he found some paper. He wrote out a bill of sale for the ranch and saloon to Sylvester Dungerhill for ten thousand dollars. When he was finished, he looked up at Sly with a menacing look. "I have this much money in my safe at the saloon. I'm not going to give you the combination to it because I'm going to need that money. I'll send someone to get in touch with you when I'm ready for it." He paused. "Just remember, if you try to screw me up, I'll send someone to kill you."

"Oh no, I wouldn't cheat you, John. Whenever you're ready for the money, I'll gladly turn it over to you." He paused for a second. "I do get to keep the profits from the saloon, though, don't I?"

"Sure, I don't expect you to do this for nothing. And if I can't ever come back you can just pay me the ten thousand and the whole thing will be yours." John headed for the door. "I got to go; just don't mess this deal up or I'll be pretty damned mad."

"Don't worry about a thing," Sly said as he folded the bill of sale up and stuck it in his vest. "I'll take care of everything."

John hurried out the door but stopped abruptly when he heard shots coming from the canyon. Diablo was waiting for him outside, and he, too, looked toward the canyon.

"Curt and Mad Dog should be here in a minute," John said as he looked back at Diablo. "There's another problem solved." He turned back to the canyon, paused for a minute, and said, "Let's ride. They can catch up."

CHAPTER 42

Sylvester sat on his horse and watched John ride off into the brush and cactus. He smiled as he patted his coat pocket where he had placed the deeds to the ranch and the saloon.

"You fool," he muttered. "Do you really think that I will hang around this forsaken country and wait for you to come back some day?" Sylvester reined his horse toward the road that ran back through the canyon and kicked him in the flanks. The horse shook his head as he took off in a trot, with Sylvester awkwardly bouncing in the saddle. He had only gone a little ways before he noticed a rider racing down the road toward him. He quickly looked for a place to hide. But it was too late, so he stopped and waited as the rider approached.

"What's going on? Where are you going?" Curt asked loudly as he jerked his horse to a stop.

"I'm going to take care of things for John until he gets back," Sylvester said. "Nobody's looking for me."

Curt paused for a second as he digested the information but glanced back the way he came. "If I was you, I wouldn't ride back that way. The posse might shoot you first and then see if you're wanted." He glanced behind him again. "Logan is right behind me. If you want to miss him, take the trail to the right there by that dry wash. It will take you back to town." Curt didn't wait for

Sylvester to say anything. He quickly spurred his horse and raced away.

"I don't need to meet up with anyone out here," Sylvester grumbled as watched Curt ride away. He kicked his horse into a trot and bounced along until he found the cutoff from the main road. The trail was narrow and wasn't used much anymore except by cattle, but it was clearly marked. Sylvester was anxious to get out of sight from the main road, and he hurried his horse down the trail. When he was out of sight from the road, he slowed to a walk and relaxed. A smile appeared on his face as he felt of the deeds in his pocket again and thought of what he would do when he got to town. The first thing would be to transfer the deeds into his name. The second thing would be to go to the Silver Dollar, get some of John's best bourbon, then drink it as he poked Juanita. He was still daydreaming about what he would do to Stella when he came to a fork in the trail. He would have to go either to the left or to the right. He thought about it for a minute, then chose to go right. The left might take him back to the road. He continued along for a while but soon came to another fork in the trail. He took the left fork this time, reasoning that he didn't want to go in a circle. Hours passed, and Sylvester was beginning to wonder if he had taken the wrong trail as he began to pass through a more rugged, mountainous country. He glanced at the sun; it was just a little above the hills in the distance, and he realized it would be dark soon. He stopped his horse; he would go back to the ranch and just take the main road back to Tucson. His spirits lifted as he turned his horse and headed back the way he had come. He rode for a while, but as the sun sank lower in the sky, he was beginning to worry again. Suddenly he saw a horse on the trail ahead of him, and that brought a wave of relief to his mind.

"Hey you, up there, could you help me?" Sylvester shouted happily. "I want to go to Tucson, and I seem to have lost my way."

The man didn't answer. Sylvester called again, but again there was no response. Sylvester became impatient. He could see someone on a horse through the trees, but the man wasn't answering. "I will pay you to guide me to Tucson," he said; still no answer from the horseman.

Suddenly he heard something behind him; he turned to see what it was. An Indian sitting on a small paint pony was staring at him with an expressionless face. Sylvester's heart skipped a beat, then raced as he realized what he had wandered into. He hurriedly jerked his horse around, but the other horseman was blocking the trail now, and he was trapped between them. Sylvester desperately pulled on his horse's reins and kicked him repeatedly, trying to make him go through the brush between the two Indians. But abruptly the Indian on the paint rode in closer and swung his war club. Sylvester's mind exploded to black as he fell from his horse.

Sylvester's head was pounding when he awoke, and he couldn't move his arms and legs. He groaned and opened his eyes to his worst nightmare. He was lying on his back and naked; his arms and legs spread-eagle tied to trees. Eight vicious-looking Apaches were standing around him, laughing and pointing at him. All at once they saw he was awake, and they began to reach for their knives.

"No, no, ahhhhhhhhhh!" Sylvester screamed and twisted his body, but the Apaches laughed as they began slashing his body with hundreds of shallow cuts.

"Stop, please stop, no, no, no, no, no, please, please, please, ahhheeeeeee, please stop!" Sylvester screamed and pleaded with them to stop as the pain intensified with each cut, but they only laughed and kept cutting. Suddenly one of them held up his hand and grunted something in Apache. The rest of them stopped and backed away from Sylvester.

The Apache looked Sylvester in the eye and spoke. "I am Geronimo. Why do you scream like a squaw, white eye?"

"Please don't kill meeeeeee," Sylvester pleaded, tears flowing from his eyes from the pain as well as his fear. "I just want to go back to New York."

Geronimo walked over to a small fire, where he picked up some of the postcards that Sylvester had been carrying in his coat pocket. He looked at them as he walked back to Sylvester.

"You take the paintings of your women lying with men and carry them with you? Are these women your wives?"

"No!" cried Sylvester through the pain. "They are women from other places. Men like to look at the pictures. I sell them."

"Do you like to look at them?"

"Yes, I look at them all the time," Sylvester gasped. "You can have them all! I'll get you more!"

Geronimo snarled then spat on the ground. He turned to Nana. "Geld him like you would a horse."

The Apache grinned and knelt down beside Sylvester. He grabbed Sylvester's testicular sack and split it with his knife. A high-pitched scream erupted from Sylvester as he realized what the Apache was going to do. He tried to squirm his body away from the knife, but the other Apaches quickly pinned him to the ground so he couldn't move.

"Ahhhheeeeee!" He screamed again as Nana pulled out his testicles and sliced the cords they were connected to.

"Look, his man things," he yelled as he held them up for everyone to see. He began dancing around the small fire as he held up his bloody trophies. Geronimo glanced at Yellow Hand and nodded. The young Apache grabbed a long knife that had been in the fire, then walked over to Sylvester, who was still groaning in pain. He slapped the red-hot blade onto the open wound. Sylvester screamed again and passed out as the pain rose to an unbearable degree.

"Why don't we just kill him," asked Nana.

Geronimo looked at Red Deer and replied, "I think he is filled with an evil spirit. He carries paintings of naked people lying together. If we kill him, his spirit will follow us. Throw him into the cactus; we will leave him here."

Nana nodded to the rest of the Apaches. They cut Sylvester's bindings and carried him to a patch of cholla. Sylvester awoke as they turned him on his belly, then he screamed when they picked him up. He screamed again as the Apaches swung him out into the spiny plants.

"Let us go," Geronimo grunted as his followers gathered up their things. Silently they rode off through the desert as Sylvester whimpered and screamed, thousands of tiny barbs digging deeper into his body every time he moved.

CHAPTER 43

"Hold it! Don't shoot! It's us, Bull, and Squeaky!" Bo eased off the trigger and lowered his pistol as he recognized the two teamsters. Both of them had their hands up in the air. They stayed frozen in that position until Bo holstered his pistol.

"You men need to be more careful how you sneak up on someone. I could have killed you both," Bo said.

"Sorry, Bo. You kind of caught us by surprise. We were both looking at the sheriff's body when you came out of that room," Bull said. "What happen to the sheriff?"

"There's not a mark on him, I think he had a heart attack. Maybe he heard the news of the arrest in town," Bo said. He looked toward the ranch house. "I haven't checked the house yet, but I think they've all gone."

"Somebody must have brought them the news," Squeaky said as he rose from examining the sheriff's body.

"You men cover me. I'm going to make a run for the house," Bo said, still looking at the house. He eased to the front entrance, then, after pausing for a second, he ran toward the cover of a well out in front of the house. He crouched behind the well to wait for a second. Receiving no response from the house, he ran to the porch, then stopped with his back up against the wall by the front door. Still no response; he turned the knob as he pushed in the door. The house was quiet. Carefully he peered into the house; seeing no one, he stepped inside. Bo carefully checked all the rooms and found them empty. In one room, a safe was open and empty. In the kitchen the food larders were open, and items were scattered on the floor. Bo stepped back onto the front porch. "Come on out, fellows. No one's here."

Bull and Squeaky appeared from the door of the barn and cautiously approached the house, their pistols ready. When they got close to Bo, Bull asked, "What do you think, Bo? Are we going to track them?"

Bo was thinking as he took off his hat and wiped his brow. Finally he turned to Bull. "Bull, they have Mary and Mary's father, Tom O'Shay. Tom has a gold mine, and John wants it. If Tom is any kind of father, he has agreed to lead John to his mine in order to protect Mary."

Bull grimaced. "Bo, you know what will happen, don't you?"

"I know, Bull. We got to hurry and get to them before they get to the mine." Bo started for the barn but stopped as he turned to Squeaky. "Draw up some water, Squeaky, while we get our horses. This may be a long trip, and we'll need to fill our canteens before we go."

Squeaky hurried to the well and lowered the bucket. By the time Bo and Bull got back with the horses, he had a bucket waiting, and Bull and Squeaky filled the canteens while Bo rode out to check for signs. He found fresh tracks heading north and followed them for a little ways, but then paused and waited for Bull and Squeaky to catch up.

"They are heading north toward Vail's station," he said as the two teamsters rode up. "They have maybe an hours start on us. I can't take the chance of being wrong on where they are headed and losing their trail, so we are going to have to follow their tracks." Bo glanced down at the tracks, then urged the gelding to follow them.

Bo's heart ached as he thought of Mary in the clutches of John and his gang. If they harmed her, he would follow them to the ends of the earth and kill them all. But Bo knew that revenge wouldn't bring her back. He needed all his skills and a whole lot of luck if he was going to save the woman he loved.

CHAPTER 44

The sun's rays beat down mercilessly on the small band of outlaws as they made their way through the desert. Diablo, who was riding next to John, sneered as he noticed him drinking the last bit of water from his canteen. "Stupido gringo," he said softly. John was getting on his nerves with all of his complaining.

"Damn that son of a bitching federal marshal," John blurted for the tenth time. He glanced around as he heard someone shout. Curt was coming toward them from the rear, his horse galloping fast. He slowed as he got closer, then stopped when he got up to where John was waiting.

"Where's Mad Dog?" John asked. "I hope you got that bastard Logan."

"Mad Dog's dead. The bastard was already on the canyon waiting for us, and he shot Mad Dog," Curt said. "I wasn't going to shoot it out with him face to face, so I snuck out of there."

"Are you sure Mad Dog's dead?"

"I guess so. He fell off the cliff. He was all messed up."

John frowned as he turned to Diablo. "Go back down the trail and take care of Logan, I don't need anyone following us."

"Sure, boss, I will take care of him," Diablo said. He looked at Curt. "It will only take a little while." He spurred his horse back the way they had come. He remembered a hill with lots of big rocks to hide behind where he could ambush Logan. It took him a few moments to ride back to the spot. He tied his horse to a tree well out of sight, then carefully made his way to a huge rock halfway up the hill. He settled himself behind it and checked to see if he had a clear view of the back trail. Satisfied, he leaned back and waited for Bo to come riding down the trail. Diablo was good at waiting. Little rocks were digging into his rear, but he ignored them. A fly landed on his face, and he let it crawl for a while, only blowing at it when it crawled on his mouth. Sweat rolled down his face and into the crack of his ass.

Finally he saw movement in the brush. Three riders were coming down the trail. He watched until they got close enough for him to recognize Logan in the lead. He hadn't counted on three of them, but it didn't matter. He would kill them all. He moved his Winchester into position and waited until Bo moved into his sights. He began to squeeze the trigger, but suddenly he felt something hit his head then his mind went black.

Diablo woke to a splitting headache. He began to reach for his head, but his arm wouldn't move. He tried the other arm, but it wouldn't move, either. He opened his eyes and tried to raise his head. His arms and legs were tied to stakes in the ground. An Indian was sitting on a rock watching him. A small fire was burning behind the Indian.

"No!" he screamed, "not to me. I'm the friend of the Apache." Wildly he looked around but it was only the Apache and he.

The Apache watched him for a few minutes more, then said, "Do you not remember me?"

Diablo looked at the Apache. He looked familiar, but Diablo couldn't place where he had seen him. "I don't know you. Where have I seen you before? If I have offended you; I am sorry. I will give you a lot of money and horses to pay for what I did."

"Will you bring back my wife from the dead? Will you take the shame from her that she felt as you took her by force?" the Apache said softy.

As Diablo studied the face of the Indian, trying to remember a squaw, it came to him—that day at Vail's place. The day when they killed all of the men and then had fun with the squaw before they killed her. All hope left him, and he knew he was going to die a painful death. He began to beg.

"No, that wasn't me. I wasn't there."

"You were there."

"Yes, but I told them not to mess with the squaw."

"All of the men at the station were my friends. My name is Lame Deer." Lame Deer hesitated for a second. "They call you Diablo, but today, you will meet the real Diablo from your Bible." Lame deer pulled his knife from the fire. "I have heard that you like to make a lot of little cuts on the people you kill. I think you will soon know how it feels." He paused. "But first we must cut out your tongue. It will be a long night, and I don't want your screams to disturb anyone's sleep." Diablo watched as Lame Deer approached him with the knife. Thoughts of the Bible and all the stories he had heard of hell flooded through his mind. Tears began to run down his face, and he began to pray.

"God help me!" he cried.

"Did you hear that?" Curt asked as he stopped his horse and looked back the way they had come. "I thought I heard someone screaming."

John stopped beside him and listened. "I don't hear anything." He nudged his horse with his spurs to start him walking again. "Probably just a coyote."

Curt stared at their back trail for a few seconds longer, then turned his horse and spurred him to catch up to John. He reached for his leather-wrapped canteen and put it to his mouth to take a drink. Only a mouthful of water poured from the spout. Curt shook it as if he didn't believe it was empty. "How far is it to water, John?" he said as he slapped the stopper back into the spout and hung the canteen on the saddle horn.

John looked up at the sun hovering over the horizon. "We should be at the stage stop in a couple of hours. We can refill our canteens there," John said as he guided his horse around a low arm of a Saguaro cactus. The wind was calm now, but the heat still hung in the air. He reached for his own canteen and poured a big swig of the water down his throat. He shook it when he was through, then offered it to Curt, who took a long swig.

"Thanks," he said as he handed it back to his brother. No one was talking as they trudged on through the desert, but Curt was looking ahead at the girl on the dun horse. He stared at her butt, watching it jiggle with the movement of her horse. She was wearing a light grey riding skirt that showed her legs almost to her knees. The more he watched, the more he felt the desire rising in his loins. He wondered how it would feel like to hold her down and rip the skirt off her.

She will fight, I will slap her around a while before I take her. He looked over at John, then at Sledge. He was afraid of Sledge. *By the time John and Sledge get through with her, there won't be any fight left in her.* Curt sighed as he removed his hat to wipe his brow.

The group of outlaws and the two prisoners continued to ride slowly across the desert. Thirty minutes behind them, Bo and the two teamsters followed their trail.

Bonnie was tired and hurting. She wasn't use to riding, and her thighs were beginning to get raw from the constant rubbing. She tried to relieve the pressure on her legs, but the stirrups were too long. *It doesn't matter,* she thought. *If I can't find a way out of the mess, this little pain will be nothing. I wonder what Bo is doing? One of the men said he was trailing us.* She looked over at her father, then up at Dutch, who was in front of them. She turned back to her father and said in a low voice, "Dad, what are we going to do?"

Tom turned to her, "I don't know Bonnie. We just have to wait for an opportunity and take it, whatever little one it might be. We have to try to escape." He swallowed and added, "If we can't escape, I will be killed as soon as I show them the mine. And what they do to you, I don't want to think about." Tears came to his eyes and ran down his cheeks but he forced a smiled onto his face. "We'll get out of this, Bonnie." They didn't talk anymore, both lost in their own thoughts. The sun finally disappeared behind the mountains; soon the air would become cooler.

It was nearly dark when they came to the stage station. Sledge was the first to see it, and he halted the column of weary riders and waited as John rode up to him.

"How do you want to handle this, Boss?" Sledge asked as he turned to face John.

John looked toward the light coming from several lanterns in the distance. He could make out a large tent by the corrals. "We better get some water, then go on a while before we camp. I don't know what happened to Diablo, but I don't want to take any chances on that posse catching up to us." John looked over at Dutch, then turned back to Sledge. "You and Dutch go fill up the canteens at the spring. We'll wait for you down the trail a ways." John looked over at Tom. "Which way do we go from here?"

Tom looked at John and thought for a minute. "We go to Apache Springs. From there it's only a short way to the mine."

John turned back to Sledge and Dutch. "We'll go on to Apache springs tonight. It's only about four hours, and the moon will be out. Curt and I will head out with the O'Shays. You can catch up."

"Okay, boss," Sledge said. He looked at Dutch to see if he had gathered up all the canteens, then both of them headed for the station.

John watched them fade into the dark, then turned to Curt. "Grab their reins and we'll lead them the rest of the way. I don't want them trying to ride away from us in the dark." He waited as Curt gathered up their reins. Curt handed John the reins to Tom's horse, then, leading Bonnie's dun horse, he led the way toward the Bensen road.

CHAPTER 45

Bo pulled the canteen stopper and let the last little bit of tepid water slowly drain into his mouth. He licked his dry lips as he hung the canteen back on his saddle horn. They would need to find water soon. As he glanced back down at the tracks they had been following, a thought crossed his mind. He slowed down to let Bull ride up beside him. "Bull, where is the closest water?"

Bull studied a minute as he looked at the mountains in the distance. "Over there is the Tortilla Mountains, and that is Lemmon Peak. The only water close to here is at the stage station."

"If we cut straight across to the Benson Road and then go on to the stage stop, we might beat them to it."

"Yeah, if they stop there," Bull said with a blank look on his face. Suddenly, with a look of understanding, he added, "They're bound to need water too."

"What if they don't stop there?" Squeaky said. "We don't know which way they might turn."

Bo turned to Squeaky. "I know where they're going, Squeaky. They're going to O'Shay's mine. That's the only reason Tom O'Shay and Mary are still alive."

"You know where O'Shay's gold mine is?" Bull asked.

"Yeah, I've been there." Bo paused for a second, then added, "If we don't find them before they get there, it will be too late to save Tom O'Shay or Mary." Bo looked at Bull. "Which way is fastest to the station?"

Bulled looked toward the mountains in the distance again, then pointed toward a peak that rose above the rest. "If we go straight toward Lemmon Peak, we should hit the road. The station will be to our right down the road."

Bo glanced at the peak, then turned his horse toward it as he nudged him with his spurs. "Come on, men, let's go. We're wasting time."

The sun was nearly to the mountains when the three men reached the road. Bo slid his horse to a stop and waited as Bull and Squeaky caught up. "How far is the station, Bull?"

Bull examined the landscape and nodded toward a large boulder by the road. "There's Turtle Rock. We can be at the station in thirty minutes if we don't tire out the horses."

Bo hesitated. "Okay, we'll walk them for five minutes, then speed them up until we get there." The three men nudged their panting horses to start walking down the road toward the station. It was all Bo could do to resist the urge to gallop all the way to the station, so he counted to himself to keep his mind busy. By the time the five minutes were up, his horse was breathing regularly again, and with a glance at Bull, he nudged his horse into a slow lope. He would hold him there until he thought he needed to rest him again.

The gelding was strong, and after thirty minutes, with only one rest period, Bo saw the stage stop in the distance. Motioning for the others to follow him, he rode off the road into the concealing brush, then continued until he came to the hill overlooking the stage stop. Bull and Squeaky moved up beside him as he was studying the station. Smoke was rising from a stovepipe chimney sticking out of a large tent next to the burned-out stage station. The extra team of mules for the stagecoach was in the corral. Bo didn't see any extra horses tied to the hitching post, so he slowly made his way down the hill with Bull and Squeaky following close behind. As they rode past the small cemetery, Bo noticed, with a wave of sadness, the fresh graves of Bob Vail and his brother Shorty. When they reached the large tent, Bo motioned for Bull and Squeaky to go around to the back. He dismounted and tied his horse to the hitching rail.

"Hello, the tent," he called.

"We're in here. Be out in a second." A few minutes later a man stepped outside. He was a short, wiry man wearing overalls and carrying a shotgun in his right hand. "What can I do for you?"

Bo examined the man for a second and said, "I'm a deputy United States marshal. I'm on the trail of some men from Tucson. Has anybody been by here in the last few hours?"

"No, you're the first I've seen since the stage was here about noon," the man said. "What have the men done?"

About that time, Bull walked around to the front of the tent. "I don't see any more horses, Bo." He turned to the man. "Hello, Leon. Kelsi got any of those biscuits left?"

Leon stared at Bull for a second. "Bull, never thought I would see you on a posse. Don't you have a run tomorrow?"

"I did have, but all hell has broken out in Tucson. These men we're chasing are John Skinner and his bunch."

"You mean somebody has finally decided to do something about him and his owl hoots?" Leon asked. "It's about time."

"We'll tell you about it in a moment. First we need to get our horses out of sight," Bo said. He turned to Bull. "Take the horses and hide them in the brush. We'll lay low and wait here for them to show up."

Bull grabbed Bo's horse and led him to the back where the other horses were tied. He and Squeaky then moved them down into a gully where they couldn't be seen. When they returned, Bo was already in the tent. He was sitting at a table drinking coffee as Bull and Squeaky walked in. Over at a wood burning cook stove, a pretty young woman dressed in a long blue dress and a white apron was stirring a large pot of pinto beans.

"Hello, Kelsi," Bull said as he took off his hat. "My goodness, them beans smell good. I think I smell some of them biscuits, too."

Kelsi looked up at Bull. "I swear, Bull, every time I see you, you're hungry. Don't they let you eat anywhere else?"

"I eat at other places, but their food ain't nothing compared to your cooking."

"Ha!" Kelsi said. "I bet you tell that story everyplace you eat. Come on over here and get yourself a plate, and I'll fix you up." Bull and Squeaky both grabbed a plate then pushed up to the stove. Kelsi grinned as she dished a ladle full of beans on Squeaky's plate. She reached into a covered bowl to add two biscuits to the plate.

"Squeaky, why don't you take yours with you and hide in the storage shed?" Bo said. "They might be along any minute, and we want to take them by surprise. Bull, you wait in here, and I'll go out by the harness shed and wait."

"Yes, sir. Let me get a cup of that coffee and I'm on my way," Squeaky said. He grabbed a cup already filled from Kelsi as he headed toward the door.

"Both of you wait for me to make the first move," Bo said as he got up to follow Squeaky.

"Do you want some food, Mister Logan?" asked Kelsi. "I have plenty."

"No, just this coffee will do." Bo went out the door. Bull still stood there with his empty plate. He turned to Leon. "Leon, how come Kelsi served Squeaky first and I still haven't got any beans? You better watch her and Squeaky."

Leon grinned. "Yeah, I was wondering about that."

Kelsi looked at both of them, turned her nose up, and said, "You keep talking like that, and won't neither one of you get no supper. I'll feed it to the hogs."

"Aw, you know I was just kidding, Kelsi," Bull said.

Kelsi frowned, then broke out in a big grin. "I know, Bull." She dipped the ladle into the pot to get him some beans, then she laid three biscuits on his plate. As he went to the table, she turned and frowned at Leon.

"I was kidding, too," he said hurriedly.

The sun was barely above the mountains, Bo noticed, as he walked out the door and headed for the harness shed. It would be dark soon, and the night air would be cool. He thought about Mary; she was at the mercy of ruthless, depraved outlaws who thought nothing of killing and raping. Bo couldn't understand how some people could do the bad things that they did, but he knew that such people existed. His God-fearing family believed in living by the Ten Commandants, and they had instilled the same values in him. His conscience would bother him if he told a white lie—but if they harmed Mary, he would have no problem in avenging her.

When Bo reached the shed, he found an old bench he could sit on where he could look out the partly open door. He waited as the sun slowly sank into the mountains. A full moon slowly rose above horizon from the east and cast a pale light over the desert. Leon came out of the tent carrying several lanterns. He hung them on poles that ran from the tents to the corrals, then he went back inside the tent. Bo wondered if he was expecting a stagecoach this late or if he was providing more light for his sake.

Fifteen minutes passed, and Bo was wishing he had his coat. Another ten minutes passed, and Bo was feeling around the shed for a horse blanket. Finally he heard a horse coming. He peered into the darkness where the sound came from, hoping to see Mary. He felt for his Colt and tried to remember if he had checked the chamber for bullets.

Suddenly Bo tensed as a horse and rider appeared in the light. It was Sledge! Bo remembered the big man at the café one night when Ronald had pointed him out and said that Sledge worked for Skinner. A second rider appeared carrying a bunch of canteens. Bo strained his eyes, looking for the next rider, but none appeared.

Sledge looked toward the tent and called out. "Hello, inside, we want to get some water." He crawled down from his horse without waiting for an answer. Looking at the other man, he motioned toward the spring that was between the tent and the corral. Sledge turned back to the tent as Leon walked out the door. Leon was carrying his shotgun pointed toward the ground. Bull walked out behind him, his pistol holstered.

"What are you doing here, Bull?" Sledge asked. "I don't see your stagecoach."

"I'm just passing through. Thought I might go prospecting for gold," Bull said. "You and Dutch sure got a lot of canteens. You going across the desert?"

"It ain't none of your business Bull," Sledge said irritably.

Bo watched as Dutch rode his horse to the spring and dismounted. Dutch nervously looked around as he gathered the canteens off his horse and started filling them from a pipe that ran out of the spring. Bo would depend on Squeaky to take care of him. Bo stepped out of the shed, pulling his Colt. Sledge had his back to him, looking at Leon and Bull.

"Sledge, you're under arrest. Drop your gun," Bo said.

Sledge whirled, pulling his pistol. BOOM! Bo fired, but Sledge had jumped to the side as he whirled, and Bo just grazed him. BOOM! Sledge fired, and Bo felt a blow to his left side. The jolt spun him around for a half turn. BOOM! Bo managed to fire again. He saw Sledge jerk, but he didn't go down. Sledge raised his pistol again. BOOM! Bo saw fire erupt from the barrel. He felt a blow to his head, but only for a split second. Then everything went black.

When the shooting started, Dutch dropped the canteens and grabbed for his pistol. He was drawing a bead on Bo when he felt a blow to his side. He turned; Squeaky was coming toward him. He raised his gun, but before he could pull the trigger, another blow hit him and knocked him down. His life flashed before his eyes, then he gasped and lay still.

Sledge's horse was between Leon and Sledge when Bo called from the shed. As soon as the shooting started, Leon began to move to his right, with Bull right behind him. As he moved into a clear view of the action, he saw Bo go down. He saw Sledge pull back his hammer for another shot.

"KABOOM!"

Leon had quickly aimed and fired both barrels of his greener. Sledge's arm exploded from his body as the double load of buckshot tore through his arm and blew out half his ribs. He went to the ground still conscious but helpless. He slowly tilted his head down and lowered his eyes to look at his torn-open chest. He watched as his heart faithfully pumped his blood out of a torn artery onto the ground.

Leon and Bull ran over to him, with Kelsi following close behind. They stared as the blood kept pouring out of Sledge's artery. Finally the blood slowed to a thin stream and then stopped. Sledge's head relaxed, his eyes glazed over, and he was dead.

Kelsi watched for another second, then turned her eyes to look for Bo. He was lying on the ground motionless with Squeaky standing over him. Kelsi ran over to where he was lying. Squeaky turned to her with a sad look on his face, "I think he's dead."

CHAPTER 46

John paused when he heard the gunshots. He looked back in the direction of the stage station, waiting for more, but the night had turned silent once again. John wondered if a posse had been waiting for them at the station. He didn't worry when he heard the pistol shots. He thought it was Sledge getting rid of witnesses, but when he heard the boom of the shotgun and then no more gunfire, he was pretty sure it wasn't Sledge or Dutch who had done the firing. He turned to Curt, who had also halted when the shots rang out. "I think someone was waiting for them. Maybe a posse."

"You could be right," Curt said. "Let's put some miles between us and that station. A posse can't trail us in the dark, but they will be hot on our tail by sunup."

"They can follow our trail on this road by lantern light," John said. "We need to hurry and get to the cutoff. It'll be harder for 'em to follow our tracks there." John jerked his horse around as he spurred him hard, jerking on the reins of Tom's horse as he turned. Both horses leaped into a gallop down the dusty road, Curt leading Bonnie's horse close behind them. John let the horses run hard for a few minutes but eased them into a slower gait as his panic wore off and his common sense took over. A windblown horse would be useless. They maintained the slower pace until they came to the Apache Springs cutoff, where John motioned for Curt to move up beside him. "We need to stay on the road for another quarter mile, then we'll cut across the desert to the Apache Springs trail. That way, if they are tracking us tonight, it will make us harder to track. Hopefully they will think we are still headed east."

Curt nodded his head. "Good idea, John." He paused for a second. "If we ride on the edge of the road or beside it in the grass, we will be harder to track, too. In the dark they might lose our trail."

John didn't answer verbally but moved his horse and Tom's to the side of the road. Curt followed, leading Bonnie's horse behind him. They rode for a several minutes in this manner until John, seeing an opening in the brush, slowed his horse to a walk and turned him into the opening. He looked back to make sure Curt was following, then led the procession through the brush and cacti. He headed north for a while, then turned to the northwest. Thirty minutes later, they intersected the Apache Springs trail.

Tom's spirits had risen when he heard the shots at the stage station. Maybe it was a posse and soon they would be free. His hope slowly faded, though, when John continued to lead them down the road and no posse came whooping and firing their guns behind them. The hard galloping hadn't helped, either. Tom wasn't a much of a horseman, and the fast ride had increased the agony in his legs and back. He was miserable in body and in spirit, and he needed to find a way to end it one way or another. He finally made up his mind: the next time he was close enough to John, he would jump him. Maybe in the confusion, Bonnie would have a chance to get away from Curt and hide until the posse could find her. Tom watched and waited, looking for the right moment, but so far he was always behind John and couldn't try anything. He needed to get closer. He glanced back at Bonnie, and his heart cringed as the moonlight revealed her beautiful face scratched and bleeding from the grueling ride through thorny trees. Her clothes were torn, and her blonde hair was damp and dirty as it hung from under her hat. She looked at him with desperate and teary eyes, and suddenly he realized that by in the morning they would be at the mine. He would be killed, but Bonnie would have to go through a living hell worse than death.

"I have to give her a chance," he whispered to himself. "She's had it so rough she deserves some happiness." With new resolve Tom kicked his horse, trying to get closer to John, but Curt was beside him, and because the trail was narrow, he couldn't get around him. Impatiently Tom waited for his chance, knowing that they were getting closer to the mine and running out of time.

Suddenly, out of the blue, it came when John stopped his horse at the base of a small hill and looked over at Curt. "We'll rest a few minutes here."

"Why are we stopping, John? They might be right behind us." Curt said as he turned and looked back along the trail.

"I want to talk to O'Shay for a minute. We're getting close to Apache Springs." John wheeled his horse around so he could face Tom. Curt followed, but when he turned, he let the reins to Bonnie's horse drop. Tom pulled his right foot out of the stirrup, then, rising on his left leg, he brought his right knee up on the horse's neck and launched himself at John.

"Ride, Bonnie, go!" he shouted as he crashed into John and they both fell to the ground.

Bonnie hesitated for a second as her mind tried to digest what was going on. She saw her father jump John and she heard his yell to her, but she wasn't sure what she should do. She didn't want to leave her father, but she had no choice if she wanted a chance to save herself and maybe a slim chance to find help. She reached down to grasp the reins with her tied hands, but as she brought them up she hesitated, then turned to watch the struggling men. John and Tom were rolling on the ground flailing at each other with their fists. Curt had jumped off his horse and was pointing his pistol at the two men but was seemingly undecided on what to do. Suddenly Tom rolled on top of John and with an anguished yell grabbed a rock with his still-tied hands, raised it above his head, and smashed it into John's face. Bonnie watched in horror as Curt pointed his pistol at Tom. "BOOM!" the sound of the shot filled the night, then it was quiet. Time seemed to stand still as Bonnie saw her father slump on top of John, the blood seeping from his back. She knew he was dead. Curt was standing over him, smoke coming from his pistol.

"No," Bonnie yelled as she kicked the dun horse, then reined him toward Curt. When Curt heard her yell, he hastily wheeled. But Bonnie's horse plowed into him before he could complete his turn, knocking him to the ground and the gun from his hand. Bonnie took one last look at her father, then quickly turned the horse toward the trail as she kicked his ribs.

Curt, cussing, jumped up from the ground. "Come back here, you bitch," he yelled as he looked for his pistol. When he saw it lying beside him he quickly picked it up and shot at the fleeing girl but she topped the hill and never wavered; soon she was out of sight down the trail. "I'll find you, bitch, and when I do, you ain't going to like it." Curt angrily shoved his gun into his holster then turned to see about his brother. He rolled Tom off of the top of John then froze as he stared at the brains hanging out of John's head. Seconds passed, then, suddenly, he cussed and kicked Tom's motionless and bloody body. "You sorry son of a bitching Irish trash."

Curt hesitated for a second, then ran to John's horse to grab the saddlebags. He slung them over his own horse, mounted and spurred the animal, turning him up the trail in the direction that Bonnie had taken. He would surly catch her, he thought, and when he did, he would make her pay for what had happened. He would use her in every way possible until he was tired of her. Then he would skin her.

CHAPTER 47

Tears streamed from Bonnie's eyes as she thought of her father lying back there on the ground. She felt guilty leaving him, but she knew if she had stayed, she would be the next to die. She kicked the horse again as she felt him begin to slow down, and he answered with a new burst of speed. The dun horse followed the trail faithfully, and when he came to a place where the trail turned sharply to the left to avoid a boulder, he turned, but Bonnie, not being a good rider, fell. Her head slammed against the ground hard, and she was stunned.

Minutes passed until she slowly opened her eyes. At first she didn't know where she was, but quickly the horror of the last two days rushed into her mind and panic gripped her. She was struggling to get up when a voice sent a chill up her spine. She had been out too long, and Curt was standing over her, his yellowed teeth shining in the moonlight as he grinned. Slowly he pulled off his gun belt and laid it on a rock. Bonnie began scooting herself away from him but was stopped when he dropped to his knees and grabbed her leg. He struck her in the face with his fist. Stars flashed in front of her eyes, and she was helpless as he grabbed her skirt and jerked it off of her. He pitched it to the side, then reached for the top of her bloomers. He laughed as he roughly ripped them from her body and threw them to the side. Curt roughly forced her legs apart, then moved himself between them. He slowly unbuttoned his pants and pushed them down to his knees. He leaned forward just as Bonnie came to her senses. She raised her head to see what he was doing and realized what was about to happen. Quickly she raised her leather-bound hands to push at him.

"No, please, don't do this," she begged.

Curt laughed. "You bitch, you better enjoy this because it is going to get worse." He grabbed her arms and pushed them up above her head. Bonnie struggled to push back, knowing she was delaying her rape as long as she kept his hands busy. Curt laughed, then slapped her face as he held both her arms with his left hand. Bonnie was frantic with fear, and a vision of Bart Mastard trying to rape her flashed into her mind.

Slowly she quit struggling and pulled her hands back over her head. She closed her eyes.

"What? No more fight?" He slapped her face again. "Come on, this is too easy." He grinned as he reached down with both his hands and prepared to penetrate her. "This will get you fighting again."

Suddenly Bonnie's eyes flashed open as she rose up from her waist as far as she could while jabbing her still-tied hands toward him. A grin began to appear on his face as he turned his eyes toward her, but it changed to a frown as her hands struck his face.

Curt screamed and fell back away from Bonnie. He grabbed for his eye and screamed again as he touched the hat pin sticking from the bleeding orb. He yelled, "You put out my eye." Suddenly fear was replaced by a rage that overcame his pain and he looked around for his gun. He saw it with his good eye then picked it up but as he turned back to Bonnie, he felt his body grow weaker. He saw Bonnie had untied her hands and was slowly trying to get to her feet so he swung the pistol at her head. The blow snapped her head back and she slumped back to the ground. Curt cocked his pistol as he pointed it toward her. He tried to pull the trigger but his finger wouldn't move. Slowly the damage in his brain caused his body to shut down and he collapsed to the ground, his lifeless eyes staring up at the moon.

Bonnie slowly got to her feet and looked around. Her head felt as if it were full of cobwebs; her only clear thought was she had to get away. The dun horse, the reins still looped over the saddle horn, walked up to her. She crawled into the saddle and weakly kicked his sides.

The horse began to move down the trail, heading in the direction they had been going. He traveled until he got to Apache Springs, then stopped at the water. The rider, slumped forward on his back, was lifeless. After the dun horse drank, he stood there waiting patiently for his rider to give him directions, but none came.

After several minutes of waiting, Dunce became hungry. He remembered where there was some nice, green grass, so he turned from the spring and carefully went up the steep trail that led to the ledge above. When he reached the top, he made his way through the rocks to the cave. The brush blocking the entrance stopped him only for a few minutes as he pushed his head through it and plowed his way through to the cave. His rider never stirred as he made his way through the dark cave.

When he entered the valley, Dunce hesitated as he detected the scent of a stranger in the valley, but it was old and not worth worrying about. He grazed for a few minutes on the scraggly grass by the cave entrance, then moved down the old trail into the valley floor, grazing as he walked. Soon he came to the creek bank, where he grazed some more on the thick, green grass growing there. The rider on his back hadn't moved all through his journey, but now he could feel her stir. He waited for her to dismount but instead she fell from the saddle and lay still. Dunce lowered his head and sniffed her. He sensed that she was alive. He would stay with her through the night.

CHAPTER 48

*B*o *wanted to see where the sounds were coming from, but he couldn't move. Shouting and running horses, a woman's voice—but what was she saying? Pain filled his body. Something grabbed him, then he was floating in the air. He was lying on something hard, and it was bouncing him. He thought it would never end. Then more shouting, and he was floating again. The pain was bearable now. Someone was calling him, but he didn't know where to look. His mother came to him.*

"Wake up, Bo. You have works to do." Bo couldn't remember what he needed to do. He wanted to get up, but he couldn't move.

Bo slowly opened his eyes. He was lying on a bed, covered with a white sheet and a fancy handmade quilt. The bed was in a small, white painted room, but he couldn't remember how he got there. A blue washbowl and matching pitcher sat on a small table next to a wall, and hanging above it was a painting of an Indian holding a spear. Through the open window next to his bed he could see purple mountains, miles away across the desert. The tart smell of disinfectant tickled his nose. His mouth felt as if it were full of cotton, and his lips were cracked and dry. He craved a drink of water, but when he pushed the covers down and tried to sit up, pain pulsed through his shoulder and his head whirled with dizziness.

As he lay there, he tried to remember how he had ended up in this bed, and gradually it came back to him. He had been on the desert looking for Mary. Suddenly, like a burst dam, it all came flooding back into his memory. The chase, the stage station, the shootout with Sledge; he couldn't remember what had happened after that. He looked down at his body. A bandage covered his upper chest and left shoulder. He tried to move his left arm, but pain shot across his shoulder again. He felt his head with his right hand and discovered more bandages. Bo lay there for a few more minutes, but still feeling thirsty, he slowly tried to sit up again. The pain and the dizziness weren't too bad this time, and he gradually moved himself into a sitting position. He sat there resting for a moment, then, with his right hand, held up the covers while he swung his legs out of the bed. He sat there for a few minutes, then carefully stood up. He grabbed the headboard to steady himself as the dizziness returned, but slowly his head cleared enough so he could make his way over to the washstand. He filled a glass with water and took a sip. He swirled the water in his mouth and spit it into the bowl. The rest he drank. Feeling weak from his exertions, he eased back over to the bed and lay down. He closed his eyes, and soon he was asleep again.

Bo awoke with a start when he heard a rooster crowing. He had slept late, and Pa would be mad. Hastily he opened his eyes and started to get out of bed. Pain shot through his shoulder, and he sank back to the soft bed. *This wasn't his bed.* Slowly the memory of the shootout at the stage station and the foggy memory of waking up with a painful shoulder came back to him. *Where am I?*

His question was soon answered when a man wearing glasses entered the room. He was a stranger to Bo, but the man following him he did know; it was United States Marshal Rex Roberts.

"I see you finally woke up," the first man said. He was a middle-aged man with a smooth face and dark hair. He was wearing a white coat and had one of those newfangled things that doctors listened to people's heart with hanging around his neck. "I'm Doctor Holleman. How are you feeling, Mister Logan?"

"I've felt better. My shoulder hurts, and I get dizzy every time I stand up." Anxiously Bo cut his eyes to Rex. "Marshal, did you find Mary?"

"The marshal can fill you in later," the doctor said. "Right now I need to look at these wounds. Did you say you tried to stand up?"

"Yeah, Doc, my mouth felt like it was full of cotton, so I got up to get a drink of water. I was only dizzy for a few minutes, and then it passed."

"Hum, that's a good sign," Doctor Holleman said as he started undoing the bandage on Bo's head. "I'm going to change these bandages now. You can talk to the marshal now if you feel like it."

Bo turned his eyes back to Rex.

The marshal had a sad look on his face. "We didn't find her, Bo. John and most of his gang are dead, but we don't know what happened to Mary."

Bo was silent for a minute, and then he said, "Tell me everything that happened, Rex."

"When we got to the station, Sledge and Dutch were dead, and you were shot. At first they thought you were dead, too, but Kelsi, the stationmaster's wife, took care of you. It so happens she had some nurse training back East, and she knew just what to do. She probably saved you life." Rex paused for a second, then continued. "Well, anyway, we followed their tracks and found John Skinner with his head crushed in. It looked like Tom O'Shay jumped him and somehow managed to hit him with a rock. O'Shay was all shot up, but he's still alive. He's in the other room, but Doc doesn't know if he will make it or not."

"What about Mary?" Bo asked.

"I'm getting to it, Bo, but I need to tell you the whole story," Rex said. "We went a little farther and found Curt dead." He paused for a second, swallowed, and said, "Apparently Curt was trying to rape Mary. We found her clothes scattered around the ground. Somehow Mary stuck her hat pin into Curt's eye and penetrated his brain."

"He died a slow and painful death," said Doctor Holleman. "It would have taken him several minutes to die; he would have had time to do something to the girl."

Rex slowly shook his head, "We didn't find hide nor hair of Mary. Just her tore up clothes scattered around the small clearing."

"That don't make sense," Bo said. "Couldn't you track her?"

"About the time we found Curt, one of those rare rainstorms come through and washed out any tracks. We searched for two days, but we couldn't find her."

"We got to keep looking, Sage," Bo said. "She's got to be there somewhere." Bo turned to the doctor. "Hurry up, Doc. I got to get dressed and go look for her."

"You're not able to go anywhere for the next few days, and probably not then. You got to give this shoulder time to heal."

Bo turned to Rex, tears in his eyes. "You'll go with me, won't you Marshal?"

Rex walked over to Bo and grabbed his right hand. "Bo, you been out for nearly a week. Curt was slow in dying, and he had his gun in his hand. People think Curt shot her and then some animal carried her off. Others think that Indians might have found her." Rex paused as he looked in Bo's eyes. "She was hurt and she was naked; she couldn't have gone far. We had fifty people out there covering every foot, for miles in every direction. She wasn't there."

Bo closed his eyes. He couldn't believe she was dead. Somehow he knew she was still alive. He would try to rest now, but as soon as he could ride, he would look for her.

CHAPTER 49

Bonnie and Bo were sitting under a shade tree by the lake watching the children play with their pond boats. She smiled at Bo, then turned to look at a man who had walked up to her. The man grinned; there was a hat pin sticking out of his eye. She turned to Bo, but he was gone. She began to run, but suddenly she was in the desert, and the man was chasing her. He was right behind her, and she could feel his hot breath on her neck.

Bonnie woke up to the smell of fresh green grass and a bitter taste in her mouth. She was lying on her stomach with her eyes closed. She tried to remember why her body was hurting. Her memory refused to answer. Slowly she opened her eyes to see a wall of tall grass all around her. She could hear a brook gurgling somewhere close; suddenly she felt thirsty. She began pushing herself up into a sitting position but suddenly stopped as she felt something warm blowing on her neck. She dropped back to the ground, then rolled on her back, a scream ready to burst from her mouth. A face framed in sunlight hovered just above her, his mouth almost touching hers. Bonnie screamed but cut it short when she realized it was just a horse. He raised his head and backed away when Bonnie screamed, causing the sun to glare in her eyes. Quickly she turned her eyes away from the bright sunlight and discovered she was in a meadow full of green grass and surrounded by tall evergreen trees. A small clear stream ran just a few feet from her, the water gurgling as it rushed over multicolored rocks. The sky was a magnificent blue, peppered with a few cotton puff clouds. Puzzled, Bonnie gazed around the meadow, then cut her eyes to the mountains that bordered the small valley. *This place is beautiful. Am I in a park?*

Suddenly a light breeze blew through the meadow, and she felt a chill on her body. Bonnie looked at herself and realized she was almost naked. She had a blouse on and leather shoes, but nothing else. Bonnie's first thought was to look for her clothes, so with her muscles protesting, she slowly rose to her feet. At first her mind was spinning and she had to grab hold of a small tree to keep from falling, but after a few minutes her head cleared, and she slowly began to look around the meadow for her missing clothes. Not seeing them, she slowly walked over to the dun-colored horse.

"Hello, horse. I wonder what your name is," she said as she reached out to pet him. "Did I ride you to this beautiful place?"

The horse's only response was to nuzzle her hand when she rubbed his nose. He was ready for someone to take off his saddle and bridle so he could roll in the grass.

Bonnie slowly examined him, still wondering if she had been riding the horse. The reins were wrapped around the saddle horn; saddlebags and a bedroll were tied behind the saddle. Slowly Bonnie reached for the reins, undid them, and led the horse over to a small tree, where she tied him up.

"I don't want you to wander off, horse. You might be the only way out of this valley." With the horse secured, Bonnie's thoughts returned to covering herself. Remembering the bedroll behind the saddle, she untied the rolled-up blanket from the saddle, then, holding it up to her bosom, she let it unroll. Some men's clothing, along with a slicker, fell out, but Bonnie ignored them as she examined the blanket. The old, blue army blanket had a few holes in it, but she wrapped it around her waist and tucked it back under it to hold it in place.

Bonnie felt relieved now that her nakedness was taken care of, but now she was hungry. Spying the saddlebags, she pulled them from the saddle and opened them. Bonnie almost smiled as she pulled out a cloth-wrapped bundle. Quickly she opened it; a dozen tortillas, filled with beans, greeted her eyes. Bonnie held one of the dried-out tacos to her nose and sniffed. It smelled a little stale, but she didn't detect the putrid smell of decay. She cautiously bit into it; it was little tough but tasted good. Bonnie quickly downed two more of the tacos, washing them down with water from the small stream.

Her hunger sated, she paused to study her surroundings. She had never seen trees and grass like this in Arizona. It reminded her of Central Park in New York City. *Where am I? My name is Bonnie and I have a café in Tucson, but I don't know how I got here.* Bonnie raised her eyes to the tree-covered mountains that surrounded the valley. She made a slow circle, looking for an opening through the mountains, but to no avail. She turned her eyes back to the meadow. A trail wound through the tall trees to her left but stopped at the small stream.

Bonnie decided to follow the trail to her right, away from the stream, to see where it would take her. She gathered up the things that had fallen out of the bedroll, then led the horse up the trail away from the stream. She had only traveled a few yards when she spied a small log cabin nestled back in the trees. Bonnie stopped and studied the cabin for a few minutes, then cautiously made her way to it. One of the first things she noticed when she got closer was a hand-carved sign over the door that read, **Rainbow's end.** *That's curious; I wonder if that means there is a pot of gold here?*

Bonnie tied Dunce to a small bush, then went to the door and knocked. "Is anybody home?" A minute passed, and she knocked again. "Hello, is anybody here?" Slowly she pushed against the door. It wouldn't move. Frustrated, she walked around the cabin, looking for a way in. She found only two windows, but they were shuttered and fastened from the inside. As she completed the circle of the cabin and was at the door again, she wondered if she could break in the door. She scrutinized it closer and noticed a leather string coming out of a hole in the middle of the door. She reached for it and slowly pulled it through the hole. The string had something tied to it that moved. She continued pulling, and suddenly the door swung open.

Bonnie stared into a large room that took up the whole cabin. She cast her eyes about, looking for whoever lived here, but the room was empty, so Bonnie cautiously walked inside a few feet. A large fireplace set up for cooking took up half of the back wall. Shelves took up the rest. There was a rough-made table and two chairs in the middle of the cabin, and on one side wall was a bunk. A stack of firewood took up one corner, and a cupboard was on the other side wall. Bonnie walked over to the table, then ran her finger across the top. Just a little dust covered her fingertip. She decided she needed more light, so she went to the window next to the bunk and opened the shutters. Glancing at the shelves, she noticed they were neat and orderly.

"No one has been here for a while," she muttered to herself as she opened the shutters on the other window. Bonnie examined the blankets that were on the bunk, and seeing they were a little dusty, she carried them outside to shake the dust from them.

The horse, still tied in front of the cabin, nickered when he saw Bonnie. She spread the bedclothes on the ground after she shook them, then went over to him and removed his saddle. She began to remove his bridle, but hesitated for a second, wondering if she would be able to catch him again. He impatiently moved his head closer to her hands, and she smiled as she unbuckled the bridle and pulled the bit out of his mouth.

"Go on, horse, and eat," she said as she rubbed his neck. "Just be here if I need you." Bonnie gathered up the tack and went back to the cabin, where she laid the saddle and bridle on the floor by the door. Her head had begun to hurt again, so she went back outside to retrieve the blankets. She put them back on the bunk and lay down; she would rest for just a little while.

It was night when Bonnie opened her eyes again. The croaking from what seemed like a thousand frogs filtered through the open window. An owl hooted from a nearby tree. She lay still for a second, wondering what was making the sounds, but then she remembered she wasn't in her bed at the café. She remembered waking up in the meadow and finding the horse and the cabin, but she still didn't remember how she had gotten to the valley. Bonnie propped herself up on her elbow as she glanced around the room. Moonlight coming through the open windows cast just enough light for her to make out the outlines of a few of the bigger objects in the cabin. She got up from the bunk, wrapped herself in the blanket, then made her way over to the table, where she remembered a lantern was sitting. Luckily there was a tin box of lucifer matches on the table. When she lit the lantern with one of them and the room became brighter, she noticed a leather strap with a hook on it hanging from the ceiling. She hung the lantern on it, then went to the shutters to close them.

The night air had made the cabin cold, so she grabbed firewood from the pile in the corner to build a fire in the fireplace. Soon a roaring fire was warming the room, and the heat on her bare skin reminded her that she needed some clothes. Searching through the cabin, she found a worn-out pair of long johns on a shelf along with a small sewing box containing a pack of needles and a few rolls of thread. After Bonnie examined the long johns, she decided to use just the bottom half of the underwear, so she cut them off at the waist. She darned the small holes and patched the larger ones with pieces from the unused top half. When she was finished with the mending, she slipped them on. The fit was okay, but the top was ragged, so she pulled them back off. Folding about an inch of the waist over a strip of leather she had found, she hemmed it. Pleased with her work, she slipped them back on, then tied the two ends of the leather strip together to keep them from slipping down.

By this time she was tired and a little bit hungry again, so she warmed up one of the tacos and quickly finished it off. She was tempted to eat another one, but remembering what little food she had, she decided to wait until morning to eat another one. Tired but not sleepy, Bonnie went back to sewing. She tried on the pants she had found in the bedroll. They were a little big on her, but with the needle and thread, she soon altered them to fit. She slipped the pants on, and for the first time since she woke up in the valley, she felt fully dressed.

Bonnie was feeling weak again and she stared into the fire for a while, trying to remember what had happened to her. She had been waiting for Bo to come back, and she had been talking to Lupe, but that was the last thing she remembered. She sat and tried to remember until the fire was nothing but glowing coals. Finally she got up, blew out the lantern, and crawled back into the bunk.

Bonnie was sitting by the lake with Bo watching the children play with their pond boats. Someone called her name, and she turned to see who it was. She saw her father across the lake waving to her. She stood up, then walked toward him. She called to him and waved, but he walked away. Bo was beside her now, and he put his arm around her. They watched as her father walked away.

Bonnie woke and opened her eyes. She was in a strange little bed. The room was dark, but she knew this wasn't her room at the café. Slowly memories flowed into her mind as she sat on the side of the bunk. She remembered that she was in a beautiful valley and she had found this cabin. Suddenly a vision of her father, falling with blood coming from his back, rushed into her mind. It all came back now: the sheriff's treachery and finding her father, only to lose him again when Curt shot him. She remembered Curt catching her and her struggle to get away. She remembered the hat pin sticking in his eye and his hitting her, but after that, nothing. She went through her memories again, trying to sort them out. Over and over she relived the horror of her ordeal through her memories, but it always ended the same. She couldn't remember anything from the time Curt hit her until she woke up in the meadow. *I was in the desert, and now I am in the mountains. I couldn't have gone far. Bo will be looking for me. But what if Bo is dead, too? What if no one can find me? I have a horse. I will have to find my own way back to Tucson.*

Bonnie threw back the blanket and got out of the bunk. Her mouth was dry and she was thirsty, but first she lit the lantern and restarted the fire. She saw a wooden bucket by the door, grabbed it, and started walking toward the creek. The sun was already up, warming the valley. Bonnie was pleased when she saw the dun horse grazing next to the cabin. He followed her to the creek and got his own morning drink. He watched her as she rinsed the bucket out and filled it half full so she could drink from it. When her thirst was relieved, she refilled the bucket nearly to the top before she headed back toward the cabin. The horse followed her back all the way to the door, then, when she left him outside, he shook his head, snorted, and began grazing on the grass by the cabin.

In the cabin, Bonnie warmed up two of the tacos and ate them as she searched to see what kind of supplies she could find. She found only a little moldy flour, few cans of beans, and some deer jerky hanging from the rafters. She wouldn't go hungry for a while, and hopefully Bo would find her before she ran out of food.

Feeling a little better, Bonnie walked outside to explore the area around the cabin. She found the small corral and the meat drying racks behind the cabin. She walked back to the stream and looked around the meadow again. Eventually, finding nothing to even suggest how she had gotten to the valley, Bonnie went back to the cabin so she could lie down on the bunk. She was tired, and her head was hurting again.

Bonnie slept the rest of the day, then after getting herself something to eat, she went back to sleep. The next morning she decided to explore some more. This time she went farther from the cabin, but still she could find no answers. Several days passed, and Bonnie began to ride the horse when she explored. She rode completely around the valley several times, looking for a way out, but each time when she came to the cave she dismissed it as a way out. She finally looked in it one day; even walked into it a few yards, but bats began to fly around her head, and she hysterically ran for the entrance.

She finally came across the sluice box by the small stream. After searching for a few hours, she found the mine. She thought the vein of white quartz might have gold in it, but she didn't know anything about mining, so she left it as she found it. It would be a few days later when she found out for sure what had come out of the mine.

One evening as she was eating fried deer jerky, she decided to move the bunk closer to the fireplace so she could move the table closer to a window. She moved the bunk first, but when she went back to move the rocks, she was surprised to find the holes under them. She was very excited when she found the sacks of gold, but when she found the little wooden box, she hurried over to the table to open it. She pulled out the picture first, but when she looked at it she didn't recognize the young girl, so she began to read one of the letters.

My dearest father,

I hope this letter finds you well. I have finally settled down to my studies here, but I still miss you very much. I pray for you every day. I wish I could have gone out west, with you, Father. I still don't understand why you had to go and leave me at the girl's school. I have made some friends here, and I like most of the teachers, but I am afraid of Professor Dungerhill. He looks at me in a scary way.

Suddenly Bonnie's heart fluttered as she realized that she had written this letter. This was her father's cabin. This valley was his valley. The mine was his mine.

CHAPTER 50

A cavalry troop mounted on bay horses passed in front of Bo as he sat watching from the front porch of the small hospital. The blue-clad troops continued down the street and on into the main part of Tucson, the chalky dust slowly settling back to the road behind them. Farther down the street, people on the boardwalks cheered as the stiff-backed troopers passed by them. The renegade Apache Geronimo was off the reservation again, and the people were scared. It made them feel safer when the army brought in more troops to hunt the renegade down.

But Bo's mind wasn't on the soldiers; he was thinking of Mary. He rubbed his shoulder again, hoping the pain had mysteriously gone away since the last time he had rubbed it ten minutes ago. It was still a little sore to the touch, but when he tried to move it, the pain was worse. Bo wondered if Mary was hurt and in pain or if she was even still alive. He wanted to believe she was out there, somewhere, wandering the desert. Maybe someone had found her and was taking care of her. Bo wanted to go look for her, but every time he thought he was ready to leave the hospital, his wounds and the doctor wouldn't let him go. His head wound was nearly mended and his dizzy spells had finally disappeared, but his shoulder was slow to mend. It had been ten days since the day he had woken up in Doctor Holleman's hospital, and every day he grieved because he couldn't rush out and look for her. Rex had listened to his pleas and had kept people looking for Mary long after everyone else had given up hope. Finally Bo hired one of the best trackers in the territory to go out to the desert and look for her, but the man hadn't been able to find a trace of her, either. Bo sighed as he thought that maybe he should accept the fact that she was gone. He looked at his watch to see if it was time for him to see the doctor. He rose as he stuck his watch back in his pocket, then walked back into the hospital. Doctor Holleman was sitting at his desk looking over some papers but looked up when he heard Bo walk in.

"What do you think, Doc?" Bo asked. "Are you ready to release me?"

"Bo, I think your shoulder has healed enough, but don't overdo it. The simple rule is, if it hurts to do it, don't do it."

"Well, thanks, Doc. I appreciate all you've done." Bo pulled out a roll of brownbacks. "If you let me know how much I owe you, I'll pay you right now."

Doctor Holliman looked down at the papers on his desk. "I was just figuring up your bill earlier." He picked up one of the papers. "Your bill comes to fifty-one dollars. That includes changing the bandages for the next few weeks. It should be healed completely by then."

Bo shifted the roll to his left hand so he could count the money. "Here, Doc, this is for my bill. Now how much is Tom's going to be?"

Doctor Holliman took Bo's money, then looked at another bill. "Right now his bill is sixty dollars. I believe he's going to make it now, but he's going to be in here for a long time healing."

Bo peeled off another bill from his roll. "Here's a hundred dollars, Doc. If it gets to be more than that, let me know." Bo paused after the doctor took the money, then added, "Doc, I know you will do your best, but if there is anything this man needs, do it. The cost doesn't matter."

"I'll keep that in mind, Bo."

"When do you want me to come back?"

"I need to look at it every few days Bo. Just whenever you have time."

"Okay, Doc, I'll be seeing you in a few days. I'm going to get a room at the hotel." Bo picked up his bag and left the hospital. He had mixed emotions as he walked along the boardwalk toward the hotel. He was glad to be out of the hospital, but he was frustrated by his helplessness in finding Mary. Suddenly Bo realized he was in front of the Shamrock Café. He felt a lump in his throat as he paused to look in the window. He could see Juan, busy waiting on customers, and Lupe behind the counter. Bo wanted to cry as he thought of the time he had spent with Mary in the café, but he held it back as he walked on down the street toward the hotel. Maybe he would come back later and eat lunch there.

The clerk was at the counter reading the newspaper when Bo walked into the hotel. "I need a room for a while. How much by the week?" Bo asked.

The clerk wiped his mouth. "Five dollars a week, sir. I have one facing the street, or if you want one in the back, I have one available."

"Give me one facing the street," Bo said as he peeled off a bill from his roll. Here's two weeks in advance."

"Yes, sir. If you will just sign the register, please." He turned to grab a key while Bo signed his name. "You will be in twenty-one, sir, two doors down from the stairs."

Bo was still feeling downhearted as he went up the stairs to his room. He tossed his bag on a dressing table, pulled out his things, and began putting them in their proper places. Bo pondered for a second when he pulled out his gun belt and pistol, then carefully strapped it on his hip. He pulled the pistol from the holster to test the action. He half-cocked it, then checked his bullets as he spun the cylinder. Two bullets had been fired, so he replaced them with ones from his belt. He turned the cylinder and released the hammer to rest on an empty chamber. Holstering his pistol, he tried fast drawing it a few times to test his right arm. He felt a little pain in his wounded shoulder, but not enough to slow him down.

When Bo finished his unpacking, he sat down in a chair to rest. He stared out the window, but the view of the street could have been miles away because he was only seeing Mary. His couldn't get her out of his mind. He loved her, and he felt lost without her. He sat and thought about her for a long time, but finally feeling that he needed to be doing something else, he left his room, walked down the stairs, and went out to the street. Bo hadn't made up his mind where he was going yet; he just wanted to walk around a bit after being cooped up in that hospital for so long. He paused on the boardwalk and looked around, not sure yet which way he wanted to go. Slowly Bo realized that he wanted to go to the Shamrock, not because he was hungry but because he wanted to be where he had met Mary. He wanted to be where he remembered her working and living. Bo sobbed, wishing he could hear her voice again. Finally after a few minutes, he realized that he was still standing on the boardwalk, and he reluctantly pushed his grief into a corner of his mind and headed toward the café.

He was almost there when someone yelled his name. "Hold up, Bo; I been looking for you."

Bo turned to look toward the voice. Rex and another man he didn't know were walking toward him.

"Hello, Marshal. I was coming to see you, but I decided I would eat first. Would you care to join me?"

"We had the same idea," Rex said as he turned to the man who was with him. He was an older, well-dressed man with a bushy gray beard. "This is Judge Shelton. He's a federal judge from Phoenix."

"Glad to meet you, Judge," Bo said as the two men shook hands. "Come on over to the Shamrock, and I'll treat you boys to a big steak. That's what I'm going to have."

"I think I'll take you up on that, Bo," Rex said. He turned to Judge Shelton. "How about you, Judge? You up for one of our big Arizona steaks?"

"If it's all right with you, Bo, I'd like to have some Mexican food. I had the enchiladas at the Shamrock yesterday, and I swear they were the best I ever tasted. I can't wait to get some more."

"Sure, anything you want," Bo said as he nodded toward the café down the street. "Now that you mentioned those enchiladas, I think that's what I want, too."

When the three men walked into the café, Lupe was coming out of the kitchen. She hurried to Bo, a huge smile on her face. "Senor Bo, I am so glad you are out of the hospital," she cried as she grabbed and hugged him. Bo winched, and Lupe quickly stepped back. "Oh, I am sorry, Senor Bo. I forget about your shoulder."

"Oh, it didn't hurt," Bo lied. "It's just a little stiff."

Lupe smiled, then glanced at Rex and Judge Shelton. "What do you want me to fix you, Senor Bo? I know you are tired of the food at the hospital."

Bo grinned. "I shore am. Bring us all a plate of them famous enchiladas I been hearing about."

Lupe smiled as she lightly patted him on his sore shoulder. "Si, Senor Bo. I will fix them pronto," she said as she hurried toward the kitchen. Bo watched her go and then sat back down.

"I guess you heard; Judge Mills is going to prison—him and Porky," Rex said.

"No, I haven't heard anything about the hearing," Bo said. "What about Gimpy?"

"We made a deal with Gimpy. I told him if he would testify at the hearing and tell us a lot of the details, we would give him a light sentence. We had the hearing yesterday, and Gimpy told us stuff we didn't even know about."

"Yes, he did," Judge Shelton said. "Mister Mills and Mister Hogg pleaded guilty and threw themselves on the mercy of the court. I gave Mills twenty years and fined him enough to get back everything he ever got from his dishonesty. I gave Mister Hogg five years for not reporting all of Cobb's deals."

"What about Walter Johnson?" Bo asked.

Rex looked at Bo as he shook his head. "I guess he couldn't face going to prison. We found him up at the horse barn; put a pistol in his mouth and pulled the trigger."

"Well, that's a hard way to go. May the Lord have mercy on his soul," Bo said. He thought a minute. "You know, I had to take Walter's horse when I took out after Mary. He was a good horse. Did anyone bring him back to the livery?"

Rex thought for a minute. "I don't know. The boys brought you to Tucson in the stagecoach."

"What about my ole dun horse?" Bo asked. "The hostler said he rented him to the sheriff for Mary to ride."

Rex put his hand under his chin and rubbed. "I didn't know that, Bo. I don't remember seeing him. I told the boys to bring in all of the saddle horses that the Skinner bunch was riding to the livery. He might be over there."

"I'll go see about him later," Bo said. "I see our lunch coming now." Juan, looking much like a seasoned waiter, was hurrying to their table carrying a tray with two of their dinners on it. Jose was right behind him carrying Bo's. He smiled as he placed Bo's plate down in front of him, then reached out his arms. "It is so good to see you, senor. I'm glad that you are finally out of the hospital."

Bo sheepishly stood up. He knew that Jose wanted to greet him with a hug, the Mexican way, and he didn't have the heart to refuse. Juan, smiling broadly, also came over to hug him. Bo hurriedly glanced around to see who was watching as he sat back down. He didn't mind being hugged by Lupe, but he wasn't used to being hugged by men. Jose and Juan went back to their duties, and the three men began to eat. They didn't talk much for a while, only commenting on how good the food was or asking someone to pass something. Bo began thinking of Mary again. He knew he would never be sure that Mary was gone forever unless he personally looked for her—and maybe not even then. He looked up at Rex and said, "Rex, I can't believe Mary could disappear without a trace. She's a very resourceful person. She escaped from a workhouse in New York City and then made her way completely across the country to San Francisco posing as a boy."

Rex said, "Bo, I'm not satisfied that Mary is dead, either. She stabbed Curt with the hat pin. I don't believe Curt shot her after that; he would be in too much pain, and besides, there was no sign that she was carried off by an animal." He paused for a second, then said, "I think if some Indian happened by and carried her off, he would have taken Curt's horse and weapons, but they were still there." Rex paused. "Oh, and something else: we found another of John's gang dead out in the desert. The Mexican they call Diablo. Looks like he was tortured and killed by an Apache. It was the worst I had ever seen. He must have been in a lot of pain."

"But you don't think the Apaches got Mary, though, right?" Bo asked anxiously.

"No. Like I said before, Curt's horse and guns were still at the scene. Apaches would have taken them."

Bo thought for a second. "Has all of John's gang been accounted for?"

"All of them who were in his close circle are dead or in jail. Gimpy told us that there was a guy from back East named Sylvester, who had rode off with John and Sledge that day. A cowboy found him dead out close to John's ranch yesterday. He was naked,covered in cactus needles and gelded. Apaches most likely, but I guess we will never know."

Bo was quite for a moment, his mind was on something else. Finally he spoke, "I'm going to look for her myself, Rex. I'll get some supplies ready today, and I'll leave first thing in the morning."

The three men talked until they had finished their meal, then Rex and Judge Shelton had to get back to the courthouse. Bo walked with them a ways, then turned in at a general store. He purchased a packsaddle and a load of supplies for it. He told the clerk he would pick it up first thing in the morning, then he walked to the livery to see about a horse and a pack mule. When he got there, the old stableman was out back throwing hay to a few of the horses in the corral.

"Hello, old timer," Bo said as the man turned to look at him. "I need two horses—one to ride and one to carry a pack."

The old man spit tobacco juice at the ground. "You're the man stole Walter Johnson's horse. You know he killed himself right here?"

"Yeah, that's what I heard." Bo said. "I don't think he did it because I took his horse, though."

"They say he did some bad things," the old man said and spit again. He looked back at Bo. "The posse brought the black horse back; you want him again?"

"What about my dun horse?' Bo asked. "The one you gave to the sheriff for the woman to ride."

"They didn't bring him back with the rest of 'em." He spit again. "They brought in a pack mare. They said some cowboy left it at the stage station."

Bo thought for a second. He had forgotten about the mare from the valley. "Where's she at?"

"She's in the corral. Got a TO branded on her."

Bo walked to the corral. "Yeah, I left her there." He reached into his pocket, pulled out a five-dollar gold piece, and flipped it to the old man. "Can you have the black saddled for me by day-light? I'll be here for him and the mare."

The old man looked at the gold coin. "Sonny, I'll have 'em ready." He looked at the coin again. "I'll have 'em with bells on, if you want."

Bo tossed and turned in his bed most of the night, sleeping very little. Finally, at four he got up, dressed, and headed down the stairs. He stopped at the desk and explained to the night clerk that he would be gone for a few days. The still-dark morning was chilly as he stepped outside, but already a few people were moving along the streets. When Bo arrived at the café, he found people already eating their breakfast. Lupe saw him as he sat down at one of the tables, so she hurried to bring him coffee. Bo sat nursing his coffee for a while, his thoughts again returning to Mary. Although Bo wasn't hungry, he ordered breakfast and forced himself to eat it so he wouldn't get hungry later. The sky was beginning to lighten by the time he had finished his breakfast and was heading out the door. The black gelding and the packhorse were waiting for him when Bo got to the livery. He mounted the gelding, then, leading the mare, he headed for the store to get his supplies. The sun was just peeking over the horizon as he rode out of Tucson.

A cool wind blew in Bo's face as he road east on the Benton road. His first stop would be at Vail's old stage station. He would be glad to see Leon and Kelsi. He had been told that he owed both of them his life; Leon for killing Sledge and Kelsi for knowing how to take care of his wounds. Of course they weren't the only two he was thankful for. Bull and Squeaky had played their part, too. Bo unconsciously rubbed his shoulder as he thought of the shootout. If only he could have gone after Mary that night, maybe he would have found her. He shuddered and tried to clear his head. *Back home in Georgia, Preacher Johnson said that God always had a plan.* Bo looked up at the sky. "God, please let me find her alive."

The cool wind had turned into a warm breeze by the time Bo finally rode up to the station. He was ready to rest a bit. His shoulder had begun to throb with pain, and it didn't help that he had been lying around for two weeks doing nothing.

Leon was out by the corral tending the horses when Bo rode in. When he saw Bo, he hurried to him. "Bo, it's good to see you," he said. "I shore didn't expect to see you riding up out here—not the way you were shot up."

"It's good to see you too, Leon. I always was a fast healer, but to tell you the truth, right now I'm wondering if maybe I ain't healed as good as I thought."

"Well, get off that horse and come on into the tent. Some of Kelsi's cooking and a little rest will fix you right up."

"I was hoping I was in time for lunch," Bo said as he eased off the black gelding.

"Just go on in, Bo. I'll take care of your horses for you. Kelsi will be glad to see you."

Bo hesitated for a few seconds as Leon grabbed both horses and began leading them to the water trough, then he started walking toward the tent. When Kelsi saw Bo walk in the door, she ran to him, yelling his name. She raised her arms to give him a big hug but then stopped herself. "Bo, what are you doing out here? You can't be well yet."

Bo chuckled. "No, I'm not well yet, Kelsi. But you can give me a hug if you want to. Just be careful of my shoulder."

As Bo ate lunch with Leon and Kelsi, the conversation was casual, with nothing about the gunfight until afterward, when Bo asked them to tell him about it.

"Squeaky was afraid you were dead, Bo," Kelsi began. "But I saw right quick that you were still breathing and you had a weak pulse, so we stopped your bleeding, then carried you into the tent. Back East I worked with a doctor for a while, and I learned that it was best to keep a wounded person covered up, so that's what we did."

"By the time the morning stage got here, she had the bleeding nearly stopped and your pulse was better," Leon added. "We loaded you on the stage, and with Kelsi along to watch over you and Bull driving, you made it to Tucson in record time."

"I needed to get you to a real doctor, Bo," Kelsi said. "The bullet went plumb through you, and I didn't know how much damage it caused."

"I want to thank you, Kelsi," Bo said. "I think if you hadn't been here to fix me up, I would have died. Your doctoring was good enough." Bo turned to Leon. "And you saved my life, too, by taking care of Sledge."

"Well, Bo, they way I look at it, Sledge would have killed us all if I hadn't killed him," Leon said.

Bo scooted his chair back and stood up. "You're probably right, Leon." He hesitated for a second, his eyes glistening. "But Leon, I'm not so sure I care to live without Mary. I'm going out there in the desert to look for her. I'm not going to stop looking for her until I find her, either alive or dead."

They talked for a few minutes more, but finally Leon had to get a fresh team ready for the stagecoach. Bo said his good-byes, then once again headed down the Benson Road. He had learned from Rex that Curt had been found dead on the trail to Apache Springs and Mary's ripped-off clothes were found near him. Leon had told him that the first trail that cut off to the left of Benson Road was the Apache Springs Trail. Bo found it easily, and he turned the black down it looking for the place where Curt was found. He stopped when he came to the place where the posse had found John's body and a near-dead Tom. There was no mistaking the amount of blood at the location. Bo studied it for a while, remembering the details that Rex had told him of the position of the two men.

Finally his impatience won out, and he turned the black down the trail once again. A few minutes later, he came to another place that showed signs of blood. Not as much this time, but Bo was sure that this was the place he was looking for. He dismounted and looked around at all the signs that were left. A wave of sadness swept over him as he realized that this was where Mary fought for her life and eventually stabbed Curt with her hat pin. He tried to visualize what had happened here, but all of his visions couldn't explain the disappearance of Mary.

If she managed to get back on Dunce, where would she go? She wouldn't go back the way she had come because she didn't know who was still after her. She would keep running away, and because it was dark, she would stay on the trail.

Bo glanced to where the trail wound out of sight toward Apache Springs. He remounted, and, leading the mare, he continued down the trail.

The rest of the way down the trail was fruitless. Bo didn't see any signs that indicated that anyone had come down this trail in a long time. The sun was low in the sky by the time Bo reached the water hole. He dismounted, then walked around looking for tracks, but found only the tracks of coyotes and other animals of the desert that had visited the water hole recently. Bo walked back to the horses and started to mount up, but he paused to look one last time. As he swept his eyes across the miles and miles of desert, a sense of hopelessness swept through his body. He walked over to a large rock to sit down. Tears came to his eyes as visions of Mary lying hurt somewhere, waiting for someone to rescue her, flashed across his mind. He sat for a while, desperately trying to unravel her mysterious disappearance, until finally, exhausted both in body and spirit, he decided he would stop for the night and try to rest.

Having made up his mind, he looked around to find a good place away from the water hole to camp. He noticed a trail that led up the hillside and what looked like a flat spot on the hill. The trail and hill looked familiar to him. Suddenly, what his grief had kept him from seeing came surging into his mind. He looked around again. "I think this is the spring where I saw the Indians," Bo said.

Quickly he mounted and started up the trail. By the time he got to the top of the slope, he was sure this was it. He stopped at his old campsite to look below at the water hole. He remembered the dreadful feeling he had experienced when he had seen the Apaches down below and the panic he had felt when Dunce disappeared. Suddenly Bo's heart raced as he remembered that Mary had been riding Dunce on the night she disappeared.

Dunce knows where the valley is; he would remember the grass.

With hope still alive, Bo hurriedly turned the black horse towards the faint trail that would take him to the cave.

CHAPTER 51

Bonnie frowned with disappointment as she checked her last trap and found nothing in it. Her stomach growled with hunger as she thought of another day without anything to eat. Five days ago she had eaten the last of the food she had found in the cabin, and since then she had only managed to find a few berries. She had tried making primitive traps to catch the fat but speedy squirrels that abounded in the valley, but so far they had proved useless. She had seen a few cattle and deer in the meadows, but she had no way to catch them. She carried the knife she had found in the cabin with her when she went scouting for food, but she never got close enough to anything to use it. Bonnie desperately looked up at the mountains and cliffs that surrounded the valley, hoping to see a way out that she had missed before.

She had just about given up on finding a way out of the valley. The few trails up the sides of the mountains were too steep for her to climb, and her search for another way out had been fruitless. She often wondered why God had put her into such a pretty place but didn't provide a way for her to eat. She prayed every night before she went to bed that someone would rescue her. Tonight she would add food to that prayer.

Bonnie looked up at the sky and noticed that the sun was nearly down to the mountains. It would be dark soon, and she didn't want to be outside at dark. A few nights ago the quiet valley had become more frightening to her. She had heard something moving around outside the cabin, growling and scratching on the walls. The next morning there were huge tracks around the corral and Dunce was gone. He had come back later in the day, but he was nervous and spooky. Bonnie didn't know what it was, but the thought of some huge animal in the valley hastened her footsteps as she hurried back to the cabin.

A few minutes later, when she reached it, she noticed the door was open. Bonnie didn't remember leaving it open, and she hesitated for a minute as she pulled out the knife. Carefully she walked up to the open door, then looked into cabin. At first she didn't see anything, so she cautiously stepped into the room. Instantly she noticed that the shelves were turned over to the left of the fireplace. Suddenly she heard a soft scuffle to her right; slowly she turned her head to look.

"OH, GOD!" she screamed as a huge silvertip grizzly rose to his full height and let out a tremendous roar. Terrified, Bonnie turned and ran out of the cabin. The grizzly dropped down to all four legs and rushed to catch her. Mary raced down the trail toward the creek, the bear several yards behind her but closing fast. Mary looked back and screamed again. She was very afraid, and she didn't know what to do but run. She looked back again and could see the bear was closer. Seeing a small tree, she scrambled up to the upper limbs. The bear stopped at the base of the small pine, then quickly rose on his hind legs and began to push on it. The tree began swaying as it gave way to the strength and the weight of the grizzly. Horrified, Mary could feel herself losing her grip; suddenly she fell screaming from the tree.

"BOOM!" "BOOM!" The sound of shots echoed from the surrounding cliffs. Mary hit the ground, and then all was quiet. She opened her eyes, then raised her head. The grizzly was lying beside her. She screamed as she rolled away and jumped to her feet. She was ready to run, but looking at the bear, she saw blood flowing from his body. She cautiously watched him for a few minutes, then picked up a long stick and poked him.

"Is he dead?" The voice behind her startled Mary; quickly she turned. Joy poured into her heart.

"Bo!" she cried as she ran to his outstretched arms. They hugged and Mary began crying. "Bo, you found me. I have been praying that you would find me."

Bo looked into Mary's beautiful blue eyes. "I've been searching for you my whole life. I won't ever leave you again."

Mary's heart seemed to melt, and all her love for Bo filled her being as she looked back into his eyes. "I don't want to live without you, Bo. I have loved you for a long time, and I want to be with you forever."

Made in the USA
San Bernardino, CA
22 September 2013